The Jukebox Kings
DOUG ALLYN

STARK
HOUSE

Stark House Press • Eureka California

THE JUKEBOX KINGS

Published by Stark House Press
1315 H Street
Eureka, CA 95501, USA
griffinskye3@sbcglobal.net
www.starkhousepress.com

ISBN-13: 978-1-944520-17-5

Book design by Mark Shepard, SHEPGRAPHICS.COM

First Stark House Press Edition: February 2017

FIRST EDITION

It all starts when Mick Shannon—Irish Mick—loses to a knockout punch. His manager had bet heavy, and now Mick owes the mob, and more specifically, Moishe Abrams, who runs the jukes and collections in Detroit's 8 Mile. Moishe is part of the Old Guard, and not to be trifled with. But first time out, Moishe takes a blade for Mick when Mojo Johnson doesn't want to pay up. Now Mojo's dead and there's a body to get rid of and an aging gangster who needs some serious medical attention. That's when Brownie steps in to help, and so begins Mick's career with the jukes.

With Moishe on the mend, Mick handles all his collections. But he also finds himself handling Mojo's old studio… and Mojo's niece, Martika, who runs the place. Mick is beginning to see the light at the end of the tunnel—maybe some money can be made here. Trouble is, the mob boss's son, Albert Luca, also wants a piece of the action. With Brownie running interference and Moishe giving his unofficial blessing, Mick's troubles only multiply when he decides to buy a club for the studio acts to play in. Because now Albert definitely wants in—and this time he has no intention of taking no for an answer.

Dedication:

For the tremendously tough
and talented Ed Gorman,
the best friend I never met.

Doug Allyn

The Jukebox Kings
DOUG ALLYN

...sweet, strong women and keen-witted men from Canada and
Texas, California, New York and Ohio— all sons and great-
grandchildren of Ethiopia... Can you imagine a more marvelous
place than Idlewild?

W.E.B. Du Bois
From *Idlewild, the Black Eden* by Ronald J. Stephens

'Mojo come up from Mobile, in a Jukebox Cadillac
Got Lebanese boll, a fat flash roll, and a big leg woman in back,
got a slim Jim sticker and a gun in each hand,
Best not mess with no Mojo man... ah hmmm...

From: *Jukebox Cadillac Blues*

I'm "Hot Chocolate" baby, sweet, brown and sticky too,
turn me on like you do, and I'll melt down over you.

From: *"Hot Chocolate"*

DETROIT

July 1, 1963

Irish Mick never saw the punch that put him down.

It wasn't a big punch. The wild, roundhouse right barely grazed his temple.

But it did the job.

He was fighting Kid Ibo, a Nigerian middleweight out of Chicago. Black and hard as an ebony club. The Kid had deep, tribal scars gouged in his cheeks. His teeth were filed down to points.

Looked like he ate lions for lunch.

Fought like it too.

First round, Mick and the Nigerian came out swinging hard, trading heavy leather. The crowd cheered the action but it was all flash and dazzle, no real damage done. Both fighters were testing each other, probing for weaknesses. Seeing what worked, what didn't.

Ibo was short on technique but he had real *power*. Mick got that message when he slipped a right cross. The punch flashed by like lightning, missing his jaw by a hair.

But it widened his eyes.

He felt the sheer force of it. And got the message. This Nigerian was dangerous.

Put your young white ass in traction-type dangerous.

Fully focused now, Mick picked up his rhythm in the second round, taking Ibo seriously, taking him to school. Pugilism 101.

He went in low, hammering the Nigerian's ribcage with stiff body shots, short punches with serious snap to 'em, dealing out some pain. The barrage forced Ibo to drop his guard a few inches, then quickly raise his hands as Mick finished every flurry with a hard right to the head.

The attacks weren't really effective. The African was blocking most of the shots now, thought he knew Mick's game. Anticipating that final right, he started lifting his left a little sooner every time. A rookie mistake.

As the round wound down, Mick suddenly reversed the pattern. He fired off a rapid flurry of body shots, but dropped the last punch six inches lower, digging a hook under the Nigerian's elbow as he raised his guard, landing a stiff liver shot that slammed home like a battering ram, driving a fist halfway to his spine!

Ibo gasped, then quickly backed away, grinning, shaking his head like the punch was nothing. Nothing at all.

But that punch was *something*.

Mick rushed in, working the same combination again before the Nigerian could figure it out, delivering a second body shot to the same spot, flat-footed this time, a sledge hammer blow with serious steam on it.

Ibo couldn't clown this one off. Wincing in pain, he backpedaled, dancing away from Mick as fast as he could. He stayed up on his toes the last fifteen seconds of the round, then walked stiff legged back to his corner at the bell. His knees wobbled when he collapsed on his stool.

Mick nodded in satisfaction. *Gotcha cocksucker!* Ibo was definitely in the House of Hurt.

"You hooked him good there, Irish," Deacon Washburn, his manager-trainer grinned as Mick dropped onto his stool, breathing deep with his nostrils flared, sucking down all the air he could hold, inhaling the stink of the ring, the crowd, the whiskey reek rolling off Wash like aftershave. Ignoring the noise and the stench, Mick focused on the Nigerian across the ring.

Tall and rangy for a middleweight, Ibo had long arms, like Ezzard Charles. The tribal scars gleamed beneath the Vaseline on his cheeks, giving him a fierce, predatory look.

But beneath the savage mask, he could *feel* the Nigerian's pain. Ibo was keeping his teeth bared in a fierce grin to camouflage it, but his brow was furrowed and he couldn't quite straighten up on his stool, even when his trainer tugged on his waistband to relax his abdominals.

Mick knew that agony. He'd taken a punch just like it his first week of gladiator school in Jackson Prison. Pain so bad he thought the guy had ruptured his spleen. Somehow he answered the bell, stayed on his feet, but he could barely defend himself. His opponent toyed with him for a round, setting him up. Then laid him out flat in the sixth.

But this fight wouldn't have a sixth. It was a lousy four-round preliminary bout, two rounds gone already, only two left to get it done. He had to put Ibo down now, before he could shake off his misery.

Deacon Washburn was yelling instructions in his ear, had been since Mick sat down. Tuning him out, Mick looked out over the crowd.

Olympia Stadium, Detroit's answer to Madison Square Garden. Home of the Detroit Red Wings and the Friday Night Fights. Irish Mick wasn't even listed on tonight's card. He'd been penciled in as a last minute replacement.

Taking a fight on short notice for short money is a bad career move.

Makes you look hungry, and desperate. But Mick *was* hungry and desperate. His last mechanic's job only lasted three days. The car lot canned him as soon as they got tipped about his prison record. Boxing was all he had going. He needed this fuckin' purse—

"Seconds out!" the timekeeper called, slapping the ring apron with his palm for emphasis.

"Have you heard a goddamn thing I said?" Washburn yelled.

"Every word," Mick said. "Stay on him, work the body." It was what Wash always said. "How about I lay him out instead?"

"Talk's cheap," Wash grumbled, rinsing Mick's mouthpiece, sliding it in. "We need a win bad, Irish. Ibo was expecting a tune up fight. So tune his ass up!" Grabbing the stool, the old man hoisted himself through the ropes.

Mick frowned. Wash sounded worried, and Wash never worried. What the hell was that about?

He put it out of his mind. Across the ring, the Nigerian was already up off his stool, dancing in place, angry, hurting, and hungry for payback.

Worry about Wash later. Boxing's a team sport. Your corner man spots your opponent's mistakes, points them out. Plots your strategy.

But strategy's for the long run. No time for tactics in this fight. Ibo was dangerous and his flashy punches were piling up points. To be sure of a win, Mick had to put him flat on the goddamn deck.

He slammed his gloves together. *He needed to finish this!*

Right fucking now!

The bell sounded.

Ibo came charging out of his corner, throwing punches like a machine gunner. Pumped up on pain and rage, he was desperately trying to smother Mick's punches with his own, keeping him too busy to fire off another crippling body shot.

No problem. Mick let Ibo flail away. He was headhunting now, blocking Ibo's punches with his arms and elbows, looking for an opening. A clean shot for a one-punch knockout. Waiting... waiting... any second now...

Suddenly there it was! Ibo threw a left hook so hard it carried him halfway around when it missed. His jaw was wide open for a counter. Perfect!

Mick threw his right full force, swiveling his hips into the punch, giving it everything he had— but Ibo's desperation roundhouse counterpunch landed first, grazing Mick's temple.

Totally focused, Mick barely felt Ibo's glove. But it had just enough zip on it to make him miss. Big.

The force of his own blow spun him into the ropes off balance. As he straightened up, he stumbled over Ibo's left foot, and dropped to one knee.

Jesus! What the hell just happened?

Mick jumped up immediately, more embarrassed than hurt. It was a trip! Not a fucking knockdown! But the ref was already counting, giving him a standing eight.

Across the ring, Ibo was dancing in his corner, arms raised in victory, showboating for the crowd. And the audience was eating it up. Screw the battle tactics. Even your grandma can understand a knockdown. *Damn it!*

"You okay?" The ref was peering into his eyes intently.

"I fucking tripped!" Mick mumbled around his mouthpiece.

"What? Answer me, Shannon! Can you continue?"

"Hell yes!" Mick roared around his mouthpiece, nodding vigorously, desperate to get the ref out of the way and get back into the fight. Grabbing his gloves, the ref wiped them off on his white shirt then stepped back and waved the fighters on.

Mick charged into Ibo's corner, but the Nigerian danced out of reach, grinning, hot-dogging around the ring for the last half minute of the round.

"You're blowin' it, Irish," Wash yelled as Mick sagged on his stool. "Dammit, I told you— "

Mick leaned back, closed his eyes, tuning Wash out again.

Shit! Decked by a dumb-ass lucky punch. Ibo hadn't laid a glove on him all night. And he wouldn't have to, now. The knockdown would decide the bout. Wash was ranting at him, practically frothing at the mouth, more frantic than Mick had ever seen him—

"Last round," the ref said, leaning in over Wash's shoulder. "Touch 'em up when you come out. You okay, Shannon?"

"Terrific," Mick snapped.

"Good," the ref said dryly, then trotted over to remind the Nigerian's corner it was the last round. Mick noticed he didn't bother asking Ibo if he was okay. This fight was over unless Mick could nail Ibo and put him down—

But he couldn't. They did the traditional glove touch before starting the final round. It was the closest Mick came to landing a solid punch.

Ibo danced the round away, running for his freakin' life but looking good doing it. Every time Mick tried to close with him, the Nigerian got on his bicycle, firing flurries of flashy, pitty-pat punches with nothing on them, confident he had the fight in the bag.

Which he damn well did.

The ref cautioned the Nigerian about running, but that didn't mean jack squat to the fans. Ibo was still showboating at the final bell. Five seconds to confer with the judges and the ref was raising Ibo's hand in victory while the ring announcer bellowed the unanimous decision. There was a smattering of applause, but the crowd was already thinning, headed for the johns and beer booths before the next no-name bout.

CHAPTER 2

"Lucky goddamn punch," Deacon Washburn said glumly, cutting the laces off Mick's gloves in the shabby dressing room. "You rocked him in the second. What the fuck happened? I told you to work Ibo's body— "

"Screw it, Wash. It was my fault. I went for the knockout. I was a second late— "

"And you always will be," the old man said.

"What?"

"Listen to me, Mick. We're quits after tonight anyway, but you gots to hear this. You punch hard, you got heart and a white boy can always get a fight in this town. You a damn fine club fighter, but that's all you ever gonna be. You too slow to make it big in the pro ranks. You got good skills and I can teach you more, but I can't teach you *quick!* You're born quick or you ain't. And you ain't."

"Christ, Wash, it was only one fight— "

"No! You're catchin' leather every round, Mick, and these are only prelim fights. Next step up, against better talent, you'll get your brains scrambled. You got the heart to stand in there and trade with anybody. And that same heart gonna land you in Palookaville inside a fucking year. Do you understand what I'm sayin'?"

"Okay, okay, I know I'm not good enough yet! That's why I'm payin' you— "

"Not no more you ain't. We're done."

"What the fuck, Wash? You wanna quit me, go ahead! You aren't the only corner man in Motown. Try working a fight sober, maybe I'll win a few."

"Don't be raggin' on me, boy. I didn't duck you into that sucker punch."

"I know that, I— goddamn it. Look, I'm sorry, Wash. I know I blew it. Give me my money, I'll buy you a beer, we'll talk this out."

"That's the rest of it, kid," Wash sighed. "There ain't no money. It's gone."

"Gone? What are you talking about?"

"I bet the advance on you, Mick. I *knew* you could take Ibo, he was perfect for you— " He swallowed. "Anyway. Our money's gone. Every damn dime and then some."

"Dammit, Wash, you had no right— *fuck!* Wait. What the hell does that mean, 'and then some?' What did you do?"

"Ibo's a nobody from Chicago, you're nobody from Detroit. I had to give odds to get any action." Wash was an ex-pug, stolid as a water buffalo. But he was sweating now, avoiding Mick's eyes.

"You gave odds?" Mick asked, swallowing. "How much?"

"Four to one."

"Four! Sweet Jesus! To who?"

"Ron Ducatti. Used to fight some himself, he's a promoter now. Do you know him?"

"Ronny Duke? I know who he is. And he's not just a promoter, he's mobbed up. How much are we out, Wash? Exactly?"

"The advance was six. It's gone and we're down eighteen hundred, Mick."

"Sweet Jesus, Wash! Why not a freakin' million? Have you got eighteen hundred? I haven't got eighteen bucks."

"I ain't got squat neither. I figured you'd clock Ibo, we'd clean up. But maybe it'll still work out. Ronny's backin' a new fighter, a stud from L.A., Calvin Kroffut. Dude looks super bad, tattoos, dreadlocks. Learned to fight in prison, like you. Kilt a Mexican fighter down in Tijuana. Killer Kroffut, they're callin' him now. Killer K. A bad-ass name sells a lot of tickets."

"What's that got to do with us?"

"K's wins are all nobodies, Mexicans from Cali or south of the border. Everybody's down there is fifty and one and Kid Gavilan's they daddy. I hear Ronny's lookin' for some...local bouts."

He looked away, unable to meet Mick's eyes.

"My ass," Mick groaned. "You mean Ducatti's lining up tomato cans his boy can knock down to pump up his win record."

"It don't matter what he's doin'," Wash said. "Bein' down eighteen to Ronny Duke ain't like owin' the Bank of Detroit, Mick. We in deep shit here. You gotta talk to the man."

CHAPTER 3

Mick found Ronny Duke holding court at a third tier table overlooking the main floor. A dozen people around him, all as drunk as he was, except for his new fighter seated at the end of the table. Wash was right. Even in a slick new sharkskin suit and tie, Killer K Calvin Kroffut looked bad to the bone, prison yard hard, iron-pumper muscles straining the seams of his tailored jacket.

Ron Ducatti looked bad too, in the original sense of the word. Big and fleshy, with thinning blond hair, he was on a downhill slide. His cheeks were splotchy from booze, seamed with smile lines from his salesman's grin. Brows were shiny with scar tissue from his time in the ring. Looked like he was carousing himself into an early coronary, laughing all the way.

"Mr. Ducatti? My manager said you wanted to see me?"

"Irish Mickey Shannon," Ronny said, not bothering to offer his hand. "Hey everybody, say hello to Irish Mick."

A couple of drunk chicks at the table glanced up. Cleaned up, in his best white shirt and jeans, Mick could pass for roughneck handsome. Square jawed, with a lanky frame, he looked almost boyish, if you missed the scars around his brows and the deep nick in his upper lip. A nightstick souvenir from the Jackson pen.

"Siddown, have a drink," Ronny slurred. "You'll probably want a shot to go with the one put you on your ass."

"A beer'll do," Mick said, swallowing his anger. "And it's Mick, not Mickey." He took a chair opposite Ducatti.

"Beer here," Ronny bellowed at a passing waitress, stuffing a ten down her bra. "Have you met Killer K yet, Irish?"

Kroffut offered a paw the size of a smoked ham, but there was no contest of strength. K shook gently, Spanish style. "You had him in the second, Shannon. Bad luck. You don't fight like no white boy. Got you some chops, some rhythm. Pick up that shit in the joint?"

Mick eyed him, didn't answer.

"Want some advice?" Kroffut said, leaning forward, his massive mahogany face only inches from Mick's. "Get out while you can. You a step slow, Casper. Keep fighting, you'll get your brains scrambled. Get yourself killed. Maybe I'll kill you."

"Maybe you'll fuckin' talk me to death," Mick said.

"You got a smart mouth, pretty boy," Kroffut grinned, not backing off an inch. "Might be fun, bustin' you up."

"Hey, hey, let's not start no fights at the fights," Ronny Duke inter-rupted, with a bleary grin at his own wit. "Wash tells me we got a prob-lem, Shannon— "

"He bet on me and I lost, so I owe you," Mick said, turning to Ducatti. "I get that. If you want me to fight this gorilla, I'll do it for free. But I won't dive, Mr. Ducatti, not for you or anybody else."

"Dive? For Killer K?" Ducatti snorted. "Hell, kid, he'd knock you into left field. And with your half ass record I couldn't match you with Shirley Temple let alone the Killer. I got a job for you, though. Guy I know needs a driver who can handle himself. You can drive, right?"

"Whoa, we've got a mix-up here, Mr. Ducatti," Mick said, flushing, "I'm a fighter— "

"Not from what I seen," Kroffut said.

"If you want to try me, bring it!" Mick flared, whirling on Kroffut.

"Damn it, Irish, cool your jets!" Ronny Duke snapped, waving Krof-fut back to his seat. "You're into me for eighteen, Shannon, which your corner-man lost bettin' on you. Have you got my money?"

"Not tonight, but— "

"Then you two gambled money you don't got, which means you're in the toilet, swirlin' around. Want me to flush you down?"

Mick turned away a moment. Had to, to keep from punching Ronny Duke's lights out. But he knew what would happen if he did. He'd be dead meat a second later. And so would Wash.

Out on the arena floor, acres of boozy spectators were cheering or curs-ing two gladiators in the ring. Fight night, Motown style. Shirtsleeves and summer dresses, not a tuxedo in sight.

Half an hour ago he'd fought an African warrior to entertain these stiffs, tripped over the guy's foot... And now he was in a deep, deep hole. With only one way out.

"I drive for a guy?" he said, facing to Ronny Duke. "That's all I do?"

"You'll drive, and do as you're fucking told," Ronny said, handing him a slip of paper. "You call this number. Ask for Moishe Abrams."

Mick swallowed, his heart dropping like an elevator in free fall.

Ducatti caught the look. "You know Moishe?"

Mick shook his head.

"But you've heard the stories about him, eh? Forget 'em. Moishe was bad ass back in the day, but he's past it now. Washed up. Guess you two got somethin' in common."

He chortled at his own joke.

Mick couldn't even fake a smile.

CHAPTER 4

Mick was waiting outside his fleabag rooming house in Ecorse the next night, when Moishe Abrams rolled up. In a hearse. Or close to it.

The old man's ride was a slab-sided '61 Lincoln Premiere estate sedan, big as a boxcar, black as a casket. Looked like he bought it second hand from a funeral home.

Which was appropriate.

Mick grew up hearing Moishe Abrams stories around the neighborhood the way other kids heard about the bogeyman or monsters under the bed.

Old time hard guy, street muscle for the Purple Gang. Back during prohibition, Abrams ran booze down from Canada, drove it across the ice of the frozen Detroit River, at night. No lights. Must've had brass balls back then. Not so different now. Didn't look washed up to Mick. Looked square and gray as a cement block, and just as hard.

"You drive," Moishe said, climbing into the shotgun seat. "I don't see so good at night."

'Or daytime either,' Mick thought. Moishe's black framed glasses had lenses like Coke bottles.

"Where to?"

"Idlewild," the old man said. "The spade Las Vegas. You know it?"

"I can find it."

"Ray Charles could find it and he's fuckin' blind," Moishe said. "Head west to Grand Rapids and swing north. Wake me up at the exit."

Tipping his New York brim down over his eyes, the old man folded his arms and conked out, dead to the world. A three hour run straight west, then north on 131. Moishe never twitched.

Forty miles out of Grand Rapids, Mick felt the old man's eyes on him. Moishe shifted around, sitting up, loosening his shoulders, looking Mick over.

"Ronny Duke says you're a fighter," Moishe said. "You any good?"

"Not good enough, or I wouldn't be here."

"You good for anything else?"

"Cars," Mick said. "I can wrench anything with wheels, take it apart, set it to rights. Your Lincoln's due for a lube job and a tune."

"If you're a mechanic, why were you fightin'?" Moishe snorted. "Plenty of grease monkey jobs in Motown."

"Getting hired is no problem. Staying hired is a different thing."

"Why? You a juicer? A junkie?"

"Neither one. But every place I sign on, an Ecorse cop will show up in a day or two to warn my boss I'm an ex-con, a violent felon, they should cut me loose."

"Are you a violent felon?"

"I did a nickel in Jacktown," Mick sighed. "Assault with intent to do great bodily harm. I was seventeen, tried as an adult."

"Who'd you assault? The judge's wife?'

"A cop. Three of 'em, actually."

"You jumped three cops?" Moishe snorted, eyeing him. Curious now.

"I only jumped one," Mick sighed. "An Ecorse city cop named Spivak. He was dating my ma, slapped her around, blacked her eye. I went after him in a diner, busted him up with his own billy club. The other two cops mixed in, they got what they got."

"So you wrecked all three?" the old man smiled, shaking his head. "Not real smart."

"I was seventeen," Mick agreed. "How smart were you at seventeen?"

"Smarter than that. And this Ecorse cop— ?"

"Spivak," Mick said.

"He's still got a hard on for you?"

"Him and his pals have gotten me canned three times so far," Mick said. "I hear his arm's still messed up."

"Probably thinks of you every time he pounds his pud," Moishe grunted. "Take the next exit."

They swung off the highway, in the middle of nowhere. Not a house in sight, nothing but woods. But there was traffic. Other cars rolling west on the same back roads, headed toward the Lake Michigan shore. They passed tourist cabins now and again, plus an occasional cottage or mobile home up on blocks, more of them as they approached the Idlewild village limits.

Traffic was getting heavy here. The main drag through the village was a river of headlights, everybody cruising past the clubs and liquor stores on Lake Drive, seeing and being seen.

And definitely checking out Mick and Moishe. They were the only white faces in sight.

Most of the rides were newer models, late fifties to showroom-new sixty-threes. Swooping tailfins, wild ass two and three-tone paint jobs Simonized to a high shine. Pimped out with gold plated grilles, fat-boy whitewalls, continental kits from Warshawsky's or J.C. Whitney. Gaudy as jukeboxes on wheels.

Windows down, radios up, music swirling in the night air. Bo Diddley shouting down the Shirelles and Jackie Wilson. CKLW and WLAC clashing in the sweltering July night.

Suddenly Mick slammed on the brakes, bouncing Moishe half out of his seat. A clown in a lime green '58 Fairlane had veered off the road onto the shoulder, skidding broadside, then wheeling back into traffic, weaving like a wino in a windstorm.

Definitely had a load on, slowing down, speeding up again. Mick reached over to turn up the Lincoln's radio— the Fairlane's taillights flashed cherry red!

Fuck! Stomping the brakes, Mick whipped the wheel hard right, skidding the big sedan to a halt, his door only inches from the Ford's rear bumper.

"Asshole!" Mick yelled out the window, leaning on the horn ring.

The Ford's driver, a bleary-eyed black in a turquoise Borsalino brim toasted Mick with a beer bottle, then matted his gas pedal, spraying buckshot gravel all over the Lincoln as he roared off, cackling.

Whipping the wheel around, Mick floored the Lincoln, muscling it back into its lane, tires howling.

"Whoa!" Moishe barked. "what the fuck you doin'?"

"I'm gonna run that fat bastard down and kick his ass."

"Not on my time, you ain't, junior. He's trashed out of his tree. Half the Ubangis in Idlewild stay loaded from May to Labor Day. Cool off. This ain't no hot rod."

No, it wasn't. But the big Lincoln's outsized 430 cube V-8 engine had nuts. The biggest American mill in commercial production, it was plenty fast enough to run down a Fairlane. Mick's knuckles were white on the wheel as he rapidly gained on the Ford.

Moishe gave him a look. Didn't say jack squat. Didn't have to.

"Okay, okay," Mick sighed, easing off the gas. "What's the deal out here? I lived down south awhile, but I never seen so many black faces in one place."

"Idlewild's the only town outside Harlem they can really cut loose. Shoulda seen this burg back during the war. Duke Ellington, Count Basie, Cab Calloway all played here. Big bands. Real bands. Not like the shit on you hear on the radio nowadays." On the Lincoln's radio, Little Eva was *dooo*-ing "The Loco-motion." Moishe switched it off. "I hate that noise. Two junkies and a drum."

Mick dug that noise. Picked up a taste for black music in the joint, but he left the radio off. He preferred hardcore blues anyway, and the old man was as square as his ride.

"That's the joint up ahead on your left. Regency Lounge," Moishe said.

"The bandleader in there owes me. You haul his ass out, we beat it out of him, we're gone. Piece o' cake."

Slowing down, Mick felt a jolt of unease. The Regency was a full blown nightclub, its parking lot jammed with high end rides. Imperials, Cadillacs, big Packards and sleek Studebaker Hawks painted every color of the rainbow. A freakin' metallic gold Rolls Royce was parked near the entrance.

A hundred cars meant two, maybe three hundred people inside. All black. He glanced at the old man. What the hell was he thinking?

"Mr. Abrams, I don't know what all Ronny Duke told you, but— "

"He said you're a fighter, you owe him and can't pay. Some part of that wrong?"

"I'm also fresh out of the joint. I don't want trouble— "

"Won't be no trouble. Get your ass in there, tell Mojo I want to talk to him. That too tough for you, junior?"

"I— no, okay," Mick said grimly. "How do I find him?"

"He'll be onstage. Big, treetop spade playin' a white guitar. Maurice Johnson, the Mojo Man. Blacks call him Mojo but I'd go with Mr. Johnson, I was you. He's usually strapped, carries a .38 Smith. Plus a hideaway blade up his sleeve."

"He's packin' heat?" Mick swallowed. "Look, I'm—"

"You been in the ring, that makes you a pro," the old man snapped. "I figure that makes you about even. Time to earn your fuckin' keep, Irish. Haul Mojo's bad ass out here. Get my money."

"Fine." Jamming the big Lincoln angrily in park, Mick climbed out.

"Where you goin'?" Moishe asked.

"You want him, I'll fuckin' get him."

"You wouldn't get past the door, dumb-shit. These shine clubs got bouncers the size of buildings. I just wondered if you had balls. Hold on, I got this covered."

Mick waited as Moishe levered himself stiffly out of the Lincoln. The two men were a contrast in styles. Barely twenty-three, Mick was decked out in his redneck best, sharkskin blazer, pegged pants, pointed Dago boots from Flagg Brothers. Black silk shirt, snaky tie.

Moishe Abrams was square, gray and myopic, with coarse features, blunt hands. Old-timey gray pinstripe suit and a New York brim. Still dressing like swing was the thing.

Music hit them like a wall of noise as they pushed through the club's double doors. Bass drum thumping a heartbeat, blues guitar moaning like a woman in pain. Sad, sweet and eerie. The sound gave Mick goose bumps.

A slick black in a tuxedo was working the greeter's station. Tall, slim dude with processed hair, bow tie. Elegant. Beyond him, Mick could see a vast ballroom, white table linens glowing in the candlelight, the dance floor packed with colored men in tailored suits or tuxes, their women in high style, dazzling colors against dusky skin, exotic as African birds. A six piece electric blues band was onstage, fronted by a tall black singer in a white suit, wailing on a white guitar, shouting out lyrics.

"Welcome to the Regency, gentlemen," Tuxedo said. "The ballroom's full, but if you'd care to wait at the bar— "

"This ain't no social call, blood," Moishe growled. "Need a word with your bandleader, Mo Johnson."

"Regarding— ?"

"Business. Mine and his, not yours. Don't I know you?"

"My name's Brown, sir," the greeter said carefully. "From Detroit."

"Don't narrow it down much, does it?" Moishe snorted. "You get Johnson out here. Now."

Tuxedo gave a barely perceptible nod. A mountain-sized bouncer eased out of the shadows. Looking them over. Didn't say anything. Didn't have to.

"The band will finish their midnight set in…ten minutes or so," Tuxedo said smoothly, glancing at his watch. "There's a service door at the rear of the club. I'll send Mojo out as soon they break. We won't have any trouble, will we, sir." It wasn't a question.

Moishe didn't answer, took his time looking the bouncer up and down instead. Then turned to Mick, grinning.

"I like big fellas like this one. Can't hardly miss 'em, even in the damn dark."

"Sir— ?" Tuxedo called after him. But Moishe was already headed out, He didn't look back.

CHAPTER 5

Gunning the Lincoln past a gleaming line of pricey rides, Mick crawled the Lincoln around the building, still hearing the blues band in his head. Hot flashes of fine, dark-eyed women, swaying to the music like they all felt the same heartbeat—

"Whoa up," Moishe barked, straightening in his seat as Mick hit the brakes. "That's Mojo's car."

"Which one?"

"The red Eldorado, in the alley by the back door. He cut a record about it a few years back. "Jukebox Cadillac." See the big fuckin' gold 'M' on the door? Definitely his ride. You said you know cars? Can you boost that one, hotshot?"

"Boost it?" Mick echoed, trying to follow the sudden lurch in logic.

"He owes me six large. Puttin' a beating on him won't get me a damn dime. If we cop his ride, he don't pay up, I keep the car. You said you can wrench anything with wheels, right? Can you cop his car or not?"

"I— yeah. I can get it going."

"Then what's the holdup? I don't see no anchor on ya."

Parking at the mouth of the alley, Mick trotted to the red '58 Eldorado Brougham. It was pimped to the max. Wire wheels, fender skirts, continental kit on the trunk.

The music was louder back here, the bass drum thumping through the walls. Great tune, a cover of B.B. King's "You Upset Me." Hot shuffle.

Using the wire loop on his key ring, Mick went to work on the driver's door lock, humming along with the song.

Music to steal cars by. Jesus, how did he into this? He had the door popped by the second chorus.

Sliding in quickly behind the wheel, he groped under the dash for the wiring harness. Jerking it down, he tried to remember the starter sequence. Yellow to white? No. To black. Flicking open his pocket knife, he scraped away the insulation, baring the yellow wire.

Sweat dripping in his eyes. In the dim light, couldn't tell the black wire from blue. Risked switching on the interior lights a second. Whoa! Blinding white on white upholstery, showroom new. The blues man treated his wheels right. Finding the black wire, Mick scraped a bare patch on it.

Different song on the jukebox now. "Come to Me" by Marv Johnson. Great tune to get laid to. Which would be easy to do in a ride this fine.

Turning his face away, Mick touched the bared wires together. Sparks popped! The engine grumbled a few seconds, then coughed and died.

Damn it! The Eldorado had probably had dual carbs. They jacked the horsepower to 325 but made it tricky to start. Pumping the gas pedal twice, then holding it halfway down, Mick sparked it again. This time the V-8 caught with a roar that quickly gentled down to a smooth rumble.

Twisting the wire leads together, Mick straightened up behind the deep-dish wheel, revving the engine to signal Moishe that he had it.

"*Come to me…*" Something about that song was bugging Mick. It was still high on the charts when Johnson died in a car crash down in Arkansas—

Fuck!

If the jukebox was playing, the band was on break!

Mick was fumbling for the gearshift when the driver's door flew open and a fist crashed against his jaw! His world winked out for a second. Felt himself being hauled out of the car, then slammed up against it!

Mick gave his head a quick shake, trying to clear it. A huge black guy was towering over him. Bad motherfucker in a white suit, his big fist already on the way—

Prison yard reflex. Mick ducked under the punch as the blow whistled past. Countering with two stiff hooks to the big man's belly, he followed with a right cross that just missed Mojo's throat, bouncing off his shoulder. Grunting at the impact of the body punches, Johnson retreated a step, but only one.

"Punk-ass honky fuck! Steal my car? You're dead meat!"

The guy was a fucking giant, six-five at least, conked hair piled above a wide forehead, an under-slung jaw like a bulldog. Broad shoulders, pencil thin Little Richard moustache. He was a head taller than Mick and topped him by a hundred pounds. Street hard. Fists the size of catcher's mitts. *Goddamn!*

Hunching his shoulders, Mick dropped into a boxer's crouch, flicking out a stiff jab to keep Mojo backed off as he edged along the Caddy. He had to get clear of the car, buy himself some fighting room... Or running room.

Eyeing Mick's stance, the big man's shook his head in disbelief, his face splitting in a broad grin, white teeth against dark skin. He gave his wrist a quick flick and a shiv flashed into his palm like quicksilver magic. A nine inch Arkansas pig sticker, double-edged blade.

Holy shit!

"Wanna dance, white boy? Well, come on, show me some moves."

Mick's jackknife was in his pocket. Might as well be on the moon. He'd be gutted out if he reached for it. Mojo was no amateur, looked to be a stone pro with a blade.

Shifting the dagger from hand to hand, he was mocking Mick's boxing moves, the shiv flashing back and forth like heat lightning. Slashing the blade at Mick's face, Johnson backed him up, a step, then another, until his back was against the Cadillac. The next thrust zipped down Mick's forearm, laying it open, the blade grating on the bone— Headlights blazed on at the alley mouth! Freezing Mick and Mojo in the glare. Shielding his eyes with his free hand, Mojo man squinted into the lights. But the blade point never wavered, keeping Mick pinned against the car.

"Mr. Johnson, how you been?" Moishe stepped into the lights. Looking like what he was. Old time thug, busted nose, busted knuckles. An army .45 in his fist. The gun was at his side, aimed at the ground. But it was there all the same.

"Moishe? What the fuck, man? Is this punk your dog?"

"He is tonight. Cut him again, I'll have to charge you for stitches and you're upside down already. Lose the blade, Mojo. Let's talk."

"Sure. No problem." Johnson shook his wrist and the shiv vanished up his sleeve as magically as it had appeared. "Ain't nothin' here we can't work out."

"You're down six large, Mojo. Vig's fifteen this week. You got it?"

"I can knock half the vig down for you tonight," Johnson said, licking his lips. "Bump you a couple hundred more in a few days."

"Playin' that nigger noise must be making you deaf, Mojo. I said your vig is fifteen. Now. Tonight. Not in a few days or whenever you fuckin' get around to it. I cut you slack last month. No more."

"Damn it, Moishe, I had problems gettin' my studio open, but it's goin' now and it's earnin' good. Two, three weeks, I'll be in high cotton. I'll double your vig. Give a brother a break— "

"Two weeks? Your ass. I can't go back to my people with short money again," Moishe flared, cocking the .45. "You know who I'm with. You know they don't play. I'm takin' your ride and bumpin' you a yard for wastin' my time. Give the kid your keys."

"I play Cincy tomorrow, Moishe, Naptown next week. How'm I supposed to get there?"

His voice was drowned by jukebox music as the club's back door opened, spilling light into the alley. Tuxedo, the greeter, stuck his head out.

"Hey, Mojo, the crowd's getting— " He didn't finish. One look at Moishe's gun and the blood streaming down Mick's arm, Tuxedo ducked back inside. Slamming the door on Mojo's last hope. Darkening the alley and his mood.

With a move so quick Mick could barely follow it, Mojo snaked a snub nosed .38 from under his coat. Cocking the hammer, he jammed the muzzle under Mick's eye.

"Whoa up, now!" Moishe said. "What the fuck you doin'?"

"Listen up, Moishe," Johnson said quietly. "Y'all ain't in Dee-troit now, old man. You in Idlewild. Five hours from nowhere. You got no juice out here, pops. Nobody to back you up. I can blow this kid's head off before you make a move."

"He's just a driver I borrowed. He's got nothin' to do with this."

"You want him out of it? Fine, you put your piece away, I do the same, we work somethin' out. But you ain't takin' my ride."

Mick could almost see the wheels turning in the old man's head. He swallowed, half expecting Moishe to just cut loose, spray and pray, likely cap them both. But he didn't.

"Okay, okay," Moishe said, holding up the .45, then sliding it back into his waistband. "No need to get crazy here. Your turn now." He kept his hand on the butt of his weapon until Mojo grudgingly matched his move.

"We're back to square one, Mojo," Moishe said. "You owe, can't pay. I didn't come all this way for nothin'. You want to walk away from this, hand over your damn keys!"

Johnson glanced at Mick, then back at Moishe, gauging his chances. Decided he didn't like the odds.

"Screw it," Johnson grumbled, pulling a key ring out of his pocket. "Car ain't worth dyin' for. Take the damn ride." He tossed the keys in Moishe's direction. But as the old man reached up to snatch them out of the air, Mick glimpsed the madness in Johnson's eyes.

"No!" he shouted. Too late!

Flicking the knife out of his sleeve, Mojo whipped it across the alley like a lightning strike, burying the blade in Moishe's belly! The old man staggered back, stunned, staring down at the sticker. Then he dropped to his knees, moving like he was underwater.

Mojo reached for his .38, but before he could jerk it, Mick lunged, tackling the big man chest-high, grappling for the weapon. Johnson wrenched the snub nose out of Mick's grasp, then lost it as Mick lifted him off his feet, body-slamming him into the alley wall.

Cursing, Mojo hammered Mick with both fists, trying to shake him off, frantically scanning the ground for the gun. Mick buried his face in the big man's shoulder, jamming him against the wall, trying to avoid the blows. If he got loose, got to his gun—

But Mick couldn't hold him. The punches were raining down like a hurricane. Keeping Mojo pinned, he couldn't duck or defend himself. Felt the darkness rolling in as the blows kept coming— an elbow slammed into his temple.

Flashbulbs flared in the air round him. Mick felt his grip slipping as his consciousness flickered. Clawing desperately at Johnson's jacket, he tried to keep his feet as the ground seemed to melt beneath him. He clutched Mojo's belt, trying to haul himself up— Mojo landed a hard right to his temple, breaking his hold. Breaking free of his grasp, Johnson kicked Mick in the chest, sending him sprawling. Then he snatched up his .38, his eyes wild with triumph!

Grinning, he eared back the hammer, his eyes locked on Mick's—

The alley exploded with gunfire!

Mick flinched, knowing he was fucking dead—

But he wasn't! He opened his eyes, looking around wildly—

Sweet Jesus! Somehow Moishe had staggered to his feet again, reeling towards them, blasting away with the .45, the big automatic bucking in his bloody fist.

Johnson stumbled backward as the heavy slugs punched into his chest, pulping his heart. Still he stayed upright, fumbling the .38, holding it two-handed now, aiming straight at Mick's face— a wild round slammed into his shoulder, spinning him around, bouncing him into Mick, carrying them both up against the Cadillac.

Then Mojo was toppling like a tree, bearing Mick down with him as he fell.

Moishe fired off a last wild round at Mojo, missing the big man as he dropped.

But he didn't miss Mick.

A white-hot iron seared Shannon's side as the slug ricocheted off the pavement, slashing across his ribs. Instant agony! Which doubled as Johnson crashed down on top of him, driving his breath out.

Blood was bubbling from Mojo's mouth as he struggled to rise...then he went suddenly rigid, shuddering in a final, violent seizure.

Mick felt the big man die. Felt the fetid dampness of Mojo's last gasp hot against his cheek. The ragged sigh as his soul fled. Felt his body slacken, settling onto Mick gently as a lover, pinning him to the ground with his bulk.

Dead weight.

A sudden gush of warmth flooded Mick's legs as Johnson's bladder let go.

Jesus! Jesus! Jesus!

Recoiling in horror, Mick tried to squirm free but couldn't shift Mojo's corpse. Pain was scorching his ribs like a blowtorch with every movement.

"Help me."

For a crazed moment Mick thought Mojo had spoken. He scanned the vacant brown eyes but they were already glazing over, lifeless as ball bearings.

Across the alley, Moishe was on his knees, the gun forgotten, holding the ivory hilt of the Arkansas pig sticker, dark blood pulsing between his fingers, soaking the crotch of his old-timey suit.

"Help me. *Gott in himmel!*"

Groggy from the punches, sick with horror, Mick's eyes locked on

Mojo's face, watching the bloody froth dribble from the corners of his mouth.

"Forgodsake, Irish."

The agony in Moishe's voice cut through the haze, snapping Mick back to reality. Inside the club, the jukebox was still thumping through the walls. James Brown. "Please, Please, Please!" The whole fucking scuffle hadn't taken much more than a minute or two.

Pulling himself together, Mick managed to wriggle out from under the corpse, kicking free of it, blood soaking his jacket, his slacks, even his shoes. Ripping his shirt open, he checked his rib cage. An ugly gash, oozing red. A flesh wound, though, not much penetration, like a gouge from a jailhouse shiv. It hurt like hell, but he wasn't dead yet.

Mojo was though. And Moishe too. Or damn near.

Stumbling to his feet, Mick helped the old man stagger to the lee of the building, easing him down with his back to the wall. Moishe moaned with every movement, his hands clasping the knife hilt, keeping it steady, trying to hold back the red stream of his life.

Grabbing up the .45, Mick stuffed it in his waistband. Had no fucking idea what to do next. James Brown's voice grew louder as the alley door opened.

Jerking out the gun, Mick aimed it at the gap. "You!" He motioned with bloody fingers. "Step the fuck out, right now! I'll blow your ass away, swear to god!"

Tuxedo hesitated, then edged warily out. Still impeccable, slender as a riding crop. Eying Mojo's corpse, he shook his head. "Oh, man," he murmured, looking more saddened than surprised.

"You got a doctor in this town?" Mick demanded.

"I probably got ten doctors in the house tonight, boy. Got lawyers, judges, CPAs. Likely a few cops. But ain't none of 'em about to mix into this white trash bullshit." Keeping his hands in plain view, Tuxedo crossed the alley to kneel beside Moishe.

"He's real bad," he said quietly. "We can't fix this. He needs a hospital fast."

"Then call a fucking ambulance!"

"No time. It'd take an hour to get one here from Clare, *if* they bothered to come at all. Shit happens in Idlewild, white folks don't wanna hear about it. 'sides, the old dude can't wait. He's Moishe Abrams, right?"

"You know him?"

"Everybody knows him. His people own the jukes, the vending machines. You with him? Mobbed up, I mean."

"What's that to you?"

"Boy, we in the same pigpen here. I got my own place in Motown. Summer weekends, I run this club for some Chicago people. Serious Chicago people, know what I'm sayin'?"

"No! What— ?"

"So neither one of us wants Moishe Abrams dead with the law and the Outfit all over our ass— "

Mick wobbled, his knees going rubbery. Tuxedo reached out to steady him. Slapping his hand away, Mick shoved the gun in his face. "Back the fuck off me!"

"You'd best put that piece away and see to yourself, white boy. You're about to bleed out."

"Fuck that! I'm all right!"

"Fine, It's your funeral. So? You got the gun. What do we do, tough guy?"

Mick stared at him, blinking, barely able to stand.

"Got no clue, have ya?" Brown sighed. "Jesus. Okay, listen up. I'll tell the band Mojo took off. Wouldn't be the first time. We'll put Moishe in my car, I'll run him back to Motown to a hospital. But if he dies on the road I'm dumpin' his ass in a ditch. I ain't takin' the weight for this."

"But— "

"But what? Keep screwin' the pooch, you both gonna die on me. I'll see to Moishe, but Mojo's your problem. You know the country around here?"

Mick shook his head.

"Then listen up! Five, six miles east of town, there's a dirt road that turns off to the south, leads into a marsh. No guardrails back there, no nothin'. That swamp will swallow 'bout anything, even a big ass Cadillac. You understand?"

Mick didn't. But he nodded. Too groggy to think straight.

"Ditch Mojo's ride in that muck," Tuxedo went on. "Nobody'll find it for awhile, maybe never. By the time you hoof it back here, the town'll be shut down for the night. Take Moishe's Lincoln car and fade. You were never here. Got it?"

"Wait! I need to think— !"

"No time for that shit!" Brown snapped. "Old man's bleedin' out. Make up your mind, white bread, or I'm leavin' you."

Mick couldn't focus. His ribs were ablaze, his wrist dripping red, his brain getting fuzzier by the second from the beating and blood loss.

A thousand possibilities were whirling wildly in his mind, all bad.

He was in way too deep. Had no idea what to do—

"A-zor li," Moishe moaned softly. "Help me."

CHAPTER 6

Mick stared down at the Samaritan Hospital parking lot five stories below. Gleaming car roofs, toy-sized people. He hated hospitals. The disinfectant, the institutional buzz. Nurses talking past you like you weren't there. In the prison infirmary, they— he felt someone's eyes on him and turned from the window. Moishe was awake. Staring at him.

Mick crossed to the bed. "Hey, Mr. Abrams, how you doin'?"

Dumb ass question. Moishe looked like crap on a cracker. A thousand years old. His wild days were history now, he was just another sick old man in a hospital bed. "Want some water? A nurse?"

Closing his eyes, Moishe shook his head with a barely perceptible movement. No. But when he opened them again, his gaze lanced into Mick like an icepick. Asking the question.

Mick glanced around quickly, making sure they were alone. "Idlewild?" he whispered. Remembering the nightmare.

He'd helped Moishe into the shotgun seat of Tuxedo's gleaming Studebaker Silver Hawk, the knife still stuck in his belly.

"Leave it be," Tuxedo ordered. "Bleedin's slowin' a bit. Pulling it could kill him."

After Tuxedo and Moishe roared away, Mick wrestled Johnson's corpse to the rear of the Caddy. But the trunk was crammed with boxes of Mojo's 45 records. No room at all. So Mick crammed the body down on the floor between the seats, folding him in half to get the damned door closed. The singer's knees were a good six inches above the window frame. Soaked with blood.

One-thirty in the morning, the wild-dog traffic scene had slowed some, but plenty of black folks were still cruising Lake Drive and Mick got the hard eye from a few brothers. He averted his eyes, hoping to Christ they were too busy staring him down to notice Mojo's bloody knees.

As he left the village limits, traffic began thinning out, and after he turned off onto the dirt road it vanished altogether.

Fighting the wheel as he bounced along the narrow track, he drove ever deeper into the boondocks, woozy from blood loss, fading in and out. Ribs on fire, seeping red. Forearm, too. Tuxedo was right, he should have wrapped his wounds. Too late now.

Mist was roiling up off the soggy ground like a goddamn vampire movie, couldn't spot the swamp if his life depended on it. Which it did.

He kept stopping the car, scrambling down the embankment to look for water. Wondering if the slick spade called the law the second he was out of sight.

Couldn't find any swampland at all. Brushy flatlands broken by clumps of tag alders and jack pine. On his fifth stop, he found water the hard way, stumbling into muck up to his knees, losing one of his shoes. Swamp water rolled away into the murk, dimly lit by the quarter moon. Steep banks on both sides of the road, no guardrail. This had to be the place.

It damned well better be.

Wedging the Caddy's gas pedal down with a rock, Mick let the engine rev up to the max, then he slammed the gearshift into low, leaping back as the big red machine went howling down the embankment, smashing through the underbrush, plunging into the water in an explosion of foam and debris.

But it didn't sink.

Mick stared in numb horror as the big sedan pinwheeled slowly away from the bank, engine screaming, tires churning the murky water to froth. Mojo's bloodstained corpse was clearly visible through the rear window.

For a gut-wrenching moment, he thought the big man was moving. Trying to get up. But it was only the car rocking as it settled into the ooze, bellowing like a dinosaur dying in a tar pit, until the swirling mud finally flooded the big V-8, choking it to deathly silence.

Swamp slime was inching up the Caddy's sides, gushing through the open windows, sucking the Eldorado down under the ooze.

Dazed, his guts in knots, ribs and wrist dripping blood, Mick watched as the big Caddy finally disappeared, leaving oily bubbles swirling in the ooze.

And still Mick stared, waiting for the red Cadillac to rise again. With Mojo at the wheel... he shook off the vision. Jesus, he had to get it together. This wasn't over yet.

He limped the five miles back to the Regency, wearing only one shoe, ducking into the brush to avoid headlights. Finally made it back to Moishe's Lincoln sometime after four a.m...

Realized Moishe was staring at him now. Waiting for an answer. Taut as a guy wire.

Mick swallowed. "Everything's covered, Moishe. It's handled."

"What— ?" He coughed weakly, hocking up a glob of spittle that drooled down the corner of his mouth. "Nurse said a black guy brought me in. Who was that?"

"The tuxedo guy from the bar. Brown? You don't remember?"

"Crazy bits and pieces...." He swallowed, wincing at the effort. "Who stuck me? Johnson?"

Mick nodded.

"And him?"

"He's gone. You won't see him again."

The old man absorbed that, considering it. "Okay. God. What a cock-up. My coat's in the closet, got a straight razor in the pocket. Get it."

"What— ?"

"Give it to me!"

"Okay, okay." Mick found the pearl handled straight razor in the jacket and handed it over. Moishe clasped it the way another man might grasp a rosary. He slipped the blade under the blanket. Armed now, and still dangerous. If only in his mind. Sagging back, he closed his eyes.

"I'm tired. Mick? You did good....."

His voice faded. For a second Mick thought the old man had died. But Moishe was still breathing. Barely. Taking a tissue from the bedside tray, Mick wiped the spittle from the corner of his mouth. Then leaned over him.

"It should be me in this bed, not you, Moishe," he whispered. "You saved my ass back there. I won't forget that."

He knew Moishe was zonked, that he was only talking to himself. But as he turned away, the old man grabbed Mick's wrist with his gnarled paw. With no more strength than a child.

"Wait," he murmured.

Mick scanned Moishe's face. Nothing. The old hump was still deep in dreamland. Probably waltzing with Rita Hayworth.

But he didn't pull away.

When the nurse looked in half an hour later, Mick was still there. Sitting at the bedside. Holding the old man's hand.

CHAPTER 7

When Mick walked in the next day, Moishe was sitting up in bed in a white terry bathrobe.

"You're late," the old man growled, greedily spooning down tapioca pudding. "Visiting started twenty minutes ago."

"Sorry, I didn't think you'd be— "

"Breathin'? Well, I am. Got a helluva bellyache, but it ain't my first."

"Good to see your mood's back to normal."

"Fuck my mood. I got trouble."

"What's wrong? What do the doctors say?"

"That I'm lucky to be alive. Some fuckin' luck. I'll be stuck in this dump a month."

"Beats bleeding out in that alley."

"You don't get it! I can't be off the street three days, let alone three weeks. When word gets around I'm laid up, nobody will pay. I'll lose everything."

"But when you're back on your feet— "

"Won't be nothin' to go back to. My action comes down through the Italians in Grosse Pointe. I fall behind, they'll hand my turf over to one of their own. I'll be lucky if they leave me breathin'."

"Jesus," Mick said.

Neither of them spoke for a moment.

"Look, I owe you big, I know that. Let me make it right. I'll cover for you, till you're on your feet."

"Fuck that, you're Ecorse Irish, Shannon. You wouldn't last five minutes inside 8 Mile. Half my accounts are jailbirds with a hard on for anybody white— "

"Good," Mick said, interrupting the old man's rant.

"Good?" Moishe echoed, baffled.

"Since you're already fucked, I won't worry about makin' it worse."

"Except for the part where some deadbeat kills your ass."

"I did five years in Jackson, Moishe. Never stepped off or bent over. I ain't easy to kill either and the way I see it, neither one of us has squat to lose anyway. I got this."

Moishe eyed him a moment. Then shook his head.

"You'll be dead in a day."

"If I can't pay Ronny Duke, I'm dead meat anyway. Tell me what to do, Moishe. It ain't like we got a choice."

"On your head be it," the old man said grimly. "Listen up."

Closing his eyes, Moishe recited forty-eight names like a rosary. Where to find them and how much each one owed to the last dime. Did the whole thing through without a pause, showing off. Then walked Mick through the first six names a dozen times, strictly by rote, nothing on paper. Until Mick had them nailed.

"All blacks or beaners," Moishe explained. "Nickel-dime neighborhood businesses, bodegas, bars, blind pigs. If they're short, always get something— " He broke off, coughing again, visibly tiring. "*Nem de gelt.* Get the money, Mick. If they ain't got it, take something worth more than

the vig. I know people who can peddle any fuckin' thing. You got
wheels?"

"A beater '57 Chevy— "

"Fuck that. In darktown, a man's ride has to show class. Take my Lincoln, but treat it right. Car's worth more'n you are. And get some de-
cent threads. Mannheim's, on Cadillac Square. Ask for Sol. He's my
cousin. Pick out a nice gabardine. Maybe a pinstripe."

"Pinstripe, right. Anything else?"

"Just one thing." The old man took a deep breath, wincing at the effort. "Mojo."

"What about him?"

"Deals can go south real sudden. Don't forget how it went with him."

"Not likely," Mick said.

CHAPTER 8

Mick drove Moishe's Lincoln but passed on the suit from Mannheim's.
Moishe dressed like George Raft, didn't know squat about style.

Knew about money, though. By Mick's reckoning, Moishe had over
sixty thousand on the street. Five hundred here, five grand there. Every
loan at five points a week.

His first stop was Moishe's rundown office on Dequindre, a storefront
building backed up to the D&R tracks. Abrams Vending Machines in
gold stick-on letters on the grimy glass door. A Salvation Army desk, a
phone, a torn sofa patched with a flannel turquoise blanket. A back room
with an army cot, a hot plate and a cheap transistor radio.

The dump smelled like a bus station. Dead hopes, dead ends. Forty
years of sharking, busting heads and god knows what, and this is all
Moishe had to show? No need to lock it up. Nothing in the place was
worth stealing.

Except the gun. Mick found a 1911 Army .45 where the old man said
it would be, in the top drawer of his desk. A rough piece but servicea-
ble, serial numbers filed off. Mick popped out the magazine, a full rack,
recently cleaned and oiled.

Jacked the cartridge out of the chamber, caught it before it fell. The action was loose, but still functional. A million of these pieces came
through the big war and Korea. His uncle Jerry brought one home from
Okinawa, where he'd lost a leg and most of his friends. He and Mick
had cranked a lot of rounds through it.

Mick hefted the piece. It felt familiar as a boxing glove. Common as dirt. Inside 8 Mile, you could buy one on almost any street corner. Fifty bucks.

Or five years.

As a felon in possession of a firearm, getting busted with a piece would cost him five years automatic, on top whatever else they could pile on. And he knew cops who'd roust him anytime they saw him.

Five more years in the joint? Still beat hell out of being dead forever.

He slammed the magazine into the butt, jacked a round into the chamber, and slid the piece into the small of his back.

Time to hit the street.

Chapter 9

Named for its distance from the river, 8 Mile marks the border between the dark heart of Detroit and the whiter suburbs. Inside the line, everybody knew who Moishe Abrams was. Knew he was a dinosaur from the Purple Gang days, mobbed up with the Italians now. He was a legend in the 'hoods, a hoodoo man in a snap brim hat. The monster hiding in your bedroom closet. Every mope in Motown had a Moishe Abrams story. Street kids traded 'em like baseball cards.

But there were no neighborhood sagas about Irish Mick Shannon.

In the slam and the ring, looking boyish had worked for him. Bigger men didn't take him seriously until they were flat on their ass, sucking wind, wondering what the fuck happened.

Mick might be a step too slow to be a top pro, but he was tough enough for the street.

Or so he'd thought. Until Idlewild.

He knew different now. In the alley behind The Regency, Mojo wasn't trying to knock him out, beat him down or win a decision on points.

He wanted blood. If Moishe hadn't stepped in, Johnson would have cut Mick's throat or blown his damn head off.

Death wasn't an abstract idea anymore. Its reality struck home as Mojo's dead weight settled onto his body, pressing him down, as he tasted the big man's last breath, felt the heated flush as his bladder emptied.

In Moishe's world, tough didn't mean squat. Only winning. Winners get to wake up in the morning, put on the coffee, catch the news on WJR.

Lose? Even once? And there's no round two. You end up in the bottom of a swamp in a jukebox Cadillac.

The big car had suicide doors and wide seats. Plenty of room for one more.

The first name on Moishe's list was Maceo's Market. A corner party store, pop, potato chips, day-old bread. Stroh's and Mick's Malt Liquor by the bottle, ninety-nine cents for a short dog, paper bag included. Maceo Willis was a roly poly black old timer in a dirty apron and raggedy goatee, processed hair going gray.

One look at Mick's boyish face, the checked sport coat and Dago boots, and Maceo was instantly all attitude.

"I hear Mr. Moishe's laid up in the hospital," Maceo groused, arms folded, making no move to open the register. "Might not be comin' out, neither. Cut real bad, I hear. People say he's shittin' in a bag."

"I'll tell him you're concerned about his health. I'm here today on business."

"Yeah, well that's a whole 'nother thing, youngblood. You look a little green to be collectin' up in here. I got two boys older'n you. An' they both a whole lot badder. Know what I'm sayin'?" Two bruisers ambled out of a back room as Maceo spoke, both built like fullbacks. One flipped the *Open* sign on the door over to *Closed*. Stood with his back to it, blocking the exit, giving Mick the eye.

Mick glanced at them, wincing as the gash along his ribs twinged at the movement. Maceo smiled, misreading the look, thinking it was panic.

The black plastic Motorola radio on the end of the counter was tuned to WCHB, Inkster. Joltin' Joe Howard introducing "Before You Accuse Me." A Bo Diddley blues tune Mick remembered from the joint. Great jam. The memory of it, hearing it in the joint, relaxed him.

"Way I see it," Maceo continued, "Maybe I'll lay back in the weeds a few days, see how ol' Moishe makes out. Maybe he sicker than you say. Maybe he dead. I mean, how I even know he sent you?"

Leaning over the counter, Mick motioned Maceo in closer.

"Mr. Willis, Moishe fronted you four large to cover your numbers bank last August," he said, keeping his voice low, barely above a whisper. "Your vig started at two cees a week and you been paying down a yard a week off the front. I need two forty today— " Jerking Moishe's army .45 from his belt, he jammed the muzzle hard under Maceo's chin. "Plus twenty extra for wasting my fucking time. If I don't see the two sixty on the counter in the next five seconds? Those big ass boys are gonna be scrapin' your brains off the ceiling with a spatula. Is there any part of that you don't understand?"

One of the thugs started toward them, but froze as Mick cocked the hammer. Maceo frantically waved him off, feeling the .45's muzzle ice cold against his chin.

"No questions," Maceo grumbled, straightening up slowly, keeping his hands in plain sight as he popped open the register to count out the cash. "You definitely Moishe's boy all right."

Number two on the list was Maloof's Barber Shop. White tile floors, mirrored walls. Three white-coated barbers working on clients, a half dozen black men waiting in chairs against the wall. The sweet scent of bay rum, lilac water and cigar smoke hanging in the air. Nat King Cole murmuring "Stardust" on one of Moishe's jukeboxes in the corner, background music for the easy banter between the barbers and their customers.

Which stopped dead when Mick walked in. Every man pausing to give the white boy the eye. Only Nat kept crooning.

"Can I help you?" the nearest barber asked. Big guy, light skinned, tight, curly hair, thick moustache. Algerian, Moishe said, a black Arab.

"Mr. Abrams sent me."

A long moment as Maloof sized him up. He'd been shaving his man, still had the straight razor in his hand. But Mick was still wired from the bodega, and the anger showed in his eyes.

Maloof moved slowly to retrieve an envelope from the drawer under the cash register. He held it tightly for a few seconds before letting go, showing class. But no trouble.

By mid-afternoon, Mick felt like he'd been working the same damn street for a year. Some people griped, some didn't. But everybody paid.

Cooley's was last on his list, a beer bar off Cass Avenue. The name on the license was Cyril Cooley but the real owner was Cyril's brother-in-law, Duwayne Jenks.

"Jackson Prison grad, a coke smoker with a serious case of jitters," Moishe said. "Got his eye gouged out in some prison yard thing, wears a black patch like a goddamn pirate. His drug habit keeps him jumpy, like he's only a twitch away from havin' a seizure. Looks mean, but won't be no trouble."

Dead wrong.

Mick sensed it the moment he pushed through the front door. A dark tension in the air, black as the mood in the Jackson showers before a gang rape.

The bar was nearly empty but the old Seeburg juke was cranked to the max, John Lee Hooker shouting "Smokestack Lightning", his guitar ringing off the walls like a damn anvil factory. Deafening. No reason for it to be so loud. Nobody was listening.

Jenks was at the far end of the bar next to the register, easy to spot because of his eye patch, head shaved smooth as a cue ball. Three men at the counter, all soul brothers, all big. Two were on stools down at Jenks's end, batting the breeze, their summer shirtsleeves rolled high to show off their iron-pumper biceps, decked out with crude prison tattoos. One was wearing a black do-rag, the other a bright yellow golf shirt, a huge mole on the bridge of his nose. A third stud was drinking alone at the far end of the bar, well away from the others, like he didn't know them. Wearing a blue Hawaiian shirt and a Detroit Tigers baseball cap.

Mick came on slowly, trying not to aggravate his sore ribs, giving his vision time to adjust to the gloom. Feeling the rhythm of John Lee's guitar, timing his breathing to its beat, letting the music settle him down. Put him in the mood.

In the joint, black fighters always shadowboxed to music, either live or in their heads. The music tuned 'em up, literally. Kept 'em loose, but focused. Ready for Freddy. Ready for anything.

Mick scoped out the shadows for trouble, trying to nail down why the setup felt so wrong. A long, narrow room, a dozen scarred Formica tables, wooden chairs. A hazy cloud of blue-gray smoke in the air. Jenks, the mole man and Do-rag were trading hits on a joint. Sucking down the smoke, holding it in for the rush. The three of them working a single doobie. Paying no attention to the guy sitting alone at the far end.

And that was it. Most of the blue haze was hanging over the tables, away from the bar. Butts were still smoldering in one ashtray, empty beer glasses beside it. More glasses at a table nearby, one half full. Other customers had been in here up until a very few minutes ago. Gone now. Somebody tipped off Jenks that Mick was coming, and he and buds must have cleared everybody out.

No witnesses.

With Moishe down, DuWayne Jenks was looking to break his deal, Detroit style. Disappear the new boy somewhere, maybe in the same swamp as Mojo. Claim you paid him off. Who could say different? For a split second, Mick could almost smell the rank stanch, hear the sigh of Johnson's last breath.

He got a powerful jolt of adrenaline, stark fear mixed with a rising tide of red-eyed rage.

"What'll it be, young stud?" Jenks called. A signal. At the far end of the bar, Tigers cap rose casually, tossed down a dollar, headed out. But he didn't actually leave. At the door he apparently changed his mind, strolling over to the cigarette machine. Loitering in front of it, like he'd forgotten his brand.

All this happening in the few seconds it took Mick to stalk the length of the bar down to Jenks and the other two. He stopped six feet away from them, glancing back at Tigers cap, who was still dawdling at the cigarette machine, trying to look nonchalant. Mick guessed the front door was locked now. Felt his wounded forearm tensing, palms itching to make a fist, throw the first punch.

Jenks was just as edgy, wired up on bennies or cocaine, fidgeting, wired up for action but trying not to look it. Do-rag and the guy in the yellow golf shirt swiveled slowly on their stools to face the new kid, Mick. Seen up close, Yellow Shirt's mole had hair growing out of it. The blemish gave him an alien, three-eyed look.

"I'm Shannon. Moishe Abrams sent me. You got something for me."

"Sure do, boy, sit yourself down, you can check the count right here," Jenks said, tossing an envelope on the bar. Next to Do-rag. Mick didn't move.

"Bring it to me."

"Hey, I ain't no fuckin' mailman," Jenks said, glancing nervously at the other two. "I'm payin' y'all way too much anyway, layin' out hard cash money for a junky fuckin' jukebox I could buy for twenty dollars at the Goodwill. Ol' Moishe never changes no records, same shit on it as when I took over the place— "

Mick tuned him out. Jenks' rant was strictly a distraction. The barman was working himself into a fury while Tigers Cap slowly edged up from behind on Mick's blind side.

Moving too slowly to suit Do-rag.

"Fuck this white punk!" Do-rag growled, coming off his stool with a six-inch switchblade in his fist. "We gettin' paid for the man. This one's just a kid."

Mick jerked the .45 but Do-rag kept right on coming, so buzzed on reefer and rage he didn't see the Colt. Or maybe he was too stoked to care.

"Slow up, stud! Back off!" Mick warned. Do-rag lunged at him instead, hooking upward with the blade, trying to open Mick's guts. Hurling himself backward, Mick stumbled into a table, falling as Do-rag slashed wildly at his face— the Colt exploded like a thunderbolt, once, twice, bucking in Mick's fist, the copper jacketed slugs punching into Do-rag's torso, sending him stumbling back against the bar.

Stunned, clutching his chest, his mouth bubbling red, Do-rag stared in stunned surprise at the gouts of blood pumping out between his fingers. He turned to Jenks, tried to speak but didn't have enough breath. His knees buckled and he collapsed to the dirty Linoleum floor, the blade clattering down beside him.

For a split second, nobody moved, Mick every bit as shocked as the others, running on adrenalin and reflexes now. Yellow Shirt was only a step away, a Bowie knife in his left hand, eyes wide. Centering the muzzle on the hairy mole, Mick let him stare down the barrel.

"Drop that pig sticker and sit your ass down, stud. I won't say it twice."

After a moment's hesitation, Yellow Shirt tossed his knife on the floor and eased slowly back onto his stool at the bar.

"You! By the cigarette machine, get the fuck over here."

"Hey, mister, I got nothin' to do with this— " Tigers cap babbled, edging toward the door, desperately measuring the distance.

"You won't make it, dumbshit. You locked it, remember? But if you want to try, go ahead on. I'm in the mood." And he truly was. He was only a word away from killing them all. And they damn well knew it.

Moving very carefully, Tigers cap walked back to the bar, holding his hands waist high, palms up, fingers spread. Stopped a few stools down from Yellow Shirt and Jenks.

"Look, white boy— "

"Shut up!" Mick snapped. "You wanna live through this?" he asked Yellow Shirt.

The man nodded, swallowing hard, his golf ball Adam's apple bobbing up and down.

"When we're done here, you and Tigers cap are gonna pick up your buddy and stash him in the same place you figured to stash me. Then you're gonna fade. Out of Detroit. If I ever see your face again, I'll be the last thing you ever see. Understand?"

Yellow Shirt nodded again, his eyes still locked on Mick's, reading the mix of fear and killing rage. Knowing he was only a split second from being as dead as Do-rag.

"The guy on the floor?" Mick said, gesturing with the weapon. "He said he was here for the man. He meant Moishe, right? You weren't expecting me?"

"No man," Jenks said, "it wasn't nothin' personal, just a job, you know? On the old man, not you— "

"Shut up. I'm guessing Moishe's money isn't in that envelope. Is it, Jenks?"

One-eye Jenks thought about lying, then just shook his head.

"Too bad. Your note just came due. Every fucking dime of it. Nine thousand six, plus the fifty rent you owe for that piece of shit jukebox. You got it?"

"Not today, but— "

"Fuck that. You're out. This joint belongs to Mr. Abrams now. I'll be at his office at five. You and your brother-in-law bring the nine six, or the title for this place and sign it over."

"You can't— "

Mick fired! The slug ripping past Jenks' face so close the muzzle blast seared his cheek before it slammed into the cash register, rocking it, popping the cash drawer open.

Ka-ching.

"Okay, okay, Jesus!" Jenks babbled, backing away, palms raised to ward off the next slug. "We'll bring the damn papers over. We'll bring 'em!"

But they didn't. Mick waited until seven, then went back to Cooley's looking for Jenks.

He found the place deserted. The cash register drawer was open and empty. The floor where Do-rag fell had been hastily scrubbed, but the signs of violence were clear enough if you knew where to look. They'd dragged him out the back way to god knows where, hadn't even bothered to mop up all the blood.

But the lease and liquor license were on the bar.

Signed over.

And notarized.

□   □   □

Mick didn't go back to his flat in Ecorse that night. He crashed on the cot in the back room of Moishe's office instead. The way the day had gone, it might be safer not to be where he was expected to be.

Couldn't sleep, though. Stared up at the water-stained ceiling. Sorting things out.

Three days ago, he'd been a club fighter, a pug without much of a future. Now? He knew exactly what his life was worth. Nothing. And how quickly it could end. In a Motown minute.

He tried to summon some regret for the thug who'd come at him in Cooley's. Or for Mojo. Couldn't quite manage it. He hadn't asked for it. They'd tried their luck, his had been better. This time. Maybe tomorrow it wouldn't be.

Maceo had called him Moishe's boy. And maybe that's what he was now, like it or not. If so, there were worse things to be. Like buried in a swamp outside Idlewild. Or dead on a barroom floor. He hadn't chosen any of it, but he was in it now, ready or not.

Back in the joint, he'd made big plans. Figured he could fight his way up the ladder to the serious dough. Maybe even a championship.

Right. Now he'd be lucky to live through the week.

Definitely time for a new plan. Tomorrow. He'd come up with one tomorrow.

It was eleven o'clock. Lights out. Jailhouse habits are hard to break. Pulling Moishe's cheap plastic Motorola close to his ear, he tuned in WLAC Nashville. John R. on the mike. Blues in the night, all night, Jimmy Reed, Howlin' Wolf, Muddy and the Kings, B.B. and Albert.

And the blues queens, Mamie Smith, Ma Rainey, Alberta Hunter. "Copulatin' Blues", "Blacksnake Blues." Hard people singing about hard times.

Mick could relate.

He kept volume low, though there were no guards to hear. Another jailhouse habit. Finally drifted off with his cheek pressed against the tube-warmed plastic case, while Ruth Brown crooned a lullabye... The same way he'd slept every night for five long years. The radio his only lifeline to the world outside.

Fell asleep dreaming about the dance floor at the Regency, brown-eyed handsome men and their high-style women, dancing to Mojo Johnson's blues, as colorful and exotic as African birds...

CHAPTER 10

Next morning, Mick was in Moishe's room, on time. He'd had some misgiving about bringing cash to the old man in the hospital but it was the right thing to do. Wounded and sick, holding the money clearly gave Moishe a lift.

He riffled through it expertly, confirming the count. He quickly scanned the title and liquor license from Cooley's. Then glanced up at Mick.

Reading him like a parole officer.

"What happened with this?"

"Not much," Mick said. He'd decided not to talk about Cooley's. He didn't know Moishe well enough. Didn't know anybody that well. "They couldn't pay. They gave me the paperwork."

"Bullshit," Moishe said bluntly. "I know Jenks. He didn't hand over the bar. I asked you what the fuck happened?"

"I handled it, Moishe. That's it," Mick shrugged.

The old man eyed him suspiciously, then shook his head, smiling.

"What?" Mick asked.

"Nothin'. You're learnin', is all. You have to use the .45 I gave you?"

Mick nodded.

"Lose that piece, then," Moishe said. "All the tests they do nowadays, a gun's like an eyeball witness. That's why I use army .45s. Big slug, lotta power. Million of 'em around so they're hard to trace. Ream out the barrel to fuck up the rifling, then bust up the frame. Throw the parts away, different places."

Another nod.

"You did good, getting the paperwork, but cash is better."

"They didn't have cash."

"Figures. Jenks is a deadbeat mother. Thing is, with cash, there's no way to say who got how much. Paperwork like this, I gotta send up the line to Grosse Pointe. Mr. Luca's lawyers check it over, make sure it'll transfer straight up and legal."

"Then you get it back?"

"Not these days," Moishe said sourly. "I'll be lucky to get a taste. Is Jenks still breathin'?"

"Was, last I saw of him."

"Too bad. That fuck always was trouble. Next time, *nem de gelt*. Get the cash." He winced at stab of pain. "I ain't bustin' your balls here. You made it past Jenks, you gotta be tougher than you look," the old man conceded, waving the paperwork from Cooley's. "But take a lesson from seein' me in here. You can't do business from a hospital. Or a hole in the ground. I make our count six grand. The Italians take twenty percent. If they offer to cut me a break, you say no. I don't need it. Got it?

"No break," Mick nodded.

"How much are you down to Ducatti?"

"Sixeen. Eighteen now, with the vig."

"All right," Moishe said, counting out the bills, putting them in a separate envelope. "Pay him off."

"I haven't earned this— "

"I know you ain't earned it! But as long as you owe Ronnie, he owns a piece of you. I don't want no confusion about who you work for."

"There's no confusion on my end, Moishe. How about yours?"

"What do you mean?"

"Jenks was laying for me. Only he didn't know it would *be* me. He was expecting you. Said it wasn't personal. Just a job."

The ole man looked away a moment, then nodded.

"Okay. You know the St. Clair Club, in Grosse Pointe?"

"I— know where it is, sure."

"You go there this afternoon. See Mr. Luca at a table in the back, give him these envelopes."

"The title too?"

"Their lawyers will go over it, make sure it can't be traced back us, then sell it off. Go alone. And clean up. Wear a jacket and tie."

"Why? What's— ?"

"Shut up and listen. It's like a fuckin' job interview and I need you to pass. If they ask questions, you play dumb. *Don't* tell 'em nothing about my business, understand? Years ago, I had a crew workin' the street for me. Far as you know, I still do, understand?"

Hell no he didn't understand, but Moishe's energy was fading, swirling down the drain.

"I got this, Moishe. You get some rest."

"I can rest up when I'm dead," the old man growled. "Deal with old man Luca, Irish. And don't fuck me up."

CHAPTER 11

The St. Clair Shores Club is a sprawling bar-restaurant a few blocks from the Ford plant in River Rouge. Strictly blue collar, its taproom did a heavy shot-and-a-beer trade, boilermakers, schnapps or whiskey triples. Waitresses bustling between the pine tables with laden trays. Shop rats in flannel shirts and baseball caps loading up to face the din and dirt of the assembly lines, or getting hammered after a shift to forget it. Men arguing sports or talking shop. A big Seeburg jukebox thumping out pop tunes of a decade earlier, Sinatra, Perry Como, the Mills Brothers' singing "Paper Doll."

Mick heard buzz about the St. Clair in prison, knew it was a mob front. One corner of the dining room was blocked off by a spindled divider, as tough to get past as the Berlin Wall. Four tables in that corner had permanent 'reserved' signs on them. Two goons lounged near the divider to make sure they stayed private.

Union stewards, local pols and even cops could pop into the St. Clair to wash down a quick lunch, do some glad-handing. Some would pass an envelope to one of the men playing pinochle at the rear table. Or pick one up.

Taking Moishe's advice, Mick cleaned up. Wore his best houndstooth sport coat, black button-down shirt, snake-skinny necktie. His wounds from Idlewild were taped up tight. His ribs were sore and still weeping fluid, but his jacket concealed the bandage as well as the one on his forearm. Good to go.

At the St. Clair, he threaded through the crush to the rear dining area. One goon on duty, watching him come. Older guy, Moishe's generation. Stone gray hair combed back in Polack waves, thick glasses, brown leather bomber jacket. He stood up, blocking the aisle. Jerked a thumb at the 'reserved' sign.

"I'm Shannon. Moishe Abrams sent me to see Mr. Luca."

Bomber jacket glanced past the divider, got a nod.

"Open your jacket." Mick did, expecting to get frisked. A look was enough. Brush cut waved him past.

Four card players at the table. Ronny Duke, big and blonde in a blue sharkskin suit, short Princeton haircut and a bloody-eyed hangover. The stud next to him was fifty-ish squared-off thug in a bulky Local 54 Teamsters jacket, salt and pepper flat top, his pasty face mottled as a pimento loaf.

A college kid in a University of Detroit navy blazer was dealing. Hair trimmed short, Sinatra style, with the same narrow face, pouty mouth. Despite the smoky dimness, Joe College was wearing sunglasses. He glanced up at Mick, cocking his head like a crow to look him over. Then went back to shuffling the cards without comment.

At the head of the table, The Man. John Luca. Fifty-ish and elegant, with dark, silver-streaked hair in a perfect pompadour and a nose like a Roman emperor. White alpaca sweater, manicured nails. A familiar face. He'd been headline news in Detroit for years. Called as a witness at Jimmy Hoffa's racketeering trial, Big John took the fifth amendment twenty-six times. Gave the prosecutor his name and address, period. Luca's sunlamp tan couldn't conceal the broken veins on that classic nose, though. Mick made him for a juicer. Luca nodded at him.

"You're...Shannon? Do you know who I am?"

"Yes sir. Seen you on TV."

"Not as dumb as he looks," the college boy cracked.

"This is my nephew, Albert," Luca said, nodding toward the college kid. Things work out, maybe you'll be working for him one day."

"Not in that greaseball haircut," Albert snorted. "The Elvis look is over, Tex." He fanned his cards, scanning his hand, knowing Mick wouldn't say anything.

"This is Charlie Musso, and I guess you know Ronny," Luca senior continued. Musso was the squared off union hood. Ducatti glanced up, nodded a bleary hello. None of the others bothered.

"How's Moishe doing?" Mr. Luca asked.

"Good. Not quite a hundred percent, but good."

"Really?" Luca's eyebrows went up. "From what I've heard— well. Glad he's doing better. He worked for my father back in the day. A real old timer."

"He's a fucking dinosaur," Albert snorted.

"Maybe you should tell him that," Mick snapped. "To his face, I mean.

See how it goes."

"Are you going to cover the old man's end if he comes up short?" Musso asked.

"Not likely," Ducatti snorted. "He's the fighter who lost his ass betting on himself."

Mick ignored the dig, still watching Albert. And suddenly his sunglasses made sense. One lens was darker than the other, masking a milky, sightless eye. A white worm of scar tissue curled out of the puckered socket, nestling in his brow.

"Settle down, guys," Luca said, waving them to silence. "A few years ago, that thing in Idlewild wouldn't have happened. Albert's right, the old man's probably past it. We'll give him a breather on the vig."

"He said you might offer," Mick said, taking two envelopes out of his vest pocket, sliding one in front of John Luca, the other across to Ronny Duke. "Said he didn't want any favors."

Ronny checked his count, then nodded, surprised. "We're good, Shannon. Does this mean you're out?"

"It means I owe Moishe now," Mick said.

Luca thumbed his money without counting. But he fished the title to Cooley's out of his envelope, scanned it, then eyed Mick curiously. "What's this?"

"A title to a bar. Cooley's. We had to close out the account."

"Did something go wrong?"

Mick wasn't sure what to say, so he said nothing. Which is sometimes the right thing.

"My people been askin' around about you, Shannon," Luca said, folding the title into an inside pocket. "Nobody knows anything. Why is that?"

"I've been away."

"In Jackson, for a nickel," Ronny Duke said. "Assault on a police officer. What was that all about?"

"Personal," Mick said.

John Luca glanced up, then nodded to Musso.

"Shannon jumped his ma's boyfriend in a coffee shop. Ecorse cop. Busted him up, plus two of his cop buddies. The judge said it showed 'contempt for authority.' Sentenced him as an adult. Did I miss anything?"

Mick shook his head. The man had done his homework.

"Five years?" Albert snorted. "I hope the old lady was worth it."

Mick almost backhanded him out of his chair. Barely caught himself. "She's gone, actually," he said evenly, measuring his words. "Passed while

I was inside. And if you've got anything else to say about her, you'd better stand the fuck up."

Everyone at the table caught the edge in his tone.

Albert flushed an angry red. "Get your dog on a leash, Ronny."

Ducatti started to say something, but Musso waved him off.

"Do you know who you're talking to?" Musso asked, his pig eyes narrowing dangerously.

"Nope," Mick said. "And neither does he, or he'd watch his fucking mouth."

"It's all right, Charlie," Big John said quietly. "The boy's right. Albert was out of line. And he'll apologize. Won't you, Albert?"

"Sure," Albert said, more annoyed than angry. "Sorry about that, sport."

"This cop you jumped," Musso went on. "Spivak?"

"I thought you didn't know much about me."

"Charlie knows more shit than Mr. Wizard," Ronny Duke said. "He's just showing off."

"Word is, Spivak's still pissed off," Musso said. "He's looking for you."

"Make sure he doesn't find you," Luca added. "We have useful friends in most departments. That's why Moishe's incident went into the books as an unsolved mugging. If there's any blowback from Idlewild, you two take the weight for it. And for this," he added, holding up the title for Cooley's. "Any questions?"

Mick had a big one. About the clowns at the bar waiting for Moishe. Paid to do a job... . Albert was watching him, with a barely concealed smirk. Like he was reading his mind.

"No," Mick said. "No questions."

"All right then," Luca said. "Moishe sent you, but you're new to the work. Maybe someone else on his crew should be handling it. Someone older. Who's he working with now?"

Mick didn't answer.

"My uncle asked you a question," Albert Luca snapped.

"I'm the new guy, haven't met everybody. Moishe tells me what to do, I do it. That's it."

"You may work for Moishe, but he works for us," John Luca said pointedly. "Our end of his action stays the same, no matter who's collecting."

"I'll see to it."

"You won't have to. Not all of it, anyway. While Moishe's laid up, Charlie Musso will take over East Detroit and Highland Park. You handle his Grand River accounts, the blacks, the Spanish. Any shortages come out of your end, not ours. When Moishe can show up himself, we'll talk again. Carry your weight, you'll make out, Shannon. Fuck up and bad things will follow. Understand?"

Mick nodded.

Luca arched an eyebrow, waiting. Exactly like a punk ass Jackson hack, Mick thought.

"Yes sir, Mr. Luca. I understand."

"Good. Ronny will be your contact from now on. Don't come back here again."

"Yes sir, Mr. Luca," Mick said again, but no one noticed. To the men at the table, he was already gone.

CHAPTER 12

"They fucked you," Moishe groaned. "Bent you over and done you like a dog. I shoulda known."

"You didn't agree to anything. If I got the deal wrong, I'll straighten it out."

"You don't get it. Sending you was the same as going myself. But Luca made you for a rookie and screwed us both. Gave my white accounts to Musso, left me the ghetto. If I'm a nickel short he'll take the rest. He's looking to squeeze me out."

"Why?"

"Because his fucking nephew wants my territory and John's a greedy fucking Sicilian *gonif*, that's why! His father was Greaseball Joe Luca. Ran whores, numbers for the Licavolis. A fucking *pimp*. After the Collingwood war killed off most of the Purple Gang, Greasy Joe took in us that was left. Smart guy, Joe. Good with books. We all made money. And if he fucked you, he did it to your face. Not like his weasel rat bastard— " Moishe broke off, coughing, redfaced, hawking up gobs of tapioca and spittle on his hospital pajamas. "What did you tell 'em about my crew?"

"The truth. I'm the new guy. Know from nothin'."

"Got that right, at least," the old man said sourly. "That's the key to a thing. What the other guy don't know, he don't know."

"There's more," Mick said. "At Cooley's, what Jenks said about laying for you? I think they already knew. Albert did, anyway."

"What did he say?"

"Nothing. Just a feeling is all."

"Look, I know this ain't what you signed on for. If you want out— "

"I don't. I'm as jammed up as you are. Musso says that Ecorse cop Spivak, is looking for me."

"If he finds you, we're both fucked," Moishe said flatly. "If you go down— " He didn't bother to finish. "Anything else?"

Damn straight there was. Mick wanted to know who else on the list might try to cap him, what else Moishe was holding back. But he didn't ask. The old man looked ready to drop and Mick'd had all he could handle of the stuffy room, the reek of antiseptic and the drainage from Moishe's wound.

"You take it easy, Moishe. I got this."

"Did you use that piece? You gotta ditch it."

"I know, you told me."

"Then why you loafin' around here?"

"The names, Moishe," Mick said patiently. "I need the next six names."

"Right," Moishe said absently. "I was just checkin'. You ready?"

Hell no he wasn't ready.

But he memorized the next six names anyway.

CHAPTER 13

After the hospital, Mick headed out to his rented digs in Ecorse. Needed to crash. The punches were coming too fast. Ibo's fists. Idlewild. The fight at Cooley's. And now Spivak, hunting him? Jesus. He needed a standing eight count, time to get his head around it all.

It felt like a bomb had exploded in his life, blowing his whole world sky high. And now the wreckage was crashing down around him. Images flashing into his memory like slides from a broken projector.

Smokestack Lightning thundering on the jukebox at Cooley's. The stunned look in Mojo's eyes as his legs gave out— Mick shook off the vision. Think about that later. A whole lot later. Maybe never.

Right now, he needed to keep moving, keep punching. But he was running on empty, hadn't eaten a damned thing all day.

Which was one problem he could solve. Maybe two. He was rolling up on Scotty's Diner, just inside the Ecorse limits.

The place where his young life went wrong. If Spivak was hunting him, maybe he should return the favor. Pop in, say hello. He slowed, and pulled the Lincoln into the lot.

Climbing out of the Lincoln felt like time travel. The diner looked the same. Finished in stainless steel with a rounded roof like a railroad club car, it had a half dozen hot rods parked out front. A chopped '58 Mercury Turnpike Cruiser with the electric rear window, painted two- tone pink and black. Metallic gold '53 Olds Fiesta, with Frenched tail lights.

Inside, a gleaming red Formica counter, chromed stools, varnished plywood booths. Roy Orbison on the jukebox, *Only The Lonely*, a great make-out song. Mick let the tune lift his heart a bit as he made his way to a booth in the corner.

Felt like his own ghost. Used to hang in this place with his buddies on high school nights. How long ago? Six years? Nearer seven? It seemed like a lifetime had passed, but from the look of the place, he could have walked out yesterday. Shop rats in coveralls and work boots chomping burgers at the counter, bobby-soxers in poodle skirts and ponytails sipping sodas and giggling at a corner table. A crew of young toughs were huddled in a booth near the door, black nylon jackets and Elvis style ducktails, greased back. Collars turned up. Trying to look bored and hard. A few years ago, he could have been one of them—

"What'll you have?" A perky blonde waitress in a pink uniform, matching cap. Honey colored hair tied back in a ponytail. Oval face, bright eyes. Good looker. And vaguely familiar.

"Coffee. Cheezeburger, apple pie. I know you, right?"

"Puh-leeze," she sighed, jotting down his order.

"No, really. American History, second hour. Mrs. Gibson's class."

She gave him a quick once-over. "I don't remember you."

"I wasn't there much. Mick Shannon. You're— " he glanced at her nametag— "Leanne something." He offered his hand. She ignored it.

"Back in a jif." She marched briskly back to the counter, looking really good going away. Round, firm ass, great legs. The hoods in the booth were watching him, watching her. Mick turned away. One of them waved Leanne over, asked her something. About him? Probably. She shrugged and kept going.

But he noticed her checking him out as she poured his coffee at the counter.

"I remember you now," she said when she brought his order. "But not from school. You're the bad-ass who busted that cop's arm with a ball bat."

"A billy club, actually," he corrected. "His."

"You went to jail."

"A long time ago."

"I'll bet Sergeant Spivak doesn't think so. His arm never did straighten out right. Cops come in here sometimes. You'd better be gone when they do."

"Can I finish my burger?"

"I'm serious."

"Maybe you oughta do like she says, pal. Take a hike."

One of the hoods from the bunch in the corner had moved up behind her. Tall, slender kid, with teenage acne. Bait. They sent the easy meat over to sucker him in. After the jailhouse games he'd seen in Jackson, it was almost comic. Leanne moved back behind the counter, watching them as she wiped it down.

"Take a seat," Mick offered. "I won't hurt you."

"Hurt me? What are you smokin'? I'm not afraid of you."

"Then sit. You can do your act from there."

"What act? What the fuck you talking about?" The guy glanced uneasily over at his buddies, then slid into the booth across from Mick. Giving him the hard eye. Wasn't half bad at it, either.

"C'mon, we both know the game. You give me some shit, maybe smack me one, we step outside to dance, your buddies kick my ass, rip me off. Only you don't wanna do that."

"Why not?"

"Because we're family. I'm your second cousin on your mama's side."

"Bullshit. You're no kin to me."

"I am now," Mick said, leaning in, keeping his voice low. "Because that's what you'll tell your friends. You didn't recognize me because I've been away. In the joint. For bustin' up a cop. The sorry truth is, I can break every bone in your face before your pals make a move. Whatever happens after that, you'll be a mouth breather the rest of your life. But there's no need for it. Because I'm your second cousin, Mick Shannon. The one who works for Moishe Abrams. You've heard of Moishe, right?"

The name obviously registered. The kid blinked, confused now.

"Don't look at them, look at me. At the scars on my hands." He laid his palms flat on the table. Scarred knuckles, enlarged joints. The kid swallowed.

"What's your name?" Mick asked.

"Al— " He coughed. "Aldo."

"Cousin Aldo," Mick smiled, giving him a love slap on the cheek. "Tell your mama I said hi. Now go back to your friends. They're beginning to wonder."

Aldo rose, nodded at Mick then swaggered back to his crew. To tell them about his tough guy cousin. They eyed Mick as they listened, then went back to jiving each other.

Leanne brought a coffee pot to Mick's booth.

"Don't mix it up with those guys," she said, topping off his cup. "They're bad news."

"They're just kids."

"They're as old as you are."

"Not anymore. I'm a lot older than I look. What time do you get off?"

"None of your business. Besides, you're leaving."

"I am?"

"A cop car just pulled in. Might even be Sergeant Spivak. Do you wanna find out?"

"Probably not," Mick sighed. "Does this place have a back door?"

"Through the kitchen. Come on, I'll show you."

Tossing a five on the table, he followed her around the counter into the steamy kitchen. The Mexican fry cook didn't even look up.

The screen door opened onto a loading dock. "Thanks for helping me out."

"Don't get a big head about it, I just don't want any trouble on my shift. Where's your car?"

"Over there. The black Lincoln."

"No kidding?" she said, curious at last. "That's a really nice ride. What do you do, exactly?"

"I'm in the collection business. Do you work here every night?"

She looked him up and down. He looked back. Nice view. Blonde hair, bold blue eyes and built for speed.

"Most nights, I'm on two to ten. Fridays and Sundays off. Not that it's any of your business."

"You're right," Mick nodded. "It's not."

But it might be.

And later on, as he crashed on the cot in his hole-in-the-wall rented room, he thought about what it really looked like. What his life would look like. To a hot blonde, built for speed.

CHAPTER 14

Mick expected a fresh round of trouble making his rounds the next day, but surprisingly, he had no problems at all. A pool hall, couple of mom and pop groceries, a barber shop-numbers bank. Everybody had the money up, ready and waiting, already counted, in envelopes. Inside 8 Mile, word on the street passes faster than jungle drums. Even the gash on his ribs was closing, feeling a bit better.

Late afternoon, a gleaming '63 Pontiac Bonneville rolled up outside

Moishe's office. Convertible, metallic blue, split grill, split tailfins. Waxed to a high shine.

Ronny Duke climbed out, looking as sharp as his ride. New mohair suit, wing tips, blonde hair neatly trimmed. Mick was behind Moishe's scarred desk in shirtsleeves, his checked jacket hanging on a wall hook.

"How they hangin', country boy?" Glancing around the office, Ronny shook his head. "Love what you've done with the place. You got something for me?"

Mick slid an envelope over. Resting a haunch on the corner of the desk, Ronny did a quick count of the money, nodded when he finished.

"All here. And I've got something for you." He passed Mick an envelope.

"Six grand," he said, after a quick count. "For what?"

"Your end of that Cooley's thing. Big John's lawyers already found a buyer."

"Why six?" Mick asked, feeling his blood rise. "I've worked in bars, know a little bit about 'em. That place is worth twenty-five, thirty grand."

"Not to you. Title had to be laundered. It's under new management now. Elmo Suggs bought it. Heavyweight contender a few years back. Cooley's has a bad rep, needs a guy like Elmo to handle the rough element."

"But it was on Moishe's turf, his account. Doesn't he get a say?"

"Not your problem, sport. Like you said, you're the new guy. But you're not as green as I thought. I know Jenks and those bad-ass cons he was runnin' with. How'd you get past those fucks?"

Mick didn't say anything.

"C'mon, it's on the street you took 'em apart. Put one in the ground, ran the others off."

"Don't believe everything you hear."

"Long green's all I believe in," Ronny grinned, flicking the wad of bills with a fingertip.

"You like it so much, you should try collecting it."

"Not me, I'm with management." Ronny slipped the envelope into an inside pocket. "Can I ask you somethin'? That night at Olympia Stadium, second round? Your body shot nearly broke Ibo in half. Where'd you learn that punch? The slam?"

"No. Bull work on my grandfather's farm. Gym rats pump iron for an hour, think it's a workout. Summers, I was in the fields at first light, heaving eighty pound hay bales up on a flatbed wagon. Compared to that, a six-round bout barely breaks a sweat."

"Sounds too much like work," Ronny snorted. "So does working the ghetto with Moishe's crew. How many guys is the old man running these days?"

Mick just stared.

"Don't be a chump, Shannon. The old kike's history. Even if he scrapes by this time, Moishe he can't last much longer. Albert wants his action and sooner or later Big John's gonna give it to him."

"I can't see Albert working 8 Mile."

"He won't be. You'll work it for him."

"Not likely. We didn't exactly hit it off."

"He can be pushy, sometimes," Ronny nodded.

"He looks like somebody pushed back. How did his eye get messed up?"

"High school scuffle. Albert was whompin' some kid with a brick, kid's big brother grabbed it away from him, smashed Albert's face, wrecked his eye. He's been a scary sumbitch ever since."

"I'd worry more about the guy who clobbered him."

"No need. Me and Musso grabbed that punk up, took him to Musso's garage in Dearborn. Albert jammed the kid's head in a machinery vise, squeezed it one turn at a time till his fuckin' eyes popped out. I damn near puked. Boxers like Killer K dig puttin' the hurt on people but when it comes to pain, Albert's in a whole different league. He's like one of those old time Dago princes in history books."

"All the more reason to stay clear."

"Won't be able to for much longer. The mob's action in Detroit has always been the unions; skim money, pension funds, no-show jobs. But fuckin' Bobby Kennedy and the feds are puttin' the screws to that. Dave Beck's doin' a nickel at McNeil Island, Jimmy Hoffa's goin' away for jury tampering. Without that union money, the family will have to take back the streets. Dinosaurs like Moishe will get pushed aside for new blood."

"I can't see Moishe stepping aside for Albert or anybody else, and if it comes to it, I'm with Moishe."

"Seriously? You'll stick in Darktown with that old Yid?"

"Darktown's fat city compared to places I've been. Anything else?"

"Any colored cathouses around here? I got the urge."

"I'm not a pimp."

"You're not as smart as I thought, either. Tell you what, let's hit a couple hotspots tonight. Kill some brews, talk some more. Have a good ole howl at the moon."

Mick eyed Ducatti, knowing he was selling something, not sure what.

"I can howl," he said.

□   □   □

He wound up as a barroom babysitter instead. He hooked up with Ronny Duke at the Chesterfield Lounge at ten. Brother Jack McDuff's Hammond organ-based quartet was cooking hard, big Red Holloway on tenor sax.

The band was too jazzy for Ronny's taste so they moved on, and none too soon. Ducatti was already half in the bag, hitting on black chicks, mouthing off to their boyfriends, practically begging to have his head handed to him. Mick had a mild whiskey buzz going, but he wasn't too wrecked to read the looks they were getting. Time to move on.

By the time they wobbled into the Flame Show Bar at midnight, Ronny was barely coherent. They shouldered their way to the bar near the small stage. Dinah Washington was crooning "What a Difference a Day Makes." Mick thought the old torch singer looked down and out, but her velvet blues voice suited his mood.

The music spoke to him, of sadness and loss. But there was an odd comfort, in knowing he wasn't the only one with troubles. The blues make the rounds. Sooner or later, they'll find you too.

Ronny Duke wanted to push on to the Gold Coast to catch Nolan Strong. Mick let him go. Lost in Dinah's lyrics, he was content to sit and listen forever. Didn't even notice when Ronny shoved off on his own.

Mick woke the next morning with a savage headache and a sour stomach. Re-taping his gashed ribs didn't improve his outlook. During their pub crawl, Ronny'd babbled on at length about Moishe's sinking status with the Luca crew, which made Mick's own situation even shakier.

Working for Moishe might pay better than spinning a wrench or fighting in the prize ring, but you could also end up in a swamp or bleeding out on a barroom floor. And for what? A piece of paper the Lucas would grab up anyway? If he was going to put his ass on the line, he wanted more to show for it than Moishe's flyblown office.

He decided not to tell Moishe about Ducatti's chat. The old man had enough trouble. So did Mick.

He hadn't asked for any of this, but he owned it now. He'd gone through a swinging door into a whole new world, every bit as tough as Jackson. On these streets, he was fresh meat, the fucking new guy, starting at the bottom.

And looking around? He didn't care much for the view.

CHAPTER 15

Four days later, Cooley's reopened. Under New Management, the sign said. The new management was even bigger than Jenks, tougher too. An ex-heavyweight named Elmo Suggs, twenty-two wins, fourteen losses. Big Elmo hung pictures of himself over the bar, sparring with Joe Louis, clowning for the camera with Rocky Marciano. An affable lug, he was a good talker, good with customers. And clearly, nobody to mess with.

Mick thought Moishe might bitch about the petty payoff the joint brought, but the old man was still using a walker to make it to the john. He took the money and shut his mouth. Mick did the same, but down deep he was seething. He'd paid one helluva high price for Cooley's. Paid it in blood. Elmo Suggs hadn't done dick.

He was even more concerned about what it meant. Ronny said the Lucas would squeeze Moishe out in time. Was this the start of it?

On collection day, he tried to chat Elmo up, pump him for info, but the big man was no help. The old heavyweight seemed ill at ease when Mick came for the skim and the jukebox money. Actually seemed nervous, Mick thought. Which made no sense. Suggs had gone toe to toe with Archie Moore and Joe Louis, two of the toughest studs on the planet, and he outweighed Irish Mick by a hundred pounds. If it came down to a scuffle, Elmo could knock him through the wall.

But after years in the ring Elmo understood violence up close and personal. Hearing the street talk about Mick, he expected him to be a foaming-at-the-mouth psycho.

The truth was a lot simpler. Irish Mick was a middleweight.

In a serious dustup with Elmo Suggs, Mick would lose and both men knew this. Which made him risky as a junkyard dog with his growl cut out.

There wouldn't be any push-and-shove, no warm up or warning. Mick couldn't afford to lose a single round. Not a one. He'd have to bring it all from the git-go.

The way he did with Jenks and his pals.

So Elmo didn't like having Mick around, but didn't mind talking about him. Enjoyed telling people about the day he took over the bar, and found blood on the floor and a bullet hole in the cash register. Four bad-ass brothers run off by Moishe's white boy made a great saloon story. One that grew a little each time he repeated it.

Suggs had the register repaired but left the bullet hole untouched. A conversation piece. And Elmo made a lot of conversation.

The rumors weren't the kind that got back to Mick. But he noticed that day by day, collecting was getting easier.

Then Moishe came back. Ten days after Idlewild, the old man limped into the office to find Mick at his desk. Moishe was moving like a zombie, leaning on an aluminum cane, wincing with every step. His gray pinstripe suit hung on him like death camp pajamas. Even his fedora looked a size too big.

"Why you loafin' around here?" the old man growled. "You got no work to do?"

"I'm doing it," Mick said mildly. "Just finished over on Piquette and I'm checking the tally before I go back out. You want to do the count?"

"I'll know if it's off by a nickel, you just remember that." He winced at a spasm of pain, waited for it to pass.

"Why didn't you tell me you were getting out? I could've picked you up."

"My sister came for me. I'll be staying with her until... For awhile. How far down the list are you?"

"We're halfway through the month. Two dozen names to go."

"You're falling behind."

"Maybe a little. It's my first go around."

"You're too green. I should've found somebody older."

"Hell, you're older, we can do it together. If they cut you loose, you must be feeling better, right?"

"Do I look better, dumbshit?"

"Your disposition's back to normal. What's wrong, Moishe?"

"Everything," Abrams sighed, leaning heavily on his cane. "That bastard in Idlewild fucked me up. I'm sewed together inside like a rag doll. Docs say I'll be a year healin' up. Meantime, I can't lift nothin' heavy, can't eat nothing that ain't mushed like baby food or I'll be shitting in a bag the rest of my life."

"I'm sorry, Moishe."

"Sorry don't help, but it means you get your shot. You ain't ready, not even close, but the fuckin' doctor bills are eatin' me up. Here, look this over." Fishing an envelope out of his pocket, he tossed it on the desk.

"Black Kat?" Mick frowned, scanning the legalese. "What is it?"

"Mojo Johnson's sorry ass recording studio. Mine now."

"All legal?"

"Close enough. Mojo won't be fightin' us in court, and I sure as shit ain't runnin' it past the Lucas. Get your ass over there, take an inventory. I know people who can unload any damn thing. Maybe we can sell off the gear, salvage a few bucks."

"I'll see to it."

Moishe glanced around the seedy storefront. Rented by the month for more than twenty years. Mick behind the battered desk now, little radio playing, black music, black DJ. Moishe felt like a trespasser. Like his own goddamn ghost.

"I was like you once, you know," he said quietly. "We all were. Tough Jewboys from the block. Me, Dave Weinstein, Shorty Huyck. From Hastings Street north on Congress, Jefferson to East Grand? all Jewish then. Paradise Valley, we called it. Now it's all blacks and beaners. Know why? Because Kikes are smart. They see how this life plays out and they get the fuck out. Send their kids to college. Doctors and lawyers don't worry about bein' dead by dark."

"If it's the smart move, why didn't you get out?"

"Probably should have," the old man admitted. "But down deep, you and me ain't so different, Shannon. I got hooked on the action. A junkie for trouble. And look what it's got me."

"I seen worse, Moishe. Anything else?"

"Try not to get yourself killed, eh? Just my lousy luck, you're all I got."

CHAPTER 16

Mojo Johnson's studio was on Hastings Street north of Piquette, the heart of Darktown. A shabby two-story house with a fake brown-brick facade, sagging porch. The ramshackle garage out back looked like a stiff breeze would flatten it. Place was easy to find, though. A giant hand-painted canvas banner draped over the front porch read *Black Kat Recordings! Home of the Hits!*

Mick parked the big Premiere in front. Rolling up in a funeral home Lincoln isn't a bad move when you want people to take you seriously.

He half-expected to find it closed but he could hear music thumping through the walls as he trotted up the steps. Then he stopped, listening intently. He didn't know the song but he definitely recognized the voice. From the Regency Club in Idlewild.

It was Mojo Johnson, shouting a blues jam from the dark side of hell. Mick shook off a shiver as he pushed through the front door.

The foyer had been converted into a make-do waiting room. A red vinyl sofa with matching chairs. Black woman at a beat up secretary's desk, wearing oversized horn-rimmed glasses that gave her an owlish look. Pixie hairdo, short as a boy's. Navy blouse, Capri pants, a sweater draped over her broad shoulders. A big woman, with heavy breasts. Queen size.

She eyed Mick a moment. Then turned down Mojo's voice on the portable plastic phonograph on the corner of her desk. "Can I help you?"

"My name's Shannon. Who are you?"

"I'm Mr. Johnson's secretary. He's not in, but if you'd care to make an appointment— "

"He won't need any more appointments. Mojo got behind on a loan, lost the business to my boss, Moishe Abrams. I'm here to take an inventory. I'll need a tour."

"Whoa up, youngblood. You don't just walk in off the street and tell me to jump. Do you have any paperwork?"

Surprised by her calmness, Mick tossed Moishe's envelope on the desk. She took her time scanning the forms. From her deepening frown, he guessed she actually understood them.

"Damn," she said softly. When she looked up again her eyes were liquid and unreadable, dark as a forest pool.

"Okay, Mister...? What was your name again?"

"Shannon."

"Right." Opening the desk drawer, she took out a metal cash box, a ledger and a checkbook, and slid them across. "Here's the calendar with all our bookings from day one, plus the sessions I have scheduled for the next few weeks. The checkbook is for the business account at Michigan National, nine hundred and eighty four dollars, plus I have about...four hundred and eighty-six bucks and change on hand, petty cash. Mojo paid me forty a week plus four hours free studio time. It's Friday, let's call it thirty-five even. Okay if I take it out of petty cash?"

"No, it's not okay. What's your name?"

"Martika Daniels."

"Look, Martika— "

"*Miss* Daniels, if you don't mind. I don't know you."

"Okay, *Miss* Daniels. What's your rush? Nobody fired you."

"Nobody has to. I quit."

"Fine, quit if you want. But if you expect any cut and run money, you're gonna walk me through this setup first."

"You don't even know what this place is, do you? Why am I not surprised?" Shaking her head, she opened the cash box, started counting out bills. Mick flipped the lid closed on her hand, pinning it with his forefinger.

"Is there some part of what I just said you missed? You'll get paid, *after* you show me around."

Their eyes locked, and for a moment, he thought she might clock him with her free hand. She was big enough. Almost as tall as he was, with hips as wide as her shoulders. Not overweight, just... big. A substantial package.

"Alright already, no need to break my bones," she said, massaging her knuckles as he released her. "A tour won't take long, anyway. C'mon."

Mick followed her into the living room, scanning the account book as he walked. The room was sealed off by a crudely assembled wall of mismatched windows, obviously salvaged from the trash. Made it look like a museum exhibit. Inside on display, were an ancient upright piano old enough to actually belong in a museum and three microphones on stands. A drum kit was crammed in the corner, half hidden behind a mattress.

"This is studio P for parlor, which is what it used to be," she said. "The musical accompaniment is played and recorded here. Sidemen bring their own axes— "

"Axes?"

"Instruments. Guitars, saxes and such. The drums and piano are permanent because they're too clumsy to move. The closed door at the far end is Studio B., for bathroom. We're recording in there right now. Listen up, maybe you can hear it?"

Mick listened. "I hear...somebody wailing, sounds like."

"Studio B's supposed to be soundproof, but it's not quite. Gracelle Taylor from Bethel Baptist is taping her lead tracks."

"In the bathroom?"

"In the shower, actually. Lot of natural echo in there."

"She's singing in the shower?"

"Haven't you ever sung in a shower, Mr. Shannon?"

Mick flashed to the showers in Jackson, guards grinning at the new meat on their knees, sucking off...

"No," he said. "Can't carry a tune."

"But you know what echo is, right?" Stepping up to the hall door, she sang a line— "*I'm "Hot Chocolate" baby, brown and sticky too, warm me up and I'm gone melt all over you...* " She broke off. Mick was staring at her.

"What?"

"Martika Daniels? *"Hot Chocolate"*? You're *that* Tika Daniels?"

It was her turn to stare. "That was, quite awhile back," she said. "Where'd you hear it? It never got played on white radio."

"Where I was, a lot of guys were into blues. When they weren't howlin' like dogs."

"Where was that?"

He shrugged off the question. "It was a good tune, *Chocolate*. Whatever happened with that?"

"My drunk ass uncle Mojo happened," she said, facing him squarely. "We played a show in Covington, headed out to the next gig. On the road to Knoxville Mojo fell asleep at the wheel, rolled the car. I got busted up pretty good, my leg mostly. Kept me out of the business a few years. Now I'm here, tryin' to work my way back up to the bottom."

"Tough break."

"That's why they call it the blues, white boy." She started to say something else, then broke off, shaking her head smiling. "Lord."

What?"

"All your pals who were diggin' on "Hot Chocolate"? I don't even want to think about what they were doin' while they listened."

"No," Mick agreed, smiling in spite of himself. "You probably don't."

"Anyway, you heard the way my voice echoed off the door?"

"It rang. Like down a hallway."

"The word is reverberation. Reverb for short."

"Reverb," Mick nodded, looking around curiously. "And... you actually make records here?"

"We tape the music here, the records are pressed in a plant. Why?"

"I thought they came from— I don't know. Fancy places. Big halls and such."

"Some records come from studios in New York or L.A. Others get cut in garages or dumps like this. Motown Studios is only a few blocks from here, and it's not much bigger than this place. You *have* heard of Motown, right?"

"Smokey Robinson, The Temptations? Everybody's heard of 'em. You know those guys?"

"Went to high school together. The cable running along the wall to that other door is from the lead microphone in the shower. Miss Taylor sings her part in Studio B, the signal runs to a four track mixing board in control room K, for kitchen." She eased open the kitchen door, giving Mick a glimpse of a rangy black kid with a scraggly goatee, wearing headphones over a gray Kangol beret. Frowning, he waved them off and Martika quickly closed it again.

"That's Jerome. He's still in high school but he can mix up red beans and rice in there or mix a tune down from four tracks to two. That was a joke, Mr. Shannon. Are you following any of this?"

"I think so," Mick nodded, closing the ledger. "You record the music on different mikes in different rooms, then mix it down to stereo. Why's what's her name singing alone? Where's the band?"

"The studio's too small to tape instruments and vocals at the same time. Drums and guitars would leak into vocal mikes, muddy up the tracks. To get clarity, the musicians recorded their parts earlier— "

"So they don't drown out the singers," he nodded. "Got it. Go on."

"A four-track recorder can handle small combos or doo-wop groups, but it limits the work we can do. Motown has better gear. Mr. Johnson was planning— by the way, where is Mojo, anyway? Why isn't he handling this?"

"He's…on the road someplace. Playing."

"Where?"

"I don't know. Let's get on with this, I got places to be."

She eyed him thoughtfully. An uncomfortable experience. The brown eyes behind her horn rims were intelligent, penetrating. Wide forehead, coffee brown complexion, full mouth. A formidable woman.

"Mojo planned to rent a bigger board as soon as our lease on the four track runs out. We need an eight track deck— "

"Whoa up. What lease are you talking about?"

"All the studio gear is leased or rented. Didn't Mr. Johnson mention that? Even the house is a rental."

"Rented," Mick echoed. The Daniels woman looked away, to hide a smart-ass smile. Like she was way ahead of him. Which she probably was.

"All the lease agreements are in the front desk, Mr. Shannon. Top left hand drawer. That's all there is to see. Unless you want to check out the upstairs?"

"What's up there?"

"A storeroom for extra gear, and my room. The nightstand and radio are mine. I'm taking them with me."

"You live here?"

"I crash here sometimes. Musicians play in the clubs till closing, then record here afterward. Sessions can start at three or four in the morning, run till morning. My cousin Jerome does the engineering, I deal with the customers, book the dates and collect the fees. That's the whole deal. Can I have my money now?"

"A couple questions first. You say Motown Records is only a few blocks away. Are they set up this same way?"

"More or less. It's a bigger house and Mr. Gordy had the basement remodeled— "

"But it's just a house? Smoky Robinson doesn't sing in somebody's bathroom, does he?"

"Actually, he does. Or he used to. Sometimes he records in big New York studios with a full orchestra now."

"I liked his early stuff better," Mick said absently. "What about the nine hundred bucks in the checkbook?"

"Nine eighty-four, actually. It's our take for the last ten days, minus the rent on the gear."

"And who paid you, for what? Where did it come from?"

"My god, you really don't know— never mind. People pay us to record their music on half-inch studio tapes," she explained slowly, as if talking to a child. "We send the master tape to a company that cuts the phonograph records, 45s, LPs, EPs, whatever the customer wants. We collect up front for studio time, cash on delivery for the master tapes plus a twenty-five percent kickback from the record company. Which, by the way, they never pay. Mojo was going to talk to them."

"How do your records get into stores?"

"Mostly they don't. Our customers peddle their records at gigs or at church, or give them away to get their names around. Music shops get their records from big distributors out of New York or Chicago... is something wrong?"

"Why?"

"You're staring at me."

"Sorry. I was thinking."

"Looks like it hurts. If there are no more questions— "

"Just one. What's with the attitude?"

"Which attitude would that be?"

"C'mon, sister, you've been busting my chops since I got here."

Taking a deep breath, she faced him. Eye to eye.

"I know who you are, Irish. You're Moishe's boy, the crazy ofay who's been tearin' things up along 8 Mile. Everybody's talkin' about how you ran DuWayne Jenks and that trash out of Cooley's."

"Friends of yours?"

"*Hell* no! You did the neighborhood a favor."

"Then what's your problem?"

"When I took this job, Uncle Mo promised I could cut my own music. I busted my ass for a month, for *free*, to get it up and running. Now that it's finally making money— " She broke off, shaking her head. "Anyway, you're in, he's out. So am I."

"Why?"

"Why? Because you don't know from Shinola, white boy! You don't play, you don't sing. Don't look big enough to be a leg breaker either but that's what people say. Do you know *any*thing about music?"

"I know what I like and now I've got a rough idea how this place works."

"Rough is right."

"What do you know about cars?"

"What?"

"Cars. You can drive, right? But how much do you know?"

She eyed him, but didn't answer.

"Right," he nodded. "You know to crank the key, step on the gas, right? Which is all you need to know."

"I am not following— "

"A V-8 engine's got fifteen hundred moving parts," Mick said, waving her off. "I can tear one down and rebuild it in a day. Compared to a big block Ford, this business isn't so complicated. And I don't even have to turn the key. It's already running."

"It's not that simple. A gospel quartet from Bethel Baptist will be here in an hour to dub background tracks behind Gracelle's vocals, then Jerome has to mix down twelve songs for their LP and choose four for an EP they want to sell at a fund-raiser next Sunday. That's six fifty total, minus the deposit we have to front the pressing plant. I've got a street-corner quartet scheduled at six and a jazz trio from the Chit Chat Lounge booked for an after-hours session at two a.m. They're bringing a Hammond B-3 organ so you'll have to rent two more mikes for its Leslie speaker... are you following any of this? Do you even know what I'm talking about?"

"No. Ever been in a blind pig?"

"Hell yes. Sang in a million of 'em, back in the day."

"Then you know every pig's got vending machines, slots, a jukebox. The man I work for owns them."

"Moishe Abrams. And I wouldn't be braggin' on that if I was you. What on earth you gettin' at?"

"Point is, I don't know squat about jukeboxes. I just collect the money, once a week. Maybe we can do that here."

"How do you mean?"

"Mojo owed Moishe serious dough. The gear's all rented, so we can't sell it. Only way I see to squeeze a nickel out of this place is to keep it going. How much do you clear a week?"

She stared at him as though he was speaking Swahili, her eyes huge behind the horn rims.

"You're serious?"

"Dead serious. How much can it clear?"

"If things keep going like they are, it can do...four fifty, maybe five.

After expenses."

"A week?"

"Or ten days. Depends on the trade."

"The guy taping in there? Can he run this place?"

"Jerome's still in school. He only comes in to do the mixing."

"Then we're stuck with you."

"Say what?" she demanded.

"If your nut's four fifty, can you deliver that every week?"

The woman opened her mouth to argue, then closed it again, thinking. "Yes," she said at last, "It can do four-fifty. But if I stay, I want a raise."

"For what?"

"Combat pay. Working for Uncle Mo was one thing. Working for you is something else. I want an extra twenty a week."

"Half the mopes in this town don't make twenty a week."

"Then hire yourself a mope," she said briskly, picking up her purse. "Good luck with that."

"Hold it! How about this? You clear the four and a half, you get forty a week. Anything over, you take twenty percent. How's that?"

"It's... fair. More than fair, actually. How come? You don't know me."

"Sure I do. You used to be "Hot Chocolate" Tika Daniels. You live around here, so you'll be easy to find and you already know who I work for. So you know jacking me around would be a huge fucking mistake."

She glanced away, mulling it over. "If you're serious about making money, we'll need better equipment, and you'll have to advertise— "

"Lady, I don't know if my boss will go for any of this. I'll take the four-fifty. If Moishe okays it, I'll be back for the same every week. Cash, no checks. Any questions?"

Surprisingly, she smiled, looking away. "Man, you really are as crazy as people say. What happens if business gets slow? You gonna break my legs?"

He shrugged and headed for the door without answering.

"Hey!" she called after him. "I was just kiddin', you know?"

CHAPTER 17

"Something wrong with your ears?" Moishe rasped. "I said take an inventory, sell it off. You make a few collections, think you're runnin' things now?"

"It's not like that," Mick said patiently. They were in the storefront office the next day, Mick at the desk, Moishe leaning on his cane. He didn't like sitting down. Too hard to get up again.

"If we close it down, all we get is what's in the bank. The house is rented, the gear's rented, there's nothing to *sell*, Moishe. But the place is making good money. I saw the books."

"Fuck the books. I don't know dick about no record business. Do you?"

"It can't be that complicated. If a mope like Mojo can make it pay, how tough can it be?"

"I'll ask, next time I see him. Look Mick, we loan money, we collect the vig. We don't buy into no ghetto action. Too risky."

"Fine. Close it down, send the paperwork to the Lucas, see what it gets you?"

For a tense moment, Mick thought he might get clipped with Moishe's stick. But he didn't.

"We wouldn't get squat," the old man admitted.

"Not if we play it like Cooley's. But it doesn't have to be that way. The St. Clair doesn't know squat about your turf, Moishe. All they do is count their end of the vig. They don't care where it comes from."

"Maybe not, but we both know where that studio came from. I don't want nothin' that can tie us to Johnson. Dead or alive, that prick's bad luck for me. Close it out."

"For a one-time payout? When we can make that much every week?"

"Tell you what, kid. You think that business is such a hot shit idea? I'll sell it to you. Mojo owed me six large. Take that over, plus say...another three? It's all yours."

"You know I don't have that kind of money. I still owe you for Ducatti."

"I'll take it out of your pay. Say...two hundred a week for a year, half vig you. But I want no part in the business. You go bust, you still owe me the full stroke. Fair enough?"

Hell no, it wasn't fair. Moishe smiled sourly, waiting for Mick to say no.

Mick glanced around the storefront office instead. After twenty years, Moishe had money on the street and this dump. And Mick had even less.

Owing Moishe was a huge risk. So was every goddamn day inside 8 Mile. Walking into Cooley's, say.

"Nine's too high. How about I cover the six he owed you?"

"Fuck your six. You can have it for seven-five for the next ten seconds. Going...going...."

"Seven!" Mick said.

"Done, you stupid bastard! Just when I thought you might have some smarts. Made your mind up awful quick though. That *shvartza* over there pretty hot?"

"She's big and brown as a Hershey bar, Moishe. Not my type."

"Got somethin' against chocolate?"

"Screw yourself, Moishe, it's not like that."

"What it's like ain't my problem. But you got a problem you ain't even thought of."

"What are you talking about?"

"If you go bust, you'll have to break your own fuckin' legs."

Moishe chortled all the way out to his sister's '59 Buick wagon. Leaving Mick shaking his head. Knew the old shylock had played him like a two dollar fiddle. But for the first time in his life, he actually fucking *owned* something.

It might not be much, but it *had* to be easier than fighting Kid Ibo for short money.

CHAPTER 18

Stepping out of the Dequindre office to make his afternoon run, Mick spotted the pair as he was locking the door. Two suits climbing out of an unmarked car parked down the block. Cops, plainclothes. One Irish, one Mexican. Ducking back inside, he just managed to slide the .45 into an office drawer as they pushed in.

"Raid, motherfucker," the Irishman said, grinning. "Turn around, put your hands on the fucking wall." Big, copper-haired boozer, crowding fifty, running to fat, watery eyes, busted veins in his cheeks and nose. Wearing a rumpled, off the rack Sears sport jacket.

The Mex looked sharper, tailored suit, dark tie, hook nose, hard eyes. He hung back, leaning against the door. Watching.

Easing down behind the desk, Mick faced the Irishman. "You must be Becker."

"That ain't how it works, bog trotter. I told you to kiss the fuckin' wall!"

"Not a chance."

"What?"

"You've seen my sheet, Sarge. I did time at Jackson. I've kissed all the walls I'm going to."

"You want it the hard way, I'm up for that." Becker's boozy grin widened, as he jerked a snub-nosed thirty-eight out of his shoulder holster, giving Shannon a good look at it. "You know the drill, cunt. Assume the position. I won't tell you again."

Mick swallowed, feeling the half-healed gash along his ribs from Moishe's slug. But he stayed put, his eyes locked on Becker's.

"Fuck this, Bud," the Mex said. "Why work up a sweat over this mutt?"

"He's new, Loop," Becker snapped. "He has to learn who's boss."

"He knows who's boss, don't you, Shannon?"

"I know who my boss is. Same guy that gave me an envelope for you two. Do you want it or not?"

Greed and anger warred for a moment in Becker's eyes. Greed won.

"Give it up," Becker said, holstering his piece. Mick took the envelope out of the top desk drawer, slid it across. Becker quickly riffled the bills, then slipped it into his jacket. "Okay, here's the score, asshole. This here is street tax. You can do business, but that's it. We been hearin' stories about what a bad-ass you're supposed to be, but me and Garcia seen a hundred punks like you come and go. Tough boys don't last on the Corridor, Shannon, only smart ones. Stay smart, maybe we get along. Fuck up and we bust you like any other piece o' shit. Clear?"

Mick nodded.

"And next time I tell you to do something, boy, you better fuckin' do it."

Mick didn't answer. It was just guff now and they both knew it.

"See you in two weeks, sonny. Have my money ready and the count better be right. Let's go, Loop."

The Mex opened the door to let his partner pass but didn't follow him out. Turned back to Mick instead.

"Just so you know, Moishe's deal is with Becker, not me. He takes money, I don't."

"Not my business," Mick shrugged.

"This might be. A mob crew out of Chicago muscled into South Bend last summer. They're in Benton Harbor now. Darktown, both places. Rumor is, they're coming here next. You heard anything?"

Mick just looked at him.

"Right," Garcia sighed. "Go ahead and slaughter each other, just don't bleed on my sidewalks. If you hear anything— fuck. Why am I wasting my breath?"

CHAPTER 19

The roust rankled Mick, rekindling ugly memories of Jackson. Reminding him of his place in the world. Still at the bottom of the fucking barrel. It gnawed at him through the day as he made collections, making him sullen and curt. Which actually worked in his favor.

Until the last collection of the day. A corner bar called Brownie's.

It was dim in the lounge, dark paneling, maroon carpet and dark oak furniture. Bobby Blue Bland on the jukebox, crooning *Stormy Monday Blues*. Mick felt himself relaxing, absorbing the down home feel of the room and the music.

The woman behind the bar was ripe and full figured, a café au lait belle who gave Mick a welcoming smile wide as a grand piano. He was still returning her smile when he felt the cold kiss of a gun muzzle against the back of his neck.

"Keep walkin', stud. Straight to the office at the end of the bar."

No choice. Mick walked, his guts coiling into a knots, expecting a bullet with every step. Feeling dumber than dirt.

The men's room. He'd walked past it without giving it a glance. Too busy eyeballing the black beauty behind the bar. Letting her boyfriend slide out right behind him. Jenks? Couldn't tell. Couldn't risk looking back. The woman turned her back as the gunman pushed him through the office door, slamming him up against the desk, kicking the door shut behind them.

"Hands flat on the desk."

Patting him down quickly, he found Mick's forty-five Colt and yanked it. A second frisking, more thorough this time. Touched his wallet but left it. Nothing else to find.

"Okay, sit yourself down in that chair, motherfucker. Keep your hands on the desktop where I can see 'em. Nothin' sudden."

Mick sat. Facing a tall, slender black guy in shirtsleeves, a narrow silk tie that matched his claret vest. Holding a nickel plated .38 Smith and Wesson. Cocked. Thin face, aquiline features. Like the old Chuck Berry song, a Brown-eyed Handsome Man. With beads of sweat across his brow.

Odd. He looked as scared as Mick felt, which was damned strange since he was the one holding the gun— and then his face registered.

"Idlewild," Mick said. "You're the guy in the tuxedo, right? Brown?"

"Took you long enough to remember, white boy. We all look alike to you?"

"Tuxedos look alike to me. And it was a rough night."

"Rougher for Mojo. That why you're here? To settle up?"

"I came to collect three sixty. The vig and a yard off the end plus the jukebox money."

"Vig? Jesus H. Christ! I save that old kike's miserable fuckin' life and he wants his fuckin' vig? Is that all he wants? Or are you supposed to cap me after?"

"Why should I?"

"Maybe so I can't say nothin' about a certain guitar playin' mother-fucker who won't be appearin' *live* again, anywhere. Ever."

"I just came for the money. Moishe gives me a list, this joint is the next name on it. I didn't even know it *was* your place. I thought you were from Idlewild."

"Nobody's *from* Idlewild, it's strictly a resort. I run The Regency on summer weekends. And I'm still thinkin' Moishe sent you to close the books on that mess."

"Truth is, Moishe doesn't remember much about that night."

"Man wakes up in the hospital, don't wonder how he got there?"

"He was too sick to care at first, and now he's got other shit to worry about."

"Like what?"

"Like none of your fucking business."

"You're right, youngblood, it's not." Brownie shook his head slowly. "Jesus. I ain't slept for a week worrying about ol' Moishe comin' around to cash my ass in. Then I hear stories about Moishe's new boy, runnin' DuWayne Jenks and his jailhouse crew out of Cooley's. Figured it must be you and I'd be next. Only that ol' man never gave a thought to me, did he? I'm just another no-account nigger owes him money."

"What did you expect? Flowers and a card?"

"Hell no! I expected to get my head blown off! How well do you know that old man you work for?"

"I don't know him. I owe him. That thing in Idlewild? He got cut savin' my ass. I'd be dead in that alley if not for him."

"Lucky you. But that ain't the first time I seen Moishe in action. Hot August night, six, seven years back? I was tendin' bar at a blind pig in Dearborn. Some bullshit argument starts up, next thing I know, dude's dead on the floor. Ol' Moishe's standin' over him with straight razor in his hand. "Driftin' Blues" playin' on the jukebox. Cuttin' was done be-fore the song was."

"What was it about?"

"Who the fuck knows? It was a hot night, the guy says a wrong thing to Moishe, a second later his throat's open to the bone. Me and the night manager loaded the poor bastard in the trunk of his car. '57 De Soto, with two-tone fins, black and gold? Sweet machine." He shook his head, remembering the car.

"We ditched it in an alley off Twelfth, left the keys in it. Probably wasn't there five minutes. Dumb fuck that copped it got himself a real fine ride with a helluva surprise in the trunk. The stiff floated up a few days later in the Rouge. No fuss. A nigger gets knifed in East Detroit? Do tell."

"What's this got to do with me?"

Brownie eyed him a moment before answering. "Here's the thing, white bread. After the killing? While I'm still moppin' up the blood? Ol' Moishe sat his wide ass down at the bar to finish his drink. With a dead man bleedin' out not five feet away. The look on his face... Hell, he didn't have no special look. Empty eyes. Nobody home. Moishe killed that dude just because he was black or because he was in a mood. Or just because, you know?"

"Moishe's got no beef with you, Mr. Brown. Neither do I. I give you my word."

"Say what?" Brownie chuckled in amazement. "You give me your fucking word? You really are one redneck motherfucker, ain't' you? Your fucking word." He shook his head slowly.

Deciding.

Live or die.

"Here, take it," he said abruptly. Reversing Mick's Colt in his hand, he slid it across the desk, butt-first. "If we're gonna bleed each other, let's get to it."

"If my money's ready, we've got no problem, Mr. Brown," Mick said, slipping the piece back in his belt. "I owe you one anyway. Maybe two."

"For what?"

"For bailing me out of that jam in Idlewild. And again today."

"Today?"

"I was careless when I walked in here. That won't happen again."

"Best not, a Casper workin' 8 Mile. Your money's in the top drawer. What's your name?"

"Mick Shannon." Mick slid the drawer open, found the envelope.

"I'm Leo Brown. Brownie to my friends, and most everybody else." He hesitated, then offered his hand. Mick ignored it, riffling through the cash in the envelope instead. "We're good," he nodded, pocketing the money. "You want me talk to Moishe about Idlewild?"

"Hell no! Hope he forgets I was ever there. What was that about, anyway?"

"Mojo owed big, couldn't pay. Or wouldn't."

"I know he opened a recording studio, tried to sell me a piece. What happened with that, anyway? Moishe take it?"

"Not exactly. I did."

"You?" Brownie's eyebrows raised. "How'd that happen?"

Mick just looked at him.

"Yeah, right," Brownie said, raising both hands, "ain't none of my business. I worked for a jazz label a few years back, lost my ass. Take care out there, hear?"

"Worried about me, Mr. Brown?"

"Every day I see you comin' is a day I *don't* see ol' Moishe comin'. And that's one fine day, far as I'm concerned.

CHAPTER 20

Mick hustled through his last collections of the day, trying to get back to the Black Kat studio before closing.

Didn't quite make it. Martika Daniels was locking the front door when he rolled up in Moishe's Lincoln.

She straightened, facing him.

"Are you here to close us down?" she asked.

"Not yet. Hop in, we need to talk."

"I don't hop no-place on your say so, sonny, especially not in no hearse. Come inside, I'll buy you a coffee. It's your coffee anyway."

He followed her through to the kitchen. The place was stone silent, a rundown, cobbled up house in the heart of the ghetto. Christ, what was he thinking?

"Coffee's fresh," she said, pouring two cups. "I've got an all-night session scheduled. I was just going home to check on my mother, catch a catnap. What's your news?"

"I'm buying the business from Moishe," Mick said simply. "Now we've gotta make it go."

"You're... *buying* it? With borrowed money from that old man? You gotta be crazier than I thought. Or punchy. People say you're a boxer. Irish Mick Shannon?"

"You a fight fan?"

"My neighborhood, we get fights every night for free. Why do they call you Irish? Ever meet a Shannon who wasn't Irish?"

For a moment, he considered running the usual bullshit line about his fighting Irish ancestors. But there was something about her eyes. She wouldn't buy it. He decided to go with the truth instead. This once.

"Irish on a fight card means I'm white. Most Motown fighters are black, so white fighters sell tickets. And a lot of redneck shop rats always bet on white boys. Brothers generally bet the other way."

"Which way do you bet?"

"I don't. Last time I bet on me, I lost big. Are you writing a book?"

"Just trying to get a handle on this thing. People say you're a wild dog. And that old man you work for? Folks spit when they say his name. He's like the devil up in here."

"I'm just a guy trying to make a buck."

"You'd better make it quick. There's a pool on you, you know. Folks laying bets on how long you'll last, which day you'll get capped."

He scanned her face, wondering if she was jerking his chain. She met his eyes straight on, with that dark, unreadable gaze. And he realized she was dead serious.

"What's the cutoff?"

"The fall. Ain't nobody bettin' you'll last past Labor Day."

"Maybe they're right. Now walk me through this business again, tell me how I make it pay."

CHAPTER 21

Scotty's was jumping, shop rats lining the counter, booths full of teenyboppers, air rich with roadhouse aroma, burgers and onions sizzling on the griddle, black coffee bubbling in the percolator. Juke box thumping out white-bread pop. Bobby Vinton, "Blue Velvet."

With Spivak looking, he knew the smart move was to stay clear of Ecorse. This place, especially. And he would. Soon.

But for now, he wanted one more quick visit back to the time before prison wrecked everything. He took a stool at the counter, and just for a moment, caught a flash of a separate reality. The life he might have had if he hadn't gone after Spivak that night.

A straight John job at a garage, stopping here after work with his buddies, maybe hooking up with a looker like Leanne.

She was at a back booth taking an order, joshing with some older guys in bowling shirts, looking fine as a fox in her pink waitress outfit. She spotted Mick parked at the end of the counter, but instead of a smile, her eyes darkened. Brushing past him like he wasn't there, she vanished into the kitchen, emerging a moment later with a take-out box. Parked it in front of him as though he'd ordered it.

"The guys in the corner booth are cops," she said quietly. "It's their bowling night. The bald one works with Sergeant Spivak."

"Seeing you might be worth the trouble."

"You'll never find out if the trouble happens in here," she said briskly, sliding the bill under his order. "Call me sometime." A phone number was printed neatly on the back of the bill.

Heading out, he glanced casually at the table in the corner. The porky, bald cop was eyeing him oddly, frowning. Mick could feel his gaze all the way out the door. He didn't look back. Didn't have to.

Knew he'd been made.

                        □   □   □

On edge now, he headed for his flat in the Sun Valley apartments. But he drove past the converted motel first without pulling in, scoping out the area. Nothing looked out of place, no lights showing in his unit, no blue TV glow— *a match flared in a parked car.*

It was sitting on a side street, facing Sun Valley. Facing the door of Mick's flat. '62 Chevy Biscayne, navy blue, black-wall tires. No decals, but it didn't need them. A police ride, unmarked. Two men in it, the man at the wheel, smoking.

Watching Mick's digs? From where they were parked, there wasn't much else to see.

Averting his face as he passed the Biscayne, Mick quickly swiveled his rear view for a glimpse back. Felt his chest constrict, his breathing go shallow.

Spivak. Even at this distance, Mick knew the set of his bull shoulders, the flattop brush cut. Could almost see his freckles in the dark. Deputy Wes Spivak. No. Not deputy anymore. Leanne called him Sergeant. And he wasn't alone. A second man was riding shotgun. Mick couldn't make him out, but the lawmen were of a size. Two of them waiting for the kid who'd broken Spivak's arm five years ago.

Tough years for Mick. Hard time in prison, almost as hard since. But Spivak wouldn't see it that way. He'd figure he had a payback coming. A beating or a broken arm to make them even.

So. How to handle it?

Take his lumps?

Mick had serious fighting skills now, knew how to duck and cover, take shots on his arms and elbows. After what he'd been through in Jackson, he could probably survive anything Spivak and his pal could dish out.

But they might not settle for a beating. They could rough him up, then bust him for assaulting an officer. An ex-con's word against two cops? He'd get ten years in Jackson this time.

Not a chance. He wouldn't do another day for Spivak. He'd die first. Or somebody would.

He chewed that one over. He could go back to Moishe's office, grab up the .45, edge up on Spivak. Solve the problem permanently.

Only it wouldn't. He'd be an obvious suspect and truth was, he wasn't quite ready for that anyway.

The killing in Cooley's was one thing. It happened in a heartbeat, with no choice at all. Do or die. But walking up on somebody, capping 'em cold? Even a piece of crap like Spivak?

Moishe could do it. Pop a guy, take a seat at the bar, have a drink on his luck. So could Ducatti and Albert and a thousand thugs he'd known in the joint.

But bottom line? Mick honestly didn't know whether he was down for that or not. Or just wasn't ready to find out.

Neither man had glanced up as he drove past, so they weren't looking for the Lincoln. The cop in the diner saw his face, not his car. He couldn't risk driving by again, though. The Lincoln was too conspicuous. He'd have to come back later.

But knowing where Spivak was, he also knew where he wasn't.

☐   ☐   ☐

Scotty's had quieted down some as Mick pulled into the lot. Fewer cars, only a few customers at the counter. No law in sight, off duty or otherwise.

Easing the big Premier into a slot alongside the diner, he waited, engine idling. When Leanne stepped out the front door, he rolled up, reached across and popped open the passenger door.

She slid in, all the way across the seat, pressing herself against him. Cupping her hand on the nape of his neck she pulled his head down, kissing him hard on the mouth, holding it, her tongue flicking wetly against his. She tasted like peppermint.

"What's that for?" he asked as she pulled back, nestling against his shoulder in the center of the seat.

"I saved your life tonight so I own you. I saw it in a Randolph Scott movie once."

"Must be true then." Dropping the Linc in gear, he gunned out of the parking lot. "So? What are you gonna do with me?"

They parked in an abandoned outlet road behind Sun Valley. He found CKLW out of Chicago on the radio, Ruby and the Romantics, "Our Day Will Come."

Pulling Leanne close, he nuzzled the hollow of her throat, her milky skin delicious, the tang of her perfume blending with rich musk of the diner's entire menu. When he tried unbuttoning her blouse, she brushed his hand away, then did it herself, shifting to help him slide her breast out of her bra, closing her eyes as he nibbled on her nipple until it rose. Then he slid his kisses north from her breasts to her lips until they were both vibrating, unable to wait another second.

Sliding his palm down her back, he was slicking her panties down when the music on the radio changed. The Shirelles, "Will You Love Me Tomorrow?"

"What?" she panted.

"Nothing," he murmured, "that's a great song."

"Jesus H. Christ!" Leanne said, helping him slip her panties from around her ankles, hurriedly undoing his slacks, groping him, finding him hard.

Laying back on the Linc's broad leather seats, she splayed her thighs, using both hands to slide him inside her, already fully aroused, hot and wet.

Too hot, too wet. After a few hasty thrusts, he exploded, climaxing while the Shirelles were still in the second verse. Leanne squirmed with him, then kept on moving, her hands clamped on his buttocks, holding him inside her, rocking him like a rowboat until she finally came in shuddering waves of heated juices, her knees locked around his waist, riding him until she finished.

Sitting up as he withdrew, she quickly fished a handful of tissues out of her purse, mopping her thighs, panting, breathless, as she looked around nervously, making sure they were still alone.

"So," she said, gulping a deep breath, "I'm a slut now, right? An easy lay. That's what you think, isn't it?"

"Leave that be."

"What do you mean? Leave what be?" She primly re-buttoned her blouse all the way to the throat, a bit odd, since she was still naked below the waist with tissues clamped between her thighs.

"The whole thing was really fine. Let's keep it that way. Nice."

She eyed him suspiciously, then nodded. "It was all right. Maybe a little sudden."

"It's been awhile for me."

"That's okay," she smiled, pulling him close. "I own you now, re-

member? I'm not finished with you yet. But this time, maybe you'd better turn off the damn radio."

☐ ☐ ☐

After dropping Leanne off at her folks' place, he circled back to the motor court. Taking his time, cautiously working his way in.

A good thing.

The fucking Biscayne was still there. Parked on the street. Staked out,
no question this time. He definitely had to clear out. Fortunately, he was
on his home ground, knew every street.

Circling around, he eased the Linc down an alley a couple of blocks
behind Spivak's Biscayne. Sitting between two warehouses, shielded by
a dumpster, he settled in to watch Wes and his partner watching his flat.

He switched on the radio, keeping it low. Got a good bounce out of
Nashville. WLAC, the John R. show. Hard blues all night. Jimmy Reed,
Lightnin' Hopkins, Buddy Guy, ads in-between tunes for Red Top baby
chicks and Black Draught laxatives, ads as funky as the records. Lost in
the music, an hour slipped away. Then most of another.

Spivak and his buddy gave it up around one, firing up the Biscayne,
rumbling off into the night.

Mick stayed put another half-hour to be sure, then pulled up in front
of his flat and slipped silently inside.

Packing didn't take long. Everything he owned fit in a single suitcase.

He spent what remained of the night sacked out on the swaybacked
cot in Moishe's crummy office. The back room stank of dead-end fail-
ure, and passing trains rattled the building every hour. Still, it was better than a cell.

Thought of Leanne, naked in his bed, to pass the time.

It helped.

CHAPTER 22

He could still feel her heat the next day, the silky softness of her throat,
the convulsive gush when she climaxed. His back had welts where
she'd clawed him with her fingernails, trying to pull him deeper inside
her. He felt loose and thoroughly used up. Right with the world.

And not just because Leanne was a looker and a juicy lay.

Being with her felt like having a second chance at the life he'd blown
at sixteen. Football games, prom nights, cruising Woodward to the drive-
ins. All the things he'd ached for alone in his midnight bunk at Jackson.

Leanne was the lush, blonde proof that he still had a shot at a sweet ride. And she definitely qualified. Things were looking up.

Collections stayed simple as he worked down Moishe's list. Two quick cash pickups in the early afternoon, a numbers bank/barbershop on John R., then a party store two doors down.

Moishe's biggest account was also the hardest to find. Parking the Lincoln on Twelfth, Mick edged cautiously down a narrow service alley that led to the loading docks in the middle of the block.

It looked deserted. Eyeless windows painted flat black, trash barrels and torn cardboard boxes. A steel staircase bolted to a warehouse wall led up to a second story landing. Mick trotted up the steps, rapped twice on the freight door, then twice again. The peephole winked as someone checked him out, then the door opened a crack.

"We're closed."

"I'm Shannon. Moishe Abrams sent me about the jukebox. Tell Fatback I'm here."

A muted conversation, then a rangy black giant swung the door open. Nearly seven feet tall, he wore a coal black suit, white shirt, red bow tie, red skullcap. Arabic tattoos on his cheekbones. Casually holding a sawed-off Remington twelve gauge shotgun in one hand.

"I'm Bass," he rumbled. "I solve problems around here. You a problem?"

"Not yet," Mick said mildly.

"Best not be." Bass stepped aside to let him pass. At first glance, the bar looked deserted, chairs stacked on the cocktail tables, an ancient janitor mopping the hardwood dance floor, saloon musk hanging in the air, a heady blend of secondhand smoke, booze and perfume.

Blind pigs like Fat's place ran after hours without liquor licenses. Since the joint was illegal anyway, he was free to run slots, roulette, craps and blackjack tables, which were also illegal. Opening at midnight, the pig stayed busy till six or seven in the morning, or around the clock if a game got serious.

The big jukebox against the wall was turned down low, Little Milton wailing "Blind Man." Mick was still learning about jukes but he knew this one. A Seeburg M100A with chrome rails. The first box to offer 100 selections using the smaller 45 records, it made every 78 rpm juke obsolete overnight. Most of Moishe's boxes were Seeburgs, M100As or Bs. Bought a truckload of them in '55, hijacked in Cincinnati.

Fat was at the far end of the bar, sipping a Vernor's ginger ale, thumbing through his cash register receipts. His street name suited him. Five foot seven, three hundred and sixty pounds with a full beard, Fatback

Billups looked like a black Santa in a China blue suit, tailored to fit snug as a sausage skin. A serious man, Moishe said.

But Fat wasn't alone. Looked like he'd walked in on some kind of a meeting. A half dozen men, and two women were seated at the tables around the dance floor in groups twos and threes. All black, every one of them watching Mick come.

Not street toughs. Well dressed, in tailored suits, Stetsons and homburgs. Older men, for the most part, the women too.

"Take a load off, Irish," Fatback said, swiveling on his stool to face Mick. "We were just talkin' 'bout you."

"About the Labor Day pool?" Mick asked.

"If I'm you, I'd be more worried about makin' it to suppertime. Today."

Mick eyed him curiously. His words were a threat, but there was no edge in his tone.

"In that case, I'll sit by you," Mick said, taking the stool next to Fat. "In case I need cover."

"Nobody means you harm up in here," Fatback said. "We're all business people. Kind of a blind pig posse. These folks here all own spots up and down the Corridor, so we all do business with Moishe. But business first."

Fat slid him an envelope. Mick checked the count, a sweet one, eighteen hundred.

"We're good," he said, rising.

"Sit your young ass back down," Fat said. From the corner of his eye, Mick noted Bass watching from the doorway, still cradling the shotgun. He sat his young ass back down.

"What?"

"We need to talk about your hassle at Cooley's, youngblood. Word's around what happened. Ain't nobody cryin' over Rasheel fuckin' Dellums— "

"Who?"

"The stud you burned down," a woman's voice from the posse said. Mick couldn't make out her face. "You don't know his name?"

"We weren't introduced."

"You didn't miss much," Fat said. "Dellums was a sorry-ass sumbitch, sorrier now, I expect. You got no trouble from our side of the street over him. This one time. But if ya'll plan to make any more management changes along them lines, you should know we ain't all as stupid as DuWayne Jenks. And definitely not as easy."

"I'm just the collector, Mr. Billups. If the count's right, I've got no problem with you, or anyone in this room."

"You tell that old man you work for, it's a new day." The voice from the posse again. "We got boys comin' home from the war and from prison. Hard boys. We ain't farmhands up from Alabama no more."

"Maybe you'd rather pass that message in person, I can arrange it."

One of the women chuckled, a low rumble of laughter that ricocheted around the room. A tall, spare woman in a leopard coat, hair piled high in a French do, red horn-rims.

"I believe he'll pass on that idea," she said. "But Cooley's? If it wasn't a move, how'd them Lucas end up with the place?"

"They didn't. Elmo Suggs bought 'em out. The fighter?"

"Elmo used to fight for Ronny Duke," she said. "Which means he never kept two nickels to rub together in his damn life."

"Elmo's just a front," Fatback said. "Name on the license downtown is Luca. Albert Luca. Big John's boy... " He broke off, reading Mick's face. "Hell, you didn't know, did you?"

Mick didn't answer. Got up from the stool instead, staring Fat down. "Anything else?"

"Nah, we're done here," Fat said, still smiling. "But just so we're clear? Anymore problems like Cooley's? You'd come talk to us first. We'll see you get your money."

"I don't work for you."

"Everybody knows who you work for, youngblood," Fat said, turning back to his receipts. "Just tryin' to keep peace in the valley, like the song says. You ain't got nothin' against peace, have ya?"

Mick glanced around the room, at the dozen dark faces. All sizing him up.

"No. I can do peace," he said, turning to head for the door.

"One other thing," Fat called after him. "Brownie gave me a buzz. Says he wants a sit down with you. Papa Doc's, whenever you say."

"What's Papa Doc's?"

"You serious?" Fat glanced up from his receipts. "Little joint on Canfield, sweetest hickory barbecue north of Biloxi. Hell, you don't want to go, send me. Dude say he's buyin'. What time?"

"Five," Mick lied. "I'll be there at five."

CHAPTER 23

With the meet set for five, Mick showed at four to scope out the ground. He'd had enough surprises for one week.

From the outside, Papa Doc's Hickory Hut looked like a rundown storefront diner. The inside was no better, scarred pink Formica counter, a row of backless stools, checkerboard linoleum floor, homemade plywood booths along the wall.

But the moment he stepped through the door, Mick got the appeal of the place. A long open-faced grill beside an honest-to-god Dixie barbecue pit. Sizzling chickens and racks of ribs rotating slowly above a cherry red bed of hickory coals. Juices dropping and popping in the fire, scenting the air with an aroma like southern smoked heaven.

Mick's mouth was already watering as he headed for the back booths, wanting a view of the room. The corner booth was already occupied. Leo Brown was sipping a cup of black coffee, reading the Chronicle, Detroit's only black-owned paper, looking elegant in a fawn silk vest and matching tie. Watching him come.

Mick slid in across from him. Didn't offer to shake hands.

"You're early," Brownie said, folding his paper. "A cautious young man."

"You're earlier."

"Nah, I own this booth. Do a lotta business up in here. Swimmin' like a fish in the sea of the people."

"What?"

"Chairman Mao said that, in the Red Book? You oughta read it. One smart, slant-eye motherfucker. He says jump, a billion Chinamen say 'how high?' He also says power comes from the barrel of a gun. Which ain't exactly news this part of town."

"What do you want, Mr. Brown?"

"To buy you some dinner. Talk some business."

"Our business is done till next month."

"Nah, that's Moishe's business. Our business ain't got started yet. You said you takin' over Mojo's recording studio, Black Kat?"

"What's that to you?"

"Nothin', yet. How much you know about the record biz, Irish? And the jukes?"

"I'm learning. What's on your mind?"

"A history lesson. Back in the day, jukes were real important. Them old 78 records were so big and heavy a box couldn't hold but twenty tunes. People used to jam the joints the day the jukebox man brought the new sides. After the war, everybody got TVs and the new 45 rpm jukes could hold a hundred plays so folks don't pay so much attention. Except inside 8 Mile. In Moishe's territory."

"Why is 8 Mile different?"

"We got a special situation up in here. Know how many black radio stations we got in Detroit? One. CHB in Inkster, daytime only. Frantic Ernie Durham at WJLB plays some rhythm and blues but he's a white cat. Ain't but a half dozen black stations in the whole U.S. of A."

"So?"

"So when black folks want to hear black music, it's hard to find on the radio. Gotta go out to clubs, cafes, catch live shows. But suppose their local neighborhood jukebox had some hot tunes? Your tunes. I figure y'all own what? Maybe three hundred twenty boxes, give or take?"

Give or take his ass. It was three twenty two on the nose. Brown knew his business. Mick sipped the strong coffee, waiting.

"Thing is, ol' Moishe only supplies the records that came with the boxes in the first place. Some business owners buy a new side now and again but most don't bother."

"I still don't— "

"I'll cut to it. I worked in the record business a few years back, ran promotion and sales for a jazz label till it went broke. But it's a new game now. Motown's crankin' out Oreo pop hits and English boys are playin' blues, but it's still tough to get black singers on the air. Anywhere."

"So?"

"You, on the other hand, can get a record played all over this town without buyin' radio time or payin' off a single DJ. If a singer cuts a record at Black Kat, that tune can be on every fucking jukebox in Detroit. Set it up for automatic play, it kicks on twice an hour whether anybody plays it or not. Folks like it, ask for it at the local record store, call up DJs askin' to hear it. It can give a tune one helluva jump start."

"But only on the jukes," Mick countered. "You'd hear it around town, but that's it."

"Every hit starts out local. The trick is to get it heard at all, and you could do that. There's more. There's maybe sixty black clubs inside Grand Boulevard. My place, Fat's, the Chit Chat, the Flame Lounge? It'd take me an hour to list 'em all. We all use entertainment. If Jackie Wilson's gonna be at the Chit Chat for two weeks, we could tag the owner for some extra green to put Jackie's songs on automatic."

"We?"

"That's what I'm saying. We, my man," Brownie leaned back, relaxing. "That's where I come in. The business end? I can handle that. Sales, changin' the records, all of it. I'm a club owner myself, I know everybody in the biz and they know me. This deal's a license to steal and it won't cost you a damn dime. In fact, you'll be money ahead from the git-go." He paused, waiting...

Mick waited him out.

"I'll buy in," Brownie finished, bridging his slender fingertips, eyeing Mick over them. "I'll give you five grand for a half interest in the studio. You keep every cent you're makin' now, we split the new biz I bring in, fifty-fifty. Partners."

"For ten you can buy me out, be your own boss."

"Haven't got ten, and I ain't got the boxes. You do. Anyway, I don't want to buy you out."

"Why not?"

"A studio's a lot for one guy to handle, especially if that guy owns a bar or works the street for Moishe Abrams. Partners share the weight. That's why you need one and so do I. Berry Gordy's got his whole damn family workin' for him over at Motown, and they printin' money there. Piles of it."

Mick hesitated, knowing something wasn't quite right, but not what. Couldn't get a read on Leo Brown. He'd done time with black men, trained with 'em, fought them.

But Brown was no pug. He was streetwise, and smart. He read books. Dressed well. Owned his own business. Using the jukes to promote the studio might work and he was willing to back it with hustle and his own cash. It sounded too good to be... Ah. And there it was.

"You want to buy in. Be my partner," Mick said. It wasn't a question.

"That's right."

"And partners should be straight with each other."

"Right again."

"I know I'm missing something, Mr. Brown— "

"My friends call me Brownie."

"We're not friends. We're not partners either. And that's the thing. You know how Moishe got the studio, so you also know I don't know squat about the business. With five thou you could buy into any studio in town, make your own deal with Moishe. You don't need me. Why make me the lucky one? What do you really want from me?"

"I knew it," Brownie nodded slowly, smiling. "Knew you had more goin' on than guts and muscle. Okay, straight up. My jazz label didn't go broke because we didn't *make* money. We just couldn't collect it. The music biz is full of chiselers, some are mobbed up, some claim to be, but they all stall you on payday. Havin' you as a partner will solve that problem. You'll know who's mobbed up and who ain't, and collecting is what you do. Word is, you're real good at it."

"Is that it?"

"Hell no. The big thing is the jukes. Moishe owns 'em, but he don't know or care about what's on 'em. We can put money in his pocket... "

He broke off. Mick was smiling.

"What?"

"I wondered what the bottom line was, and you just hit it. This is about Moishe, isn't it?"

"Damn straight it is," Brownie admitted, leaning back in his chair. "I told you about seein' Moishe in action before. You say he don't remember Idlewild, but he will. You're on his good side now, but I've seen his other side. Someday soon that old man will get to feelin' righteous, go back to bein' his bad self."

"And he'll remember you saved his life."

"Or he'll remember I'm a nigger who knows too much," Brownie said, leaning in, his eyes intense. "If that comes up, I want to be on his good side already, earning for him. And you'll be there to remind him I'm worth havin' around. We'll be partners, we both earn, and I get an insurance policy. Northwest Mutual of Irish Mick Shannon."

Mick laughed out loud. Knew he was being played, that there was more going on behind those brown eyes, but... Fuck it.

"Not fifty-fifty," he said. "Not for five grand."

"Give me a number then."

"For five large? I might go to a quarter interest."

"Batshit," Brownie smiled, both men relaxing now that they were down to it. "We both know the dance, white-bread. I'll drop to forty percent, you come up to thirty. Let me give you the full five for a one third interest, and I'll buy us the best fuckin' rib dinner you ever ate. Deal?"

CHAPTER 24

Five thousand fucking dollars. Cash money.

Driving away from Papa Doc's, Mick spread the neatly bundled packets out across the Lincoln's seat, glancing down at them now and again. Smiling. His biggest single payday in the fight game was the six hundred he earned for getting clocked by Kid Ibo and Wash gambled that away before he ever saw it. Things were looking up.

Back at the office, his first move was to cut out fifteen hundred for Moishe. When the old man stopped the next day for the tally, Mick slid an envelope with the extra cash in with the take.

Moishe expertly riffled through the bills without comment. He was looking better, getting some color in his cheeks, gaining back a few pounds. He was still using a cane to get around but it was a burled oak stick now, thick as a man's wrist with a brass pommel. Armed and dangerous again.

Mick expected a smile when Moishe finished the count. But when the old man looked up, his eyes were narrow, glittering with rage.

"I make it fifteen hundred over, kid."

"The thousand's off the front of my loan for the Black Kat studio. The five's your end for putting me in the deal."

"A bonus? You're tossin' me crumbs off my own goddamn table? You said we couldn't make a dime dumpin' that place."

"I didn't dump it, Moishe. I sold a piece, took on a partner."

"What partner?"

"Leo Brown, owns Brownie's Lounge."

"Brownie? The *schvartz* manager from Idlewild?"

"He saved your ass that night, Moishe. Mine too."

"He had to. The Chicago Outfit owns the Regency. Any trouble there, Brown's in deeper shit than us. But he knows what happened to Mojo and now he's buyin' into our action? I don't like it."

"Not our action, Moishe, my action. I'm payin' through the nose for it, remember?"

"Because you said there was no money! Only now there is. You think I'm banged up enough you can piss in my ear, tell me it's rainin'? I was running booze across the river before you were born."

"And nowadays you can buy booze for five bucks a fifth at the A & P. Like the song says, the times are a' changing."

"Only change I see is you. Gettin' too big for your britches. Taking you on was a mistake."

"Fine. Cut me loose. I've got three more stops this afternoon. Have at 'em."

"These are my streets. You think I can't take 'em back?"

"Not today. Not walkin' with a fucking cane."

Moishe flinched as though Mick had slapped him, his face reddening. "You smartass Irish punk! You'd be dead back in Idlewild, wasn't for me."

"I know that, Moishe. You got fifteen hundred in your hand that proves I know it. You're already money up on this deal and I still owe you the six for the studio. What the fuck's your problem?"

"Gettin' tipped by a mouthy punks who should be washin' my car, not drivin' it."

"Hell, if the fucking money's such a big insult, give it back. I'll never offer you another goddamn dime, I swear to Jesus." Mick held out his hand, half expecting Moishe to smash it with his stick.

He didn't, though. Instead the old man looked away, smiling grimly, shaking his head. "Fuck you, Shannon. You can insult me with money anytime. Probably skimmin' twice that anyway. But this thing with Brown? The St. Clair Club won't have it, Mick. No blacks in the business, rock solid rule."

"It's not their business, Moishe. The Lucas got no part of Black Kat. It was Mojo's deal, now it's ours."

"Everything we got goes through them."

"They get their cut of the street money, but we both paid the freight for this. I didn't see any Lucas that night in Idlewild. Or in Cooley's. If we cut 'em in, they'll cut us out again."

"What are you talkin' about?"

"Cooley's. They told you Suggs bought it for basically nothin', gave you a chump change cut. But he didn't buy it at all, he's just a front. John handed it off to Albert. They fucked us out of it, Moishe."

"Where'd you get this?"

"From Fatback. But I checked it out. It's true."

"It don't change our situation."

"I don't have a situation. Luca said it himself, you work for them, I work for you. I owe you, Moishe. I dropped a guy for Cooley's, and Luca just handed it off to his nephew. Tipped you like a bellboy."

"You don't understand."

"I understand gettin' fucked. Been to that dance more than once. Look, I owe you, and I'm down for doin' any damn thing to take care of *your* business. But not theirs. Are you okay with that, or do we have a problem?"

Moishe shook his head slowly, unwilling to push things to a break. He needed the Lucas for protection, but needed Mick too. Shannon was a tough kid, with some smarts, but he had a fire in his belly, hungry as a Doberman off its chain.

Moishe remembered that hunger. A young man's ambition. Every stud in the old Purple Gang had it... and they were all dead now. The crazy dreams and the wild-ass boys who had them. Moishe knew what street dreams could cost.

Wasn't sure what to do. So he took the simplest option. Do nothing for now. Let it ride, see what happens.

Pocketing his envelopes, he limped out to his sister's car, wondering if hiring Irish Mick Shannon was the biggest mistake of his life.

Wondering if he'd get them both killed.

CHAPTER 25

"Garbage," Brownie said. "None of this noise will fly. Put it on a juke, folks'll kick the boxes to death."

They were in Studio K (for kitchen) the next afternoon. Brownie in shirtsleeves and a silver silk vest with Martika Daniels and her cousin Jerome. Mick had popped in on a mid-afternoon break. They'd been listening to Jerome's Sony reel-to-reel tape deck to groups and singers who'd recorded at Black Kat over the past weeks.

Lanky, with a prominent Adam's apple and a scruffy goatee that looked glued on, Jerome dressed like a hipster from the fifties, sporting a Dizzy Gillespie-style tweed beret and black turtleneck. His square, black framed glasses were even thicker than Martika's.

The look was definitely quirky, but the kid was sharp about the music.

"Mojo never planned to make no hits here," Jerome said. "The studio's too small to get a clean sound. With this setup, we're pretty much limited to renting mike time to amateurs."

"All we need is one," Brownie shrugged. "Maybe do a ballad, without much background?"

"I can do ballads," Martika said quietly. "I had a record— "

"Ten years ago," Brownie said.

"Eight," she continued. "Look, I had some bad luck, but I only took this job because Mojo promised— "

"If Mojo's promises meant doodly-squat, this white boy wouldn't own the joint, sugar," Brownie said. "Thing is, the first group we put on automatic play has to *belong* there. They gotta be able to run with it, make personal appearances in clubs, and malls and street dances, maybe even TV. You know the drill, you've been there. How's your leg doin'? Still a little gimpy, I noticed."

"Let it be for now," Mick said flatly. "I need you to run the shop, girl, keep the cash flow coming in. We'll find something for you later."

"Assumin' you make it to later, Irish. So now I got Mojo's word and yours too? Lucky me."

Mick gave her a look and she turned away. Angry, but not intimidated.

Just smart enough to fold a losing hand.

"I might know somebody," Jerome said. "Remember Varnell Mack from the Sultans?"

"Who are the Sultans?" Mick asked.

"The Sultans of Soul," Brownie said. "East Detroit boys, been bangin' around singin' at weddings, lodge halls since high school."

"Never heard of 'em," Mick said.

"You'd know 'em if you grew up in the Bottom," Jerome said. "Varnell left a demo tape... Jerome changed tapes, deftly threading the leader over the playback heads. "It's a gospel tune, but..."

The recording wasn't much better than the others, a doo-wop group, singing unaccompanied, with a lead singer whose voice soared like a songbird learning to fly.

"Didn't know they were still together," Brownie said.

"Back together," Tika amended. "The group went broke working the chitlin' circuit a few years ago, busted up. Varnell came around last week, lookin' for Mojo. Wanted to trade backup vocals for free studio time."

"He's still got some chops," Brownie mused. "More important, they have a name."

"If the Sultans were offerin' to work for free, their price sounds about right," Brownie said. "They playin' anyplace I can hear 'em, Jerome?"

"The Chit Chat this week, opening for Jackie Wilson."

"What do you think, partner?" Brownie asked. "You up for some clubbin' on the Corridor?"

CHAPTER 26

Mick felt a jolt of electricity the moment they stepped into the Chit Chat Lounge. The music and smoke, the buzz of the crowd. Couldn't help smiling. He'd brought Leanne, thinking a hotspot would impress her. But she'd gone all wide-eyed on him, spooked as a doe in the headlights. The club was nearly full and they were the only white couple in sight.

Just up the street from Berry Gordy's Motown studio, the Chit Chat was twice the size of Brownie's Lounge, with a lot more style. White linens, candles glowing on cocktail tables, waitresses in perky French maid outfits. An uptown crowd, black men in suits, women in vivid, high fashion dresses and heels. A raised tier around the outer rim of the room offered every seat in the house a clear view of the bandstand.

Onstage, a four-piece combo was cooking, piano, guitar, bass and drums jamming on a jazz riff Mick didn't recognize. Their music was rock solid in the pocket and the crowd was with them, feeling every beat.

Spotting Brownie at a table near the dance floor, Mick led Leanne through the crush, turning more than a few heads as they passed. In her pink sack dress and beehive hair, Leanne looked big-blonde and busty as Mamie Van Doren. Dead sharp.

Brownie rose as they made their way through the crowd. In a gunmetal gray suit and matching tie, he looked stylish as an ESQUIRE ad. Mick was in his Robert Hall jacket, pegged slacks.

"Damn, Country, don't you own a freakin' tie?"

"I can swing one if I jack your action a few points."

"I only buy outfits for ladies and you don't qualify. Hello, miss, I'm Leo Brown, Brownie to my friends and everybody else," he said, holding Leanne's chair like a maitre d'. "And you are…?"

"Leanne. Skiba," she added taking her seat, clearly uneasy.

"Lovely name," Brownie smiled, resuming his seat. "This is Jerome Daniels, and his cousin Martika."

Leanne nodded, unimpressed. Jerome looked like the underage beatnik he was. In her plain navy shift, horn rims and plastic pearls, Martika looked thrift shop presentable. Easy to overlook in a roomful of overdressed women. Yet there was a dignity about her. Mick couldn't put his finger on it. He shook it off.

They were still exchanging quick introductions when the drummer kicked into a solo, closing off the set with a bang as a tuxedoed emcee trotted onstage.

"Ain't they great, folks? Let's hear it for Benjy Jefferson and his Motown All-stars! Live and in living color at the Chit Chat for one night only. Give it up for 'em!"

"All-stars," Jerome snorted. "Three dopers Benjy slapped together to play for drinks."

"Which one's Benjy?" Mick asked.

"The drummer, the Cuban-looking guy with the gunfighter moustache. Used to book all Motown's studio sessions but the boy never met a bottle he didn't like."

"Has Motown cut Benjy loose?" Brownie asked.

"He still plays on sessions but he isn't booking gigs anymore."

"He's half crazy but he's the best session boss there is," Brownie said. "Think he'd run a gig for us?"

"Gordy don't let his musicians work other studios," Martika said.

"Benjy needs the action, though," Jerome added. "I hear he's got expensive habits."

Onstage, the band shifted into a driving hitch-hike beat, Jefferson grinning broadly as he heated up the tempo. Energy rising, the audience was buzzing with anticipation.

"And now, the opening act of our star-studded night, directly from the Rochambeau Hotel in Atlanta, Georgia! Hometown boys, you know 'em, you love 'em, can't get enough of 'em! Give it up for...the Sult*aaaans* of *Soooul*!"

The band was cooking hard now, Benjy Jefferson ripping off manic drum fills like a machine gunner, the bass player locked rock solid on a four-beat hitchhike pulse.

But onstage, confusion reigned as the emcee looked around desperately for the act he'd just introduced, Benjy laughing out loud at the panic in his face.

The Sultans were on their way. Four studs in eye-popping lime-green leisure suits, thumbs in the air, came hitchhiking through the crowd from four different directions, as laughter and applause crackled around the room.

Vaulting onstage, grabbing the mike from the emcee, the heavyset lead singer tore into Barrett Strong's "Money!" as the rest of the group lined up behind him in a dance step, echoing *'that's what I want'* with more energy than accuracy.

"They're still rough," Brownie observed, "but better than before."

"Some," Martika agreed. "They'd be better if Varnell quit trying to carry the act. Doesn't have the pipes for it."

And that was it. Mick got it. Got her, for the first time. And smiled. She met his eyes. "What?"

"This isn't a show, is it?"

"Sure it is. They do a good show."

"But that's not all it is. You're like a fighter watching a bout. You're sizing 'em up. In case you've gotta take 'em on."

"I haven't been on a stage in a long time."

"But you can't turn it off, any more than I can. Can't help sizing up the competition. Probably will till we're eighty."

"She'll get there a lot sooner than you will, hon," Leanne cracked.

"Easy sweet thing," Tika smiled, her eyes glittering. "You're a long ways from 'billytown.'"

The moment passed as the Sultans ended their opening song. The crowd applauded politely, but Martika rose to her feet, whooping her approval.

"Sit yourself down, girl," Brownie said wryly. "We're about to talk business with those boys. Don't get their heads all swole up."

The crowd response was mild, like a warm up fight, Mick noted, scanning the room. The Chit Chat was filled wall to wall now with well-dressed black couples plus a few tables of white frat boys from U of Detroit, out scouting for brown sugar.

Onstage, the bullet-headed lead singer introduced himself as Otis De-Witt, then ripped into the next number with as much energy as the first. "Motown Mama." A good song, but not one Mick knew. DeWitt sang his lungs out, storming around the stage but the applause was thinner for the unfamiliar tune and the Sultans quickly shifted back to mainstream material. Their chubby little bass singer kicked off the Marcels' *Blue Moon*, clowning the *bow-bapa-bow* introduction with a comic stutter, trying for laughs and getting them.

Playing it safe for the rest of their set, the Sultans covered pop hits by the Coasters, The Temptations and Little Anthony, finishing up with Marvin Gaye's "Chicago Hitchhike," dancing off through the audience during the last chorus to enthusiastic applause as the emcee raced back onstage to milk the crowd for applause and pump up the volume for the main act, Mr. Love Light, Jackie Wilson, coming on in half an hour.

Brownie and Jerome split to track down Benjy Jefferson and the Sultans' leader, Varnell Mack, leaving Mick in the uncomfortable silence between Leanne and Martika.

"What did you think, babe?" Mick asked.

"Not really my thing," Leanne sniffed. "A little too..."

"Black?" Martika offered sweetly.

"Crude," Leanne flared. I didn't care for them, that's all."

"I thought they were strong," Martika countered, "but maybe they're just 'my thing.' How about you, Irish?"

"I liked their energy," Mick said cautiously, catching the friction between the two women. "The lead guy, DeWitt, worked the crowd and the chubby guy, the bass singer? A good showman, got some laughs."

"I figured you for a Sinatra fan," Leanne said.

"No, I'm more into blues. The Kings, Howlin' Wolf."

"Did you hear blues in that place you mentioned?" Martika asked. "Where the other boys howled like dogs?"

"And before," Mick shrugged. "Growing up in Ecorse, Bobby Vinton doesn't say much to you."

"Don't believe a word of it," Leanne said, taking Mick's arm possessively. "He can barely manage his business when a love song's on the radio— "

She was interrupted by Jerome returning with the drummer in tow. Benjy Jefferson dropped into the seat facing Mick, a whiskey glass in each hand. Up close he looked more Spanish than black, a thick mustache, processed hair, eyes sparkling with mischief. Eyes that met Mick's dead on.

"And here he is, the nastiest cat in Motown," Benjy grinned. "The brand spankin' new juke box king. How you doin', Mr. Shannon? Heard a lot about you. All bad. You as evil as everybody says?"

"Your mama doesn't think so," Mick shot back. "She cried for me to stay on, but I hated to keep all them boys in line waitin'."

"Man even knows the dozens," Jefferson said, with a grin that didn't touch his eyes. "Where'd you learn that mess, cowboy? Jail?"

"Had a cell right across from your daddy."

"Whoever that sumbitch was," Benjy nodded, passing one of his shot glasses to Mick. They touched 'em up and knocked back at a swallow.

"You have a great band, Mr. Jefferson," Martika said.

"Thank you, sweet thing," Benjy said, taking her fingertips, kissing her hand. "It's not a band, though, just a pickup group. I remember you, right? You Mojo's girl? The one runnin' that crackerbox studio for him?"

"I'm his niece," Martika corrected, "and it's Mr. Shannon's studio now."

"We're wondering if you can do some dates for us," Jerome added.

"Y'all got health insurance?" Benjy asked. "From this boy's reputation, I might need extra."

"All rumors," Brownie said, rejoining them with the tallest of the Sultans in tow. "Mr. Shannon, meet Varnell Mack."

Mick rose to shake hands, but even standing he was still looking up. Tall, gaunt and dazzling in the lime green suit, Mack towered over him by half a head. High cheekbones, narrow face and jaw, and sad, gentle eyes. If he'd heard the street talk about Mick he showed no sign. He folded his long frame gracefully into the last chair.

"You're the boss?" Mick asked. "I thought Otis DeWitt— "

"Otis sings lead," Varnell said, his voice a mellow murmur, "I handle the business. Brownie told me what y'all got in mind. How many jukeboxes we talkin' about?"

"All the ones that count," Brownie said. "We can't promise you Broadway lights, but we can build you a name in this town."

"What material?" Varnell asked.

"You'll have to do covers," Benjy said flatly. "If we know the material, my group can cut three, four backup tracks in a few hours. I'm booked for two more sets at Fatback's after we finish here, but we could cut some tracks at the studio, say, eight tomorrow morning? You boys come in at ten, we'll— "

"Yo! Irish!" Ron Ducatti bellowed, weaving through the crowd, leaning drunkenly over Mick's shoulder. "Me and Albert came down for Jackie Wilson's show but there's a line out front. Make room, okay?"

"Yo, Stretch?" Benjy asked. "This a table for four, we got six and we're talkin' business here."

"You must have a friend someplace, sport," Ronny slurred, flipping his coat open to show the automatic in his waistband. "Go find 'em."

"Whoo-ee, lookee that!" Benjy said, wide-eyed, comically stroking his mustache. "The big dude's packin' iron. Problem is, most of the brothers in this joint are strapped too, Blondie. Includin' this one." He unbuttoned his jacket. Didn't show a weapon, didn't need to. "Take off."

"What's the holdup?" Albert Luca demanded, shouldering through the crush to stand with Ducatti, looking sharp in a Sinatra suit, designer shades. "We need two seats, Shannon. Lose these people."

"I just told your girlfriend we got no seats," Benjy said, standing up. "Now I'm tellin' you, shorty. Fuck off, the both of ya."

Albert reddened, as if he'd been slapped. "Do you know who I am?"

"Let me think. Hell no. Guess you ain't as famous as you thought. Shorty."

"I'm Albert Luca. John Luca is my uncle. Does that name register with you?"

"Big John? Hell yes! I've heard of him. He here tonight?"

"No, but— "

"Then he won't be needin' a chair. I'll keep this one warm in case he shows. Meanwhile, you and Blondie go dance someplace else."

"Who you calling Blondie, you nigger fuck?" Ducatti flared.

"Everybody chill out!" Mick said, grabbing Ducatti's wrist as he reached for his automatic.

"Get off me!" Ronny snarled, jerking free. "Who's side are you on?"

"Mine! You start up in here, we'll all get capped!"

"How about it, Albert?" Ronny asked. "Want me to pop this numbnuts?"

Luca glanced around at the staring sea of black faces, all drawn to the drama. "Not now. Shannon, with me. We need to talk." He turned and headed for the door without waiting for an answer.

Giving Brownie a look, Mick trailed Albert and Ronny Duke out through the crowd. In the vestibule, Luca wheeled on him, his narrow face flushed and furious.

"What the hell was that? Why didn't you back us up?"

"Back what? Ronny's drunk and that drummer's strapped. You don't really want a shootout in there?"

"I want that mouthy motherfucker dead! In the fucking ground! Tonight!" The cords in Albert's neck were taut as guy wires. Above his ruined eye, the white worm scar was writhing like it was alive, burrowing in deeper.

"You want him gone, he's gone," Ronny said. "Me and Mick will take care of it."

Mick stared from one to the other. Ronny was too loaded to care but Albert was in a murderous rage. Dead fucking serious.

"No problem," Mick agreed. "I've got no plans for the next twenty-five to life. How about you?"

"What are you talking about?"

"Prison. The House of Many Doors. Ronny got into it with Jefferson in front of a hundred witnesses, and you just told them your goddamn name. I know he pissed you off, but you got nothing serious ridin' on this. You'd better cool out and think it over."

"Don't tell me what to do!" Albert snapped. "You're hired help!"

"You're right. I'm just a driver. But I'm not dumb enough to cap some mope over a damn chair! If you want to try sticking my head in a vise over this bullshit, bring it. But I'm not a high school kid, pal. And I work for Moishe Abrams, not you."

"Not for long, Shannon. You just made a huge fucking mistake. Let's go, Ronny." He stormed out the door.

"Christ, Irish," Ducatti sighed. "You got a death wish?"

"No, but he does. You weren't serious about whacking that schmuck in there?"

"Won't have to. Albert'll cool off. You don't have to worry."

"You're the one I'm worried about, not Albert. If he makes a move on me, I don't figure he'll come himself."

"No," Ronny admitted. "He'd send me. Which would be a shame. I kinda like you."

"You'd get over it."

"The minute my check cleared," Ducatti grinned blearily, straightening his tie. "I'll see ya Tuesday, Mick."

"If not before," Mick murmured, watching Ronny wobble out.

The emcee was revving up the crowd for Jackie Wilson's show as Mick eased back down at his table. Leanne's chair was empty. Mick glanced the question at Martika.

"Powder room," she said.

"Nice friends you got," Benjy grinned broadly, enjoying himself.

"They're not friends and you've got a big mouth."

"Do we have a problem?" Brownie asked.

Mick shrugged.

"He does that a lot," Martika said. "Answers questions by not answering questions."

"That big blonde dude must be super bad," Benjy went on. "No other way his punk-ass boyfriend could have lived this long."

"Goddamn, Benjy," Brownie sighed, "do you know who that guy was?"

"Some hood's nephew, so fuckin' what? Half the chumps in the music biz are mobbed up and the other half claim they are to knock your price down. You start kissin' everybody's ass, your face turns brown...oh hell, I'm sorry, man. Is that why folks call you Brownie?"

"Fuck you, Jefferson."

"Same to ya, Mr. Brown. You ready to talk some business or what?"

The two men leaned in, conferring quietly. Leanne returned to her seat just as Jackie Wilson's band kicked off an easy shuffle. Wilson strolled out of the wings to a roar of applause, fine as wine in a beige continental four-button jacket, knife-edged slacks, gleaming patent loafers.

Opening his show with "(she was) Only Sixteen", he was totally at ease, singing to the men in the crowd, knowing he already had the women. He upped the tempo a bit with the next tune, "Lonely Teardrops", finger-popping, dancing gracefully to the music.

A *stone cold pro,* Mick thought. The Sultans knocked themselves out to earn a smattering of applause. Wilson was winning over the same audience without breaking a sweat.

By the time he closed his show with "Higher and Higher", he had the crowd on its feet cheering as he danced offstage to a standing ovation, people cheering, yelling for more.

No encore. He sauntered back out, took a quick bow, but that was it. Benjy's quartet had already replaced Wilson's band for the final set.

"Always best to leave 'em wantin' more," Varnell Mack said wistfully, folding his lanky frame back into his seat.

"You guys did an encore," Mick noted.

"We're hungry for the love," the older man admitted. "Down south where nobody knew us, we had a ton of tough nights. Cleavon clowned us out of trouble more times than I can count, when Dexter couldn't talk our way out of it."

"Maybe we can change your luck," Brownie said.

"If it wasn't for bad luck, we wouldn't have none at all," Varnell smiled, rising. "See you at the studio tomorrow, Brownie. Nice meeting you, Mr. Shannon, ladies." Mack moved off through the crowd like a gentle giraffe, affable and dignified, even in a lime leisure suit.

"How'd y'all like Jackie's show?" Brownie asked, glancing around the table.

"Him I like," Leanne gushed. "He sings like he's from Las Vegas."

"Too slick for me," Mick shrugged. "Worked the room like a pool hustler, thinking two shots ahead. The Sultans' lead singer, the burly guy? What's his name?"

"Otis DeWitt sings lead, Dexter Jaquette's the second tenor." Jerome said. "The little guy, second from the end."

"Otis laid it all out there, like a fighter, savin' nothin' for next time. Sang every tune like it was their last chance."

"If they're working for you, maybe it is," Martika sniped.

"We'd better go," Leanne said. "I have a long day tomorrow."

"Nice meeting you miss," Brownie said, rising politely. But Leanne was already heading for the door.

CHAPTER 27

In the Lincoln, Leanne stayed over on her own side of the seat, giving him the silent treatment. He waited her out. Had a fair idea of what was up.

"You could have warned me about the coloreds," Leanne said at last. "I'm not prejudiced but I don't care to socialize with them."

"I thought you liked Jackie. Mr. Las Vegas, and all."

"That's not the point."

Switching on the radio, he found WCHB in Inkster, Long Lean Larry Dean murmuring sweet nothings between love songs—

"Enough of that for tonight," Leanne said, sliding over to switch the radio off.

Mick let it pass because she stayed in the middle of the seat, her thigh warm against his, her hand on his knee. Pouting or not, she was still hot to trot. Two minutes of small talk and she'd slide that dress up around her neck.

He was more worried about Albert. At the St. Clair Club he'd made him for an arrogant punk. As Big John's nephew, he could afford to be cocky.

He'd discounted Ronny's story about Albert crushing the kid's skull but he damn well believed it now. He'd met enough whacks in jail to know Albert was definitely off the rails. Question was, what to do about it?

With the Luca crew behind him, bucking Albert would be suicide. Unless it came down to it, do or die, and it just might. He'd seen guys shanked for a lot less—

A siren yelped behind him, gumball flashers swirling. Prowl car! Fuck! He glanced at the speedometer, five over. What the hell? Jerking the .45 out of his waistband, he shoved it out of sight between the seats. Leanne's eyes widened but she didn't comment.

Easing the Lincoln to the curb, Mick kept it in drive, engine idling. They were in a residential area, houses all around.

Two Ecorse cops climbed out of the prowl car, white guys in tan summer uniforms carrying flashlights. One was in his forties, six foot but running to fat. His partner was much younger, early twenties, scrawny with a weak jaw, his bird face pitted with acne.

The older cop came up on Mick's side, his hand on his gun butt. "Driver's license. And turn off your vehicle, please." Mick shut the Lincoln down, passed his license out the window to the older cop. Sergeant L. Gorski on his nametag. The cop who'd made him at Scotty's.

The younger cop was flashing his light through the passenger side window, checking the interior.

"Hiya, Leanne, how the heck are ya?" he asked, leaning on the door frame.

"Good, Cody," Leanne said. She didn't sound good. Had a quaver in her voice, kept looking from one cop to the other, jumpy as a cat on a freeway centerline.

"This your vehicle, Shannon?" Gorski asked.

"Belongs to my boss, Moishe Abrams. The title's in— "

"Step out of the car."

"What's the problem?"

"No problem. As long as you step out. Right now." Gorski patted the butt of his service revolver.

And Mick knew what was coming. And felt suddenly sick for knowing.

"You'd better walk home, Leanne," he said. "It's only a few blocks."

"I don't understand— "

"It's okay, babe, " Cody said, opening her door. "We got an all-points lookout for a car like this one. Might take awhile to clear up. You don't want to miss your beauty sleep."

"I do have to work in the morning," she said uneasily, sliding out. "I'll see ya, Mick. I had...." The rest was lost as she hurried off, high heels clicking on the sidewalk.

"You deaf, Irish?" The younger cop drew his revolver, waving it in Mick's general direction. "My partner told you to get the fuck out."

Mick considered trying for the .45, but knew he'd never make it. He climbed out of the car instead, slowly, being careful not to give them an excuse.

"Assume the position," Gorski said. "You know the drill."

Mick leaned on the Lincoln, his hands on the hood. Cody came around the car to pat him down. A sloppy search. Didn't check his boots or sleeves. Cody had to be green as grass.

Gorski wasn't much better. Kept his hand on his gun butt but he was standing within easy reach. Hobby cops, both of them. Okay for writing speeding tickets or rousting drunks but neither one would last a week in Jackson. And Mick'd survived five years there.

"He's clean," Cody said, straightening.

"Search the car."

Mick's heart sank. If they found the gun— Headlights flashed as a second patrol car pulled up behind the first. And Sergeant Wes Spivak stepped out. In civvies, jeans, cowboy boots, a plaid short sleeved shirt. His reddish hair was rumpled, eyes watery. Looked to be about half in the bag.

Keep them out of the damn car, Mick thought. *Push his buttons.*

"How you been, Wes? Or do I call you Sergeant now? Did you get a promotion for bustin' me?"

"Shut up," Cody said.

"Did you frisk him?" Spivak asked.

"You bet, Sarge. Nothin'," Cody said.

"Put him in your car, we'll take him— "

"Why stall around, Wes?" Mick prodded. "You've been waitin' years for this dance. Get to it, if you got the nuts."

"You don't give orders here, punk," Gorski said.

"Neither do you. This psycho fuck's dyin' to tune me up. What's the matter, Wes? You only swing on women? Or doesn't your arm work anymore?"

"Hold him!" Spivak barked, snatching a nightstick out of his prowl car.

"Easy now, Wes," Gorski warned, grabbing Mick's right arm as Cody seized his left. "A witness knows he's in custody."

"Fuck your witness!" Spivak grunted, jamming Mick in the gut, driving his wind out, doubling him over. "And fuck this punk. You're right, Shannon, I've been waitin' for this. I've thought about it every time I shave, every time somebody asks me how I fucked up my wrist! See?" He shook his fist in Mick's face. Then punched him full in the mouth, splitting his lip.

Mick shook his head to clear it, then spat blood on Spivak's shirt.

"Cocksucker!" Spivak roared, flailing away with the stick, hacking Mick across the biceps, the thighs. Squirming, Mick struggled against Cody and Gorski, working the angles to avoid taking the blows squarely. Realized Cody's hands were slipping down his forearm. The young cop didn't know how to clamp on properly. His thumbs were overlapped, an easily breakable hold. And neither man was blocking his legs. Strictly weekend warriors, they didn't have a clue.

Tiring, Spivak stepped back, wheezing, bleary-eyed. Definitely half drunk, the booze reek rolling off his sweat. Mick hocked up a gob of blood and mucus, spat it at his feet.

"Okay," Gorski panted. "I think this punk got the message."

"Fuck that, I'm just getting warmed up," Spivak growled, slapping the nightstick against his open palm. "Hold his arm out, Cody."

"Now wait a damn minute, Wes!" Gorski warned. "The witness— "

But if Gorski was worried, Cody wasn't. His eyes were bright, eager to deal out some pain. Setting his stance, he slid his grip down to Mick's wrist, then yanked his forearm out straight to give Spivak a clear swing at it. Mick struggled enough to let Cody think his grip was solid, knowing he'd only get one chance.

"Payback time, you fuck," Spivak growled. "Listen close! You'll hear the bone snap!" Wading in, he jabbed at Mick's face with the nightstick, wielding it like a fencing foil, trying to mash his nose, grinning hugely, enjoying himself. Mick ducked and bobbed, making Wes miss a few, but one jab laid open his cheekbone, another grazed his forehead, hot blood streaming into his left eye.

Tiring of the sport, Wes stepped back, slapping the stick into his palm, then grasping it like a baseball bat, two-hand hold. Widening his stance, he took a couple of warm up swings, Mickey Mantle style, halting the stick at the last second, inches above Mick's wrist, watching his face.

Mick felt Gorski and Cody bracing themselves, tightening their grips, for the big finish. No need for Mick to get ready, he was already taut as a revolver at full cock.

"Batter up!" Wes roared, raising the nightstick high to get a full swing. But as Spivak stepped in, Mick lashed out! Using Gorski as a brace, Mick drew up both legs and stomped Wes's left knee with both feet, hearing the crunch of bones as the joint buckled backwards. Wes screamed, stumbling into Cody, carrying him down as Mick wrenched his wrist free of Cody's grip.

Whirling on Gorski, who was clawing for his weapon, Mick grabbed his lapels, head-butting the fat cop full in the face, jerking the pistol from his fist as Gorski dropped to his knees, gagging in a welter of blood.

"Don't even think it!" Mick roared, leveling the piece at Cody, who was fumbling for his sidearm with Spivak still writhing, half on top of him. "Move half an inch and I'll splatter your brains all over the curb!"

Staring down the gun muzzle, Cody froze, then slowly raised his hands. Moaning, Spivak rolled off of him, clutching his shattered knee.

Jamming the Police Positive against Spivak's temple, Mick cocked the hammer, turning his face away to avoid the muzzle blast—

"God, don't," Wes groaned, cowering, shielding his face with his forearms, as though they could ward off a bullet. "Please— "

"Don't do it, Shannon," Gorski panted, blood bubbling from his broken nose. "I got kids— "

"Shut the fuck up!" Three seconds. Three more. No gunshot. Mick was gripping the .38 so tightly his arm was quivering like a power line in a gale. But he didn't fire. He wanted to so bad he could taste it. Couldn't quite do it.

"Jesus, kid." Spivak moaned. "I'm beggin' you— "

Jerking the weapon up, Mick kicked Spivak in the belly, burying his boot ankle deep in Wes's guts, nearly breaking him in half. Spivak went white, his mouth working like a beached carp, vainly gasping for air. Then he retched, spewing booze and bile on the pavement.

As Mick leapt back to avoid the vomit, Cody tensed, sliding his right hand toward his weapon—

Found himself staring down the gun muzzle again. The hammer still at full cock.

"Go ahead, try it, dumbfuck," Mick panted. "Gimme half a reason."

Blinking, Cody shook his head, raising his hands again.

"All right," Mick nodded. "Take out your piece with your fingertips and hand it over. Easy."

The young cop did as he was told, shaking so badly he nearly dropped the weapon.

Snatching up the revolver, Mick backed off a step, a gun in each fist, covering the lawmen.

"Wait!" Gorski pleaded. "Don't be crazy, Shannon. Nobody's dead yet. We can still fix this."

"Last time Spivak fixed things, I did five years."

"But that's settled now, swear to God! I thought he was going to rough you up, but I'm not down for this. Wes had his shot, and came up short. Call it even! But if you take this any further, there's no way back."

Mick wobbled, Gorski's voice fading in and out.

"Jesus, look at you. You can barely stand up. You better get out of here while you can."

"Get on your knees."

"What? Oh man— "

"Get the fuck down! You, Cody! Get in my car, behind the wheel. Move!"

"What are you going to do?" Gorski asked.

"Your partner's gonna drive me out of here. When I'm in the clear, I'll cut him loose. But just so you know? I did five years for Spivak's busted arm. I'm not doing another day. If you call this in, if I hear a siren or see a prowl car, I'll cap your pal's punk ass so fast— "

"We won't call it in, I give you my word! Just don't— "

But he was talking to the air. Stumbling around the Lincoln, Mick collapsed into the shotgun seat, Cody at the wheel.

"Drive." he said, jamming the pistol against Cody's crotch.

□   □   □

Cody was crying. Silently. Tears and snot dripping down his nose. Probably didn't even know he was doing it. Weaving, slamming on the brakes at stoplights, he was driving like a robot with its brain shorted out. As soon as they crossed West Grand, Mick ordered him out of the car, afraid he'd get them busted for a traffic violation.

Which may have been a mistake. Alone behind the wheel, woozy from the gash on his temple with blood dripping in his eyes, he could barely keep the Lincoln on the road. Knew he had to hole up someplace, but couldn't think where. Didn't dare go back to his place in Ecorse or Moishe's office. The cops knew about them both.

Parking the Lincoln in an alley on St. Antoine Street, he stumbled the last few blocks to Mojo's studio. Black Kat was dark, no lights showing. Couldn't find his fucking key. Hammered on the door with a gun butt. When it finally opened, he fell through it. Hit the deck hard, but never felt a thing.

□   □   □

Footfalls dragged him up out of the blackness. Someone was sneaking up the stairway. He could hear the creaks. Dazed, every inch of him aching, it took him a moment to grasp where he was. Upstairs at the Black Kat studio, Tika's room? With somebody coming.

He was groping vainly on the nightstand for a weapon when the door inched ajar. Then opened wide.

Martika Daniels. Wearing her work duds, black sweater, poodle skirt, horn rimmed glasses.

"You still alive, Irish?"

He didn't answer. Sagged back on the pillows. "What the hell happened?"

"I should ask you that," she said standing beside the bed, frowning down at him, dark eyes huge behind her horn rims.

"I had trouble. How did I get here?"

"You showed up at three, pounding on the door like a crazy man, then passed out on the porch. I dragged you in, Jerome helped me haul you up here. You said no doctor. but— "

"No! No doctor. No hospital. My car— "

"Jerome hid it around back in the garage. But you really do need help, white boy. You're bleeding all over my sheets. I've got a cousin who was a medic in the army, works nights at Samaritan Hospital. I called him. Left a message."

"Has anybody been looking for me?"

"Like the police, you mean? No, nobody. They probably figure you're dead. You sure look it."

"Where's my gun?"

"Forget it. You'll only get yourself killed. If somebody comes looking, you climb out the window, lay flat on the roof. Nobody can see you out there."

"Damn it, Martika, where's my goddamn gun!"

"It's down at the desk! If there's any trouble, you'll hear it go off! Then you'll know it's time to climb out the window. Right now you couldn't rassle a stray cat."

Downstairs, the doorbell rang.

"That's Calvin," she said, rising.

"What if it's not?"

"It better be," she said grimly, and stalked out.

Mick tried to sit up, couldn't quite make it, fell back on the pillows, drenched in sweat. Closing his eyes against the pain, he concentrated, trying to make the room stop rolling. Finally slowed it down a bit, then brought it under control. Kept his eyes narrowed to slits, holding things steady.

When he opened his eyes Martika was standing in the doorway, watching him. Holding a tray with a pan of water and clean towels. Big guy behind her.

"This is my cousin Calvin," she said briskly, parking the tray on the nightstand. "We'd better get you cleaned you up some or he might turn down the job."

CHAPTER 28

Martika's medic cousin, Calvin Oaks, was a skeletal black man, thirtyish with hard eyes, gentle hands. He wore an army fatigue jacket, combat boots, and an orange keloid burn scar on his cheek, a keepsake from combat in Laos.

"How bad does your head hurt?" Oaks asked.

"Compared to what?"

"If you can crack wise, it can't be too bad. From those scars around your eyebrows, you done some fighting in the ring. How many times you been KO'd?"

"What's the difference?"

"I don't give a damn about your record, pal, I'm askin' about concussions." Calvin had already stitched the gash on Mick's temple, the cut on his cheekbone and was carefully closing up a wound on his shoulder with a butterfly bandages. "How many?"

"I've been decked a few times, only knocked out once. And that was a body punch."

"Liver shot?"

Mick nodded.

"Better there than your head. These welts on your arms and shoulders? I'd say a nightstick or an iron pipe. Which was it?"

Mick hesitated. "A stick."

"Lucky again. Nightstick's lighter, less likely to break bones. This half-healed gash along your ribs? That's a bullet wound, a ricochet from the looks of it. When did that happen?"

Again, Mick hesitated. "A few weeks ago."

"You didn't see a doctor?"

"I've been busy. It's coming along all right. I heal fast."

"Good thing, the life you're in. That wound should've been stitched up, but it's too far along to fix now. You're gonna have a nasty scar. Okay, here's the scoop. Unless your body bruises start to bleed out subdural and swell, they should heal on their own. They won't kill you, but the next few days, you're gonna wish you were dead. The gash on your head is trickier. What time did it happen?"

"I'm not sure. One or two a.m., somewhere in there."

"It's nearly six now," Oaks said, glancing at his watch. "If your skull was fractured, you should be showing symptoms and I don't see any. But sometimes symptoms can take eighteen hours or more to develop. You really should get X-rayed."

"Can't risk a hospital."

"Why not?"

Mick just looked at him.

"Okay, it's your funeral. Don't take anything stronger than aspirin for the pain. Martika will check you every hour. If his eye starts to bulge or you can't wake him, call an ambulance— "

"I told you, no hospital— "

"Then she can call a hearse, run you straight to the morgue," Calvin said, pressing down the butterfly bandage with a flourish. "Y'all owe me a cee for this."

While Martika took Calvin down to the desk to pay him, Mick picked up the bedside phone, called Leanne at home.

"Mick? My God, what happened? The police were here."

"Which police? Ecorse or State?"

"Sergeant Gorski, the one who stopped us last night. He looked all beat up. My dad is furious. Really gave me the third degree."

"I'm sorry about that. What did he want?"

"He wanted to know why the police came. Who you were, how long I'd been seeing you— "

"Not your dad, Leanne, the cop! Gorski. What the hell did Gorski want?"

"He wanted to talk to you. He wasn't in uniform. He wanted to know where you lived or your phone number."

"And you said...?"

"That I didn't know! All I could tell him was that you worked for Mr. Abrams."

"Don't worry about it, Leanne. I'll handle it."

"Okay, but— look, the way things are, maybe we shouldn't see each other for awhile. My dad's really sore about the police and all. I like you, but— "

"Not enough," Mick finished for her.

"It's not that, it's...well. After things settle down, call me sometime."

"Right. I'll do that."

He hung up the phone very carefully, to keep from smashing it. And realized Martika was watching from the doorway. "What?"

"Calvin told me to check your eyes every hour, to see if your brain's bleeding out. How do you feel?"

"Worse than I look. Anything else?"

"Not a thing." And she was gone.

□   □   □

He desperately needed sleep, but every time he started to nod off, his mind flashed back to the street in Ecorse, the two cops holding him while Spivak jabbed at him with the nightstick— damn. Just thinking about it hurt. So did laying in any position for more than two minutes at a time. Felt his limbs stiffening, seizing up like an overheated engine. Finally managed to doze off. Thought he heard music from the studio downstairs. He was trying to make out the song when he fell off the earth, all the way back to Mississippi, sitting up with his grandfather's coffin in a roomful of strangers. With a band playing softly somewhere.

Snapped awake an hour later with his right calf locked in a savage charley-horse. He managed to knead it out, then swung his legs over the side of the bed and stood up. One inch at a time. *God-oh-god-oh-god...*

The bedside clock said nine o'clock. If the cops hadn't come for him by now...? He wasn't sure what that meant. Good or bad? His head was too fuzzy to figure it out.

Wobbling to the nightstand, he checked himself in the mirror. Sweet Jesus. His cheek was swollen, straining at the stitches, blood and fluid oozing out both ends. He looked like Frankenstein after a four-story fall.

Found his bloody pants from the night before and borrowed an oversized shirt from the closet. Dressing himself was an agony but he managed, then he trudged ever so slowly down the stairs. Baby steps. Moving like Moishe minus his cane, aching and stiff. And hungry as a stray dog.

Downstairs, the Sultans' recording session was already underway. Otis DeWitt, the burly, bullet-headed lead vocalist was at the far end of Studio P for parlor, singing into the solo microphone. Stately Varnell Mack, chubby Cleavon Gates and little Dexter Jaquette were huddled around a second mike in the opposite corner of the glassed-in room.

All four Sultans were stripped down to tee shirts and slacks, sweating like field hands in the afternoon heat. No fans in the room. Too much noise.

Brownie, Jerome, Martika and Benjy Jefferson were clustered intently around the recording console in the kitchen, listening to the vocal mix through a pair of monitor speakers. Despite the heat, Brownie was impeccable in an aqua silk vest, and shirt, Jerome was wearing his tweed beatnik beret above a black muscle tee.

They glanced up as Mick shuffled in, exchanged looks with each other. Benjy was bleary-eyed, sipping from a hip flask, wearing the same dark suit from the Chit Chat, probably hadn't been to bed yet. He nodded hello to Mick, then looked away, smiling. But nobody said a thing. Not word one.

They pointedly concentrated on the playback while Mick foraged in a cupboard, found some Wheaties, filled a bowl, added some milk then joined the group at the table, wolfing down the cereal as he listened.

His head was killing him. So was the playback. It sounded godawful. The song was one from the night before, "Motown Mama", but Otis was dragging the beat, singing flat. The background harmony had been ragged at the Chit Chat, but it was worse now. Even Cleavon, the chubby, boisterous bass singer, seemed subdued.

"What's happening?" Mick asked.

"Benjy's band got here at eight, laid down the background tracks for five songs," Brownie said. "You didn't hear them?"

"I had a long night. What's wrong with the Sultans?"

"Ain't got it today," Jerome said, tipping back his beret. "Maybe burned out their pipes last night."

"Amateurs," Benjy sighed, smoothing down his gunfighter mustache. "That's why Berry don't use 'em at Motown. They're fine for a Elk's lodge or warmin' up for real stars like Jackie but recording's a whole different thing. No love in a studio, she's a cold motherfucker."

"They don't look cold to me," Mick said.

"Not that kinda cold," Benjy explained, taking another hit from the flask, offering Mick a taste. He passed. "Groups like the Sultans feed off the crowd, people smilin', clappin', callin' your name. Gets you high as a blast of cocaine. Stone pros don't need it. That's why I'm at Motown and y'all are stuck with them."

"You're not at Motown today, pal," Mick grated. Every word hurt. "You're on my dime here. How do we fix this?"

"Hire a better group, cowboy. Or buy a business you know somethin' about. By the way, you look like crap. That fine white girl from last night do you that way? Best gimme her number, she's too much boogie for your country ass."

Benjy took another sip, eyeing Mick over the top of the flask. Mick'd known guys like Benjy in the joint. Not the biggest or the toughest, but truly addicted to trouble. Hooked on the adrenalin rush the way the Sultans were hooked on crowds...

"Yo! Whoa up in there!" Mick said, rapping hard on the glass of the booth as Jerome hastily switched off the tape deck.

The men in the booth glanced up, startled at the interruption. "Something wrong?" Otis DeWitt asked, scowling.

"You guys sound like shit," Mick said. "What's your problem?"

In the stunned silence, Benjy burst out laughing.

"If you don't like our sound— "

"You sounded great last night, Otis, you kicked ass. What happened to that?"

"Studio's different," Cleavon, the bass singer, protested. "We have to keep our voices down. If we sing too hard, we drown out the backup music in our headsets, can't follow the beat."

"It's this lowball equipment," Jerome said. "You need— "

"What I fucking *need* is the sound they had last night," Mick snapped. "I'm not hearing it. If they can't follow the beat, turn up the music."

"It's already maxed out."

"Fine. Then put Benjy in there. He can follow the music, they can follow him."

"The drums will drown out the vocals."

"Then they'll have to sing harder, which is what they want to do anyway, right?"

"It'll muddy up the blend," Benjy said. "At Motown— "

"Fuck Motown!" Mick snapped, "I never liked that prissy shit anyway. Sounds like a tea dance. Look, you probably know every damn thing about makin' records, but I know a little about buyin' 'em. People like songs that make 'em feel good, like the singer's havin' a good time."

"Nigger music, you mean?" Benjy jibed. "Real happy, like?"

"Color's got nothin' to do with it. The Sultans were havin' a good time last night so they went over. Blues singers like Hooker and Howlin' Wolf always sound rough— "

"Because they cut their cheap ass records in garages," Jerome shot back.

"But they sound like they're playin' in your damn living room. This joint ain't Carnegie Hall, Jerome, I get that. But we didn't hire Jefferson because he's got a smart mouth. You're supposed to be the stone pro here, sport! The Sultans sounded good last night. How do we get that?"

"You don't know?" Benjy scoffed. "I thought you owned the joint? You don't know squat about recording."

"Maybe not," Brownie said, waving off Mick's retort, "but neither does our audience. My last go around, we cut cool jazz for hip cats and I lost my ass. All we need here is somethin' good enough for a fuckin' bar room jukebox. So like the man said, show us something or get the fuck out."

Dead silence. Brownie and Jefferson staring each other down like they were alone in the room. Benjy looked away first. Chuckling, he finished off his flask with a final gulp.

"Hell, Brownie, if you want crude, you can hire any fuck off a street corner. But since I'm here... " He shouldered past Jerome to the rug draped over the studio door. "Hold on, fellas, help's a'comin'."

"Keep your volume down, so you don't bleed through too much," Jerome called after him.

"The only one bleedin' here is the white boy," Benjy snorted. Settling in behind the drum set, he put on headphones that carried the soundtrack his group had cut earlier.

"Okay, here's the deal. I'll walk the bass drum, backbeat the high-hat like this." He gestured, slapping the muted cymbal with an exaggerated stroke. "Even deaf motherfuckers can follow that. Now jump on the damn tune, Otis, get some soul in this thing. And do it quick. I been runnin' on speed and Don Q for three days and I'm about down to empty."

Signaling Jerome to roll tape, Benjy tapped the high hat through the taped piano introduction, then nodded hard at Otis.

"I'm comin' home, mama..." Otis was singing stronger now, focusing on Benjy's hands, but the Sultans' background do-wops were still uncertain.

"Whoa!" Benjy snapped, zipping a drumstick across his throat. "Tighten it up, Varnell. Y'all sound like street corner trash."

"You gonna be the one on the street, Jefferson," Otis said, darkening. "After I throw your jive ass through the wall."

"Cool out, Otis," Brownie said, flicking on the studio mike. "That sounded better. Try it again."

"It's still not right," Mick complained. "Last night they sounded, I don't know. Bigger."

"It's the same Sultans, same backup band," Jerome snorted.

"But no crowd," Martika said, jumping up. "No noise. Hang on a second." Popping out to the foyer, she collected a half dozen sisters from the Abyssinian Baptist choir, waiting to record after the Sultan's session. The girls trailed Tika into the studio, chattering excitedly. She snagged Mick as she passed, dragging him along.

"You want in the record biz, Irish, here's your chance. C'mon."

Cleavon, Dexter and Otis all traded 'what the hell? looks as Martika crowded Mick and the excited girls into the studio against the back wall, but none of the Sultans griped about singing to a roomful of brown sugar.

Rolling his eyes, Jerome switched on the recorder, but when Benjy kicked the song off, the handclaps and crowd noise definitely jacked up the Sultans' energy. They delivered the tune with more drive, closing the song to a spontaneous burst of applause from the girls.

"Damn, that almost felt real," Benjy admitted, settling more firmly onto his drum throne, interested now. "One more time." This take was stronger still as the Sultans hit a solid groove, loosening up, feeling the flow.

On the final take, Benjy's grin was wide as a sunrise, bouncing on his throne, keeping the beat rock solid, adding gunshot fills to crank up the electricity. Even Mick couldn't help smiling through his split lip. At the end, the applause and cheers in the tiny room were deafening.

"That's a damn wrap," Benjy said, standing up behind his kit, stretching. "Y'all nailed it like a nine pound hammer, Varnell. Let's do the B-side same way. Otis does the first twelve bars on his own, ladies, so don't start clappin' till the turnaround. It's gutbucket blues, y'all, so do it righteous. One take. Let 'er rip, Jerome."

A lowdown blues rhythm this time, drums and bass pulsing together like a heartbeat. A blues guitar moaning softly. Mick felt Martika swaying beside him to the beat, her hip brushing his…

A chill shook him, drenching him like a bucket of ice water. Couldn't think why for a moment. Then he noticed Brownie watching him. And remembered exactly where he'd heard the song before.

□   □   □

"Did you think I wouldn't know?" Mick demanded.

He and Brownie were in the studio office, door closed. He was keeping his voice low, but he was still shaken. Furious.

"I didn't have time to tell you. You came late."

"Not so late I don't know that song. Mojo played it that night at The Regency."

"It's not his song anymore, youngblood, it's ours. *Jukebox Cadillac*, copyright by L. Brown, and T. Shannon. We're songwriters now, all legal and proper."

"What the hell are you talking about?"

"Look, Mojo peddled his records at the joints he played around the country, and some of those sides are still out there. If a singer comes across one, wants to record the song, first thing he'll do is check with B.M.I— "

"Check what?"

"The songwriters union, keeps track of airplay and such. If the tune's in our names, the singer pays a fee and that's it. Otherwise, he'll have to track down Mojo to get permission. He might have some trouble with that. So could we."

"Okay, I get it. But I don't like surprises, Brownie. Anything else I should know?"

"Only that there might be money in it. Every record's got an A side and a B side. If we own the B side, we get half the profits and those jukebox quarters add up. If somebody with a name covers the tune, we get a piece."

"You don't miss much."

"A black man can't afford to miss nothin' is this life. Neither can a white one. What the fuck happened to you, anyway? Look like you went ten rounds with a damn bulldozer."

"My problem, not yours."

"We're partners."

"Just here, Brownie. Nowhere else."

"Fine, do it on your lonesome," Brownie shrugged. "But it don't look like you're doin' so hot."

CHAPTER 29

Stomped or not, Mick still had to stumble through his route the next day. Worse, he couldn't go armed. If the police rousted him, felon with a firearm charges would send him back inside for another five years, no other charges necessary. But without a piece, with his stitched face, swollen jaw and a dozen contusions, he looked like easy meat for anybody who wanted a piece of him.

Instead, the opposite happened. When he limped into the bars and bodegas to collect, people took one look at him and got the money up, wanting him gone before his bad luck rubbed off.

The only one who didn't spook was Moishe. The old man was behind the desk in the Dequindre office when Mick gimped in, late afternoon. Moishe did a double take, then his face slowly split into a wide, gap-toothed grin.

"*Oy vey*, what the fuck happened to you?"

Mick kept it short but Moishe pestered him for details, savoring every morsel as Mick described the scuffle with the Ecorse cops.

"*Mein gott*, you've gotta be the dumb luckiest sumbitch on the planet," the old man chuckled, wiping his eyes.

"Glad you enjoyed it. Wasn't much fun for me. Could've been worse but Spivak was drunk and his two buddies were Ecorse hobby cops."

"That still counts as luck," Moishe said, serious now. "You took a beatin' but could've been dead, locked up, or on the run with every department in Motown after your ass."

"I sweated bullets every time I passed a cop on my rounds," Mick admitted. "Nobody gave me a second look."

"Because the Ecorse cops didn't call it in," the old man mused. "They crossed the line, goin' after you, but they could blow that off. Their problem is them guns."

"I don't follow."

"Service revolvers are issued by the departments. A patrolman can be fired for losing his piece and they lost two. Since they were beatin' on you at the time, they didn't report it, and now they can't. If you get picked up with their pieces, they're more fucked than you are. Where are the guns now?"

"Stashed in the garage behind the studio, why?"

"I had a call earlier from a cop named Gorski, asking for a meet up. He didn't say what it was about, but I'm guessing he's looking for a deal to get them guns back, make the whole mess go away."

"This beating ain't goin' away," Mick winced as he touched his stitches with his fingertips. "I'm not letting this go."

"Yes you are. Hell, you were too pretty anyway. Welcome to the collection business, kid."

Mick shook his head, remembering Spivak's eyes. "That cop won't let it be, Moishe. He's really crazy."

"You leave him to me. Just get me the guns, I'll handle it."

But it wasn't that simple. Moishe met with Gorski in a corner bar in Hamtramck. Traded the revolvers for a clean sheet. The traffic stop and the fight never happened. And it wasn't just talk. Gorski knew who Moishe was, who he worked for. And what crossing him could mean.

So he was very careful about what he agreed to.

"Gorski wouldn't promise me nothing for this Spivak," Moishe explained later. "The guy had a hard on for you before, and after gettin' his knee stomped, he's off the map. He'll be on crutches six months, and he'll get a medical discharge after. You fucked him up good."

"I'll send him a card."

"No joke, you stay away from him. Stay out of Ecorse, period. If Spivak sees you, he'll flip out and you'll end up dead or in jail no matter how it goes down. Understand?"

"I got it." But even as he said it, he was thinking of Leanne's creamy thighs spread wide on the Lincoln's front seat as he plunged inside her. The taste of her mouth, the salty scent of her throat. No way he was giving that up.

Wes Spivak had cost him five years in the joint and now a serious beating.

Enough. Cop or no cop, the next time Wes came at him would be the
last time. One way or the other.

CHAPTER 30

"You can't just move in here," Martika protested, as Mick lugged his
single suitcase up the stairs at Black Kat. "This is my room."
"I've been crashing in it the past three days, what's your problem?"
"You were dying then. I save your damn life and I get evicted?"
Mick almost told her to fuck off, thought better of it. She was half right.
He barely remembered falling through the door the night Spivak stomped
him. After that, nothing. Until Oaks woke him up in her bed.
"Look lady, I need a place to crash and I own this joint. I'll stash my
gear in the storeroom for now but either make me up a room or I'm tak-
ing yours."
"How did getting you a room get to be my job?"
"Because everything in this place is your job! Fix it, okay? I got places
to be."
"Damn it, slow down," she said, trailing him down the stairs. "What
kind of bed you want?"
"I don't care. But I need it by tonight or I'm crashing with you."
"In your dreams, white boy," she called after him. But she was smiling as she bustled back inside.

□   □   □

Mick spent the afternoon catching up the collections he'd missed the
day after the beating. Finished ahead of schedule. Nobody wanted
Frankenstein hanging around.
He even felt like Frankenstein. Plodding along, stiff and sore. Which
made him edgier than usual. After collecting Maceo's vig, he turned to
leave the bodega, then hesitated. A car was parked behind Moishe's Lincoln, sitting there with the engine idling. Customized '52 Mercury,
Frenched headlights, chopped top. Flat black, still in primer. Couldn't
see the driver through the narrowed windshield, only his hands on the
wheel.
White hands.
Damn. He'd known all along Spivak was too loony to let things lay.
Enough. Wes had his shot with his buddies holding Mick like a punching bag. Time to settle it.
Stepping out of the bodega, Mick headed away from his car without

a backward glance. Halfway down the block, he turned briskly into the alley as though he had business there, flattening against the bricks as soon as he was out of sight of the street. Waiting.

Not for long. Footsteps were coming on fast. Mick set himself, taut as a coiled spring. The second Spivak stepped into the alley, Mick grabbed his shirt, spinning him around, slamming him hard against the bricks!

But it wasn't Spivak. Not even close. It was the skinny kid from Scotty's Diner. Jamming the muzzle of his .45 under the kid's chin, Mick kept him frozen while he quickly checked around the edge of the building. Couple of pimps jiving each other down on the corner. No one else in sight.

He turned back to the kid pinned against the wall.

"You've got one second."

"Do you remember me?"

"Hell yes. You're the punk who tried to set me up at the diner. Where are your pals?"

"Nowhere."

Mick eared back the hammer.

"I came alone! They're all back in Ecorse, which is the same as bein' nowhere. Rolling drunks, boostin' car radios. They're gonna get busted for chump change. I'm looking for something better."

"Do I look like I'm doin' better?"

The kid licked his lips, not sure of how to answer. "Honestly? You look like you can use some help."

"To do what?"

"Anything, Mr. Shannon. I can drive for you, watch your back. Try me out a week for free. If I can't cut it, just say so and I'm gone. No charge."

Mick eyed him, wondering how this wiry kid had survived this long. Simple. He did it in Ecorse. Mick knew he should tell him to take a hike, but there was something familiar in his eyes. Hunger. The same desperation that got him hooked up with Moishe Abrams.

"What was your name again?"

"Aldo. Chaloub."

Mick arched an eyebrow.

"Syrian. If it matters."

"It doesn't. You know what business I'm in, Aldo?"

"Same as ol' Moishe Abrams. Shylock."

"Do you understand what that means? Look at my face. What's your mama gonna say, you come home looking like this?"

"I got no people. Been in foster care or on the street since I was ten."

"You can catch a beating like this any day. Or end up dead in an alley."

"I can get capped just as fast jackin' a ten buck battery out of some redneck's pickup. I need a damn job, Mr. Shannon. Can you use me or not?"

"Maybe," Mick said grudgingly, easing the hammer down, shoving the automatic back in his waistband.

Aldo waited a second, then lowered his hands. "I'm hired? Jesus, thanks."

"I'm not doing you any favors. We'll try a few days. You drive, you keep your eyes open. Forty a week for starters."

"But I offered— "

"That's lesson number one," Mick snapped, cutting him off. "Inside 8 Mile? Nothin' comes free."

□   □   □

Aldo drove the Lincoln the rest of the day. Given the shape Mick was in, the kid was worth every dime of his money. He could handle a wheel, knew the city and the streets, knew when to shut up. And when to talk.

He told Mick there were already rumors around Ecorse about his dustup with Spivak. Cody, the younger cop, was boasting he'd cap Mick on sight if he set foot in Ecorse again. Gorski didn't have much to say and Spivak wasn't talking at all, going stone silent when Mick's name came up.

Best to stay away. Maybe forever.

Aldo's chatter helped pass the afternoon, but at the end of it, Mick still felt like he'd been dragged through an alley behind a trash truck. Limping up the stairs at Black Kat, he desperately needed to crash. Just to lay down, close his eyes a few minutes. Music was drifting up from Studio P, a quavering gospel singer murdering *How Great Thou Art*, at forty bucks an hour.

But at the top of the stairs, he couldn't help smiling. Martika's door was locked. Tight. With a brand new chrome padlock. A Masterlock, yet. Masterlock ads on TV showed .357 magnum slugs bouncing off it.

The equipment room door was ajar so he pushed it open. And stopped cold. The extra gear was gone, replaced by a Navajo area rug, a sleigh bed in one corner and a squared-off Amish nightstand beside it. A rolltop writing desk stood against the far wall, complete with a row of books on top, held in place by twin model ships. A lighthouse bedside lamp gave the whole thing a cozy glow.

He sensed someone behind him.

"Okay?" Martika asked.

"What the hell is all this?"

"Better than you deserve. I gotta get back." And she was gone. Pulling off his boots, he eased down on the bed, groaning as twenty-three hundred separate aches kicked in. But as he closed his eyes, it registered that this was another first. It was his own bed. In his own room. No guards, no grandfather. Nobody to tell him go or stay.

His own place in this world.

CHAPTER 31

Three days later, Mick's second stop of the afternoon was the Royal Palms, a hole-in-the-wall bar on Beaubien. Aldo stayed with the car, watching the street.

Inside, the saloon was narrow, dim and deserted. Jimmy Reed's *Baby What You Want Me to Do* thumping on the jukebox. Could have been singing the blues for the owner, Floyd Owens. Old Floyd was falling further behind every week, but at least he had Mick's envelope waiting.

Mick did a quick count. "I make it fifty short."

"I'll catch you up next week," Floyd said glumly. But they both knew better. The Palms was on a long, slow slide. No need to muscle old Floyd, he knew the score. But as Mick turned to go, he noticed a stooped figure in the shadows at a corner table.

Moishe.

"What are you doing here?" he asked. "Keeping an eye on me?"

"I always got an eye on you," Moishe said. "Sit down. Learn somethin'."

"About what?" Mick asked, easing painfully into a chair.

"This place. The Royal Palms."

"What about it?"

"Floyd's ain't made a full payment in months. He's already upside down on it, few more weeks, he'll hand over his title and walk away."

"Probably," Mick agreed.

"A month ago, I would've sent that title over to the St. Clair club, so their lawyers could scrub it clean, sell it off, pay me my cut. But that was before Cooley's."

"Okay," Mick nodded.

"But that's only if Floyd loses the place. If somebody buys him out first, pays me off, then I'm the one sending the Lucas their percentage."

"But if you buy it, they'll— "

"It can't be me, Irish, or you either. A felon can't hold a liquor license."

"I don't follow— "

"There's more. C'mon, I'll show you." Wincing, the old man levered himself up from his chair with his walking stick. He limped off down the dingy corridor that led past the reeking restrooms to the back door. Mick followed, not moving much better.

Outside in the alley, it was even worse, piles of trash and garbage scattered around. The door of the adjoining building was broken in half, hanging by its hinges.

"Watch your head," Moishe said, edging through the narrow gap. "It's filthy in here."

Squeezing past the broken door, Mick found himself in a hallway, or what was left of one. The walls were kicked in, liquor bottles smashed on the floor, broken glass crunching under his shoes, sour stench of stale booze and piss hanging in the air like a vile mist. Moishe led him on, high-stepping carefully through the trash to an open doorway that led to...

Utter blackness. A cave? For a split second, it occurred to Mick this could be the perfect place to stash a body. His? But as his eyes adjusted to the gloom, he realized he was standing on some kind of a platform facing rows of wrecked seats.

"What is this place?"

"A movie house. It used to be called The *Maltz*. Went bust during the war. A Spanish guy, Mendez, bought it after that. Changed the name to *La Casa Mayor*, showed Mexican movies here, held dances on holidays, *Cinco de Mayo* and like that. He went broke too. Place has been closed thirty years."

"So?"

"So look at the space. This room used to hold five hundred people— "

"Moishe, what the fuck are we doing here?"

"I'm gettin' to that. Check out the west wall."

"Which way's west?"

"The far wall, with the ratty ass curtain."

"Looks like a million bats live in it. So what?"

"Forget the curtain," Moishe said impatiently, "look below that. See that line? Where the boards meet the cement?"

"Yeah, but— "

"It's not a wall, Irish," Moishe said, cutting him off. "It's only a partition. When the movie house went bust, Mendez closed off the theater side and turned the lobby into a neighborhood bar. Named it the Royal Palms. Few years later, he died, his widow sold the bar part to Floyd, who borrowed heavy from me to buy it, and is now going under."

"Okay…Floyd's going under, and once upon a time, the Royal Palms and this old movie house were one big building?"

"They still are, kid."

"You've lost me."

"If you owned the Palms, and knocked down that partition, you'd have a nightclub as big as the Chit Chat."

"You just said I couldn't take it over. Not that I'd want to," Mick said, kicking a bottle aside as he turned slowly, looking over the room.

"That's right, *you* can't. And any white face buyin' a dump in Dark-town would raise eyebrows. But you got a spade partner. Brown. He knows the biz, has his own place, and runs the Regency in Idlewild for the Chicago Outfit. He could buy it— why are you looking at me like that?"

"I'm…fucking amazed, that's all. What brought this on?"

"Cooley's brought it on, numb nuts! The Lucas screwed me out of my fair share and think I'll just take it— " The old man broke, coughing, leaning on his stick as he fought for breath.

"You okay, Moishe?"

"I'm fucking perfect. Or I will be when we put this thing together. You talk to Brown— "

"Slow down, Moishe. I can talk to him, but even if he's willing— "

"Willing's got nothing to do with it. He's in because we need him and because I say so. You tell him that." Mick wanted to argue, but Moishe's furious glare put 'paid' to that idea.

"Okay, say, he goes along— "

"He will."

"What about the money? How much— "

"You still don't get it! We're buyin' this motherfucker from ourselves! We won't need money! It's all paper. Brown buys out Floyd for chump change, then pays me off, all on paper. I pay the Lucas their cut of the chump change *Floyd* owed, which takes them out of the picture. Then Brown runs the place a few months, sells it on the quiet— "

"Sells what, Moishe? It's not a bar, it's a dump."

"But it's a big room. Have Brown fix it up nice. Like the Regency."

"The Regency," Mick echoed, realizing the old man had completely lost it. He was so set on fucking the Lucas, he really thought— It didn't matter. Once Moishe was set on an idea, there was not backing him off it.

"Okay," Mick nodded. "I'll talk to Brownie about it. See what he says."

"He'd better say yes."

"Fixing this place up won't be cheap, Moishe— "

"I'll front you whatever you need, you and Brown. Hell, I'll even cut you a break on the vig. Make this work, Mick. You owe me!"

CHAPTER 32

"He's out of his everlovin' mind," Brownie said, turning a slow swivel, eying the wreckage of the old theater.

"Want to tell him that?" Mick asked. "You were the one who wanted to be in business with him."

"As life insurance, Irish, not a death wish. This place is the freakin' Titanic."

"It's definitely big," Martika noted.

Mick had brought the crew from the studio to eyeball out Moishe's brainstorm. Martika was onstage, looking around. Jerome had already scrambled up to the catwalk, checking out the overhead equipment.

"Jeez, you gotta see the speakers up here," the kid yelled down. "Gotta be thirty-inchers, at least. Bet they haven't made these in fifty years."

"Every damn rope holdin' up that platform is fifty years old too," Brownie called up. "Come on down from there. Hate to cheat that crazy old man out breakin' our necks personal."

"Maybe it's not totally crazy," Martika mused. "Back when I was pushing *"Hot Chocolate"*, I worked the chitlin' circuit with Mojo. I swear we played places worse than this. Thing is, a big old movie house like this? It's got a few things working for it."

"Like?" Mick asked.

"It's already got a stage, and spotlights overhead. If you tear out the first row of seats at ground level, you've got a dance floor. Put cocktail tables around the upper tiers, it could pass for a show bar."

"We could bring the studio sound system over to record here after hours," Jerome said. "Hey!" he yelled, his voice ringing around the room. "See? Natural reverberation. Sounds like a giant hall up in here, because... well. That's what it is."

"So, stage, seats, sound," Mick said, ticking them off on his fingertips. "What else?"

"Jukes," Brownie said. "The acts from Motown Records play at the Chit Chat a lot. We could do even better here, because we could put any act that played here on every jukebox in town. Free advertising."

"The only act we've got is the Sultans."

"I've been hearin' their record up and down the street," Jerome said. "People are diggin' on your raunchy-ass sound. They say it sounds like a party goin' on. It draws people inside, to see what's happening."

"I've worked in clubs, bounced in 'em, fought in 'em," Mick said, shaking his head at the shambles. "I know some about this business. It would cost a pile just to clean this place up, then you'd need staff to run it. If it doesn't make money right off, it could bleed it just as fast."

"Moishe's money," Brownie pointed out.

"To start with," Mick nodded. "Moishe ain't big on charity. He'll expect to be right side up in a hurry."

"And I ain't big on crossing that old man. So? Floyd owns the bar, who owns the rest of it?"

"The City of Detroit," Mick said. "It was seized nine years ago for back taxes. Eighteen hundred and seventy-three dollars. It's been on the city auction list the past four years, without gettin' a single bid. It's on the charity roll now, which means you can buy it on time. Half down, pay the balance off monthly over three years. Nine thirty-five down— "

"And twenty-seven a month," Martika finished for him. "And I want in."

They both glanced at her in surprise.

"Look, I do the books, so I know how much you've got in the bank," she said. "I'll work free, but I want a share. Ten percent."

"To do what?" Brownie asked.

"The same damn thing I do at the studio. Book talent, book everything. I'll book a cleaning crew for openers. Unless you'd rather shovel the place out yourselves," she said, facing them, her fists on her hips. "Ten percent. And I want to sing."

"Sing?" Brownie said. "How long since you've been on a stage, lady?"

"Awhile. But I still know way around. I ain't looking for a star slot, but back in the day, I was good. You can always can me if it don't work. But I want my shot. Let me know what you decide. You know where I'll be."

◻   ◻   ◻

"That old man could be onto somethin'," Brownie said. They were parked in his Studebaker Hawk in front of the Royal Palms after doing a walk-through of the tumbledown theater. "Big freakin' gamble, though."

"Not taking it could be bigger. Unless we want to go up against Moishe?"

"Pass on that, brother," Brownie nodded. "All right, say we do this thing. For openers, turn Martika loose on it. She's smart, she's got contacts in the neighborhood. To keep this off the Luca's radar, we'll have to use people from the block. Inside 8 Mile."

"What about the money? How much do you figure to get it up and running?"

"Three for the buy, maybe ten for the rest. And borrowing from Moishe's one helluva gamble."

"Every day I work these streets is a gamble. Hell, they've got a lotto going on my fucking life."

"I know. I laid fifty on August 17th."

Mick turned sharply to stare at him.

"C'mon, I'm screwin' with ya," Brownie grinned. "I only bet twenty-five. But if we do this, you deal with Moishe. I want nothin' to do with that man."

"The liquor license will have to be in your name. Ex-cons can't hold one."

"You trust me that much?"

"Oh, hell no."

"That's good," Brownie smiled. "'Cause I got no use for stupid partners. How much will them Eye-talians from the St. Clair want?"

"They've got no part of this. That's the whole point."

"That's Moishe's point. But is it smart? Cuttin' them out?"

"It's payback."

"That wasn't the question, Irish. I've heard a million stories about what a bad ass motherfucker Moishe Abrams is. Never heard a one about his genius IQ."

"I'll handle Moishe."

"What about Martika? She said ten percent, but that singin' business ain't carved in stone."

"Let her do the work, then cut her out?" Mick asked.

"This is your deal, Irish. Your call."

"She gets her deal, and sings, if she wants. And the next time you wonder if I'd weasel on my word, just ask me. Don't play me, Brownie. I don't like it."

"Fair enough. Cutting Tika in is a smart move anyway. Girl's bright as a dime. I'd tap that myself if I wasn't already tied up. *And* if she ditched those glasses and lost twenty pounds. So what do we call this place?"

"What does the name on the marquee mean in English?"

"*Casa Mayor*? The Big House."

"Like prison?" Mick winced as his grin strained his split lip. "Hell, let's keep the sign, then. We'll probably end up there anyway."

"Assuming we live that long," Brownie nodded.

CHAPTER 33

Buying Floyd Owens out of the Royal Palms took twenty minutes. The old geezer was terrified of Moishe, and when he realized he could escape the vig's crushing weight and come out a few bucks ahead, he couldn't sign the title over fast enough. Wished Mick luck and walked away whistling.

The Casa Mayor building was trickier. After chasing his tail around city hall half a day, Brownie got the message. He chatted up a few secretaries, figured out which cog in the civic machine needed grease, and finagled a title for twenty percent of the back taxes plus a five cee campaign contribution. Cash, no checks. No receipt.

The next morning, Tika and a small army of her relatives ripped into the cleanup like a flock of locusts, quickly filling a twenty-five yard dumpster, then a second, with decades of accumulated trash.

Minus the broken bottles and smashed fixtures, The Casa actually looked worse. The pitiless glare of the overhead theater floodlights revealed stained walls, ragged curtains and a tile floor crusted with thirty years of grime and rat crap.

Which Martika took as a personal affront. Dressed for combat in overalls and tennis shoes, her hair bound up in a bright red bandanna, she led a soap and water assault. Within ten days, every square inch of the old theater had been scrubbed, waxed or repainted. The damaged walls and ceiling were refinished in flat black that made the room seem both darker and larger.

Three weeks into the remodel, on a tip from Moishe, Mick, Aldo and Brownie made a midnight run to Dearborn to smuggle a truckload of fixtures out of a club tied up in a foreclosure.

With the commandeered furniture, The Casa suddenly began shaping up. Cocktail tables replacing trashed theater seats, wall sconces for romantic lighting, gleaming checkerboard tiles for the dance floor and matching carpet squares onstage to continue the motif.

Instead of buying curtains to mask the back wall, Martika suggested lowering the old theater screen and playing film clips between the live shows, silent snippets of old Laurel and Hardy movies, W.C. Fields, Harold Lloyd. The clips were fast, funny, authentic, and best of all, free, since the old films and projectors came with the building.

Jerome's idea of transferring the sound system from the Black Kat studio didn't go as smoothly. The system sounded gigantic in the old theater, but he had problems hooking it up. Buzzes, hums and deafening pops at odd moments. Jerome begged for a new, more powerful amplifier but the partners had run through Moishe's front money. They'd have to make do till the club started earning.

With the main room in good shape, Tika made two final changes. The theater's original office was an eight by eight cubbyhole near the entrance. After clearing out the desks and file cabinets, she cut the door in half, converting it into a cloakroom. Then she had the carpenters triple the size of the old projection booth, high above the dance floor, finishing off the room with walnut paneling and plush carpet.

Shielded by one-way mirrors, the new office had a clear overview of the entire ballroom, a virtual guard tower, where Mick could keep an eye on things without being seen. It even had its own private exit, enclosed fire stairs, that led down to the alley behind the club.

When Mick asked her about the escape route, she just arched an eyebrow. Which was answer enough.

Brownie made the lion's share of business decisions, ordering liquor, hiring wait-staff and kitchen help. But he didn't do it on his own.

The partners hooked up every evening at the club to discuss every move.

"You can trust me," Brownie explained, "but we'll all get along better if you don't have to."

Brownie kept him up to speed every step of the way. And in fact, Mick wasn't a total amateur. The last few summers he'd worked on this grandfather's Mississippi farm, he'd picked up pocket money boxing in backwoods joints. He'd learned the basics of the bar business and how it worked. The hard way.

Now Brownie was giving him an advanced course, Nightclub Management, 201.

Mostly, Mick absorbed the information without comment, blending it with what he'd learned down south. Soaking it up the same way he'd learned about cars, boxing and the collection business. Filing facts for future reference like a pack rat. Nightclubs were a lot simpler than tearing down a big block V-8.

As the remodeling neared completion, they hit a major snag. In a town full of nightspots, first impressions were everything.

"We need to make a splash," Brownie said at the partners' meet that night. "Open with a big name. But I talked to every booker I know, and we ain't in the ballpark. Sam Cook gets three grand a night, Jackie Wilson and Marvin Gaye want even more. I dickered my ass off, couldn't knock 'em down a dime."

"How much is left in the kitty?" Martika asked.

"We're underwater," Mick said. "I'm into Moishe for three grand, over and above the front money, full vig. If we borrow any more, we might as well sign the title over now."

"Then it'll have to be the Sultans," Martika said quietly. "You put "Motown Mama" on the jukeboxes because locals knew their name. It's been playing on automatic for weeks. With all that background racket on the record, it sounds like a party goin' on up and down the corridor. Put that to work."

"The Sultans are okay for a backup act," Brownie conceded, "but they can't carry a whole night— "

"They won't have to. Hire Benjy Jefferson to put a house band together. He can open the show, then I'll do my set— "

"Whoa," Brownie said. "We might want to hold off on that. An opening weekend's do or die, girl. You only had the one tune, and that was years ago."

"I can cover Motown tunes, do some Supremes, Mary Wells. Benjy knows those songs cold and they've had enough hits to fill a set. And we had a deal, Irish."

Brownie glanced the question at Mick.

"I'm not sure we've got a choice," Mick said. "If the place doesn't earn from the git-go, we'll both be dead in a ditch anyway."

And so it was settled.

The Casa would rise or fall with its home-grown talent.

Because they couldn't afford to do anything else.

But later, when Mick had time to mull over the decision?

The crack about ending up dead in a ditch wasn't so damned funny.

CHAPTER 34

Opening night. A Wednesday, third week of October. Mick hated the mid-week idea, wanted to open on a Saturday night to make a bigger splash.

Or a bigger bomb, Brownie countered. Openings nights are always rough. Orders get lost, drinks get dropped, swampers get the flu? It'll be a mess. Better to open Wednesday, use Thursday to repair the damage, then hit big on the weekend.

Brownie was only half right. Opening night wasn't rough, it was a total train wreck. At eight o'clock, The Casa Mayor was barely a third full.

A few curious black couples with a sprinkling of U of Detroit college boys. Wearing a new sharkskin suit, Mick took the bouncer's post at the end of the bar, stone-faced and watchful. A whirlpool of emotions churning in his gut. Fear. Excitement. And pride. It was just a rehabbed movie house/ show bar in a ghetto neighborhood. But it was his. Or half, anyway.

Brownie was working the door, tuxed up and sharp, hair slicked back, patent leather loafers gleaming like glass. Greeting and seating couples, lighting candles at their tables, lighting ladies' smokes. A gentleman's gent.

Onstage, Benjy Jefferson's house band kicked off their opening set. Calling themselves the In Crowd, the group featured Benjy on drums, Jerome on keyboards, a tall old timer on upright bass and a young, very nervous white kid playing a Fender Strat.

They came out kicking. After opening with their title song, they swung into "Green Onions" by Booker T. From his sentry post at the bar, Mick gauged the audience response. Smiles and nods, fingers snapping to the beat. They did a third tune, a Meters cover before Benjy switched on his microphone.

"Good evening, ladies and gent— " The mike shorted out! Static crackled over the PA like a lightning storm. Jerome hurried offstage to kill the power and find the problem. Leaving the crowd eyeing one another doubtfully, the energy bleeding out of the night like a fizzled firecracker.

And that was the high point of the night.

After three false starts, Jerome got the stage microphones working but the band sputtered badly afterward, shaky as a fighter who'd been decked in the first round. At the bar, Mick was sweating through his new jacket, cringing at every sour note. Felt like he was fresh meat back in Jackson, a human punching bag again.

Two more lame tunes from Jerome, then it was Martika's turn.

"Ladies and gentleman, tonight, taking the stage for the first time in the all new Club Casa Mayor, the Motor City's own *"Hot Chocolate"* girl, Tika Daniels with the In Crowd!"

Martika came onstage slowly, in a too-tight Supremes-style miniskirt, with knee high boots, that only underscored her limp.

'*Wrong dress,*' Mick thought. And the wrong damn song. She opened with "Where Did Our Love Go?" A perky little Supremes number, but the wrong tone for a grown-ass woman. Mick could feel the audience chilling in the first few bars. She followed it with Mary Wells' "My Guy", which barely drew a smattering of applause. Her third tune "Hot Chocolate", a slow grind, actually worked. Sort of. A few couples were threading their way to the dance floor, but two bars into the second verse the mikes cut out again, more buzzing and crackling.

Tika soldiered gamely on, trying to shout over the noise, but the short circuit kept squelching her voice, making her sound like a munchkin with the hiccups. Then a deafening *hummmm* over the PA system drowned her out altogether. The band blundered to a halt, stranding her in mid-verse. And still she didn't quit.

Dropping the useless microphone on the floor, she moved to the front of the stage and attempted to close out "Hot Chocolate" solo, but without a mike, her voice was lost in the cavernous room. Benjy tried to restart the band, but the dance floor was already clearing off.

"Amateur night," a drunk down the bar muttered. Mick glared at him but couldn't argue. Halfway through the song, Benjy mercy-killed the set. Waving the band and Martika to silence, he shouted an apology for the technical difficulties but promised they'd have it cleared up for tonight's main attraction, the Sultans of *Soooul!*

The announcement drew a patter of polite applause, but most of the crowd were already voting with their feet, clearing out.

Seething, Mick tracked down Brownie backstage, where he was huddled with Jerome and Benjy Jefferson, trouble-shooting the PA system.

"What the fuck happened? Everybody's leaving! We were supposed to be ready!"

"Welcome to showbiz, youngblood," Benjy chuckled. Mick almost clocked him.

"Nobody's ever ready for opening night," Brownie said calmly. "Shit always shows up, just like tonight. We'll get the Sultans through their set and straighten things out. "

"Straighten what out?" Mick growled.

"Dump Martika for openers. Her act's not strong enough, Mick. She was dyin' from the minute she gimped onstage. The mikes cutting out didn't help, but— "

"No," Mick said.

"No what?"

"We can't cut her act. It was part of our deal. "

"But she killed the night, Irish. We'll find something for her later but our grand opening's gotta break big. "

"I know that! You're the one who said openers are always rough. "

"Rough doesn't cover Martika's act. It bombed. "

"She was okay. The songs were lame. "

"What are you talking about? Except for 'Chocolate,' they were all Motown hits. These tunes are burnin' up the charts. "

"For the Supremes, maybe. Diana Ross look like a fashion model. Tika's a grown-ass woman, with a limp. She can't sing that 'baby, baby' crap. When she did 'Chocolate,' couples got up to dance. Have her sing more of that."

"Blues?" Brownie snorted. "That tired old shit will clear the room."

"It's sounds old to you because you've been hearin' it on black radio. White folks haven't heard it. It'll sound new to them."

"Actually, mister leg breaker here might be onto somethin'," Benjy Jefferson put in. "Half the British Invasion bands are *named* after blues tunes, the Rolling Stones, Lovin' Spoonful? White folks dig blues, they just can't play it worth a damn."

"The music's a downer— "

"Everybody's had their heart broke at least once," Benjy grinned. "Besides, it's great music to fuck to, and who don't like to fuck? I can play whatever you say, guys. Figure it out, lemme know." He peeled off to the bar.

"Keeping her is a mistake, Irish," Brownie insisted. "Let me get somebody else."

"We've got no money for anybody else!" Mick snapped. "If I can't pay Moishe somethin' come Monday, we could be swimmin' the Rouge wearin' cement boots."

"If it's do or die, then she'll have to do," Brownie said. "I'll tell Benjy."

"And get her a better outfit," Mick called after him. "Those white boots look ridicul— " He broke off, spotting Martika standing in the shadows backstage. Wasn't sure how much she'd heard. But from the deep maroon hurt in her eyes? She'd heard enough.

□   □   □

Mick spent the rest of the night working the streets with Aldo, collecting in blind pigs and back alley clubs that never saw the sun. Moishe had money in more than a dozen after hours joints and they hit them all, finishing up well after first light.

He tried to clear his head of the static from The Casa's disastrous opening, but couldn't shake the image of Tika limping to center stage... then later, trying to salvage her set, belting out her song without a mike.

Damn it.

He didn't poke his head back into The Casa until late afternoon. Found it nearly deserted. After the beehive madness of the previous weeks, it was strange to see the club almost empty. He hoped like hell it wasn't an omen. Jerome was onstage working feverishly with an electrician, rewiring the PA system, checking every circuit.

Carolina Shaw, the bartender from Brownie's place was tending bar, looking luscious.

"Is Brownie around?"

"He was in earlier. He and Martika went to meet with some lady from Motown Records."

"Motown? About what?"

"No idea. Brownie's on it, Mick, that's all I know."

"He'd better be," Mick said grimly, looking around the empty club.

CHAPTER 35

By Friday night, Mick was wired into knots. His vig payment to Moishe was due on Monday and he didn't have it. He'd laid his last dime on the line for this white elephant of a saloon. If it tanked again…Jesus. Couldn't even think about it.

Even collections were running behind. He got hung up in the Ford Rouge parking lot at dusk waiting for the swing shift dinner break. His slow-pay mark came late but at least he showed, and a damned good thing. The mood Mick was in, he would have stormed into the plant, hunted the dumb up, and sent him down the assembly line in serious need of repairs.

He didn't make it back to Casa Mayor until after eight. The night already looked a bit better, nearly half a house, with customers streaming in. But seeing the tables filling and hearing the expectant buzz, hardened a thought that had been lurking in the back of Mick's mind all day.

Brownie was probably right. Promise or no, they couldn't risk another disastrous night by opening with Martika. Maybe she could try again a few months down the line, but first they'd better make sure the club lasted that long. The Sultans were the hometown heroes these people came to see. Why not let them do two shows?

Hurrying backstage, he found Brownie huddled with Jerome and the gentle giraffe, Varnell Mack, finalizing the order of the Sultan's set. Varnell looked nervous, and after the disaster of opening night, he had a right to be. Seemed game though, ready to hit it again, loud and proud in his lime green leisure suit.

"We need to talk, man," Mick said, taking Brownie aside. "Look, about Martika— "

"I took care of it."

"We can't lose another crowd like— "

"I know that, Irish, it's handled. We dumped the act."

That stopped him. He stared at his partner, surprised. "Okay... You did right— "

"I got no time for this, bro. When you're stompin' some mope in a alley, I don't bug you with advice, eh? This is what I do. I'll catch you later."

Trotting off to meet and greet, he left Mick in mid-sentence. Feeling like a jerk. He hated going back on his word, even to— well, anybody. But— hell, it was business. She'd understand. She was too smart not to.

The bar was so busy some chump had taken his stool, pushing his drink aside. Mick nearly clocked the clown before he caught himself. Jesus, the schmuck was just a customer who needed a seat. He wasn't looking for trouble. But Mick was. He was ready to deck anybody who eyed him sideways. A familiar feeling.

Pre-fight nerves. Like waiting in a back room for your bout to be called. Jacked up on adrenaline, ready for war, with no one to swing at. Only he couldn't win this fight with his fists or ring savvy. The weight was on Brownie tonight. And the Sultans.

Ratcheting down his anxiety, Mick took a stool mid-way down the bar. But as Jerome and The In Crowd were taking the stage to kick off their show, a scuffle broke out between two black studs at ringside.

One was bull-necked in a dark suit, the other a shade smaller, wearing a red plaid jacket. They were in the aisle, pushing and shoving each other, yelling about...it didn't matter what. Both of them frontin', making noise to show everybody how bad they were, their dates egging them on, 'yeah, baby, you tell him, baby.'

Maybe Mick could have jawed them a little to quiet them down but they were fucking with his business and he was in no mood to chat. Elbowing through the crush, Mick slid up on the bigger one from the side. Bull-neck sensed trouble coming, started to turn, much too late. Hooking him hard under the rib cage, Mick doubled him over, then dropped him with a right cross, flush on the jaw. Big guy hit the deck like a sack of cement. Didn't move.

"You," Mick said, squaring off with plaid jacket. "Get your pal up, get him out of here. Don't come back. Ever."

"Just one damn minute, Mister Charlie," his date began, "you can't— "

"Chill, Sugar, nobody's throwing you out. Unless you say one more word... no? Good. Welcome The Casa, enjoy your evening." He glanced around quickly, scanning the crowd for trouble. A circle of dark eyes stared back, more curious than concerned. The beef was settled. They'd all seen worse. The conversational buzz picked up again.

Resuming his post at the bar, Mick got a fresh drink just as Benjy and the In Crowd were closing their first set. Confidence restored, they sounded tough and tight as a Corvette V-8, microphones working, players cooking hard, earning applause after every song.

He scanned the crowd again for more trouble. Found it, too, but of an entirely different sort.

Across the room, four white girls were sitting at a second-tier table, dressed to the nines. With a start, he realized one of them was Leanne, looking fine in a skintight blue satin party dress, her blonde hair pulled back in a chignon. Hadn't seen her since the scuffle with Spivak, or spoken with her after that final phone call. She looked terrific, blonde, busty and ready to play. The lone guy at their table was familiar too. Aldo. Decked out in a saffron Nehru jacket like a fifth Beatle. Basking in the homegirls' reflected glow.

Mick threaded through the crowd to their table, carrying his drink. The four chicks were pumped, eyes bright with excitement, hairstyles sprayed in place, makeup Barbie Doll perfect. Aldo saw him coming and stiffened.

"Relax, it's your night off. Is everything all right tonight, ladies?"

"Mick!" Leanne squealed, jumping up, giving him a quick hug. "I haven't seen you in forever. You look…different." She grimaced, touching the nearly healed gash on his cheek. "Is that from— ?"

"Cut myself shaving. What's the occasion?"

"A girls' night out, on Aldo. He said he had a piece of this wonderful new club, and so here we are. Are you working for Aldo now?"

"Not exactly," Mick said, letting the kid squirm. "We sort of…work together. The Casa's my place. I own it." He threw the line away, like it meant nothing. But it did. It was the first time he'd ever said it. About any damn thing.

"No kidding?" Leanne said, her blue eyes widening, glancing at her friends. All four girls checking him out now, interested, but a bit suspicious. Wondering if he was just another barroom bigmouth. Leanne started to ask something but her voice was drowned by the applause as Jerome stepped to the mike onstage and Benjy Jefferson kicked the band into a rock solid hitchhike beat. In total darkness, as the stage lights faded to black.

"Ladies and gentleman, tonight, taking our stage for the very first time in the all new Club Casa Mayor, give it up for the Motor City's own 'Hot Chocolate' girl, Tika and the In Crowd!"

Mick felt a jolt of rage so powerful he nearly crushed the glass in his fist. Banged it down on Leanne's table instead. That lying sonofabitch!

"Excuse me, ladies, gotta go. Business."

"Don't be a stranger!" Leanne called after him.

He barely heard her. Pushing through the crowd, he headed for Brownie's greeting station at the door. He wasn't there.

Mick spotted him across the room, seating a well-dressed older couple on the third tier. Chasing him down, he caught up to him at the bar, grabbed his arm and spun him around, face to face.

"What the fuck is this? You said you canned her!"

"Get off me!" Brownie said, pulling free. "I said we dumped the act! You said have her sing blues, that's what she's doin'."

Mick risked a glance over his shoulder— and stopped.

Martika wasn't limping onstage, she was already at the mike when the spotlight found her. Her dress was a full length, glittering metallic sheath with spaghetti straps that emphasized her ample bosom. She was a queen sized woman, and tonight every inch of it showed.

He scarcely recognized her. She looked like her own foxy older sister. And it was more than the dress. Even her hair was different, a sleek, sophisticated hairstyles with C-shaped 'guiche' curls, like Audrey Hepburn's in *Breakfast at Tiffany's*.

But she wasn't singing Motown covers tonight. Benjy kicked off her set with *Rock Me Baby*, the old Bobby Blue Bland jam. Tika slid into the verse like a woman on fire, moaning the turnaround, making it a powerful turn-on. The dance floor filled before the second chorus, couples grinding to the music, getting hot and bothered.

She got a strong hand for the opening tune. Thanking the audience over the applause, Tika announced the next number as Benjy counted it off, nailing it on the beat as though they'd performed it a thousand times. Totally confident.

Jackie style. Mick recognized Wilson's microphone technique from the Chit Chat, but her delivery was warmer, more feminine, with a kick all her own. She owned that stage and the audience sensed it, nodding in time with the music, smiles lighting the room. Eating her up.

She drew an even bigger hand for the second song, whistles and foot stomping. Coolly taking it in stride, Martika waited for the crowd to quiet, then slid into her signature tune, *"Hot Chocolate."*

For a paralyzing moment, Mick thought the mike had failed again. It hadn't. She'd deliberately lowered the volume, making the audience quiet down to listen. Her voice had been inaudible opening night, but folks were hearing her now. Almost a whisper...

"I'm Hot Chocolate baby, sweet brown and sticky too,
turn me on like you dooo... .I'm gone melt all over you...."

Mick felt his breathing go shallow as the room faded away, shrinking down to the spotlight halo on the stage. Music had moved him his whole life. He didn't always understand why he liked a song, but he knew real power when he heard it, sensed it the same way he could hear an engine humming in perfect tune. Martika had... whatever it was. The Real Thing.

He heard traces of Mojo's phrasing in her delivery, but her style was her own. Mick had the feeling that if she turned her blues up one more notch, she'd break every heart in the room. Including his.

He turned away, scanning the crowd, trying to shake off the song's spell. It didn't help. The audience was as entranced as he was. Dancers were packed on the floor now, the whole room only a few notes away from climax.

At the finish, the audience erupted, couples standing up to applaud. The dance floor stayed filled up she did a final tune, an upbeat "Further on up the Road" to close her show, the audience clapping in time with Benjy's backbeat, rocking in their seats.

As the song ended, the stage lights dimmed again as Martika walked slowly off, her limp barely noticeable. But she paused at the curtains, to look back at the crowd, still applauding. And even after she disappeared, Mick couldn't take his eyes off the place she'd been. Still seeing her in his mind's eye, glittering on center stage.

He'd spent time with the woman nearly every day for months, but he'd never really seen her at all.

Or heard her. When she was singing he felt like he could see all the way to the center of her soul. And he had no fucking idea what to do about that. But he wanted...hell.

He had no idea what he wanted. None of it made any sense to him. Even to him.

Joining in the applause when Tika finished her set, Mick glanced at Brownie, who was clapping even louder.

"Yeah!" Brownie shouted. "That's what we're talkin' 'bout!"

"Okay, okay, you did good," Mick admitted. "You're a fucking genius, man."

"Nah, genius is what we just saw up there. The girl's freaking' magic. I just feel sorry for the Sultans. Those poor bastards gotta follow that act in twenty minutes. And one more thing? I ain't one of your deadbeats, Mick. Don't ever put your hands on me again."

"No," Mick nodded. "Sorry about that. Are we okay?"

"Oh hell yes!" Brownie yelled over his shoulder as he bustled off through the crowd. "We're solid fucking gold!"

Backstage, the four Sultans were huddled up, hurriedly reconfiguring their set to take advantage of the energy in the room. Tika was making nice with a circle of white college boys from U. of D. Everyone hoping to get lucky, Mick guessed, slowing his pace. Tika saw him coming, waved her admirers away, and waited. In heels, she was early as tall as he, standing eye to eye. And hers were flashing.

"So what's up, boss man? How did I do?"

"You were...wonderful, I've never— "

"Brownie was ready to can me Wednesday night. Wanted me gone. He said you saved my ass. Why was that?"

"Actually, I changed my mind," he admitted. "I was ready to cut you loose too."

That brought her up short. "Why didn't you?"

"I was trying, then you started to sing, and...well. I heard you."

"You've been hearin' me sing around the place since day one. A flashy new dress and all of a sudden your hearing got better?"

"Maybe it did, but— look, I'm trying to apologize here and I haven't had much practice at it. What are you so mad about?"

"Because this was a wonderful night! A magic night! I've been waiting for it half my life. And you're saying it almost didn't happen?"

"You're right," Mick agreed, taking a deep breath. "I nearly screwed things for you— hell. All I can say is, I'm sorry. I'm not real quick, but I try not to make the same mistakes twice. I underestimated you, Miss Daniels. I won't do it again. So. Can I make it up to you? Buy you some champagne to celebrate? Or are you havin' too much fun breaking my balls?"

She looked away, trying to hang onto her anger. Couldn't quite manage it.

"No, I think I'm about done with that. And champagne sounds really nice. Get enough for the guys in the band. Benjy will— "

"I was thinking... it could be just us."

"Us?" she frowned, surprised. "What are you talking about?"

"That I'd take you someplace nice, buy you some champagne. Unless you're got other plans? Boyfriend?"

She cocked her head, reading his face. Liquid brown eyes. He had no idea what she was thinking.

"The Sultans are partying in the dressing room. I can't change clothes."

"Are you kidding? You look terrific. Come on, let's get out of here."

CHAPTER 36

"Where are we heading?" she asked. They were in Moishe's Lincoln, cruising Grand Boulevard.

"Someplace classy, candles and tablecloths, waiters. How about the Ponchartrain?"

"With me? In this dress?"

"What's wrong with it?"

"Men," she sighed. "There's nothing's wrong with it, it's maybe the prettiest dress I've ever had. But if we go into a restaurant? A white guy with a colored girl in a dress like this? Everybody will take me for a hooker."

"That's crazy."

"No, that's how it is. And this night's been really special and I don't want anything to ruin it. Can we just go back to Black Kat? I was so jumpy before the show that I lost my lunch. I'm starving."

"Are you okay?"

"I'm fine, it was only nerves. But right now a tall stack of hoecakes sounds a whole lot sweeter than champagne."

□ □ □

In Studio K for kitchen, she stepped out of her heels, going from six-one back to five-eleven. Putting an apron on over her sheath, she busied herself at the stove, humming while she whipped up flapjacks from scratch. Mick got a beer out of the fridge, sat at the table, watching her. Truly seeing her for the first time.

"You think The Casa's gonna do okay?" she asked.

"I think it's gonna be a goldmine. I should be there right now."

"Brownie's got it covered. It's his thing. It'll be fine."

"You like him?" The pang of jealousy caught him by surprise.

"Brownie? I don't really know him. Carolina's been with him six years and *she* doesn't know him. There's a lot goin' on with that man that doesn't show. He's like you that way."

"Me? I'm not complicated."

"You're like a stray dog runnin' the streets, Irish. No tellin' what you'll do next. Sometimes you bark, sometimes you bite. But nobody owns you. Or knows you, either."

"So I'm a dog?"

"All men are dogs," she smiled, pouring the batter into the pan.

"Every woman knows that. We like dogs. Can I ask you something?"

"Sure."

She hesitated, then turned to face him. "Mojo's gone, isn't he? For good, I mean. I won't see him again. Ever."

Mick blinked, taken totally by surprise. Didn't know what to say. And then realized his silence had already said it.

"That's kind of what I thought," she continued calmly, turning back to her pancakes, deftly flipping one from the skillet to a plate. "You say more by sayin' nothin' than anybody I've ever met."

He didn't say anything to that either. Unsure of his ground now. The truth might wreck everything. But he guessed trying to lie would be even worse.

"It's okay," she said. "I think I knew it that first day. Mojo was my uncle but he was mean as a snake with a backache. He and my father didn't speak, he wasn't welcome in our home. My folks hated my working for him. We were together for awhile, back when I was singing. Did you know that?"

He shook his head.

"I was only sixteen. And after the wreck, he ditched me. Hadn't seen him in years when he showed up, offered me this job running the studio. I almost didn't take it, I mean, I knew what he was like but..." She took a deep breath. "I really wanted to sing again. Mojo said we'd work something out but he'd promised things before. What happened to him?"

"He owed Moishe," Mick said simply. "It was just a collection that went bad. There was a fight. Mojo would have killed me if Moishe hadn't... stopped him."

"I guessed it was something like that..." She took a deep breath. "Thank you for telling me."

Mick had no idea what to say next. None at all.

"Mojo was headed for that place his whole life," she said. "I'm sorry it happened, but..." Again, a deep breath. "If it had to happen? I'm glad it was him and not you."

He just stared at her. "I'm not following."

"I mean, I cared for him once, so maybe it's wrong to feel that way, but I can't help it. I knew you were special that first day you came stompin' onto my porch. Knew there was... somethin'going on between us, but I had no idea what. Good or bad. But I knew you were... somethin'. Knew it to my bones."

"So, you're a witch?"

"No, just a colored girl getting by in this life," she said, carrying a steaming plate of flapjacks to the table. "Which means I've gotta have it all goin' on, all the time, just to keep up. Sure you don't want some of these?"

"No thanks, I'm good," he said, smiling as she doused the stack with maple syrup and ripped into it like a wolf. "So you liked me that first day?"

"Hell no! What was to like? Throwing your weight around when you knew absolutely nothin' from nothin'."

"I've done all right."

She glanced up at him, munching a mouthful of flapjacks. Didn't say anything.

He started to take a sip of his beer, then paused, the bottle frozen in midair. As he got it. Really...got it.

"It's been all you, hasn't it," he said slowly. "The studio, the club. I wouldn't have any of this if not for you."

"You might. You're smarter than people think."

"That's not saying much."

"Maybe not," she admitted, sopping up the last drop of syrup with the last bite of hoecake. "God, that was good." And their eyes met across the kitchen table. The challenge in the open between them. And the electricity.

"So," she said quietly, "you want to chat me up some more? Or should we see about the rest of this?"

"The rest?"

"Us. How we are together. It's been coming since that first day. Unless I'm reading this all wrong— ?"

He answered by leaning across the table, cupping the nape of her neck in his palm, and kissing her. Her mouth tasted like maple syrup and sugar. The kiss lasted a year, and seemed the most natural thing in the world. Until the urgency set in, and he blundered around the table and wrapped her in his arms, clasping her body against his, holding her until it hurt. For a moment, their eyes met and held, and the hunger was in the open between them.

"Slow down, sonny. Don't be wreckin' my new dress. I need it for tomorrow night. My room?"

"Are you sure this is what you want?"

"It's exactly what I want, sugar. Whether we're any good or not? It's going to be fun to find out. Just do me one favor?"

"What's that?"

"Don't you dare try to carry me upstairs."

CHAPTER 37

Mick woke slowly, rising to the surface of a deep sea dream. Martika's bedroom was aglow with morning light. She was at the window in her shift, arms folded. Looking out at the street. The light wasn't kind to her face and he wondered how old she actually was. Thirty-five? Maybe forty?

It didn't matter. He'd had girls before. Once, after a Mississippi fight, he'd done two at a time. Sisters? He couldn't remember. Because it didn't mean anything. To him, *or* them, probably.

He'd never been with a full grown woman who knew what she wanted. Martika was a whole 'nother thing. A different league, different weight class. She'd fucked him out of his mind for most of the night. He'd poured himself out on her until he was done. Could barely move. And that was only the beginning.

Wildest ride he'd ever had. She took everything he had to give, wrapping her ankles around his waist, her energy driving him until they both exploded. And then doing it all over again. The pulse of it rising and falling like waves on a shore. And somewhere in the midst of the sex, he caught a glimmer of what "Hot Chocolate" was *really* about.

She was the best he'd ever had. Or ever would. And he wanted her again. But...

Now she was at the window in her robe, staring out at....who the hell knew? They were totally different people. He had no insight into what she was thinking. Couldn't read her any better than he had on that first day. Her soul was as deep and dark as her eyes.

"Look at you," he said softly. "Anything wrong?"

"Not one damn thing," she said, glancing back at him. "Everything's really, really right. The most right it's ever been. It was a wonderful night."

"Which part?" He lay back, laced fingers behind his head, watching her.

"All of it. The audience, the band. The applause. Oh, and you weren't so bad either. In fact, truth be told? You were maybe the best of it all. But everything looks different in the morning. You can have the sweetest dreams at night, but when that old sun comes up...? And you gotta deal with what is." She turned to face him. "I need to know some things, Irish."

"Like what?"

"Whether we're about anything. I was good last night. Onstage, I mean. People liked me. And what happened with us afterward was maybe a part of that. And if that's all it was, it's okay. I'll understand. I'm not asking you for anything, but…"

"But?"

"I won't be your whore, Mick. Your part-time colored girl. I saw you talking with that blonde, your date from the Chit Chat?"

"Leanne? What about her?"

"Nothing about her. She's pretty, and she's your own age. You and her together makes a whole lot more sense than you and me. But you can't have us both. I won't let you do me that way. I won't let you break my heart."

"I won't."

"Mmmm. I believe I've heard that old line in about a thousand blues tunes. Thing is, we're nobody's idea of a match. But I think we might be good together. You need me, you know. You're tough and quick but a lotta boys come off the Corridor like that. Look at yourself, still healing up, got scars on top of scars. The way you're going, you won't see Christmas— what are you laughing at?"

"I'm not laughing. Smiling maybe."

"You think I'm funny?"

"Sure. And you're big and you're damn sure beautiful, but mostly? I think you're smart. I think you might be the smartest woman I've ever known."

"But…?"

"Your butt's nice too. About perfect, I'd say."

"I'm serious, Mick."

"So am I. Everything you said is dead right. About me, about everything."

"What about your white girl? She's younger than me. Prettier, too."

"Not to me. And anyway, you're a lot smarter."

"What's that got to do with anything?"

"It's got everything to do with it. Look, I don't know if I can explain this right, but… What you said last night about me being sharper than people think? Maybe that's so. I'm quick about some things but I'm damn sure no genius, and I know that. But you might be. I picked up on that the first day. How smart you were. To a guy like me, you've got no idea how sexy a smart woman is."

"Let me get this straight. All that thrashing' and crashing' around we did last night, you on top, me on top, that was all because…why? You think I'm smart?"

"Something like that. Look, if some dumb chick wants to jump a guy's bones, so what? What does she know, right? But if a really intelligent woman thinks you might be worth something— that you might be special? Do you see how different that is? Why it matters more?"

"That is…the strangest damn compliment I ever heard. If that's what it was."

"I told you I wouldn't say it right."

"No, you're doing fine. As long as we're straight with each other, we might have a chance. Now, about that white girl? I've been thinking."

"Why am I not surprised?" Mick groaned.

"Don't be like that, you might like this. In the club business, two week gigs are pretty much standard. Singers, bands all book for two weeks at a time. If they do good, you hold 'em over, or ask 'em to come back. Maybe we could do that. A two-week deal."

"Two weeks?"

"We might not make it that long."

"Okay. What happens at the end of two weeks?"

"Nothing. If we're not happy, we're done. But if we're both okay with it, we renew. Just like at the club. But it's exclusive. You'll have to be true to me. For two weeks."

"That's it? We try it for two weeks?

"That's all I'm asking," she nodded. "How hard can that be?"

"I don't know. I've been places where an hour can seem like a year. Maybe you can help me make up my mind."

"I'll be happy to try," she smiled, letting her shift slip to the floor. She was tall and strong, and her body was sweet chocolate, built for action, full breasts, more than his mouth could hold. Queen sized, top to bottom. And every damn thing about her was exactly right. She was the hottest thing he'd ever seen.

"Okay, deal," he said, swallowing. "Moishe knows lawyers if you want it in writing."

"No need," she said, climbing on top of him, straddling him, sliding his quivering erection inside her juicy, electric warmth. "Your word's good with me."

CHAPTER 38

Sitting at his desk in The Casa's office high above the dance floor, Mick spotted the guy the moment he stepped into the club. Hard to miss him. Big bull of a black guy, shaved head, square face. His crappy blue suit looked two sizes too small and he wasn't wearing an overcoat, despite December gusts outside that were howling in from the Rouge River like a pack of rabid wolves. The odd thing was, the big bruiser looked familiar. Mick was sure he'd seen him before, but couldn't place him. Bouncer at one of the blind pigs? No…from someplace though.

The big black stopped to talk to the janitor, who pointed him up the stairs to the Nest. On he came.

"Whooee, who we got here?" Brownie asked. "Man looks like Sonny Liston's big brother."

"Do you know him?"

Brownie shook his head. Their projection booth/office was plush, dark paneling, autumn gold carpet thick enough to mow. Three desks in it now, one each for Brownie and Mick, plus a secretary's desk for Martika.

The room also had a private exit and from the taut look on the big guy's face, Mick wondered if he should use it. Damn. Still couldn't place him but he was getting a bad feeling, something about this guy was all wrong.

Opening his desk drawer, he took out an army .45, jacked a round into the chamber, then laid it on his lap, out of sight below the level of the desk.

Brownie raised an eyebrow but that was all. The big guy rapped once and stepped in. Up close he looked even bigger. Had to shift sideways to get through the door. A splayed scar on his right temple that bled white into his hairline, just above his ear. Mick recognized that scar, knew it was from a broken bottle, and felt a sudden twinge of fear. The big guy seemed just as nervous. Despite the December chill, he was sweating. Mick tightened his grip on the .45.

"Mr. Shannon? Maybe you remember me? Cephus Jessup?"

"You look familiar, but— "

"Big Ceef, they call me. We fought down in Mississippi one time, backwoods joint called Bateman's. Three, four years ago?"

"Jesus H.," Mick said, stiffening, "you're the ringer. The prison champ the hacks smuggled out of Angola. No wonder I didn't remember you. You clocked me so hard I didn't wake up till Tuesday."

"It wasn't personal."

"It was damn personal to my crew. We lost serious money on that fight."

"Not to me. The hacks kept the cash, I never seen a penny of it. They let me visit my wife on the way back to The Farm, that was my pay."

"You're a long way from Louisiané, Mr. Jessup," Brownie said.

"Got paroled last year, but my wife took up with some no-good. Had to straighten things out when I went home."

"How bad?" Mick asked.

"Hospital bad, for him. Sumbitch didn't die but my parole officer vi-olated me for bustin' up his sorry ass. They were gon' send me back, five more years. I got kin in East Detroit so I come up here to lay low. Heard some noise about you and remembered your name. I'm hopin' you might have some work for me. If you ain't too mad about that other thing."

"What kind of work do you do, Mr. Jessup?" Brownie asked, amused.

"Anything needs doin'."

"How about collecting?" Mick asked. "Street money?"

"I believe a man should pay what he owes. I'd rather not kill nobody."

"What if they try to kill you?" Brownie asked.

"That happen often?"

"It's been known to come up," Mick said. "Can you handle guns?"

"Shotguns, sure enough. I grew up country. Never had much use for guns, though. If you ask people polite, they mostly do right. Pay up or whatever."

"Uh-huh. Mind stepping out a minute, Mr. Jessup?" Mick said. "I need to talk to my partner."

"You fought that man?" Brownie asked, when they were alone, shak-ing his head in amazement.

"Not for long."

"I don't doubt that. You thinkin' of hirin' him?"

"The Casa and the studio are doing good business, but I'm burning out trying to work the streets for Moishe and working here too. Maybe Ce-phus can help out with the collections."

"What'll Moishe say about that?"

"Moishe's all done with strong-arm work and he knows it. He'll be okay with it, long as he gets paid. What do you think?"

"If that nigger asked me to pay up, I'd damn sure fork it over whether I owed him or not. Seriously? You really climbed into a ring with that man?"

"Not exactly."

□   □   □

When Mick walked out the gates of Jackson Prison, he knew there was no way he could go home to Ecorse. His mom was in the ground, and if he ran into Spivak on the street, he'd be back in prison before his bunk got cold.

So with forty bucks in the pocket of his jailhouse suit, he rode a Grey-hound south to a hardscrabble farm outside Noxapater, Mississippi. His grandfather Jason Mackey's place. Hadn't been there since he was a boy. Forty stony acres, a three-room shack and a sagging barn. Kerosene lanterns. A woodstove. Hand pump at the kitchen sink, outhouse around back. Definitely the boondocks. But still better than the slam.

Jase Mackey was in his mid-seventies now, gnarled as a pear tree and just as prickly. Wore faded bib overalls, no shirt, a mat of snowy chest fur curling around the bib straps. A handsome man once, he was surly and silent now. A solitary drinker. Hadn't approved of his daughter's choice of husbands, but was sorry to hear she'd passed. Remembered the one time she'd brought Mick down for a visit. Age nine. But he was blood kin and welcome to stay on awhile. As long as he carried his weight.

Chores on the farm started every morning at four a.m. Unpaid. Hefting hay bales, weeding, hoeing. Jase doubted Mick would last a week. Too pretty. Like his mother. Called him Charles Atlas, after the wimp in the comic books who got sand kicked in his face. The old man had the names mixed up, but Mick got the drift. Compared to the crap he'd taken in Jackson, Jase's needling was a relief.

And Mick proved him wrong, tearing into his chores with a fury, working off five years of pent-up frustration. When the field work was finished he swept the house, washed the walls, raked the yard. The first weekend, he tore down the four-banger engine on his grandfather's '49 Ford 8N tractor, ground the valves by hand, reamed the jet on the gravity-fed carburetor, got the old clunker running better than brand new.

He did the same for the cherry '57 Chevy Jase kept in the barn, replacing the plugs and points, tweaking its timing till it purred like a calico cat. Jase didn't say thanks, exactly. But the Charles Atlas cracks stopped. And the second week he left a ten dollar bill on the nightstand beside Mick's cot. Chump change. But it was every penny the old man could spare and Mick knew it.

Evenings were quiet. Neither man was much of a talker and they had little in common. But they were comfortable with each other, which was no small thing. Mick's radio remained his late-night companion. Here in the south he had no trouble finding stations that aired the crude, gutbucket music he loved. Delta blues out of Biloxi and Little Rock, edgy electric blues and howls from Wolfman Jack on XERF in Del Rio, Texas. Mick couldn't tell if the Wolfman was black or white, and didn't care, he just liked the jams.

But in the morning, the songs were gone and he was still stuck on the farm, growing more restless by the day. A month into his stay, he hiked the four miles into Noxapater, and hired on as a mechanic at the Case tractor dealership.

Barely a block long, Noxapater had a two pump Mobil gas station at one end, a Ralston Purina feed store at the other, painted checkerboard red and white.

With new tractors on display and an eight bay service garage, the Case dealership was the only business on any size in town and jobs there were prized.

Mick guessed the foreman hired him for laughs. As a Yankee boy, and an ex-con to boot, he expected trouble. He got it the first day.

Most of the grease monkeys on the ten man crew were local men who'd known each other a lifetime. The muttering began the moment the foreman introduced Mick at the start of the shift. Glares and badmouthing quickly escalated to shoulder bumps, then a shove. He let it pass. Until a wrench clanged off the concrete near his head as he was unbolting an oil pan.

Fuck this!

Mick had no idea who'd thrown it, and it didn't matter. Scrambling to his feet, he stalked over to Gordie Garrison, the biggest guy on the crew. A hulking, bull-shouldered farmboy, straw-haired, red-faced, Garrison was tall as a silo and nearly as wide. Probably outweighed Mick by a hundred pounds, most of it muscle.

"Yo, numb-nuts," Mick said, looking up at Garrison. "You too stupid to hang onto your tools?"

"Who you callin' numb-nuts, you Yankee fuck?"

"You, fat boy. Is this your wrench? Or are you too pussy to own up to it?"

"Ain't mine," Garrison said, his face splitting in a wide grin. "But I know pussy when I see it. And you're about to get fucked up, city boy."

"It's my first day," Mick said calmly. "How about we wait till after the shift?"

"Nah, we're due a twenty minute break about now. I figure you'll last about two."

A ring was already forming around them, hyena smiles, wisecracks and laughter, men jostling for position, wanting a close-up of the action. No wagers on the outcome. It was a suicide match. The only bets were on how long it would take. The smart money favored two minutes or less.

But Mick hadn't picked out Garrison by accident. The big fella looked slow, soft in the middle. And guys his size seldom have to duke it out. Their sheer bulk settles most arguments. Mick made him for a good ole' boy used to friendly dustups. Rough a man around, bloody his nose, buy him a beer after. No hard feelings.

Not this time. Mick needed this job, needed the money. Which meant he'd have to whip Garrison's ass quick. Before the big man's size and strength could wear him down.

As the two men stripped off their work shirts, Mick noticed Gordie flexing his huge hands, not even bothering to make a proper fist. The big guy meant to grab him, bounce him off the concrete like a bean bag, then stomp him. He'd probably come at him in a bull rush. Straight off.

No bell, no handshake. A simple nod and both men started circling slowly, eyeing each other. A lot of racket from the crowd. Mick kept his fists moving. Garrison was grinning widely, his beefy arms outstretched, big as a bear looking to grapple.

"Whoo-haw!" he whooped, "This Yankee boy's so pretty ain't sure if I should fuck him up the ass or just fuck him up!"

Jeers and laughter from his cronies. Mick ignored them, circling closer, cutting the distance between them, giving Gordie no room to build momentum.

With a grunt, Garrison lunged, trying to pull Mick into a bear hug. Ducking under Gordie's grasp, Mick thrust upward like a V-8 piston, head-butting him full in the face, smashing his nose with an audible crunch and an explosion of blood that sprayed the circle. As Gordie staggered back, stunned, Mick hammered his midriff with a machine gun barrage of brutal body shots, hooking him hard under the ribs, driving out his wind, then chopping him down with a savage right cross to the throat that nearly snapped the big man's head off. Gordie's eyes rolled up white as he dropped to his hands and knees, spewing up his lunch out on the concrete floor.

A tense moment. Garrison down and dazed, Mick crouching over him, his fist cocked like a gun. He could have clocked him to make a statement. He straightened up slowly instead, facing the ring of baffled, angry rednecks.

"Anybody else want some?" he asked, eyeing each man in turn, knowing if the circle closed on him he'd have no chance. "Come on, guys. Anybody who wants a piece of me, take your best shot now. Because after today, I just work here. If anybody's got a problem with that, bring it." Dead silence, accentuated by Garrison's retching. "Okay then," Mick said, warily lowering his fists. "Somebody help me get Gordie to a chair. I can't shift him by myself."

"I believe you just did," one of the older men chuckled ruefully, shaking his head. "H'ep Gordie up, boys. This shit's over."

But it wasn't. The backwoods studs had grit and over the next few weeks, three more tried Mick out. And went down even harder than Gar-

rison. Using ring savvy he'd picked fighting five years in Jackson, he
ended the bouts quickly, dealing out serious damage.

He never had to fight the same man twice, or his friends either. In a
month, the garage crew were his buddies, setting up backroom scrums
with local saloon toughs, pooling every penny they could scrape together
to bet on their favorite Irish Yankee.

Matches were mostly at a pineywoods saloon a mile outside Noxapater called Bateman's. Rough plank siding and home brewed beer. Bare-
knuckle brawls in a smoky circle of sweating, screaming rednecks,
money and blood on the dirt floor, corn liquor and backslapping after.
Sometimes after a match, Mick would score some overheated pussy, frantic humps with boozed up redneck women on a pool table or the bed
of a pickup truck. Over quicker than a round in the ring.

Bateman's became Mick's hangout after work. He felt at home there,
the roughneck atmosphere, the smoke, cheap booze. Good timin' with
an edge to it.

His third bout at Bateman's, Mick took on a sawmill hand from across
the Neshoba county line. Big as a cow barn, six foot tall and four hundred beefy pounds, a Frankenstein face scarred up by a chainsaw and
an outlook to match. Everybody called him Sweet Thang.

Some of Sweet's weight was gut. Suet. An easy target. Proved to be a
hard man to drop, though. Mick's body shots sank into the blubber with
no effect, and he could feel the big man's power with every wild swing.
If Sweet Thang caught him flush, he'd knock him into next week. Tiring and desperate, Mick leapt inside Sweet's reach, driving a liver shot
under his ribcage that dropped the giant to the deck in limb-twitching
convulsions, pissing all over himself as spectators scrambled to get out
of the way.

After Sweet Thang, bouts were harder to come by, but work wasn't.
Lacey Bateman, the chunky, cheerful, bearded Alabamian who owned
the dive, hired Mick to bounce on weekends and bodyguard him on his
Monday morning run south to the bank in Philadelphia, Miss. to deposit
the weekend take.

Lacey loaned him a .44 Smith and Wesson to pack on the bank runs.
Taught him how to shoot it, too, the two of them popping beer bottles
out behind the bar. Shooting came easily to Mick. The weight of the pistol in his fist, the balance of it, felt as natural as pointing his finger. Or
throwing a perfect punch.

Bottles seemed to explode on their own. After half a box of cartridges,
Mick was already shooting better than Lacey ever would. And gaining
serious respect for the damage a pistol could do at close quarters.

Lacey taught him other things as well. A born raconteur, he held forth on their weekly Philadelphia drives on the fine art of backwoods saloon management, watching the till and the help, gauging the number of shots in a bottle and the mood of a room.

Lace also lectured him on the importance of holding onto his money to build something for himself in this life. Advice Mick took to heart. He was still carrying his chores for free at his grandfather's farm, but with his mechanic's job and working weekends for Lacey, he built up a fair sized stash. It was a killer schedule, but he was young, tough, and hungry.

The first year flew by in a wink. The only thing that changed was Mick's bankroll. It grew from a few hundred to two thousand. Then came his big chance. To double his money, in one bout.

In March, some good ol' boys from Biloxi called up Lacey to match Mick against their man, a black field hand from Louisiana. Mick looked forward to the bout, a chance to score some serious cash and work off his frustrations.

Saturday night, the Biloxi boys rolled into Bateman's lot in a battered Ford pickup truck, their black fighter riding in the back like a huntin' dog.

Big stud looked hard as a steel beam, huge hands, heavy brows, one temple scarred white by a broken bottle. Looked like he'd done some ring work, which was fine by Mick. His grandfather had been sickly lately, but wouldn't see a doc. Mick was worried about him, didn't know what to do about it. Which put him in the mood for a war.

The betting was heavy on both sides. The Louisiana man looked bad to the bone, but Mick's buds had seen him take bigger men apart.

At the bell, Mick came tearing out of his corner, ripping into the field-worker's midsection with a ferocious barrage of body punches. No effect. The big man's belly was solid as a sack of cement and Mick caught a left hook counterpunch that numbed his shoulder like a ten pound sledge.

God *damn*, Mick thought, settling down for a serious contest, bracing himself for some pain. They traded hard jabs for most of the round, circling, working in close, both men looking for an opening. Then things winked out.

Afterward, Mick could remember ducking under a roundhouse left, then nothing until he woke up on a cot in Lacey's office with an ice bag on his swollen jaw. He'd stepped into a straight right, dropped like a box of rocks.

Lacey found out later the Biloxi men were actually guards at The Farm,

Angola State Prison. The 'field hand' was the Angola champ, Big Cephus Jessup. Might have been funny except for the money Mick and his friends lost.

A few weeks later, plowing his south pasture on the Ford 8N, a cholesterol bomb exploded in Jase Mackey's chest, seventy years of grits, gravy and chicken fried everything, shattered his heart, stopping his breath in an instant.

As the tractor rumbled mindlessly on, Jase slumped on the seat, then toppled off backwards, splitting his skull on the iron drag bar. He was dead as a beaver hat when he hit the ground. Which was just as well since the harrow plowed him under, grinding his blood and bones into his own stony field.

Mick stayed long enough to see what was left of the old man planted properly, then loaded his few belongings into the old Chevy and headed north—

And now Cephus had made his way here, looking for him, and Brownie was staring at him.

"Yeah, I fought him once," he said, "and I sure as hell don't want to do it again. Hire him?"

"Hell yes," Brownie agreed. "And do it quick. Before he gets mad."

CHAPTER 39

The following Friday night, the line outside The Casa Mayor stretched beyond the marquee into the snowy December streets. Good vibes, nobody pushing. Christmas coming in a few weeks, holiday spirit in the air.

Working the door, tuxed, and razor sharp, Brownie's guts iced up when he spotted the two ofays shouldering their way to the front of the line. He remembered them from the hassle at the Chit Chat. Mr. *"do you know who I am?"* Albert Luca and his blonde bodyguard, Ducatti. Dark continental suits, belted jackets, pegged slacks. *"And here we go,"* he thought.

They had a girl with them, a high yellow hooker in a red satin sack dress, chocolate hair piled high. Lenore something. Call girl, not street traffic. Brownie'd seen her around, usually with fat-cat white johns.

"Good evening, folks," he murmured. "Welcome to The Casa Mayor. Table for three?"

"Front row seats, pal, ringside, best in the joint," Ronny said, slipping him a ten. Neither man recognized Brownie. No surprise. Brothers looked alike to them.

"This way, sir" Brownie said, palming the bill as he led them in, listening closely. The two men were discussing The Casa's décor. Why were they so interested? As customers? Or was Mick getting some new partners?

He seated them at the last ringside table near the stage. Ronny griped because it wasn't stage center but Brownie explained the table was reserved for special guests, the mayor and his party had used it last week. Total bullshit but the arrogant pricks bought it and settled down. Lords of the manor.

They ordered a round of single malt Rob Roys, and a magnum of champagne, started knocking it back like beer and soon ordered another around. Brownie noted that Ducatti and the hooker, Lenore, were doing most of the drinking. Albert was sipping his drinks while they guzzled theirs. If he was here for fun, he was doing it mostly sober.

Albert caught Brownie eyeing them once, but didn't react. Looked right through him. Like he wasn't there. To Albert, he probably wasn't.

But not all brothers were invisible. Albert stiffened when the band started and he spotted Benjy playing drums. Leaning over, he said something to Ducatti, who swiveled for a better look. Both men giving Benjy the hard eye. A wasted effort. Busting whiteboys' balls was one of Benjy's favorite things, right up there with making music and getting buzzed. He'd forgotten his hassle with Albert five seconds after it finished.

But Luca clearly hadn't. And after seeing Benjy, he started checking out The Casa more intently, scoping out the setup.

Tika was back as the opening act after a two week run in Cleveland and the audience response was strong. She'd added new tunes and even a dance routine but the high point of her act was still her tear-the-house-down version of "Hot Chocolate."

As Tika sashayed off to a second ovation, one of the waitresses tapped Brownie's arm.

"Them two honkies at the front table want to see you."

"Is there a problem?"

"Other'n them bein' drunk, white and pushy, you mean?" She flounced off. Waving Cephus over to cover the door for him, Brownie headed into the club.

"Is everything all right, gentlemen?"

"It damn sure ain't," Ronny said, blinking, trying to get his eyes to focus. "We're light."

"I beg your pardon?"

"Our party, pal. We're a girl short. Or can't you count?"

Brownie noticed Albert watching him, mildly amused. And cold fucking sober. "Maybe your ladyfriend can call a friend," Brownie suggested. "Lenore has lots of friends."

"I've seen the one I want," Albert said, pinching the lapel of Brownie's tux, pulling him closer. "That singer. What's her name? Martina?"

"Martika."

"Whatever. Here's twenty bucks for you. Get her ass out here to join the party." He jammed a folded bill into Brownie's vest pocket. "Tell her there's some change in it for her. And more for you, too."

"She's a singer, not a hooker, Mr. Luca. I can't tell her what to do."

"Are you saying no, sport?" Ronny asked, straightening up, a dangerous edge in his tone.

"Not at all," Brownie said smoothly. "Her manager's backstage, I'll send him over. I'm sure you can work out an arrangement."

He backed away before they could argue, heading for the greeting station.

"Cephus, we got a situation," he said, taking the big man aside. "Two mobbed-up Caspers are lookin' to buy out Martika."

"Where they at?"

"Sitting up front, but be cool. You just tell 'em you're her manager— "

"You mean them two she's talkin' to now?"

Brownie turned. Martika was already at Albert's table. "Goddamn! They must've sent a waitress after her with the same message. Come on!" Brownie hurried back inside with Cephus right behind him. But it was already too late.

Brownie didn't know what Albert said but he could guess. Martika threw a drink in his face, then upended the champagne bucket in his lap before storming off. With a roar both men exploded out of their seats, Ducatti clawing for his gun just as Cephus grabbed his wrist, clamping it.

"Leave it be, sport," he rumbled. "Anything you pull's goin' right up your ass."

Ronny was furious and half-loaded, but one look at Cephus's battle-scarred face sobered him fast.

"Snotty bitch ruined my dress," Lenore griped, brushing ice off her lap.

"This'll cover it," Brownie said, jamming Albert's twenty down her cleavage. "The show's over, gentlemen, time to go."

"I want that black bitch fired!" Albert snapped, enraged. "I want— "

"I'll certainly look into it, sir," Brownie said, cutting him off as Cephus seized Albert's arm. "Right now you'd best get your ass gone before her fans stomp you to death."

"You can't throw *us* out!" Albert said, incredulous. "Do you know who I am?"

"I don't even know who y'all *think* you are, motherfuck," Cephus growled, hustling both men toward the exit. "But I definitely know where you're goin'. Keep movin'!"

But it wasn't that simple. When Albert's driver, Artie Infante, saw his boss and Ronny getting muscled out of The Casa by a couple of spades, he came charging out of the car, a snub nose .38 in his fist.

Spotting Infante coming on the run, Cephus swung Albert around, tossing him like a rag doll into Artie, knocking both men sprawling on the sidewalk. Grabbing Artie's collar before he could recover, Cephus clocked the driver with a short right that flattened his nose, spraying Albert with blood.

Raising both hands, Albert stayed down, but Ronny backed away, reaching for his weapon.

"Bad idea, mister."

Ducatti felt a sharp nudge in his ribs. Brownie was behind him with a piece pressed hard against his spine. A fountain pen, but Ronny didn't know that.

Enough. Raising both hands, Ronny helped Albert to his feet and headed for their car. Artie Infante stumbled along after them, his blood splattering the sidewalk with Lenore right behind him, bitching every step of the way.

CHAPTER 40

Moishe phoned first thing the next morning. John Luca had called them in for a sit-down. Right fucking now.

Mick picked him up an hour later. Moishe was dressed for winter, a Homburg, a muffler, a heavy overcoat and his gnarled walking stick. Mick wore a new black mohair suit Brownie'd helped him pick out. No topcoat. Wanted his shoulders free, a piece at hand.

Moishe didn't say squat in the car, obviously steamed. And worried too. As they pulled into the lot behind one of Musso's pawn shop in East Detroit, he told Mick to leave his .45 in the glove box. No weapons at a meet.

"What if there's trouble?"

"If we got that kind of trouble, it's already too late. Do like I tell ya for once, Mick. Leave the fucking piece."

Inside the pawn shop, Moishe led the way through counters piled with cheap Jap transistor radios, Mix-masters, Melmac kitchenware. Cheesy guitars from Korea hanging in rows overhead. Racks of rifles and shot-guns against the side wall. Perry Como murmuring '*Peace on earth, goodwill to men,*' in the background.

An elderly black couple were the only customers but there were sales-men behind every counter, all oversized white guys. All of them strapped.

"A lot of firepower for a hock shop," Mick said, looking around.

"Rough part of town," Moishe shrugged.

Mick felt a sudden chill, wondering if Moishe had already cut a deal with Luca. To serve him up on a plate.

But there was no backing off now. He followed Moishe down a hall-way at the rear of the showroom to a steel door with two goons posted outside it. They waved Moishe past but patted Mick down for weapons before letting him through.

Inside, the stockroom had cardboard cases stacked to the steel beams overhead. John Luca was at a utility desk in the center of the room, wear-ing a cashmere sport coat over a snowflake pattern sweater. Very festive. Albert was beside him in his designer shades, along with Ducatti and Charlie Musso, the surly union thug from the St. Clair. Artie Infante, the driver Cephus decked, was standing well off to one side, a bandage across his swollen nose, a purplish bruise the size of an avocado under one eye. Four more Musso goons were posted around the room, not counting the two guarding the door.

Too much muscle for a chat, Mick thought. Moishe didn't seem spooked, but it was hard to tell what Moishe was thinking, now or ever.

"Good to see you up and around again, Moishe," Luca said, waving him to a metal chair. There was no seat for Mick. He took a position at Moishe's shoulder.

"Coulda seen me sooner, if you stopped by Henry Ford there," Moishe griped, leaning on his cane to lower himself onto the seat. "Any of ya could've."

"Fucking feds," Luca shrugged. "They stake out everything now, weddings, funerals. Even hospitals. No class, those mopes, no courtesy."

"I ain't much on courtesy either, John. Get stiff if I sit too long, so get to it. So what's this about?"

"Your boy Shannon has gone outlaw on you Moishe," Musso said, his pudgy face flushed and angry. "While you been laid up he went out on his own. Got himself a nightclub, a recording studio."

"No shit?" Moishe said. "You telling me my business now, Charlie, like I'm some kinda schmuck?"

"You know about these ventures?" Luca asked coldly.

"The kid works for me, John. What do you think?"

"What I *know* is, that you never brought any of this to us, Moishe. I never okayed it and we haven't seen a dime. Is Shannon going independent, or are you?"

"You called a meet over this chickenshit?" Moishe asked, glaring around the circle, not a bit intimidated. "Musso bitched, I bet. Why didn't you just fuckin' ask me about it, John? Save us all a trip."

"He's asking you now, pops," Albert snapped. "So stop dancin' and answer up."

Mick stiffened. If Albert wasn't afraid to mouth off to Moishe...

"Nobody's dancin', young Junior," Moishe said mildly. "The studio's nothin', a nickel-dime operation we took off the spade who cut me at Idlewild. Cost me forty grand in medical bills and clears a few hundred a week. You'll get your end *after* I break even, we should all live so long. The Casa Mayor ain't much more. These nigger bars come and go. Figured it'd run in the red for a year but it's doin' better than expected. You'll get your taste."

"That isn't how it works, Moishe," Luca said dangerously. "You didn't come to me or show us any paperwork. Even now, all we've got is your word."

"You wanna see the books, John, you can read 'em anytime you want. Send fat Charlie. He knows the bar business. Is that what this beef's really about? The Casa coppin' some of Charlie's East Detroit saloon trade?"

"It's about doing things the right way," Luca said.

"Yeah," Musso chimed in. "You never asked no permission— "

"I don't have to ask for dick in Darktown!" Moishe barked, cutting him off. "8 Mile's mine! It was part of my deal comin' into this bunch when most of you were still stealin' hubcaps. I sent you paperwork for Cooley's, John. Shannon buried a guy to get that place, it should've been sold off and shared out. Instead, it goes to your nephew. Do I complain, call a big fucking meet to bitch about it? No. I get it. It's time Albert got something of his own, so good luck and god bless. When I got cut up, Musso took over my white accounts. I ain't seen dime one since and I ain't holdin' my breath. There's no paperwork on The Casa because on *paper* it ain't ours. We got a partner holdin' the license. We're still upside down on the club but I'll start your percentage if it'll make things right."

"How come we're only hearin' about this now?" Musso demanded.

"If you got off your ass and stopped by my office for a coffee, you'd know all about it, Charlie. I got no secrets from anybody in this room."

"Or so you say."

"You calling me a liar, you fat guinea fuck?" Moishe asked quietly. His tone hadn't changed. He was still an old man with a cane, but Musso paled under that stare.

"Enough," Big John said, "no more *agita* over this. Darktown's got more nigger bars than TV's got westerns. Gunsmoke, Maverick and all them. We're the cowboys, spades are the herd. You start the payments next week, Moishe. Backdated to catch me up. We're done here."

"Wait a minute!" Albert said. He'd been slouched down, observing the byplay, but he was bolt upright now. "Shannon's spooks roughed us up. He has to answer for that!"

"Mick works for me," Moishe said mildly, "so any beef is with me. Way I hear it, you and Ronny made your own trouble, tryin' to buy out some singer like she was a whore. Even shines won't stand for that. If you wanted satisfaction, you shoulda got it on the street instead of lettin' poor Artie get his face rearranged. You got Cooley's as a fucking gift, Albert, you got nothin' else comin' from me." Moishe groaned, levering himself to his feet. "Except maybe some free advice. Give up chasin' them colored whores, boys, they wear your ass out. You end up needin' a cane to get out of your damn chair."

John laughed and everyone joined in. It was over. Albert read the room, then gave Moishe a grudging nod. The others moved to the coffeemaker, relieved it was settled without bloodshed. A Family again.

"*Until next time,*" Mick thought.

Moishe chatted up Luca and Musso, sipping espresso from a tiny cup, chuckling at Big John's jokes. Even slipped the battered Artie Infante a few hundred for his pains.

Mick hung back, still wary. Albert was standing outside the circle too, with Ducatti at his shoulder. He caught Mick's eye and sauntered over, Ronny a step behind.

"You dodged a bullet today," Albert observed. "I thought sure that old man would throw you overboard."

"And I thought you were supposed to be smart. Guess we were both wrong."

"Don't push it, Shannon, you got lucky. You should be working for me anyway. We're in the same business. I swapped Cooley's to Charley Musso for one of his East Detroit nightspots, and I'm buying into a joint in Dearborn. There's a lot more money in clubs and drugs than the union rackets. But you already know that."

"Actually, I don't. And trying to follow the way you think gives me a headache, Albert. Maybe I'm not smart enough."

"You're smart enough to go after the right action. I just think bigger.

I'm willing to let this pass, make room for you at the table. If you shape up."

"It wouldn't work, Albert. You like bossing people. I don't like bosses."

"Moishe's your boss."

"You're right. Maybe it's you I don't like."

"You've got a big mouth, plowboy," Ronny said, jamming a finger in Mick's chest. "Just because the old farts gave you a pass— "

"Hey! What's all this *tsouris*?" Moishe said, shouldering in between them. "Don't you know what 'over' means, Ronny? I thought you young punks knew everything."

"We've got no beef with you, Moishe," Albert said. "Shannon's spades roughed us up. Nobody lays hands on me."

"I'm layin' a hand on you," Moishe said, fingering Albert's lapel. "Nice fabric, too. So what you gonna do? Knock an old man around?" He smiled up at Albert, but Mick could feel the chill from three feet away.

"No, it's over for now," Albert said, carefully removing Moishe's hand. "Another time." Backing away, he rejoined the crew at the coffee machine.

"Anytime you feel lucky, sonny," Moishe called after him. "Let's go, Irish. Christ, I can't take you anyplace."

As he held the door open for Moishe, Mick glanced back, meeting Albert's stare. Nothing showed. No anger, no hate. It was like trying to read a fucking statue. But he knew damned well this wasn't over.

□　□　□

Outside, Moishe seemed to deflate, his legs turning to rubber. Mick took his arm. Big mistake. Moishe whacked his hand away with his cane, hit him so hard he nearly broke his wrist.

In the car, Moishe twisted around in the shotgun seat, snaking an Army .45 from the small of his back and his pearl handled straight razor out of his sleeve, slipping them both into his overcoat pockets.

"You said no guns," Mick said.

"Thought they might search you," the old man shrugged. "If they ever frisk me, I might as well start bangin'. I'm dead meat anyway."

"If you don't trust 'em, why are you still with those guys?"

"I got no choice, neither do you. You're in the Outfit for life, which won't be long if you keep fuckin' up. I should've let them pop you."

"Why didn't you?"

"Because they wouldn't stop with you! I brought you in, I'd go too. They say dogs can smell a bitch in heat five miles away. That's how the fuckin' Lucas are with money, Mick. Keeping it from them was as stupid as havin' a black partner. We use spades, we don't mix with 'em."

"Brownie's forgotten more about the club biz than Musso ever knew. And we owe him. You'd be dead if not for him."

"You go behind my back again, you'll wish I was."

"I've got nothing to hide from you, Moishe. Luca took Cooley's and tipped us like waiters. The Casa is Brownie's and mine. We built it. You're almost paid off, but if you want in— "

"Fuck no! You give me enough heartburn as it is. Just keep my vig paid up. But if you jam me up with that crew again, we won't have no sit down about it. I'll fuckin' cap you myself."

"No you won't, Moishe. Admit it. You were bored out of your skull before I came along."

"Fucking mouthy Irish punk," Abrams muttered, shaking his head. But he couldn't quite hide his smile.

□   □   □

The meet at Musso's Pawnshop marked a change for Moishe and Irish Mick. The older man stepped away from the day to day business, leaving Shannon free to operate as long as he kept his payments up.

Mick made damn sure he did. He honored Moishe's deal with the St. Clair crew as well, paying Luca a percentage of The Casa's action the first of every month, resenting every dime of it.

It wasn't chump change, either. During the holidays, business at the club picked up. Then Tika got a surprise Christmas present. "Girl Talk", her first single, jumped from Moishe's ghetto jukeboxes onto local radio station playlists, first in Detroit, then spread outward to Cleveland and Toledo.

In early January, it broke onto Billboard Magazine's Top 100 list. The Black Kat label was too small to market the tune nationally, so Brownie sold the distribution rights to Chess Records in Chicago. The extra hustle from the Chess brothers' sales crew got "Girl Talk" radio play across the midwest; Naptown, Cincy and K.C., then onto the east coast, Philly, Boston, and even New York, climbing the charts the whole time.

To number forty-six. Where it peaked for a week, then began sliding back down again, finally falling off the charts in February without cracking the Top Forty.

Still, it was a promising start for a new singer on a new label. And a very hectic time. With Mick and Martika scrambling from city to city to promote the record, Cephus and Aldo took over street collections while Brownie worked double shifts to keep both The Casa and his own club humming.

Her brief brush with success only made Tika hungrier for more. Rehearsing long hours at the club, she sharpened their act, working in new songs as fast as she could write them. With the Chiffons and the Crystals scoring Top Five hits, Tika was convinced she was only a song away from the big time.

But her luck wasn't contagious. Varnell Mack and the Sultans of Soul had been in the same game a dozen grueling years, working freebies for local DJs, promoting their tunes on the chitlin' circuit, without scoring even a modest hit.

As The Casa Mayor's house group, they'd become hometown heroes in Detroit, drawing sellout crowds night after night. But none of their records made the leap from Moishe's jukes to radio. 'Too rough,' the DJs told Brownie. A polite way of saying 'too black.'

Jealousy would have been natural, but it never came up. Varnell and the Sultans reveled in Martika's success, proud as new parents. They took it as proof that lightning could strike, even in the ghetto. And worked all the harder to score a hit of their own.

Be careful what you wish for.

CHAPTER 41

March 8, 1964

"What would you think about having a child?" Martika asked. They were in the studio kitchen. Tika at the stove in her robe, barefoot, whipping up breakfast. Mick was in pajama bottoms, sipping coffee as he scanned the Detroit News, trying to wake up.

He was wide awake now. Groping for a proper answer. And realizing the time for one had already run out.

"That's what I thought," she said.

"Whoa, cut me some slack, babe. I was working the street till three in the morning, just crawled out of bed. What brings this on?

"What do you think brings it on?"

"Okay...." Sometimes talking with this woman was like sparring with Joe Louis. Blindfolded. "How long have you known?"

"I don't know yet, not for sure. But my flow is late and I'm usually pretty regular. I've never been this late before, Mick. So I'm asking."

"Okay, I...honestly? I don't know. I think kids are great, I just never really— "

"You thought I was too old?"

"No," he said *very* carefully. "It's not like that. Things have been smokin' along so well, I haven't had time to think of much else. The club is doing business seven nights a week, your records are breaking onto the national charts, I guess I never— "

"Forget it, lover," she snapped, cutting him off. "It's my problem. I'll take care of it."

"Slow down, lady. I didn't say anything like that!"

"You didn't say anything at all, Mick. As usual. And as usual, you sayin' nothin' says a whole lot."

"Not this time, it doesn't. You...caught me by surprise. Do you want this baby?"

"Yes," she said flatly, her eyes locked on his. Not a shadow of a doubt.

"Okay then."

"Okay? *Okay?* What the hell does that mean?"

"It means... okay. Yes. If you want the baby, we'll have it."

"Oh *hell* no!" she said, slamming the skillet down. "You're not laying this on me! You'd best think this through, white boy. Our baby will be brown, you know that?"

"And I've suddenly got some big problem with brown?"

"Not now, maybe. But babies change things. You gonna take us to visit your kin out in Ecorse?"

He hesitated. "No. Probably not."

"I didn't think so."

"It's got nothing to do with the baby. Most of 'em quit speaking to me when I went inside. They grew up poor white in Mississippi, Tika. They can't change."

"You did."

"I grew up with black people."

"In Ecorse? Freakin' Billytown? How many brothers were in your school?"

"I didn't grow up in Ecorse, babe, I grew up in jail. Plenty of brothers there. Look, I don't want to fight about this, Tika. If you want this baby, then I do too. Simple as that."

"Nothing with us is ever simple," she said, turning away.

And it wasn't. Living with Martika was the finest time of Mick's life.

Street smart and talented, she was the hottest lover he'd ever had and the age difference and flashes of racial friction between them only cranked up their passion. They were in love with each other and the music and the action and he was still young enough to think he could fuck or fight his way through anything.

But Tika was right. A child would change things. He only had one ancient aunt who was even speaking to him. His mother's sister. He sent her money at Christmas, took her to lunch now and again. But he had no illusions about her. Flora Mackey was a Mississippi redneck who said 'nigger' as casually as 'pass the salt.'

He tried to picture himself taking Martika to visit Aunt Flora with a brown baby in his arms. Or maybe he'd pop into Scotty's Diner, show off the kid to his high school buddies. Right. That'd go over big. Still, if Tika wanted a child, he'd have to find a way to make it work.

But then, he didn't have to.

In early April, after a sold out show at The Casa, Martika started bleeding in her dressing room. Mick rushed her to the emergency room at Henry Ford.

Later, out in the hallway, an elderly doctor told Mick it had been a near thing, a few minutes more and they might have lost them both. Martina was weak from blood loss, but barring complications, she'd recover. As he turned away, the old doc paused, and almost as an afterthought, said, "I'm sorry for your loss, Mr. Shannon."

"Right," Mick managed. "Me too. So, um, what... ?"

"The child was a girl," the doc said. "A daughter, stillborn. She simply... came too early to survive. I'm very sorry."

Mick didn't say anything to that. There was nothing *to* say.

In the beginning, he wasn't even sure he wanted her. But now, her death felt like a piece of his soul had been torn away.

He couldn't even imagine how Tika must be feeling.

She'd been desperate for this child, bled for it, nearly died for it. And he wondered if any part of what they had together, could survive this loss.

Or if their love affair would be buried with the child Martika could never cradle in her arms, or nurse, or sing to.

Or...

Anything.

CHAPTER 42

Sitting on a gray vinyl couch in the Henry Ford waiting room, his head in his hands, Mick sensed a sudden tension in the room. A rustle, people shifting, nervously.

He glanced up. Cephus Jessup had stepped in, filling the doorway. The big man jerked his head, motioning Mick outside.

"How's our girl doin', Irish?"

"She's resting. They've got her pretty heavily sedated. What's wrong, Ceef?"

"I don't know, but somethin's up, Mick. You need to see some people. They won't talk to me or Aldo. Only you."

"What people?"

"Maceo and Fatback, for openers. Might be more, we're still in the middle of the route."

"I— can't leave here now, Ceef."

"Man, I wouldn't bother you at such a dark time 'less it was dead serious. You need to handle this, Mick. Personal."

◻   ◻   ◻

Marching down the alley to Fatback's joint with Aldo and Cephus, Mick hunched his shoulders against the wind off the Rouge River, forcing himself to keep to a walk. He felt like charging. Mad enough at the world to smash his fist through a fucking wall.

A gray day, the leaden overcast trapping the stench from the auto plants over the city. Rain coming on, charcoal skies matching Mick's mood.

The loading docks in the center of the block looked abandoned. Trash cans, torn cardboard boxes scattered around. Windows blacked out. Yet Mick felt eyes on them, knew they were being watched. Maybe over shotgun sights.

Trotting up the cast iron staircase that led up to the second story warehouse, Mick rapped twice on the metal freight door. Then twice again. And waited.

The peephole winked as someone inside checked him out, then Bass, Fatback's Black Muslim bouncer opened the door. As tall as Cephus, but lankier, looking very dapper in his black suit, white shirt, red bow tie. A sawed off Winchester twelve gauge pump gun cradled in his arms.

"Mr. Shannon," Bass nodded politely, showing them in. "I know y'all are strapped, so I'd appreciate it if nobody does anything sudden. Things are a trifle tense up in here."

"Looks like it," Mick said. Across the dance floor, Moishe's jukebox was on its face, smashed glass scattered around it. Fatback was on his usual stool at the end of the bar, all three hundred fifty pounds of him cased in a wine velvet leisure suit. A nickel plated .38 on the counter beside his beer mug.

"We left the box where it fell," Fat said. "Figured y'all best see it that way."

"What happened?"

"Two white guys come in around three-thirty this morning. Took a table near the dance floor, ordered up. One of 'em comes over, ax me if I'm the owner. I say yeah, next thing, the jukebox crashes over, them honkies got pieces out, coverin' the room, plus two more who already here, settin' off by theirselves."

"Stickup?"

"That's what I figured, but the guy says I need a new juke and he'll supply it. Says you and Moishe are out of business."

"News to me. You get a name?"

"He made damn sure I did. Savuh— Fat glanced at Bass for help.

"Savarese," the Muslim finished. "Philip Savarese. From Chicago. I've heard the name before."

"Where?"

"Benton Harbor. I have a cousin there, this same line of work. The Chicago Outfit moved in last fall. Buried a few people. The town's theirs now. So is Lansing, pretty much."

"But not Detroit," Aldo put in.

"Not yet, maybe, but they comin'," Fat said. "Look, I ain't forgettin' Moishe backed me when I opened this joint, but this thing with the jukes is between y'all and them Chicago guineas. I hope it works out for ya, Mick, but I ain't about to get caught in the middle. And I damn sure can't afford to pay you both."

"You're paying me today, Fat," Mick said flatly. "Because you fuckin' owe Moishe today. How you handle Chicago is your lookout."

Fat glanced at Bass, then at the nickel .38 on the counter.

"Don't even think about it," Cephus said.

"Hell, brother, I *got* to think about it," Fat countered. "I owe y'all, sure 'nough, so I'll pay you. Today. But them guineas said they'd have a new juke in here next week. So here's how it's gone be, Mick. Next week, I pay the jukebox king, whoever the fuck it is. You boys got a problem with that, let's have it now."

Bass racked his shotgun, making his point.

"No problem," Mick said, "We'll handle it."

"You'd better," Fat said evenly, sliding the envelope across the counter. "Won't be no more of these till it's settled."

"I believe your partner knows these men," Bass murmured to Mick, as he let them out.

"Moishe knows them?"

"No, your other partner, Leo Brown. The Chicago Outfit owns clubs in Idlewild, The Regency's one of them. Brownie manages that club, doesn't he?"

□   □   □

Mick sent Cephus back to Henry Ford. Wanted someone on hand in case Martika came around and needed anything. He put Aldo back on the street to make collections, pick up whatever information he could.

Mick hadn't been to Brownie's Lounge for awhile, but he remembered the first time he walked into the place. The jukebox playing blues, Carolina's smile, then cold steel at the back of his neck.

Not today though. John Lee Hooker's trio was set up on Brownie's small stage, rehearsing. The big shouldered bluesman on guitar, Tiny Little on bass, and a young harmonica player Mick didn't recognize. No drums. None needed. If you can't feel the rhythm of John Lee's size thirteen Florsheims stomping the floor, better lay down. You must be dead.

Carolina flashed him her grand piano grin, pointed him back to Brownie's office. But Mick still checked the men's room as he passed. Empty.

Brownie was on the phone at his desk, in shirtsleeves and a robin's egg blue silk vest, reading an order list to a supplier.

"How's Martika?" Brownie asked, muffling the phone against his shoulder.

"The same."

Brownie nodded, reading Mick's face. "Call you back," he said abruptly, then hung up the receiver. "What's up?"

"You tell me. Do you know a guy named Savarese? From Chicago?"

"Philly? Sure. For years. He's muscle for the Chicago Outfit. A collector, like you are for Moishe, but on a...bigger scale." Brownie bridged his fingertips, watching Mick over them.

"Bigger how?"

"You work the turf inside 8 Mile with Aldo and Cephus. Philly's got a full crew, five, six guys. He works whole towns."

"Like Idlewild?"

"The Chicago mob owns clubs in Idlewild, sure. The Regency, for one."

"So you work for this Savarese?"

"No, the Fischetti brothers own the Regency and two other clubs, Philly just collects for 'em. An underboss? Is that what you call it?"

"I wouldn't know, he's your buddy. Heard from him lately?"

"He stopped by a few days ago. Told me I'd be getting a new jukebox."

"He told Fat the same thing. Trashed his juke. I see yours is still standing."

"Like I said, Philly and I know each other."

"So do we. Or I thought we did. Funny, I don't recall you ever mentioning how tight you were with the Chicago Outfit."

"I'm not. I'm only hired help. I manage their club in Idlewild on summer weekends. It has nothing to do with our business here."

"It does now."

"I know. Ain't been thinkin' of much else the last few days."

"Trying to pick the winning side?"

"It's not like that," Brownie said, "but Phil's got five guys in his crew, all of 'em serious muscle. I don't know how many you and Moishe can raise but if I had to lay odds...?"

"You're siding with them?"

"No. I'm stuck where I am. On the damn fence. If I side with you against them, they'll kill me, Mick. It's as simple as that."

"And you think I won't?"

"Moishe might, not you. You'd do somebody in a fight to save your ass. But I don't think you'd do a friend over money."

"A friend would've given me a heads up about this."

"You've been at the hospital, with a whole lot on your mind."

"I've got a lot more now, but it's okay. If Savarese wants trouble, I'm definitely in the mood. But after today, don't count on friendship savin' your ass, Brownie. When the shit comes down? You better get behind that fence of yours. And hide."

CHAPTER 43

"Did you call this meet, Moishe? Or did Luca?"

"My idea," Moishe said. He was in the Lincoln's back seat, Aldo driving, Mick riding shotgun. Literally. A sawed-off twelve-gauge double with ten inch barrels under the front seat, loaded with double ought buckshot. "Trouble like this Savarese might work for us," Moishe continued. "Get all us back to workin' together."

Aldo took the exit road that circled Troy/Oakland Airport, a commercial field for commuter flights too small to qualify for Metro or Willow Run.

Aldo slowed as they approached a fenced-off hangar and freight yard, a man on either side of the chain link gate. No weapons showing but both men were wearing overcoats. Hands in their pockets.

Stepping to the car as Aldo rolled up, they looked Moishe and Mick over, then waved them through.

Aldo parked the Premiere in front of a hangar. A dozen cars already there, mostly Cadillacs or Lincolns. One Jag XKE, a two-seat, Brit roadster painted racing green. Mick paused to admire its lines, sleek as a 30/30 bullet.

"Stay with the car," Moishe ordered Aldo. "Keep your eyes open."

Mick waited as Moishe levered himself out of the back seat with his cane. Didn't offer a hand this time, but he shortened his pace as they walked to the hangar, Moishe shuffling along, leaning on his stick with every step.

"John's smart, meeting out here," Moishe panted. "Whole area's fenced in, with alarms. You can see anybody comin' a mile away."

Moishe was wired up, alert and animated, eager for a Family reunion. Mick didn't trust the Luca crew, but kept his doubts to himself. Bottom line, they were paying Big John's crew for protection and they damn sure needed some help.

Collections were behind, customers stalling for time or ducking payments altogether as Savarese's bunch muscled their way along 8 Mile into the inner city. Philly was operating openly, like he already owned Moishe's turf. And maybe he did.

In the hangar, the thugs around the coffee machine fell silent as Moishe and Mick walked in. Mick recognized faces from Musso's crew at the St. Clair Club, but there were others he'd never seen before. A few nodded at Moishe, the rest just looked them over.

The inner circle was at the back of the room, grouped around a conference table. John Luca, Charlie Musso, Albert Luca and Ronny Ducatti, plus three older men in suits Mick'd never seen before.

Moishe knew them, though. Went around shaking hands like a Shriner at a convention. The strangers were from upstate. Sal Benedetto from Pontiac, Jake Tricante from Saginaw, Jimmy Scotti from Flint. All Moishe's age or near enough. Last of the old guard, with crews of their own.

Luca called the meet to order, sitting at the head of the table like a prince. Mick stood at Moishe's shoulder. Albert took a similar stance, standing behind his uncle in a dark suit and designer sunglasses, his arms folded.

"You know why we're here," Luca began. "Phil Savarese's crew is muscling onto Moishe's turf inside 8 Mile. Some of you know Philly, the rest know his rep. He's a made guy, a captain under the Fischetti brothers in Chicago, plus he's got his own things going in Gary and Benton Harbor."

"What does Chicago say?" one of the older guys asked.

"Bruno Fischetti claims they know from nothing," John shrugged.

"Says anything Philly's doing is on his own."

"Which the lyin' cocksucker would say, either way," Moishe rasped, earning a few nods from the others.

"Phil's always been ambitious," Scotti said. "But from what I hear he's a good earner. Not wild, not a cowboy."

"Which means the Fischettis are most likely backing him," Luca conceded. "But if so, they're keeping it off the books. So far, Savarese's using his own crew, five guys we know of, maybe a few more we don't."

"Serious people, though," Musso put in.

"So are we," Sal Benedetto said. But Pontiac Sal didn't look serious to Mick. Looked fat. Four hundred pounds and four-eyed, tinted bifocals thicker than Moishe's. "I say we take down this fuck," Sal wheezed. "Send him back to Chicago in a box."

"And if the Fischettis are backin' him?" Musso asked. "We can't start up with Chicago, Sal, they got a fuckin' army."

"The feds are already crawlin' up my ass over the unions," Scotti said quietly. "We start a fight, we could all end up in cells next to Hoffa."

"The blacks want no part of it," Jake Tricante from Saginaw offered. "They figure if we kill each other off, they'll take over our territory."

"Nobody's taking a square inch of my ground, Jake," John Luca snapped. "Not the blacks and not Philly. He wants our turf, we'll bury him in it!"

"Actually, he's not taking *our* turf, exactly," Albert said coolly. "In Gary and the other towns, Philly's kept to the ghettos. Dope, protection, jukes. Strictly the black trade. Is 8 Mile worth a war with Chicago?"

"It's my damn territory!" Moishe protested.

"But it doesn't have to cost you anything," Albert countered. "With a five man crew, Savarese isn't a serious threat. Squeezing the blacks is all he can do. Have your boy Shannon whack the first shine who stalls and the rest will fall in line. If they want to pay Philly too, that's their lookout. Some are paying both sides already."

"It beats going to war," Musso agreed.

"Not a chance," John said flatly. "If we let Savarese muscle in, we'll be hip deep in those Chicago fucks. We need to send Don Bruno a message. Philly's gotta go and that's it. I want him dead."

"Then let Moishe handle it," Albert said. "If we all rip into Savarese, Chicago can claim *we* started a war. But if Moishe does him, it's a turf thing between two captains. The cops don't give a damn about Darktown. That'll be the end of it."

"You want me to take on Savarese alone?" Moishe protested. "That's nuts!"

"You didn't have no trouble goin' in the club business on your own," Musso spat. "Or keepin' back our share till we busted your balls about it."

"That's old news, Charlie," Luca said firmly, "but Albert's got a point. It's Moishe's turf and he's buried more guys than Forest Lawn. How about it, Moishe? Can you take this asshole?"

"I can loan you some people if you're short," Musso offered.

"I've had all the help from you I can afford, Charlie," Moishe said bitterly. "Shannon thinks he owns my territory already. We'll see if he can hold onto it."

"That's it, then," Luca nodded. "Savarese goes, Moishe handles it. Any other business?"

□   □   □

"What's your beef with Albert?" Moishe asked quietly. They were in the Lincoln, Aldo at the wheel, Mick in front, headed back into Motown.

"I don't have one, he does," Mick said over his shoulder. "I blew him off once, about capping a guy, and Brownie ran him out of The Casa."

"I heard his beef that night was over your woman, Martika what's-her-name, the singer? I hear she's in the hospital. How's she doin'?"

Mick swiveled in his seat to stare at the old man.

"Think I lasted this long being stupid?" Moishe asked. "I still walk the neighborhoods, talk with a few brothers. Know what else I hear?"

"No."

"I hear a lotta talk about Moishe's boy. Funny they call you that. Not the Irish boy or Irish Mick. Moishe's boy. The jukebox king who makes 8 Mile sound like one big party. Them Sultans singin' in every bar on the Corridor. And makin' money like he U.S. mint. Maybe that's why Albert hates you. Jealousy. It must be something serious, because he definitely wants you dead."

"What are you talking about?"

"Savarese won't settle for my turf," Moishe snorted. "He wants it all. And fuck what Don Bruno says, Chicago's backing Philly, they just ain't ready to show their hand yet. Savarese's starting in Darktown because he knows we're thin on the ground there. How do you suppose he knows that?"

Mick thought of Brownie, but said nothing.

"Big John probably figures Philly will pop us, then they'll cut a deal to split up my action between him and Albert. John's been skimmin' the unions so long he thinks everything's negotiable. But Philly's a street hood. He don't cut deals, he just takes. He'll burrow in like a blood tick and suck Motown dry a block at a time. What Albert said about some people paying us and Savarese both, is that true?"

"I think so, yes."

"But how would Albert know that? Does he have contacts down here?"

Again, Mick considered Brownie. "None I know of."

"Me neither. But there's another way Albert could know about those double payments. From Philly."

"I don't follow."

"They could be working together. Albert helps Savarese take my territory, then together they whack John out and split the city. It's a smart move. That's why Philly's comin' on so strong. He thinks we're all alone."

"We are alone, Moishe. You just saw to that."

"Use your head, Mick. Do you really want Musso or Albert standing behind you in a fight? This way, we got an edge."

"What edge?"

"Me. Albert promised Philly it'd be easy. He's like you, thinks I'm a fuckin' dinosaur. But them big lizards were bad sumbitches. And I'm still worth any five punks like Albert. Or you."

Mick stared at the old man, wondering if he'd lost it completely.

"I don't mean in no street fight, junior. Wars get won up here," Moishe smiled, tapping his temple. "Chicago tried to muscle us once before, back when the Purple Gang was mostly Jewboys. After the feds put Capone away, Nitti sent word Chicago wanted a piece of our action. Or else. Chicago had an army in them days. No way we could win a fight with them and we all knew it. So Nitti sent three guys to work out a deal."

"What happened?" Aldo asked.

"Harry Kirsch and Sol Wenner met their train, treated 'em like big noise, even carried their damn bags for 'em. The second they were in the car, *bam, bam!* Harry caps all three. Sol wrapped their heads in hotel towels to keep 'em from bleedin' on the upholstery, then we ran 'em straight over to Lipinski's."

"The funeral home?"

"Piled 'em into double decker coffins, Aunt Goldie on top, Joe Chicago in the false bottom. Buried 'em Orthodox, the same day at Mount Zion. No bodies, no investigation, no nothin'," Moishe said, chortling at the memory. Aldo and Mick exchanged a glance.

"Nitti never figured it out?" Aldo asked.

"Hell yes, he knew somethin' happened, but he didn't know what! And we were real polite. 'Your guys never got here, Mr. Nitti. Don't know where they got to, Mr. Nitti. Send us a few more.' Only nobody wanted to come. Nitti had no idea how strong we were or what was up with us. In time, the whole thing went away."

"Savarese isn't coming on a train," Mick said. "He's already here."

"I didn't say I had it all figured. But I know how he works. He'll cap a local everyone knows first, like Big Maceo or Elmo Suggs. Scare hell out of everybody, make an example to 'em. Then he'll come after you. Might not even bother with me."

"And you know this how?"

"It's what I'd do," Moishe shrugged. "Us dinosaurs been around a long time."

"Okay, what do we do?"

"We stay out of sight. Duck and run, keep moving. Try to find Philly before he finds us."

CHAPTER 44

Staying out of sight wasn't difficult. For the next three nights Mick slept on a sofa in the waiting room at Henry Ford. Not that it mattered. Tika was so doped up she barely knew who he was. And she wasn't talking at all. Not to him, anyway.

During the day, he joined Cephus and Aldo to make collections, all three of them strapped, keeping their faces on the street, reminding folks who they owed. But varying their routes, carefully scouting out every location before going in.

The regulars paid, but even motor-mouths like Maceo Willis and Elmo Suggs had little to say. Clearly couldn't wait for them to be gone.

The beef between Moishe's boy and the Chicago crew was in the wind. Store-keeps, pimps, even alley winos knew a war was coming, sure as baby Jesus. Nobody wanted to get caught in the crossfire.

Brownie continued working days at his Lounge, running The Casa *Mayor* at night. An obvious target because he was Mick's partner, Brownie was on edge twenty-four/seven, but especially at The Casa.

He doubted Phil would come at him personally. Brownie knew him by sight, knew Red McGee and Gus Buono, too. There were guys in Phil's crew Brownie'd never seen, but they wouldn't be difficult to spot. Philly didn't work with brothers and Red was the only Irishman. That left five tough looking' Chi-town Dagos, packin' iron. Inside 8 Mile, they might as well wear signs.

But the week crawled past with no sign of Philly or his crew. If they were collecting in the ghetto, they were timing it to avoid Mick. By Friday, Brownie was wired tight, knowing the trouble was way overdue.

Friday had become a big night at The Casa, standing room only by ten o'clock with a line halfway down the block, party people braving the gusty city winds.

As a favor to Brownie, Florence Ballard from the Supremes was filling in for Martika. The busty diva got a strong response, too. A helluva singer, Flo, but there was only one queen in the Supremes and it was Diana Ross. Fine as a fashion model, Diana had a made-for-radio voice and Barry Gordy in her bed. If Tika stayed gone too long, maybe Flo would jump to Black Kat, take her shot at a solo.

At midnight, the Sultans of Soul were in the middle of their show, the crowd on its feet, dancing in the aisles as the homeboys covered the Contours' "Do Ya Love Me?" Varnell and the Sultans were high on the energy and applause, still hungry from the hard years on the chitlin circuit, sweating through their gold lame` tuxedos. Otis and little Dexter on their knees, pleading for love from the chicks lining the front row.

High in his eagles' nest office, Mick eyeballed every customer who came through the door. Outside, Cephus and Aldo were parked across the street in Mick's old rattletrap Chevy, watching Brownie meeting and greeting customers. Waiting for his signal.

More white faces than usual tonight, Mick noted. Word about the hot new club was spreading through the college crowd at U of Detroit and Oakland. White suburban kids coming downtown to slum, getting hooked on the blues energy. Soul music. Truth music. Nobody covered Pat Boone tunes in The Casa.

Brownie scanned the line again, wondering if he could have missed somebody. Didn't see how. The only white boys in view were college kids or street guys he knew. No strangers, no hoods. No danger that he could see. Still...something kept crawling around under his collar like a spider.

The Sultans were closing out their set with "Motown Mama", the first song they'd planted on the jukes. Had the crowd singing along, knowing the lyrics by heart now. Down front, whoops and howls erupted as a fine brown girl flashed her breasts at burly Otis DeWitt from the dance floor, flustering him so badly he choked on his verse.

Wasting her time, Brownie thought. Otis, Dexter and Varnell all had wives and kids, bore you to death with their pictures. Cleavon Gates noticed her, though. The chubby, cheery bass singer danced over to the girl's side of the stage, egging her on. Four chicks together, two white, two colored. Working girls Brownie'd seen around.

The tall one flashed Cleavon a boob-shot and he went bug-eyed, rolling on the floor as the crowd roared its approval. Never a dull set with the Sultans.

Closing their show with a group bow, they boogied off to a thunder of applause. Came back for a quick encore, then one more. Cleavon coaxing the hookers onstage to dance with him in a high-kicking chorus line.

Jerome finally grabbed the mike, emceeing the Sultans offstage, pointing out the celebrities in the house, Smokey Robinson, Sam Cooke, Mary Wells. Talking the crowd back to their seats.

But not all of them.

"Hey, daddy," the tall hooker said, catching up with Cleavon on his way backstage. "I love a man with a big, deep voice. You big all over?"

"I'm chubby all over," Cleavon grinned. "Wanna check me out?"

"I already showed you mine, show me yours. Come on back here," she panted, leading him into the shadows beside the backstage entrance. "Cindy, come here, cover for us."

"Ain't sure I got enough for two," Cleavon said, getting uneasy.

"Cindy'll keep watch, make sure nobody butts in," Lenore said, squirming her metallic sheath dress off her shoulders, baring her round, brown breasts, her chocolate nipples keeping Cleavon too dazzled to notice Cindy opening the back door.

Until Ronny Ducatti grabbed him from behind, pinning Cleavon's arms, holding him in a bear hug while Albert clamped a hand over the chunky singer's mouth, stifling his scream as he jammed an ice pick up and under his sternum, twisting it, ripping his heart open. Cleavon thrashed helplessly a moment. Then his eyes rolled up and he collapsed, without a sound.

Albert leaned down, scanning his face, then whirled on the girl. "Who the fuck is this guy? I told you to get the damn drummer."

"He's one of the Sultans," she said. "Benjy went the other way, I— "

"Let's go!" Ducatti snapped. "People are coming."

"Fuck!" Albert spat in Cleavon's face, then kicked him in the head, bloodying his cheek before he dodged out the door.

The bass singer flinched at the blow, but didn't really feel it.

He was already gone.

CHAPTER 45

Two a.m. Sunday morning. Fatback's place was nearly empty. Lightnin' Slim onstage, finishing up his last set. Few couples on the dance floor, belly rubbing to Slim's grinder blues. Two college boys from U of D at a table by the dance floor, zoned out on reefer, totally focused on every lick the lanky bluesman played, soaking it up like there'd be a pop quiz afterward.

Poker game in the corner, three local studs playing each other for beer money, not a sucker in sight. Bass, Fatback's Black Muslim bouncer, looking proper in his black suit, red bow tie, shotgun on his lap, watchful at the door. With nothing much to watch.

Fuck. Fatback stared down at the business card Philly Savarese left him, took a long, hard look at his dying business. And dialed the number.

"Yo, this is Fat. Look here, I got the message last night when y'all did for Cleavon right under Shannon's nose. Everybody in fuckin' Motown got the message. But this shit's bad for business, mister. Mine, yours, everybody's. We got to settle it. Shannon and his partner Brownie both know me. I think I can get 'em up in here for a meet."

Fat held the receiver away from his ear, wincing.

"Hey. *Hey*, motherfucker! I didn't say nothin' about *havin'* no meet! I mean Mick D. will show for one. Maybe Moishe too. What happens when they do is up to you. My joint's on the second floor, long stairway outside. No cover on them stairs. No witnesses, neither. You can set up your crew and wait for 'em. After that, it's on you."

He listened a moment.

"Yeah, Mick comes here regular, Moishe too. Been makin' payments to them bloodsuckers for years. They's a old door at the foot of the outside stairs, looks like it's nailed shut, but it ain't. You can put a man there, couple more across the alley while you wait up in my place with my fine ass as a guarantee. Once they on them stairs, they got noplace to hide."

Fat listened again.

"Hell, set it up right now, you want. I ain't goin' nowhere. But, I ain't no garbage man, neither. Y'all clean up your mess when it's over. And it ain't for free. Afterwards, you and me are done, Mr. Savarese. I don't make no more payments to nobody, and I never see your honky asses again. We clear?"

Took the phone away from his ear, staring at it, shaking his head.

"Double-cross? Hell, I'll be sittin' right here with y'all and I know damn well what'll happen if shit goes south. Like I say, I got your message. Just tell me what time you want Moishe's boy here."

Fat noticed Bass eyeing him as he hung up the phone. "Well, what the fuck, nigger? A man's ass-deep in alligators, what's he s'posed to do?"

Onstage, Slim asked the same question in a blues tune. He got no answer either.

□   □   □

A short, squared off white dude showed at Fat's place twenty minutes later. Red Mike McGee. Banty little fuck in a bomber jacket, fiery orange hair, crazy eyes. Broken nose, face scarred up from the fights he'd lost. Didn't look big enough to scare anybody, but if he was running with Savarese, he had to be bad.

Definitely knew his business. McGee checked out the loading docks first, kicking over the rotting cardboard boxes, looking inside the trash barrels. Jerked out a snub nosed .38 before yanking open the door at the foot of the stairs. Searched the empty room, then trotted up the steel stairway to talk to Fat.

Cheech Lisca, another Savarese gunman, watched every move Mike made from the alley across the loading area. Tall and gloomy as an undertaker, his collar turned up against the night, Cheech never showed himself the whole time. Very careful people, Philly's crew.

After searching every inch of the blind pig, Mike made Fatback walk him through the setup again. Only then did he call Savarese, keeping Fatback beside him the whole time.

Philly was there in five minutes. A hard-eyed bruiser, wooden faced with a dark complexion, deep seams on both sides of his mouth. His bodyguard, Gus Buono, was even bigger than Philly, paunchy, with a brush cut and a neck the size of Bass's waist, small pig's eyes. Mean eyes.

No customers in the place, only Bass, Fat, and Philly's crew. After handing his twelve gauge to Irish Mike, the Muslim doorman took a seat beside Fatback in the corner of the room, the redhead holding Bass's shotgun, covering them both.

Fat was on edge, sweating through his leisure suit. Bass used the quiet time to study his Koran. The weight for whatever the white devils did to each other this night would be on their own heads, not his. He didn't blame Fatback for selling out Shannon. A black man has to look to himself in this world, for surely no one else will. But Bass noticed that his boss was avoiding his glance. Perhaps the fat man felt some guilt after all. There might even be hope for his soul. Assuming either of them lived to see morning.

Bass figured the odds of that were about fifty-fifty. Maybe less. But all is as God wills. He went back to reading his Book.

CHAPTER 46

Mick showed an hour before dawn. Parking the Lincoln on Twelfth, he edged down the alley to the freight docks, alone, his hands deep in the pockets of a black overcoat. An icy mist drifting down, dampening his hair, the vapor of his breath phosphorescent in the dark of the alley.

The meet was set for eight, he came three hours early. Smart, but not nearly smart enough. Watching from the cracked window in Fat's place, Savarese had to admire Shannon's guts.

Knowing he couldn't match numbers with Philly's crew, he walked in alone like a nuncio, an ambassador whose life was guaranteed by the big fucking Luca army backing him up. Fifty men against Savarese's five. But Philly knew Shannon's situation with the Lucas. An outcast hired by a kike. Luca wouldn't back him in a three-legged race.

So coming in alone was a ballsy play, but a fatal fucking mistake.

"He's here," Philly said, motioning Gus Buono to the window. Red Mike stayed put, standing guard over Fatback and Bass with the shot-gun. "Watch 'em close, Irish. This won't take long."

Jerking his piece, a .38 Colt Cobra, Philly waited until he heard the clang of Shannon's footsteps, starting up the steel stairway. Nodding to Gus, he cracked the door open just a hair, his left hand quivering on the knob.

Outside, Mick continued climbing the stairs, but a few steps up, he eased out his .45, then silently wheeled, backing up the stairway now, but maintaining the same rhythm, every step an audible '*clank.*' Mick was keeping count of his steps as he climbed, with his automatic zeroed in on the doorway below. Nine steps, ten. Twelve. He was halfway up when the door at the foot of the stairs burst open and Cheech Lisca burst out, raising a shotgun!

It never got to his shoulder. Mick cut loose the second Cheech cleared the doorway. His first slug caught Lisca low in the chest, punching through to his spine, paralyzing him. Frozen in place, Cheech couldn't move or even breathe as three more slugs ripped into him, each one climbing an inch as the .45's recoil kicked up Mick's aim. The final bul-let blew through just below Lisca's eye socket, spattering the brick wall with blood and brain matter. Cheech crumpled, the shotgun dropping from his numbed fingers as he toppled backward into the alley without breath enough to scream. Dead as a brick when he hit the pavement.

Gunfire exploded from the shadows across the loading area, two rounds slamming into the wall only inches above Mick's head, stone chips stinging his face as he raced back down the stairway. A third shot blew a chunk out of the doorjamb as he leapt over Lisca's body, through the storeroom doorway at the bottom, flattening himself against the wall, sweating, breathless.

Up in the blind pig, hearing the gunfire whacking into the building, fire-haired Mike McGee bolted out of his seat, grinning like a tiger, his eyes alight with combat madness. "Cheech got the cocksucker!" he whooped, thrusting the shotgun in the air. "Come on, Philly, fuck sittin' around like pussies, let's get a piece of this. Finish it!"

Catching the little man's mania, Savarese threw the door open, charging out onto the landing with big Gus Buono close behind him. Both men wheeled to fire down the steps at— nothing. The stairway was empty. A body was sprawled at the foot of the stairs, but he couldn't make out who the hell it was.

'*Fuck!*'

Scrambling down a few steps, Philly aimed his weapon over the railing, peering down into the darkness, desperately trying to spot his guys or Shannon's. He fired two rounds into the body at the foot of the stairs, just to make sure. It jerked with the impact but didn't move. Already dead.

"Arnie! Lisca! Did you get him?"

No answer. And in that instant, Philly got it! Jesus, it was a setup! He'd spread out his crew to ambush Shannon and he'd taken them down one at a time. *Shit!*

"Get back inside!" he yelled at Gus, ducking low as Moishe Abrams stepped out of the alley with a forty-five. Using his cane as a brace, the old man opened fire, coldly aiming every shot.

On the landing, Gus Buono was frantically tugging at the doorknob. Locked! One of Moishe's slugs caught him high in the back, dropping him to his knees, blocking the doorway.

"Philly! Help me!" Gus gurgled, gagging on his own blood, still clawing mindlessly at the door. "It won't open!"

"Get out the way!" Savarese screamed. Kicking Gus aside, he fired three quick rounds into the lock, smashing it to pieces. But as he reached for the knob, the door exploded outward, slamming into his chest like a sledge hammer, smashing him backwards onto the landing.

Dazed, Savarese stared stupidly at the gaping hole in the door, blown out by a shotgun. And knew Red McGee was already dead.

Clutching at the railing, he tried to pull himself to his feet. Couldn't quite manage it. Risked a look down at his mutilated chest, torn open by the buckshot blast, blood gouting from a half dozen punctures, wood splinters sticking out of the gaping wound. God! Legs turning to rubber, he sagged slowly to his knees on the landing.

Feeling a vibration, he turned slowly, found himself staring down the bore of Shannon's forty-five.

"Give it up," Mick said softly. "It's over."

Philly tried to raise his .38 but his arm wouldn't move. Couldn't even feel it anymore. With a groan he slumped against the railing, still clinging to the gun.

"Finish him!" Moishe shouted, limping across the lot.

"No need," Mick said, taking the gun from Savarese's fist. The shattered door banged open and Fatback stepped out, holding Bass's twelve gauge. Holding the muzzle jammed against Buono's chest, he pressed a finger against the big man's carotid artery, feeling for a pulse. Shook his head.

"Who was your inside man?" Mick asked Savarese.

"Fuck you."

"C'mon Philly, what's it matter now? You couldn't risk taking us on unless you knew Luca would look the other way. Who told you? Albert?"

"You'd best answer the man," Fat said, jacking a fresh round into the twelve gauge. "You're sure enough dyin', but it don't have to be easy."

"Fuck the both of ya," Philly gasped, trying to spit at Fatback, doubling over instead, drooling blood, wracked by a spasm of agony.

"My man, you don't want to go out cursin' on folks," Fat said, kneeling beside him. "Just tell me one true thing. Who done Cleavon Gates?"

Philly raised his head, blinking. "Who?"

"Cleavon Gates, motherfucker! The butterball bass singer for the Sultans! My goddamn cousin! Which one of you Dago cocksuckers— ?"

Mick touched his shoulder.

"He's gone, Fat."

Frowning, Fatback leaned in, reading Savarese's face. Nothing. Lights out. But still on his knees, slumped against the rail.

"Goddamn," Fatback said, getting heavily to his feet. "Ain't that somethin'? Even dead that Chicago prick's too mean to fall down."

"What about the one inside?"

"Bleedin' out on my dance floor. We taped carvin' knives under every table before they came. He meant to pop us as soon as Savarese did for y'all, I could see it in his crazy fuckin' eyes. Sometimes I swear Elijah

Muhammad's right, all you white boys are blue-eyed devils from the ice lands."

"I've got brown eyes."

"Fuck your eyes, Shannon. We're even, you and me. So how about you get this white trash out my place? I got a business to run."

"Cephus!" Mick called. "Tell Aldo to bring the Lincoln up. Fat, help me get these two down the steps."

"No problem," Fatback grunted, hoisting up Savarese by his lapels, pitching him over the railing, dropping him twenty feet to the alley floor, his bones crunching at the impact.

"Jesus Christ." Mick said.

"Fuck him and this one too," Fat growled, shoving Gus Buono's heavier corpse under the railing with his foot. But before he could push him over, Cephus trudged into the loading arena, carrying Aldo in his arms. And even at that distance Mick could see the kid was dead, eyes open, sightless. The side of his skull blown away, dripping bloody fluid with every step.

CHAPTER 47

Mick drove the Lincoln, Moishe in the passenger seat, smiling, loose and easy as a sailor after a three-day leave. The big car was riding low, weighted down with Philly, Buono and Lisca in the trunk. Cephus and Brownie were following in Brownie's Studebaker Hawk with Red McGee in its trunk. With Aldo.

"Just like the old days," Moishe mused, chuckling. "Slick as a wet dream."

"Ask Aldo how slick it was."

"Tough luck about the kid, Irish, but in a thing like this, shit happens. All that lead flyin' around, could've clipped you, me, anybody. Better him than us. Have a drink to his luck. That's the only way to look at it."

"We'll have to make arrangements for him— "

"Forget that, Mick. Aldo goes with the rest."

"Damn it, Moishe, he's one of us— "

"And he had bad luck!" Moishe snapped. "Philly goes missing and we hold a funeral for one of our guys, you think Chicago won't add that up? Or the cops? Tell his people he's out of town on business."

"He doesn't have any people."

"Then what the fuck are we talkin' about, Mick? Aldo's gotta go with the others. I'm sorry, but that's it."

"Damn it, Moishe, it's not right!"

"I know," the old man sighed. "At least this'll shut up them fucks at the St. Clair, thinkin' I'm past it."

Mick glanced at him. "We can't tell them, Moishe."

"We have to. John ordered the hit on Savarese, he has to know."

"No. He was part of it, or somebody was. Savarese came straight at us. Wasn't worried about Luca at all. Knew damned well we were on our own."

Moishe was watching him. "Go on."

"He could only know that for sure if somebody was working with him. I'd guess Albert, but it could have been Musso or even Luca himself. Either way, we can't trust them anymore. He could feed Chicago some bullshit story about what happened tonight, and we could still get clipped."

Moishe turned away, smiling.

"What?" Mick snapped.

"Nothing," the old man shrugged. "But you're learning."

□   □   □

Gray dawn was breaking as they rolled into the funeral home lot. Lipinski's was a sprawling, white clapboard building that covered most of a city block, homey as grandma's farm, gingerbread woodwork in the eaves, flowerboxes under the windows sporting cheery plastic tulips.

Two attendants in white lab coats were waiting. Moishe had a word with them, then they expertly shifted the stiffs out of the trunks onto gurneys. Wheeled them inside like it was business as usual. Hell, maybe it was.

"You can take off," Moishe said. "Your spade buddies are makin' young Lipinski nervous. Leave me the car."

"What happens now?" Mick asked. "Double-decker coffins?"

"Nah, Lipinski's crematorium can toast an elephant in two hours. I'll make sure it goes right. Lipinski owes me from the old days but it'll cost us two large."

"You'll have it tomorrow. Look, about Aldo— "

"I'll have somebody say a prayer for him. You wanna watch?"

"No, I have to get back. Hey, Moishe?" But the old man was already limping off after the last gurney.

"Thank you," Mick said. To himself.

Trudging to Brownie's Studebaker, he dropped into the shotgun seat, spent, running on fumes. Looked at the blood spatters on his hands. Wiped them off on his slacks. Cephus was slumped in the back seat, his massive arms folded across his chest. Snoring softly.

"Where to?" Brownie asked.

"The hospital, I guess," Mick said, trying to focus.

"Bad idea." Brownie gunned the Hawk out onto Woodward. "You're so beat they'd probably tie a tag on your toe. Crash at my place a few hours. They won't look for you there."

"Who won't?"

"Albert," Brownie said. "If he hasn't heard what happened already, he will soon. This isn't over, Irish. He'll come after us."

Mick shifted in his seat, reading Brownie's face. "*Us?* What happened to that fence you were sittin' on?"

"I got pushed off it when they did Cleavon. That boy was just a happy little butterball who loved to sing. He had nothin' to do with this shit."

"Philly needed an example everybody would know and the Sultans filled the bill. Thanks to us."

"I'm not so sure it *was* Savarese," Brownie said, frowning. "I didn't see him or any of his guys around the club Friday night. Far as I know, he's never been there. And whoever did Cleavon *knew* the layout, knew about the back door. And why was Cleavon back there anyway? He usually heads for the dressing room after a set."

"A girl was flashing him from the dance floor just before it happened. Maybe she set him up."

"Which girl?" Brownie asked.

"Hell, I can't think. We're all draggin' ass and old Moishe's frisky as a speckled pup."

"His blood's up," Brownie nodded. "Killin' people's what that old man does best. Ought to land himself a job as a hangman. Probably live to be a hundred."

"Feel like I'm a hundred already— "

"Hush!" Brownie said, reaching over to turn up the radio.

"...saddened by the untimely death of Cleavon Gates," the announcer said, "longtime bass singer for the Sultans of Soul. Everybody in the Motor City knows the Sultans, hometown boys who've put a lot of smiles on a lot of faces over the years. All of us here at WCHB wish the Gates family our deepest sympathy. And for the rest of the night, we'll be playing all Sultans, all the time. Starting off with the first single of their new album, 'Jukebox Cadillac.'"

Benjy's drums kicked in, then the bass, then Otis jumped on the vocal: "*Mojo come up from Mobile, drivin' a jukebox Cadillac...*"

"Jesus H. Christ," Brownie said softly. "Cleavon finally got the Sultans some serious airplay."

"The hard way," Mick said bitterly, sagging back in the Hawk's bucket seat, closing his eyes. "Think it was worth it?"

"I don't know," Brownie sighed. "Guess you'd have to ask Cleavon."

CHAPTER 48

"What the hell are you doing?" Mick asked. "You shouldn't be here."

He was right. He had no idea how Martika managed the climb up to the office aerie in The Casa Mayor, but she didn't look like she could manage another inch. Gaunt, with wounded eyes, her Mary Quant A-line dress was hanging on her like a scarecrow rag. She looked exhausted, ten years older than before

"Another day in that room, they'd be talking me down off the roof," she said, easing painfully into the chair by Brownie's desk. "Catch me up, Brownie. This white boy thinks he's doing me a big favor keeping me ignorant. What's happened?"

Brownie glanced the question at Mick, who shrugged. So he told her. The push from Savarese's crew, Cleavon's killing, the payback at Fat's blind pig. All of it. The straight story. Minus the blood.

When he'd finished, she sat silent for a time.

"Aldo," she said softly, shaking her head. "My God." She drew a ragged breath. "This girl you mentioned? The one you think set Cleavon up?"

"Could have," Mick said. "She was flashing her jugs at him just before it happened, wasn't around afterward. Why?"

"Tall girl? Big boobs, hair in a beehive?"

"Lenore," Brownie said, snapping his fingers."

"Who is she?" Mick demanded.

"It sounds like Lenore. Call girl. The night I threw champagne in Albert's face? Lenore was with his blonde buddy."

"Ducatti and Albert," Mick said softly. "It works. All the way."

"Not quite," Brownie said. "Albert's still old man Luca's nephew."

"He kills Cleavon, tries to get us ambushed and gets a walk because he's connected? I don't think so."

"He'll keep," Tika said flatly. "We've got troubles of our own. What about the Sultans? Have they found a replacement for Cleavon?"

"They're not looking," Brownie said. "His funeral's tomorrow, down in Arkansas. Little Rock. Varnell says the Sultans will sing at his service and that's it. They're finished with the business, and with us."

"They can't quit," Tika said.

"They already have, sugar. Varnell said without Cleavon, they got no heart for it. Told me to stay clear of the funeral. Otis and Dexter figure it's partly our fault Cleavon got killed."

"Maybe it is," she said. "But that don't matter now. Call Metro, get me on a plane to Little Rock, Brownie."

"Are you nuts?" Mick demanded. "If you— "

"It has to be me," she snapped, cutting him off. "They won't listen to either of you. Their record's all over the radio but that won't last. They need to get back on the road to push it, or Cleavon died for nothing."

"Are you trying to end up next to him? You're in no shape to go to Arkansas or anyplace else!"

"I'll be okay, Mick. I feel better when I'm moving. Besides, it's not like I have to stay home, chase your pickaninny around the kitchen."

Mick flinched, as shocked as if she'd slapped him.

"Brownie, would you mind stepping out?" Tika sighed. "I need a word with my gentleman friend."

"Yes ma'am."

"What the hell was that?" Mick demanded, when they were alone. "Do you blame me for what happened?"

"I don't know what I think, Mick. I'm still sorting it out."

"Are you quitting me?"

"Don't know that either. You need to understand something. All I ever wanted to do was sing. But since we've been together, I couldn't help thinking I could have more. Have kids. Our kids. And when I got pregnant— "

"Look, I'm sorry about how I reacted. You caught me by surprise, that's all. It wasn't that I didn't want a kid— "

"*Don't!*" she snapped. "It doesn't matter now. Truly. Our baby's lost, and I can't have any more. Ever. I don't know where that leaves us. But right now I need to get back to business. And you have to let me. Because it's all we've got left. Can you do that?"

"Look— " He choked it off, swallowing hard. Reading her eyes. As dead as Philly's. "All right," he said at last. "You do whatever you need to, babe. I'll make the rest of it work."

"Good," she said, rising stiffly. "I have to go home and pack a bag. But there's one more thing you can do for me."

"What?"

"This trouble with the St. Clair? Brownie's right. If you go after Albert, they'll kill you for it, Mick. Luca's got an army. We only have us."

"He did Cleavon. And Aldo. I can't just...let it go."

"Then don't. But I don't give a goddamn about Albert or Cleavon or any of that. Only you. And right now you're angry, so I need you to cool down, you understand? Promise me you won't do anything crazy. *Promise me!*"

He looked away a moment, then nodded. "Okay. Nothing crazy."

"Good. I have to get going. Anything else?"

Damn straight there was. He had a thousand questions. How did she feel? What did her doctors say? Was she coming back to him afterward? They needed to talk, but more than that, he needed to hold her close, to tell her that somehow he'd make everything all right.

She was only a few feet from him, and probably wouldn't turn away. But he knew beyond doubt it would be the wrong move.

"No, nothing else, babe," he said. "Have a safe flight."

CHAPTER 49

Waiting in the lobby of Churchill's Grill, Albert felt a pang of unease. He'd sent Ronny for the car five minutes ago. What was the holdup? He was about to head back into the restaurant when his midnight blue Cadillac rolled up out front.

A pudgy black valet in a red Churchill's blazer opened the rear door and stood aside with a wide smile, his hand out.

Slipping the valet a buck, Albert started to climb in when the fat man suddenly pushed him from behind, thrusting him face-down on the Caddy's back seat. Piling in on top of him, Fatback jammed a knee between Albert's shoulder blades, pinning him while he frisked him expertly, jerking a blunt Beretta automatic out of his shoulder holster. Sitting up, Albert tried to push Fatback off him, caught a backhand across the mouth for his trouble.

"Don't do anything stupid," Mick said, swiveling in the front seat as Brownie gunned the Caddy into traffic on Woodward. "You're already dead, Albert. The only question left is whether you go easy or hard."

"Are you fucking insane, Shannon? Kidnapping me?" Albert's voice was surprisingly calm as he eyed the gun in Fatback's huge fist. "Where's Ducatti?"

"In the bar, answering a bogus phone call. All this trouble with Chicago, traveling with one bodyguard seems pretty stupid. And people keep telling me how bright you are."

"What do you want, Shannon?"

"To blow your fucking head off. My friends are trying to talk me out of it. They say it would be bad for business."

"Your friends are making sense. You should listen to them."

"Is that what you did? Listen to the wrong people? Like Savarese?"

"I don't know what—" Fat slapped him harder this time, snapping his head around, sending his shades flying.

"Listen up, you cockeye punk. Don't waste our time with no bullshit. Savarese *told* us about you before he died. One more lie, I'll blow off both your kneecaps before I pump one up yo' ass for bein' too stupid to live."

As Albert reached for his glasses, Fatback deliberately ground them under his heel. His eyes widened as he met Luca's furious glare.

"Man, no wonder you wear shades all the damn time. That is one ugly fuckin' eye you got there."

Albert touched his mouth gingerly with his fingertips. They came away bloody. "Savarese's dead?" he asked calmly.

"Dead as do-wop," Brownie said. "Told us all of it, though. Including you."

"And you think my uncle will believe a word you say?"

"We don't give a damn what he believes," Mick said. "We know it, that's enough. It'll be enough for Chicago, too. You invited Savarese in, and he ends up dead? They'll think you set him up."

"The Fischettis will know better."

"Maybe, but they'll wonder. Probably want to ask you about it up close and personal. Maybe jam your head in a vise while they ask. Pop out your other eye."

"I'd pay cash money to see that," Fat offered. "Hell, I'd turn the crank my own self."

"Just tell me what you want," Albert said, swallowing.

"I'll tell you what I don't want," Mick said. "I don't want Chicago crews all over Darktown looking for Philly. And as much as I'd like to smoke your ass, I need you alive to avoid a war. So here it is.

"You're going to tell Chicago the feds grabbed Savarese. They'll try to reach him. When they can't, they'll think he might be in custody. And they'll be too busy scrambling to cover their own asses to worry about us."

"The Fischettis have police connections," Albert countered. "It won't take them long to find out the Feds don't have Savarese. Then what?"

"Then back to square one. They'll want to talk to you, only you'll be long gone. You're marked in Motown for doing Cleavon, Albert. The brothers don't give a rip who your uncle is. If you stay in Detroit, you'll get greased, crossing the street, capped in an alley. I don't know how it'll happen, but it will."

"Maybe even in this car," Fat said. "In the next two minutes."

"You're going into exile," Brownie said. "Like Napoleon."

"What?"

"Mr. Brown reads books," Mick said. "His point is, you're leaving town. Permanently."

"And if I don't?"

"Say no and you're dead a second later," Mick said. "Say yes and try to welch, same difference. We'll find you, fuck you up, and put you with Philly."

"This is Moishe's idea, isn't it?" Albert asked. "You're not smart enough."

"If it were up to me you'd be dead already," Mick admitted. "We don't want a war so you get a pass, this one time. But you get out of Detroit, you don't come back. You've got three days to wrap things up, then I'm coming for you. Personally, I hope you're still here."

Albert glanced around the faces in the car, cocking his head to focus more clearly. "All right," he said. "I'll leave Detroit."

"For real?" Fat asked. "Or do you think you can run cryin' to your Uncle?"

"I'm not a fool. I don't have my own crew and if you took out Savarese, I don't like my odds. I've always hated this town anyway, the auto plant stink, the ignorant shop-rat rednecks and blacks. Hell, you're doing me favor, Shannon. L.A.'s wide open, I can make ten times what I have here. Detroit's just another name for Darktown. You can have it."'

"No tears for your pal Savarese?"

"Philly was a crude man, but his methods worked. So do yours, and muscling showbiz types is a lot easier than ripping off the unions. We really should be partners, you know."

"Jesus H. Christ," Fatback said, amazed.

"I'd rather drink battery acid, straight, no chaser," Mick said.

"Your loss," Albert shrugged. "Take me back to the hotel."

"Fuck yourself," Brownie said, slowing the car, pulling over to the curb. "Get out."

"Wait, I don't...have any glasses," Albert said. The first hint of uncertainty Mick'd ever seen in him.

"Man, you best get out this car while you still can, you one-eye fuck," Fat said, opening the rear door, booting Albert out, sending him sprawling in the gutter. As they pulled away, Mick watched Albert in the rear view mirror, getting to his feet, looking around trying to place where he was. Covering his ruined eye with his palm, as though it were still bleeding.

CHAPTER 50

Tika flew back from Cleavon's funeral at the end of the week. Looked gaunt and hollow-eyed as a zombie. Seething with rage. Five days of Jim Crow laws in Little Rock, drinking at 'colored' fountains, using 'colored' johns had shaken her out of the blues, fueling a grim determination to make Cleavon's death *mean* something.

The sign out front of The Casa said *closed for remodeling*. The truth was Brownie closed the club down after Cleavon's killing, hoping the bad publicity would blow over and the press would move onto a new crime. Figuring in Detroit, it wouldn't take long.

It didn't.

A shootout in Dearborn between the DEA and a crew of Latin Kings gang-bangers grabbed all the headlines a few days later. Five bodies hit the street, a fed and four bangers. Cleavon's killing rotated to the back pages, just another unsolved homicide in a town with a casualty rate running just behind the Cambodian killing fields.

Fortunately, the Sultans didn't fade as quickly. "Jukebox Cadillac" was rapidly becoming a regional hit as more radio stations aired the song first for shock value, then kept playing it as their telephone request lines lit up.

The day after Tika flew back from Little Rock, she herded the guys into the club to audition replacements, yapping at their heels like a terrier.

It was a ghoulish business, half audition, half séance. But once they were onstage as a group again, hearing their own music thumping through the sound system, Varnell, Otis and Dexter pulled themselves together like battered fighters answering the bell.

It took a day and a half, listening to a long line of singers, hopeful and hungry singers by turns. Then a skinny kid barely out of his teens took his turn at the mike. Cleavon's cousin, Porter Gates. When the boy cut loose on "Soul Stirrin'", the older men stiffened. Veterans of a thousand smoky dives, they damn well knew the real thing when they heard it. Porter's deep bass voice was richer than Cleavon's and his range extended up to a heartbreaking Billy Eckstine baritone. Varnell hired him on the spot, and though none of the Sultans would admit it, after a week of re-hearsal, they actually sounded better than before. And suddenly, two weeks away from the stage seemed far too long.

After the miracle she pulled off with the Sultans, Brownie quietly stepped aside to let Tika manage the club's entertainment. She clearly had a knack for it and with The Casa, his own lounge and the jukebox business, he had a full plate.

But after listening to her rehearse with her new band, he had second thoughts.

When she wasn't helping the Sultans rebuild their act, Tika was feverishly reshaping her own. But not with new material. She collected a combo of blues men, crude as street corner players, then never actually sang with them. Still weak from the loss of her child, humming along with the band was the best she could do. Brownie doubted she'd be strong enough to sing when the club reopened, and half-hoped she wouldn't. The Casa had a hip, uptown audience now. Singing tired old tearjerkers with a raggedy-ass crew of old timers was a recipe for disaster.

He didn't push her on it, though. The situation was too touchy. And Tika simply wasn't the same girl who'd checked into Henry Ford Hospital the month before. Didn't even look the same. She'd been a strong, energetic Amazon warrior, but now she was a shadow of that woman, gaunt as a gazelle with haunted eyes, with full breasts no child would ever taste. Fierce as a feral cat with tenacity to match.

Mick noted the changes in Tika as well, but was even less able to deal with them. They weren't sleeping together anymore. Weren't talking much, either. Exhausted after a few hours of rehearsal at the club, Martika often crashed on a cot in her dressing room, too drained to make it home. Or so she said.

It didn't matter much. Mick seldom slept there either. The Chicago Outfit might not know *what* happened to Philly, but they knew where he'd disappeared. Whose town, whose territory. If they decided to cap somebody for payback, Mick would top the list.

Albert was an even bigger worry. When Fat told him Savarese was dead, he must have expected to be next. Yet, when they'd grabbed him up, he'd barely blinked. Afterward, he'd dropped out of sight.

Brownie said he was being exiled like Napoleon. But Napoleon came back. Moishe was the coldest motherfucker Mick'd ever known but Albert ran a close second. Too bat-shit crazy to guess what he'd do next.

So Mick kept on the move, making collections with Cephus, letting customers know things were back to normal, but crashing in a different bed every night, leaving The Casa's reopening to Brownie and Tika.

He knew she was safer in the club with people around her. Far apart from him. But he ached for her, especially at night. Missed her amazing body, the quickness of her mind. He had trouble sleeping alone, haunted by dark images he couldn't shake. Savarese dying on his knees. Albert, bewildered on that windy street corner, shielding his scarred eye.

But the most troubling image of all was Martika's baby. And his. A beautiful brown daughter he'd never know. And he wondered if the lost child had destroyed his whole world without ever drawing a breath.

CHAPTER 51

With The Sultans' "Jukebox Cadillac" getting heavy radio airplay, customers were lining up in front of The Casa Mayor an hour before Cephus opened the doors. Some were club regulars, others were reporters and music buffs who'd come to see Detroit's newest rising stars, The Sultans of Soul. And a morbid few were like the gawkers who slow down to stare as they pass a wreck on the road.

Mick was there, but not in the open. Using the back stairs, he climbed to the eagle's nest, to track the action without being seen.

A dynamite night, wall-to-wall crowd. Jerome's house band, The In Crowd, filled the dance floor with their first song, a good sign. They delivered a half dozen upbeat tunes, the perfect opener for what could have been a somber night.

Mick expected Martika to go on next, but she didn't.

The Sultans of Soul came on without an opening act, taking the stage with a vengeance. The four showmen didn't give a damn why the people came. They had a packed house, their first hit song, and a crackling charge of angry energy to burn. Using every vocal trick, dance step and wisecrack they'd learned on their long, hard road, the Sultans played the capacity crowd like a piano. Two songs into their set, they owned the house.

An uneasy hush fell over the room when Porter Gates stepped up to sing Cleavon's solo, but the kid was too green to notice. It was his chance to shine and he went for it, belting out the tune with such gusto that the last doubters leapt on board the bandwagon. Even the snarkiest critics had to admit it, The Sultans of Soul were back, and better than ever.

A thunderstorm of applause called the Sultans back for two encores, and even then, the din was so deafening that Varnell led the group out to do one final unaccompanied chorus of "Amazing Grace" for Cleavon Gates, their fallen friend. It was a stunning performance. In their fifteen tough years together, it was the strongest set the Sultans had ever played.

Which left Martika in an impossible situation. No one could follow the Sultans' show. Not on this night. Brownie hustled backstage to advise Tika to delay her opening, to let the In Crowd do another set— but he was too late.

On the darkened stage, her scruffy combo of broken-down blues men were already setting up their battered gear, with applause from the Sultans' set still ringing from the rafters. No announcement, no warm up. The old-timers kicked off the opening tune quietly, dropping into a deep blue groove.

When the spotlight found Martika at the microphone a simple black sheath, the crowd barely noticed. But as she began to sing, the buzzing room quieted, then fell utterly silent. Listening.

This wasn't pop music or even soul. It was raw, inner city blues, a bloodline that flowed all the way from the Mississippi Delta to the mean streets of Detroit. A song with so much heartache compressed into every note, it was almost painful to hear. The lyrics were brutally simple, love and loss, but they really didn't matter. Tika's voice was a true instrument now, keening the melody. She could have sung it in French, or Swahili, and the audience would have understood every single word.

Watching from his office, Mick could hardly breathe. Felt his eyes stinging. Because he knew where this song was coming from, how personal it was. If Tika had stripped naked onstage, she couldn't have revealed any more of herself than she already had.

He ached for her. And feared for himself as well. Afraid her pain was so deep that she might be forever broken, and what they'd shared together was lost and gone. But he was even more terrified for her, because he didn't think this crowd could grasp a tenth of what she was showing them.

And he was right.

At the end, the very worst happened.

Nothing.

As the last notes died away, one of the guitarists shuffled his feet. It was the only sound in the utter stillness. Then a woman on the second tier stood up, and began to applaud. And in seconds, the whole audience rose, joining in. No cheers, no whistles, only applause. And hardly a dry eye in the house.

Working the door, Brownie was as shaken as the rest. He'd seen something like it once before. A few years before, a drugged-out Miles Davis stumbled onstage at Baker's Keyboard Lounge to play "My Funny Valentine", alone, on a borrowed cornet. And won the crowd exactly as Martika had. By sharing an essential human truth. Life can be sweet but pain is the price. And our only choice is to go on. Or not.

The night belonged to the Sultans, a triumph they'd earned with years of sweat, struggle, and even blood. Martika's part of it was much smaller, but it wasn't the culmination of anything. It was a beginning.

A coronation.

In a single month, Murder City had a new jukebox king. And a new Queen of the Blues.

CHAPTER 52

After its smash grand reopening, every night at The Casa looked like New Year's Eve. Crowds lined up down the block, electricity in the air. A *very* mixed audience now, party people coming for the Sultans of Soul, blues buffs for Martika, and throngs of college kids from U of D, U of M and Oakland just because The Casa was hotter than a two dollar pistol, *the* place to boogie down in Detroit.

As weeks turned into months, the crowds grew younger and whiter, becoming a true mixed-race audience in a segregated city. Wild crowds, partying like there was no tomorrow.

For some of them, there wouldn't be. With the draft expanding to keep pace with Viet Nam's body counts, young men were living with bullseyes on their backs. A feeling Mick knew well.

Mid-February, the week after Valentine's Day, he spotted a '59 Buick estate wagon, white over blue, parked up the street from Maceo's bodega, engine idling. Glancing both ways, he edged up to the car, slid into the shotgun seat. Moishe was at the wheel, wearing a new cashmere overcoat, same old snap brim hat.

"Hey Moishe, what's up?"

"News. Big John called me to the St. Clair Club yesterday. He got a call from Chicago saying Savarese dropped out of sight. The Fischettis heard he might be in federal custody. Wanted to know if we knew anything."

"And?"

"What do you think? I told John I knew from nothing."

"Think he believed you?"

"Why not? I'm just an old man, need a cane to get around. Us takin' out Savarese's crew ain't even on his radar. That's my news, what's yours?"

"What do you mean?"

Moishe shifted around to face him, reading him like a mark. A damned uncomfortable feeling. "John says Albert sold his Detroit clubs and jumped out to the west coast. Says he's already muscling into the entertainment scene out there."

"Good for him."

"That's it? You gonna lie to my face now, Mick? Like you didn't know about this?"

"After the Savarese thing, I had a talk with Albert," Mick admitted.

"You muscled John's nephew without asking me? Without even givin' me a fuckin' *heads up?*"

"I didn't want to put you in the middle."

"Bullshit! You were worried I might side with John and them. You didn't trust me!"

"I don't trust anybody much, Moishe. I had a good teacher."

"I told you what'd happen if you went behind my back again. I should fuckin' cap you right here."

"Bullshit, Moishe. All this *agita*'s got you in hog heaven."

"And you're a punk ass fuck," Moishe growled, but with no real heat. "I met Dragna once, you know. Back in the day."

"Who?"

"Jack Dragna, you ignorant shit. Boss in L.A. since the forties. Used to run gambling boats outside the three mile limit till the feds shut him down. Hung himself back in '57, or so they said. Since then, the coast is pretty much wide open. A bright guy like Albert should do fine out there."

"Good. Maybe he'll stay on."

"I wouldn't count on that."

"Why not? He hates Detroit."

"He hates you more. Ever hear what he did to the kid that fucked up his eye?"

"I heard he squashed his head in a vise. So?"

"Albert's got a serious mean streak. Even as a kid, he'd go crazy on anybody who crossed him. He hides it better now, but down deep, he's the same psycho bastard. You've fucked him up twice now. He'll come back at you for that."

"If he does, I'll give you that heads up. Promise."

"Screw that, Mick. If he comes at you, bury his ass deep, keep your mouth shut after. I don't even want to hear a rumor about it. Now get your butt back on the street. No reason Albert has to make *all* the fuckin' money."

But for the first time in Mick's life, money wasn't a problem. The Casa's nightly crowds quickly reloaded his bankroll, bigger than before. With the Sultans' *Jukebox Cadillac* a solid Top Ten hit and Martika's solo career on the rise, Black Kats Records was building some buzz in the music business as well.

Black singers too raw for mainstream studios were drawn to the up-

start young label. So were roughneck white rockers from rust belt factory towns, Detroit, Toledo, Cleveland.

Within months of the Sultans' first hit, Tika and Brownie had signed
on a small roster of raw talent and began recording them at The Casa,
after hours, shooting for a live, rough-edged sound. The records appeared
on Moishe's ghetto jukeboxes first, then on local radio stations. None
of the singles were national hits, but local DJs began airing the new music late at night as the songs attracted a cult following among college kids.
Black Kats records lacked the polish of Berry Gordy's Motown pop, but
its artists had attitude and its raw sound crackled with an angry energy
that felt right for the times. Edgy music, played by dangerous people.

The Sultans' second hit single, "Motown Mama" jacked the label's profile even higher, and soon other Black Kats artists began cracking the pop
music charts.

Mick kept a close eye on the music end of the business, but he worked
from the shadows, well aware that payback from Savarese's people or
the St. Clair could come anytime and wreck everything Tika and
Brownie were trying to build. He kept to the shadows, avoiding the
crowds in The Casa's main room, watching the shows from his darkened
office and overseeing the after-hours recording sessions the same way,
using the back stairs, haunting his own club like the Phantom of the
Opera.

He saw Martika once or twice a week, always on business. He seldom
slept in their room at the old studio and Martika hadn't been there since
losing her baby.

As his income increased, Mick paid down most of his debt to Moishe.
But he kept their loan open and kept the old man's money on the street,
earning for him. The vig was Moishe's last connection to the 8 Mile life,
and Mick knew the old man needed it. And he still needed Moishe.

Articles about The Casa and Black Kat were popping up in *Billboard*
and *Variety* now as reviews of Black Kats records earned ink around the
country. When the business section of the Detroit *News* took note, so
did the crew at the St. Clair Club.

John Luca called Moishe in to meet with Charlie Musso, pointedly ex-
cluding Mick. Musso's East Detroit joints were losing trade to The Casa.
Big John asked for a bump in Mick's payoffs to make up the difference.
Surprisingly, Moishe agreed with no argument, paying to keep the
peace.

But when Musso demanded a half interest in Mick's action, Moishe
told him he'd have to talk to Phil Savarese about that. If Phil okayed it,
Moishe would too. Musso turned to Luca for help, but the St. Clair boss

was eyeing Moishe. The old Yid might be past it, but Chicago Phil was the last guy who tried crowding him and nobody'd seen Savarese or his crew since.

"John backed Charlie's fat ass off, and that was the end of it," Moishe cackled, telling Mick the story in the Dequindre office. "The thing with Philly is over."

"Why? Because Luca knows about it?"

"Nah, because he *doesn't*, and he's already told Chicago that. If he changes his story now, they'll think he was in on it. And if he fucks with us, maybe he ends up like Philly. It's like the Purples and Nitti all over again. We're free and clear."

Mick knew he should feel relieved, but he didn't feel much of anything. The alley-cat wariness he'd adopted during the fight with Chicago was part of his character now. So were the images. Philly on his knees, Cephus carrying Aldo down that alley, dripping blood and brains. The killing at Cooley's had been a passage through a door with one-way hinges, and Savarese's death had sealed it for good. There was no way back. Not for him. Not anymore.

So he moved through his world on the quiet, the Dark Prince of Black Kats Records, making music, making money, and collecting every damned dime music biz sharpies owed his new label. But avoiding the limelight, letting Brownie front the club and the record company.

He was truly Moishe's boy now. Always strapped, always wary. And alone.

CHAPTER 53

Mick snapped awake. Sat up slowly in bed, blinking into the darkness. Wasn't sure what woke him. For a moment he wasn't even sure where he was. A motel or…. No. In his bedroom at Mojo's old studio. Another creak on the stairway. Someone was coming up. Moving quietly.

Slipping his hand under his pillow, he eased out his .45, keeping it under the blankets to quiet the *chick-chick* as he checked the chamber.

Full clip. As always.

Footsteps were whispering down the hallway now, coming closer. He thought about rolling out of bed, but he was nude, didn't feel like groveling on the floor. Raising the automatic instead, he eared back the hammer, covering the door as it inched open…

"Mick?" Martika. Wearing a nylon trench coat over her glistening black stage sheath. No hat, her curly mop tousled, glittering with raindrops. "Are you awake?"

"I am now," he said, lowering the hammer and the gun, switching on the dim nightstand light. "What time is it?"

"Around four."

"Everything okay at the club?"

"Great. Another sold out night. But I'm playing Cleveland next week and I thought we should talk first."

"Go ahead."

"No, I mean really talk, Mick. Both of us."

"About...?"

"Our thing. Us."

"Which part? The club? The Studio? Business is good— "

"Not business. This part." She gestured at the room. "You and me."

Mick hesitated, knowing he was walking in a minefield now. Blindfolded.

"I'm not sure there is a you and me anymore," he said carefully. "Your fans see more of you than I do."

"I know. I've...had a lot of things to work out."

"About the baby? You still mad with me over that?"

"Not just you. I'm mad at the world, Mick. Mad at God, I guess, for sending me the perfect gift, then stealing her away."

He didn't say anything.

"But... I can't live like this," she went on, taking a deep breath. "I thought the music might be enough for me. But it's not even close."

"Maybe not for you, but it's really....something."

"Just a little colored girl from the neighborhood, singin' her blues away," she said dryly. "Puttin' my business in the street, five nights a week."

"Whatever you want to call it, it's powerful. You reach people, babe. You move them. You move me."

"Daaamn, coming from you, that's high praise," she smiled faintly. "But you always did like your music crude."

"More honest than crude, I think. I've always known the real thing when I hear it, but I never understood the price you had to pay for that kind of truth. I know it now. I've been listening my whole life, and you're the best I've ever heard."

"That's...really nice, Mick, but I didn't come here to talk about my damn career. So don't be changing the subject, okay?"

"I'm not sure what the subject is."

"That's too bad, because it's you, pretty much."

"Okay," he nodded, absorbing that. "You're here. Does that mean you're thinking"— he coughed, trying to cover the bolt of fear that knifed into his gut. "Are you thinking about maybe coming back? Or just squaring things away, making the break for good?"

"It's not that simple."

"Nothing ever is, with you. What's the problem?"

"I'm not...who I was before, Mick. It isn't only losing the baby, I lost part of me. I'm barren now. I can't ever have children. I was older than you before, and I feel a *lot* older now. I don't know why you'd want me around. I damn sure haven't been much fun lately."

"You don't know...if I want you?"

"Damn it, don't you go all quiet on me now. I need the truth here. Straight up."

"Yeah, I can see that. Only I'm not much of a talker. You know that."

"You'd better try. You barely spoke to me at the hospital. Or since, for that matter. I know a lot's been happening— "

"It wasn't that," he said, cutting her off. "The flat ass truth is, I'm afraid to talk to you. Scared to death."

"Scared of what?"

"Of saying the wrong damn thing. Of hurting you. Of screwing things up worse than I have already. And since the hospital, you've been...so different. The way you sing, the way you are. I thought you might want to make a fresh start. On your own."

"And if I did, you'd cut me loose? Just like that?"

"I've got no real claim on you, Tika. Our two week deals ran out a long time ago."

"That's right, they did." Her thin face was a profile in the dim light.

Like a sculpture, he thought. A queen from old Egypt. And just as distant.

"Okay," she nodded, "I'm different, and so are you. Hell, after all that's happened, everything's different now. But I've been doing a lot of thinking about it. And about us. And here's what it comes down to. Of all the stuff that's happened, the best part of it was us. The place I was happiest was here. With you. And I don't know if we can have that again. Don't know if we can ever get back to that place. But that's what I want. You're what I want. So. What do you think? Any chance you'd want to try our thing again?"

"Sure. Okay."

"Okay?" she echoed, arching her eyebrows. "That's it? That's all you've got to say?"

"Not quite." His turn to take a deep breath. "What would you think about getting married?"

"What?"

"You heard. Marry me. A church, a preacher, *Here Comes the Bride.*' The whole deal."

"Jesus H. Christ." She turned away, shaking her head. Smiling. But her eyes were moist.

"You think that's funny?"

"Coming from you? Damn straight it is. Swear to god, if I'm with you a hundred years I'll never know what you'll do next."

"Now who's changing the subject? I'm asking you flat out. What do you think?"

"Seriously? Us, in a church? When was the last time you were in church, Mick? Have you ever been in one? We've never even talked about it."

"We're talking about it now."

She looked away a moment, shaking her head, then faced him again.

"Mick, half the states in this country are Jim Crow. In Arkansas, if you try to take me out to dinner, we'd eat dessert in jail. Even in Detroit, if we want to buy a house in Grosse Pointe or Ecorse, nobody will sell to a mixed race couple. It's wrong, but there it is. There's only one place we can be happy together. Right here. In this room. This bed. And I don't need a ring or a preacher or anybody's goddamn permission for this. Besides, any church you step into would probably get hit by lightning anyway. So, no, I don't want to get married. I just want to be with you. And I've had a long damn day. So? You got room for one more in that bed, or what?"

"Not so fast. Our two week contract expired a long time ago."

"Right. And?"

"So, if you don't wanna get married, we should at least renegotiate our deal to something a little longer than two weeks."

"How much longer?"

"I don't know. Two and a half weeks? Maybe even three?"

"You jive-ass turkey," she smiled, unbuttoning her raincoat. "Know what? Three weeks with you does sound like a long time. Now move the hell over, before I change my mind."

□   □   □

They didn't make love that night. Martika seemed so fragile beside him, and her touch and her warmth felt so welcome that he was hesitant, unsure of how to begin. And then it was too late. In moments, she was already asleep in his arms. And that was more than enough.

But in the morning they woke, happy, heated and hungry for each other

in the dawn light. Making love cautiously at first, then with a new fe-
rocity more fiery than before. And more desperate.

Both of them carried fresh scars, some visible, others buried deeper. And
there was distance between them now. What they'd shared before had
been wrecked and its destruction had changed them both. But the loss
of young love didn't destroy them. It only made their passion for each
other stronger, their bond more formidable.

And having a whole lot of serious money rolling in didn't hurt a thing.

□   □   □

They didn't rent a church or buy wedding rings. They bought the old
studio on Hastings Street instead, then remodeled it completely, returning the rundown studio to the comfortable home it had once been, long
before.

Upstairs, they combined two of the bedrooms into a single master suite
with walk in closets and a bathtub big enough for two. On the main
floor, they hired a retired stonemason to replace the entire wall between
the parlor and kitchen with a floor to ceiling fireplace, each rough field
stone carefully laid by hand.

New furniture, too, nothing froufrou, mostly leather and oak. Comfortable, solid and classy. Brownie said the place looked like John
Wayne's bunkhouse. But he liked it, a lot.

Other touches were more practical. Tika kept a grand piano and tape
deck in the living room for songwriting and the first floor windows were
decorated with ornate iron grates, pleasing to the eye, but also rock solid.
The front and back doors had double locks and reinforced steel cores.
A fortress against the world.

But the most dramatic change wasn't in the house at all. Mick bought
the vacant lot behind the studio, leveled the swaybacked shed, replacing it with a three-bay garage/workshop, complete with its own hydraulic
lift, air compressor and a complete array of Craftsman tools. Grease-
monkey heaven. With a small added surprise.

The day the workmen finally finished, and Mick raised the garage
doors for the first time, he found a new car sitting in the center bay. A
gleaming '64 Corvette Sting Ray, split-window coupe, fire-engine red
with a red leather interior and a 327 fuel-injected V8. The fastest freaking street machine on the planet.

He circled the Vette slowly for a full fifteen minutes, savoring its style,
sleek and slippery as a hammerhead shark. The vanity plate read T S 1.
Opening the door, he was greeted by the sweet aroma of new-car
leather. He lowered himself into the driver's seat, gripped the wheel at

ten and two and rocked it just enough to test its balance. Perfect. But when he reached for the ignition switch, the slot was empty.

Frowning, he glanced back at the house. Martika was standing on the back porch, barefoot, in Capri pants and a tie-dyed orange tee shirt, holding up a set of car keys. Waggling the keys, she pointedly checked both ways to make sure no neighbors were watching. Then she tugged her waistband open just far enough to reveal a line of black silk, before dropping the keys into her panties and dodging back inside.

But even as Mick charged after her with an erection hard as a racehorse, he couldn't help taking a last glance over his shoulder at the red Corvette. It was the first new car he'd ever owned.

Not that he had much time for joyrides.

The studio and The Casa were making money by the bale, but their new life was a lot more hectic than the old one. As fresh groups signed with the label, Tika helped them focus their talents, writing songs custom-tailored to show off their strengths. In the following year, she had two Top Forty hits of her own, three others by Black Kats artists, plus a dozen more on albums by Mary Wells, Aretha Franklin, and even one by oh-so-English Petula Clark.

None of those hits came easily. Every new record from Black Kat had to be promoted around the country, which meant non-stop traveling for Martika and the Sultans, countless one-night stands with press and radio interviews jammed into two and three month marathon tours. Fortunately, Varnell Mack and his crew were hardcore road dogs, past masters of the game.

Tall, stately, and unfailingly polite, Varnell was also a cutthroat negotiator, a meticulous planner who booked gigs back-to-back-to-back, keeping driving distances down to a manageable two to three hundred miles a day.

Occasionally, Mick traveled with the tour as a stage-manager, helping to set up the shows, making sure the equipment worked and collecting their gate money. Benjy Jefferson went along too, anchoring the local house bands, keeping the music rough, tough and tight. Sober, Benjy was a stone professional, always prepped and properly dressed onstage, and a cheerful companion on the road. But his appetites for booze, Dexedrine and other men's women made some shows a lot more exciting than they needed to be.

"When Benjy gets jammed up with somebody's husband, throw a wad of money at the biggest sumbitch in the place and run for the door," Varnell counseled. "Guarantee Benjy'll be gone before you get there. He's had plenty of practice."

But in the deep south, Mick had to leave the show. He'd lived in Mississippi, knew how deeply the root of racism grew in that red dirt. Civil rights workers were murdered by the Klan near Philadelphia, beaten and hassled everywhere else. Tika and the Sultans only wanted to sing, to lift a few hearts, but if Mick traveled with them, they'd get pulled over in every hick town in Dixie, wasting their wages on bribes or bail. Or hospital bills. So when the tour veered south, Mick headed back to Detroit to work the streets for Moishe and help Brownie run The Casa and Black Kats. Taking care of business while his heart was rattling around Georgia in the back of a bus.

Touring was a brutal grind, but Tika thrived on it, drinking in the applause like champagne at every show, giving her all, whether it was a sold out concert in Cleveland or a Biloxi barbeque joint.

As their record sales continued to rise, the venues grew bigger and the road got longer. Two weeks in New York doing shows with James Brown at the Apollo, then out to San Francisco to tour with the Righteous Brothers, riding high with "You've Lost That Lovin' Feelin'." Then over to England to open for the Rolling Stones, and on to the continent for shows in Paris, Frankfurt, Berlin.

And three years flew past like a Labor Day weekend.

CHAPTER 54

July 20, 1967

Mick was in his office nest at The Casa when the intercom buzzed.

"Two cops to see you," Cephus said, calling from his post at the front door. "One of 'em's Mexican. Garcia. Says he knows you."

"Send 'em up."

Sergeant Lupe Garcia, neatly turned out in a Hughes and Hatcher herringbone rapped once, then stepped in. A brother with him, square faced, broad shouldered, tweed jacket. Not as big as Cephus but not far from it.

"Irish," Garcia nodded, "meet my new partner, Sergeant Cordell Bennett. Cord, say hi to Irish Mick Shannon. Moishe's boy. The devil in a red Corvette. Four years on my turf, already a fucking legend."

"What can I do for you, Sergeant?"

"Actually, it's Lieutenant Garcia now, Organized Crime Division. We're making some heavy changes downtown. Prosecutor appointed a new deputy DA to our section, a redhead named Stratton. Becker thought she was a joke, some hire-the-handicapped political hack— "

"Handicapped?"

"Stratton had polio when she was a kid. Wears a leg brace but doesn't have a problem kickin' ass. First off, she opened a new investigation into union racketeering, Jimmy Hoffa, John Luca, Charlie Musso. Those names sound familiar? When Becker tried to stall her, she bounced his ass over to narcotics and gave me his slot. Looks like I'm not the only one who's been movin' up. This office is practically nosebleed country. Did you think I couldn't find you up here?"

"Why would you try?"

"Take a walk around, Cord," Garcia said. "Spread some breadcrumbs so we can find our way back. Me and Mick got some catchin' up to do."

After Bennett left, Mick slid open a drawer, took out an envelope and tossed it across the desk. Garcia made no move to pick it up.

"That's not why I came, Shannon. This ain't a social call. Does the name Bobby Fuller ring a bell?"

"The Bobby Fuller Four? Had that hit song last year, 'I Fought The Law and the Law Won?'"

"That's him. I liked that song. Lot of cops did."

"So did I. What about it?"

"Last July, Fuller was found dead in a car in front of his apartment building. He'd been beaten up, then ingested enough gasoline to drown."

"I read about it. Tough way to go."

"LAPD says your pal Albert Luca was trying to sign Fuller to his record label at the time. Albert's built up quite a business in L.A., records and entertainment. Built a reputation too, as a bad motherfucker to cross. Since Fuller's little 'accident,' singers are falling all over themselves to sign with him. Since you're a 'known associate' of Albert Luca, here I am. What can you tell me about Fuller's death?"

"Nothing."

"So I don't suppose you remember where you were last July 18th?"

"Actually, I do. I was in Europe that month, doing the first Black Kats tour with Martika, and the Sultans of Soul. On the 18th we were in Berlin."

"You're sure?"

"Not likely to forget. A German corporation tried to buy our whole damn company. Offered semi-serious bucks, too. We met with their lawyers to talk about it, in Berlin on the eighteenth."

"Sounds like a solid alibi, if it checks. What happened to the deal?"

"We turned it down. What could be more fun than this?" Mick said, spreading his hands to take in the office, the club.

"You're doing all right," Garcia conceded, "but Albert's doing better. He's muscled his way into a half dozen record labels and an entertainment agency. A real L.A. big shot."

"I read the showbiz press, Garcia. What's your point?"

"In the music biz, mob guys usually keep a low profile. Like you, for instance. But Albert plays too rough, makes too many waves. LAPD's probing his operations now, trying to nail him for racketeering. The Fuller killing was the last straw. Word is the other mob families want him gone."

"The papers said Fuller committed suicide."

"Hollywood," Garcia snorted. "If a movie star's arms and legs show up at three different landfills, the L.A. coroner calls it the worst case of suicide he ever saw. What can you tell me about Albert?"

Mick just looked at him.

"According to LAPD, Albert had plenty to say about you. Said to ask you about a Chicago hood who disappeared a few years back. Phil Savarese?"

"Never heard of him. And you work the streets, Garcia, you know Albert and I aren't pals."

"You'd top my list for Savarese anyway. Darktown used to belong to Moishe Abrams, now it's yours. Philly tries to push onto your turf, *poof*! He's gone, into thin air. And whenever bad things happen inside 8 Mile, your name always comes up."

"I own a piece of this club, I run a few jukes, make a few records and pay my taxes. I never met Bobby Fuller, don't know or care what Albert Luca's into. Congratulations on your promotion, Lieutenant. Don't forget your envelope." Mick pushed it across the desk.

"Oh, is this for me?" Picking it up, Garcia hefted it, testing its weight. Then tore it in half and tossed the pieces on the desk.

"What the fuck?" Mick blinked, grinning in surprise. "Do you know how much was in there?"

"I never did. Moishe's deal was with Becker, but he's gone and I got a new boss. If you ever give me another envelope, better roll it real tight, because it's going straight up your ass."

"Not likely," Mick said, eyeing the torn pieces ruefully. "Jesus H. Christ, Garcia, now I've gotta make this up to Moishe."

"Too bad," Garcia said, rising.

"Hold on. You warned me about Savarese once, so I'll return the favor. The vice squad's been rousting downtown clubs looking for payoffs, but this Black Power movement's catching on. A lot of brothers coming home from Viet Nam have taken all the shit they're going to. Your guys better dial it down or we could go up like Jersey. Half the Newark ghetto burned last week."

"Detroit's not Newark."

"No, it's worse. People on the Corridor got no place to go but the clubs and blind pigs, Garcia. It's gonna be a long, hot summer. Lighten up."

"Or what, you'll break my legs?"

"Don't worry about me," Mick smiled, pushing the torn ends of the envelope together. "If you're trying to be an honest cop in this town, I'm the least of your worries."

Chapter 55

July 23, 1967

No clouds. White sun cruising a sheet metal sky, scorching Motown's mean concrete all day long, hammering the heat down into the ancient salt mines beneath the city.

By noon, the auto plants were ovens. Temperatures at Ford Rouge a hundred and thirty up near the steel ceilings. Overhead crane operators were rotating down to the factory floor every half hour, their clothes soaked with sweat, heads hanging, panting like dogs.

Nightfall didn't help. Inside 8 Mile, tar was bubbling in the streets like grease on a griddle, black folks boiling out of their tenements and row houses, restless and surly. And thirsty.

The Casa Mayor was buzzing by ten, so jammed the waitresses could barely squeeze through the crowds. Brothers grabbing pitchers of Stroh's beer off passing trays, gulping them down straight, no glasses. Getting high, feeling mighty. Pumped up for the night.

The Sultans' midnight show jacked the temperature even higher. Honed on the road, their act was polished perfection now, impeccable harmony, dance steps flashy and precise. Every line of their Top 40 hits drew applause. But midway through the set Varnell could feel the crowd's focus slipping away. Edgy as an antelope herd scenting a lion, they seemed impatient for the Sultans to finish. Like they had someplace else to be.

A couple of scuffles broke out during the show. Not the usual boozy scraps either. Savage battles, guys going at it hard, snarling like street dogs, tearing at each other even as Cephus and Mick muscled them out the door.

The club closed promptly at two, waitresses and janitors vacuuming and mopping up, hustling to finish by half-past. Jerome was already reconfiguring the sound system from performance to recording mode. Had a playback of "Groovin'," a new single by the Young Rascals coming over the speakers.

"The tune's too white, Jerome," Varnell groused. Both men in shirtsleeves, Jerome in his beatnik beret and heavy framed glasses, toking on a joint. Varnell still wearing his lime green slacks, perched on a barstool, sipping an RC Cola, listening. "The boy sounds like he's on downers."

"It's the Summer of Love, man," Jerome hissed, holding in his smoke. "Mellow's where it's at. 'Groovin's a good fit for your new album and that Turk over at Atlantic is pushin' it. Listen close, Varnell. See what these white kids got goin'."

Three playbacks later the rest of the Sultans were in place, dressed casually in polo shirts and slacks, Benjy Jefferson behind the drums, still wearing his show-time suit. Benjy was half buzzed, but still wired up and ready.

Martika stalked onstage, "Hot Chocolate" in a cut off tee shirt, short shorts and flats. "Okay, guys," she said, clapping her hands sharply. "Showtime. Let's nail this sucker. One take, right?"

"Ready when you are, sweet thing," Benjy chuckled, hitting a rimshot. Then everyone went quiet as Jerome raised his hand and silently counted down from five, pointing to Benjy on one. Benjy and the bass player kicked off two easy bars alone, then the guitarist came in with the riff as Jerome comped the chords on piano.

After listening for sixteen bars, Jerome stopped the tape. "Again. And get in the pocket. Song's called 'Groovin', not some wino stumblin' around."

"We know a whole lot more about stumblin' than you do, sonny," Benjy jibed, kicking it off again. It took two more tries to satisfy Jerome. On the fourth take he nodded to Varnell. This time, when the band came in, the Sultans did too, ooh-ing the background as Otis began crooning about getting laid on a Sunday afternoon.

In the darkened office high above the stage, Mick and Martika both swayed to the beat, holding hands, listening to the blend. Brownie and Cephus were listening too, on barstools by the greeting station, quietly arguing about Muhammad Ali. Stripped of his heavyweight title by the draft board a month before, Ali'd been called a coward by fat white crackers who'd shit green nickels if Sonny Liston winked at 'em.

"Man's a Muslim priest," Cephus said stubbornly. "Should've got a deferment. Every white college punk comes into this joint's got one."

"I never heard about the priest thing till he got called up," Brownie nee-dled, egging the big man on. Both men falling silent when the music started.

Three full takes and Jerome called a break, everyone stepping away from the mikes, stretching, passing around a joint as Jerome fed the play-back through the club speakers.

"Any keepers?" Mick asked, as he and Martika strolled down the steps to join the others.

"The second take— " Jerome broke off as Mick waved him to si-lence. "What the fuck is that noise?" Mick demanded.

"What noise?"

"That popping sound between the choruses. There, hear that? It…" His voice faded as his eyes met Brownie's. "Son of a bitch. That's gun-fire."

"Hey, ya'll! Somethin's goin' down out here!" Cephus called from the front door. "Po-lice cars all over the damn place."

The whole troupe trotted out to the doorway. Cephus standing like a tree in his dark suit, flashers playing across his scarred face as prowl cars roared past, lights ablaze, sirens wailing.

"Looks to be up a few blocks," Cephus said. "Must be bad, all them cars."

"A fire?" Tika asked.

"Ain't seen no fire trucks, hon, just twenty freakin' prowlies."

"What's up that way?" Otis asked.

"Not a damn thing at four in the morning."

"There's a new blind pig, the Community League, over on Twelfth," Brownie said. "Been open since May. I'd guess Mister Charlie's about to shut it down."

"More likely put his hand out," Brownie said. "That's a lot of cars just to roust a few drunks."

"Well, we can't record with all this racket," Mick said. "Let's call it a night, try again tomorrow."

"So you can head on over there, get your young ass in trouble," Mar-tika teased.

"Never crossed my mind," Mick shot back, grinning. "But now that you mention it… "

Leaving Jerome and Varnell to close down the session, Cephus brought Mick's Lincoln Town Car around front. Gunmetal gray, the limo had the 'Presidential Package' option; armored doors, bulletproof glass. Tika's idea.

More patrol cars roared past as Mick, Tika and Brownie piled in. Cephus floored the Linc, chasing the police units down Twelfth toward Clairmont.

Never got there. Half a block from Clairmont, Cephus slowed the Lincoln, easing it over to the curb.

A raid. Cops were muscling people out of a storefront building, the Community League Civil Action Center by day, a bustling blind pig by night. The lawmen were sweating and edgy and had cause to be. Their prisoners were struggling every step of the way and an unruly crowd was collecting around the roust, already a hundred strong with more black folks pouring out of nearby tenements, steamed up and on the prod.

TV images of Newark the week before were fresh in their minds. Jersey cops blasting unarmed brothers in the streets with cars burning in the background. Change channels and you see Ali, Heavyweight Champ of the damn World being thrown in jail. Telling his draft board "No Viet Cong ever called me nigger."

More prowl cars were screaming in, policemen piling out, scrambling to form a ragged blue riot line, nightsticks at port arms to hold back the crowd.

But it wasn't working. After the scorching day, folks were in no mood to be muscled by The Man. Angry brothers were pushing back, jostling the cops, shouting "Newark!" Or "Aliiii!!!" Daring the lawmen to swing, forcing them to retreat a step at a time, crumpling the police line in on itself.

Like a fiery signal from the gods, a flaming vodka bottle with a burning rag in its throat came hurtling down from a rooftop, exploding on the street in a fiery pool of rage, boosting the heat past the boiling point.

"Back us on out of here, Cephus," Brownie said quietly. "This ride's bulletproof but it ain't fireproof and all hell's about to bust loose."

It was already too late. As the vice squad wrestled the last few prisoners into the police bus, the street cops tried backing away to disengage from the crowd. But the mob ate up every inch the lawmen gave, surging forward until the police line collapsed and their orderly retreat turned into a rout, cops breaking and running, scrambling into their prowl cars, peeling out, tires howling, while a final hardcore few tried to stand their ground.

Big mistake.

A beer bottle smashed against the side of the police bus and a hail of bricks and wine bottles followed, pelting patrol cars and the rear guard lawmen until they broke too, sprinting for their cars, running for their damn lives.

Cephus was already gunning the big Lincoln back down Twelfth, pedal to the metal with prowl cars flying past and the crowd rushing toward them like a tidal wave, coming on at a dead run.

"Get us back to the club!" Mick said. "It's gonna be a long night."

□   □   □

The next day was even longer. Angry mobs prowled the streets until dawn. Patrol cars cruised slowly past, occasionally triggering a siren whoop or flashing their spotlights as a warning. But they didn't stop. Police Commissioner Girardin had ordered his cops to avoid confrontations.

A prudent move? Or an even bigger mistake. By mid-morning, the routine dust-up at the blind pig had exploded across the ghetto like wildfire, swelling into a full blown riot. Looters, mostly young knuckleheads, were smashing store windows, snatching handfuls of merchandise and racing away.

And going scot-free. John Law didn't bust anybody or even warn them off. By dusk the inner city looked like a gigantic fire sale. Straight citizens who'd never stolen a cent were shoulder to shoulder with gang bangers, loading up shopping carts, carrying off everything from diapers to big box stereos.

Frantic store owners painted signs in their shop windows, *Soul Brother, Black Owned, Afro All the Way*. Looters trashed them anyway. The rage in the streets wasn't just about the raid or Newark or even Ali. A lifetime of frustration was exploding and racial solidarity didn't carry much weight.

After sending Martika home to Conant Gardens to be with her folks, Mick and his crew forted up in The Casa as the riot blazed hotter, spreading out to Grand River, down Livernois and east along Mack Avenue.

Whenever looters approached the club, Cephus or Brownie simply stepped out onto the sidewalk, cradling twelve gauge shotguns. Didn't say anything, didn't have to. Nobody pushed it. There were easier pickings up and down every street.

The first blaze broke out at dawn, in the rear of a ransacked shoe store. As fire trucks roared to the rescue, the crowds pelted them with rocks and bottles, treating them like alien invaders, driving them off while the flames roiled madly upward, scattering sparks and fiery debris, jumping the blazes from building to building.

Drawing on every fire station in the city, Chief Charles Quinlan hastily assembled an all-black firefighting squad. The mobs stoned them too. Skin color didn't matter, only the uniforms. A flash of blue is all it took to trigger a hail of missiles. So the inferno raged on, unchecked, keeping pace with the madness.

By dusk, the Motor City was a war zone. Smoke from a hundred arsons swirling into the night sky as gunfire began flashing from the rooftops.

Congressman John Conyers, a Detroit black with genuine political juice, stood on the roof of his car, using a bullhorn to plead with a crowd, trying to quell the rage. Had to scramble down off the car and duck underneath it, dodging a hail of rocks and bottles. Councilman Hood fared even worse. Rioters chased him down the street, pelting him with trash and curses.

Late Sunday afternoon, Governor George Romney, the former CEO of American Motors, finally clamped a curfew on the insanity. Ordering all bars and liquor stores closed, he sent four hundred state troopers and seven thousand national guardsmen marching into the city to restore order.

It was like trying to drown a fire with gasoline. Many guardsmen were green newbies who'd enlisted to avoid the Vietnam draft. They scarcely knew how to give a proper salute, let alone control a riot. Many had never even fired their M-16s.

But they learned fast.

A looter running from a store on Fourth Street was the first citizen gunned down by the Guard. Within hours, a half dozen more rioters were killed as the young troops warmed to their work.

Tuesday afternoon, Cephus was on guard at the front door, slouched on a barstool with a pump shotgun in his lap. Watching the street, half awake.

Hearing a shout and running footsteps, he leapt up, fully alert now. Inching The Casa door open, he eased warily outside.

No looters this time. An army Jeep was rumbling down the centerline in low gear, a young trooper standing in the shotgun seat, two more in back, nervously scanning the rooftops for snipers, their M-16 assault rifles locked and loaded.

More grunts were prowling the sidewalks on both sides of the street, checking doors.

"About damn time," Cephus grumbled. Waving a hello to the Jeep, he turned to go back inside. But as he reached for the knob, one of the troopers screamed, "*Gun!*"

The glass panel beside Cephus exploded as the soldiers opened up at him, firing away on full automatic. Slugs blasting past, tearing his coat, punching into the walls, shattering the neon 'welcome' sign above the door into a billion pieces.

"Get down!" he shouted. "Everybody on the damn floor!" Mick was already racing to the entry as Cephus dove behind the greeter's station. The front door burst open and two guardsmen came charging in, Mutt and Jeff in olive drab fatigues. The shorter troop cranked off a half dozen rounds into the ceiling, shattering a light fixture, sparks and glass raining down around him.

"Stop it!" Mick yelled. "What the hell are you doing?"

Both guardsmen whirled to face him, weapons shouldered, aimed straight at his head.

"Get your damn hands up!" the taller one yelled.

"Okay, okay, they're up! Christ on a crutch, cool out! My name's Shannon, I own this place— "

"A nigger with a gun ran in here!" the shorter G.I. shouted.

"This nigger, you mean?" Cephus asked, rising behind the two troopers, racking his shotgun for emphasis. "With this gun? Better point them pieces at the floor, boys. Y'all are done shootin' at folks."

"Lower your weapons, guys," Mick said quietly. "Nobody wants any trouble."

"Didn't have none till these trigger-happy fools started shootin' the place up," Cephus grumbled.

"Krabel? Jennings?" A shout from outside. "Everything all right?"

The two troopers exchanged a split second glance of triumph. Mutt started to raise his gun.

"Don't even think about it," Mick said quietly, stepping up to the taller trooper, face to face. "You won't make it."

Spec 5 Pete Jennings had a loaded M-16 set for full automatic fire, a ten-inch bayonet on his belt and the whole US Army backing him up. Irish Mick was just an unarmed civilian in shirtsleeves. It didn't matter. Jennings had a strong conviction that if he made one wrong move, very bad shit would happen to him. Very fast.

"Jennings?"

"It's all good, Lieutenant," the lanky trooper yelled back, lowering his weapon. "False alarm." Nodding to his partner, he backed slowly out the door. Both men keeping their M-16s aimed at the floor the whole way.

"Damn," Brownie whistled, "ten thousand whacks runnin' the streets and now the army's goin' nuts too? What's wrong with those guys?"

"They're young, scared, and loaded for bear," Mick said. "Bad combination. I'll take the watch awhile, Ceef."

"If you think bein' white makes you bulletproof, think again," the big man cautioned. "Those fucks are shootin' anything that moves."

"Then I won't move," Mick said. "Let's pile some tables over here, block off what's left of the doors."

CHAPTER 56

They took turns keeping watch through the night, listening to sirens and gunfire while Mayor Jerry Cavanagh and Governor Romney pleaded for calm on WJR. At 3 a.m. the following morning, President Lyndon Baines Johnson finally lost patience and declared martial law, ordering five thousand paratroopers from the 101st and 82nd Airborne to retake the burning streets. The paratroopers were seasoned combat soldiers, mostly Vietnam vets. Stone professionals compared to the Guardsmen, they were truly an army of occupation for an American city.

The gloves were off, now. Detroit's ghettos were officially designated a combat zone. Enemy territory, like Hanoi or Khe San. The fire departments received over six hundred alarms, while the butcher's bill quickly climbed to twenty dead. Then thirty. Then forty. All but one of them black.

Late Wednesday afternoon, Mick relieved Brownie at the front door barricade. Holding the shotgun against his calf to conceal it, he leaned out to check the street. Empty. Both ways. Since the army patrol the day before, things had been quiet—

A slug punched into the wall beside his head, spraying his face with splinters! Two more quick shots followed, missing him by a hairsbreadth as he dove back through the doorway, scrambling to get under cover. A bullet *spanged* off the tile floor inches behind him, whistling back into the club.

"You hit?" Cephus called, sliding up to the entrance with his back to the wall.

"I'm okay! Stay away from the door! Sniper's in the warehouse across the street."

"Army?"

"Don't know. I didn't see any soldiers in the street."

"A brother, then? What the fuck's anybody shootin' at us for?"

"Don't know that either, but I'm tired of being a target," Mick said, peeling off his jacket, tossing it to Cephus. "Give him a look at this every few minutes."

"Should I shoot back?"

"No! If it's the army, we don't want a shootout. Just keep that sonofabitch interested."

Belly-crawling away from the entrance with the shotgun, Mick jumped to his feet then raced through the club to the back door and sprinted down the alley to the end of the block, hugging the bricks all the way.

Kneeling, he peeked around the corner of the building, sweat dripping in his eyes. Caught a movement on the roof directly across from the club. The sniper was still up there, with a clear shot at the doorway. But the street was deserted. Not a soul in sight. Or a uniform.

What the hell? Had the guardsmen come back, pissed because they'd weaseled out? The shorter one seemed crazy enough. What was his name? Krabel. The bigger question, had he come back alone? Or were more of them out there covering the street?

Only one way to find out. From his sniper's perch, Krabel couldn't see this far down the block without showing himself.

Racking the Remington to make sure he had a round in the chamber, Mick took a deep breath. Then stepped out, walking calmly across the street with the shotgun pressed against his thigh to shield it from view. Just a solid citizen out for a stroll. In the middle of a riot, packing a twelve-gauge pump. Expecting to get capped any second.

A shot cracked from the rooftop and Mick took off! Dashing across the street he ducked into the lee of the building, flattening against the bricks, trying to get his breathing under control.

No more shots came, and he realized he hadn't heard a bullet hit. If the sniper'd been aiming at him, he should have heard the ricochet. Cephus must have flashed his jacket to draw fire. Maybe the shooter hadn't seen Mick at all.

Gathering himself, he trotted down the block to the alley mouth. Took a quick look. The alley was empty. A few trash cans, some boxes. They must've parked their Jeep in the middle of the block.

Inching down the alley wall, Mick peered warily around the corner. And quickly drew back.

A police car was parked not ten feet from him, near a warehouse fire door. A uniform in the shotgun seat, smoking a cigarette. Not Detroit P.D. The prowlie was from Ecorse.

The cop was one of the pricks who held his arms for Spivak the night he beat him. The fat one. What was his name? Gorski? Something like that.

Dropping low, keeping to the shadows, Mick duck-walked from the alley to the rear of the prowl car. Risking a quick peek around the trunk, he glimpsed the side of Gorski's face in the rearview. The cop could see him if he checked the mirror. But he was looking the other way, peering up through the windshield at the roof.

Edging silently along the police car, Mick tapped on the doorframe with the barrel of the Remington. Startled, Gorski turned, and found himself staring into the shotgun muzzle. He went gray as ashes, the blood draining from his face.

"Sweet Jesus," he whispered.

"Not even close," Mick said. "I know you. You're Gorski. Who's that on the roof? Spivak? Or Cody?"

"Spivak," the cop managed, raising his hands, sprinkling himself with cigarette ashes.

"We had a deal, Gorski. You promised Moishe we were done with this shit."

"We were, but Wes is crazy, Shannon! Every time he gets a load on he raves about coming after you. I've talked him out of it a dozen times."

"But not today?"

"He's drunk, wouldn't listen. Says the riots are perfect cover, he'd never get another chance like this."

"He's right, he won't. Take the gun out of your holster with your fingertips. Hand it out the window. Real slow."

Gorski did as he was told, but his hands were sweating so badly he fumbled the .38, dropping it to the pavement. Muttering a curse, Mick shoved the gun in his waistband.

"Out of the car!"

"Don't do anything nuts!"

Opening the door, Gorski slid out, hands in the air. Mick patted him down, found an ankle holster with a snub nosed .32 and threw it down the alley.

"Is anybody else with you?"

"No, we're alone. I tried to talk him— "

"Shut up! How'd he get up to the roof?"

"There are fire stairs inside that door. They go all the way up."

"How did Wes know that?"

"He's been here before, scouting your place," Gorski said, swallowing hard. "But either you weren't here or there were too many people— "

"And you couldn't pick up a phone, warn somebody?" Mick said, jamming the twelve gauge hard under Gorski's chin. "I oughta blow your fucking head off!"

"Please! He's my boss and he's crazy! What could I do?"

"What we're gonna do now. Settle this. Move it," Mick said, gesturing toward the fire door with the shotgun muzzle. "Walk soft, fat boy. If Wes hears us coming, you'll be in the middle of it."

"For God's sake, Shannon, I've got kids."

"Good. Then you'll know to be quiet. Because there's only one way I'm leaving you behind me."

Gorski stumbled to the building, sweat stains already darkening his armpits. Easing open the fire door, he inched through.

Inside, an open square stairwell led up to the roof. Iron pipe railings welded to steel steps, two flights per floor, circling the stairwell at right angles. Six stories straight up.

Gorski turned to plead but Mick jabbed him in the ass with the shotgun.

Swallowing, the porky cop started up the stairs, using the handrail, hugging the wall. By the second flight he was panting. Overweight, out of shape and scared spitless.

Two stories up. Three. Trailing a few steps behind, Mick could see Gorski's knees turning to rubber, wobbling with every step now. Hoped to Christ the fat cop wouldn't have a heart attack—

Gunfire exploded from the roof! Spivak blasting away again. But then came the pop-pop-pop of return fire from across the street, and a yelp from above. A hit?

Had to be. Footsteps came pounding across the roof, heading for the stairwell. Jesus! They were only halfway up with no cover at all. Grabbing Gorski's belt from behind, Mick held him in place. Above, Wes Spivak burst through the rooftop door, packing an M-1 police carbine.

Wild-eyed, his tan summer uniform stained with sweat and filth from the roof, Spivak was streaming blood from a gash on his temple. Looked like half his ear was blown away. His shirt had bloodstains too, but Mick couldn't tell if it was another wound or blood from the gash. Flying down the stairway in a panic, he was coming straight for them.

Raising the Remington, Mick centered his sights on the landing of the floor above. Wes would come around that corner directly into the killing zone. Dead to rights. Mick squeezed the trigger gently, taking up the slack.

"God," Gorski gasped, dropping to his knees, shielding his face with his arms to avoid the blast. Suddenly Spivak burst onto the landing a flight up, disheveled, his face bloodied, a mask of pain.

Spotting them, he stumbled to a halt in stunned surprise. He was in the open, no cover. But Mick didn't fire. His hands were quivering, squeezing the Remington so tightly he thought the stock would splinter. But somehow he couldn't— then it was too late!

Breaking free of Mick's grip, Gorski ran, blundering up the stairs, into the line of fire! The fat cop was babbling, probably begging them not to shoot but so breathless that neither man could understand a word.

Nor were they listening. Separated by a single flight with Gorski between them, Wes and Mick stared at each other through the black iron railings and ten years of hate.

For a frozen moment, neither man moved. Eyes locked, hearts hammering, minds racing.

Mick thought it might end in a standoff— snarling a curse, Spivak threw the carbine to his shoulder! Had to hold it one handed, his left arm hanging useless.

"Get out of the fucking way, Stan!" he shouted, blasting past Gorski like he wasn't there, the gunfire deafening in the narrow well, slugs whining off the walls and the steel railing.

Terrified, Gorski turned to flee, stumbling mindlessly down the stairs as fast as his wobbly legs could move.

"Get down!" Mick roared, flattening against the wall to let Gorski pass, the Remington ready. Just one clear shot.

Spivak kept firing wildly, struggling to control his weapon with his good arm. Mick couldn't return fire without hitting Gorski, couldn't run without giving Wes a clear shot at his back.

Fuck this. Mick touched off a blast in the air, hoping to drive Spivak back. Big mistake! Flinching, Gorski tripped and blundered into Mick, clutching him as he fell, dragging him down. Both men tumbling down the steps to crash on the landing in a tangle, the shotgun skidding free.

"That's it! Hold it right fucking there!" Spivak roared, aiming down over the railing. "Don't move, Shannon! Get the hell away from him Stan."

Dazed, Gorski stared up at Spivak's face, the blood streaming from his torn ear, a killing madness in his eyes.

"Don't, Wes," Gorski sobbed, scrabbling sideways on his hands and knees, trying to get clear.

Dazed from the fall, Mick looked around for the shotgun. The Remington was across the stairs against the rail, with Gorski in the way. No chance. He'd lost the pistol was too. It was down a few steps. Out of reach.

"Stand up, you fuckin' Irish punk," Spivak taunted. "I want you to see it comin'."

"Jesus, Wes, you can't!" Gorski pleaded. "It's fucking murder!" Stumbling over the shotgun, he tried to grab it— and it went off! The blast hit the wall, spraying Spivak's legs with stone chips! Startled, Spivak cut loose with the carbine, but Mick was already moving, scrambling down the steps, scrabbling for the pistol, knowing he was too late—

The shotgun blasted again, this time catching Spivak full in the chest!

Stunned, he fumbled the carbine away, clinging to the railing, staring at Gorski in stunned surprise. His life drained over his hands as they lost his grip on the rail and he toppled over it, cart-wheeling through space, banging off the steel banisters like a pinball before crashing down on the concrete floor, four stories below.

Wes writhed a few seconds in the widening pool of his own blood, mindless as a crushed insect. Then went utterly still.

"Jesus Christ," Gorski sobbed, "I didn't mean— I just wanted..." He collapsed on the stairway, hyperventilating, only a word away from hysteria.

Mick warily took the shotgun out of Gorski's quivering hands. The fat cop looked up at him helplessly. "I didn't want any of this. You gotta believe me— ."

"It doesn't matter now, " Mick said sharply, kneeling beside Gorski. "We're both in it up to our eyes now— " He dodged aside as Gorski vomited, spewing a sour yellow stew down the steps.

"I've never even fired my service weapon at anybody," Gorski blubbered, "I— "

"Knock it the fuck off," Mick snapped, seizing the fat cop's shoulders, shaking him hard. "You did what you had to! Does anybody know you're here?"

"What?" Gorski swallowed hard, suddenly aware that they were alone on the stairway with Spivak bleeding out below. And Mick had the guns.

Shannon caught the look. "Relax, sport, I've got no beef with you. This was a long time coming, bad luck you got in the way. But we gotta get clear of this or we'll both rot in jail while they sort out who did what. Clear?"

Gorski nodded, swallowing.

"Okay. Did you guys check in with the army or anything? Do they know you're here?"

"No, there are cops are all over, nobody paid attention to us."

"Okay then. We have to lose Wes. The way the army's shooting up the town, he'll be one more stiff on the pile. But we'll have to use your prowlie. They're stopping civilian cars."

"I can't do that!"

"Yeah you can," Mick said grimly. "Anyway, it's not like you've got a choice."

□   □   □

They drove boldly through the ghetto, Mick at the wheel, Gorski sig-

naling thumbs up as they passed other police cars and soldiers pa-
trolling in Jeeps. On the outer rim of the riot zone, they ditched Spivak's
body in a dumpster, covering his corpse with trash. Gorski fled home to
Ecorse, leaving Mick to work his way back to The Casa through the
smoking city, skulking through the shadows like an alleycat after an air
raid.

At the club, Brownie tried to question him but Cephus waved him off.
Mick's face told him all he needed to know. Spivak's corpse wasn't dis-
covered for a week. Because of their history, Mick was questioned
briefly by Garcia and Bennett, but the detectives didn't push it. By then,
the administration was desperate to downplay the riot violence, so Spivak wasn't lauded as a fallen officer. Like Cleavon Gates, he went into
the books as an unsolved homicide in a city with a long, long list.

CHAPTER 57

Detroit burned for five days. Most of the city survived without a mark,
but the ghetto looked like Nagasaki after the bomb. Stores looted,
trashed and torched.

No rhyme to it. Cohn's Jewelry on Woodward had fine china on display. Untouched. A Dollar Shop around the corner with nothing on the
shelves worth more than a few bucks was stripped to the walls. Rolls of
toilet paper left strewn in the street.

Maceo Willis' bodega was firebombed the second night of the riots,
front windows shattered, the interior gutted by the blaze. And that was
the easy part. The next afternoon, his youngest son was gunned down
by a wired-up guardsman as the kid stood watch over the smoldering
wreckage.

"Them soldier boys claimed he shot at them," Maceo said quietly as
he poked through his charred merchandise, salvaging what little he could.
The paunchy store owner hadn't shaved, the gray stubble around his
goatee making him look a decade older. "All the kid had was a busted
pool cue. Lyin' honky bastards. No offense."

"None taken, Mr. Willis," Mick said. "I'm sorry for your loss."

"You about to be sorrier. I got no money to pay you this week, Shannon. Don't know when I will have. If you gotta bust me up, get to it.
Can't hurt much worse nohow."

"There's been enough bustin' up, Mr. Willis. Get your business squared
away. We'll get straight later."

"What about the vig?"

"No vig, no nothing till you're right-side up. Fair enough?"

"Ain't nothin' fair about this shit, Irish. But thanks. I appreciate it."

Walking back to his car, Mick saw Moishe Abrams limping through the smoke down Dequindre, headed for his office. As Mick hurried to catch up, Moishe heard his footsteps and whirled, eyes wild, raising his stick in his gnarled fist. His old timey suit was dusty with ashes, his nose ringed with a black circle of soot.

"Moishe? What are you doing down here?"

"Seein' what's left of my action," the old man said bitterly. "Swear the sons of bitches had a list of every stiff owes me money, burned 'em out just for spite."

"A lot of people got hurt."

"Only in Darktown. All these years, the boys at the St. Clair calling me Nigger Moishe behind my back and me laughin' all the way to the bank. Ain't so funny now."

"It'll come back, Moishe. In a few months— "

"A few months maybe the crazy spades burn the rest of the town! And how do I pay Big John and them in the meantime? Dammit, I never shoulda done business down here. I gotta cash out before somethin' worse happens. But can't walk a fuckin' block without a damn cane. You gotta squeeze the marks hard, Mick. *Nem de gelt*! Get the money!"

"Moishe, there's no money to get. A lot of people have lost everything. Maceo Willis is burying his youngest boy tomorrow."

"He's got more boys. What have I got?"

"You've got me. I'll get your money, Moishe. In a few months we'll collect it all. But right now these people need a breather."

"A few months might be all the time I got! Either get my damn money or I'll hire somebody who will! Nobody stiffs me!"

"Don't get crazy on me, Moishe, nobody's trying to stiff you. You want out, give me a number. Maybe I can cash you out."

"It don't work that way. Luca decides who gets what."

"Luca's never given us anything but trouble. But go ahead, ask Big John to buy you out. See what you get."

"No," Moishe said slowly. "They'd hose me. Forty fuckin' years and all I can do is lay off my action on a punk kid."

"Life's tough. Ask folks around here."

"You ask 'em! They're your people now. You had balls when I took you on, Shannon. That *schvartza* singer's turned you into a pimp."

Flushing, Mick barely held himself in check. But he read the wildness in the old man's eyes. And the fury. And realized Moishe *wanted* a fight. Enraged at the destruction of his world, Moishe needed to lash out at somebody, to feed his adrenaline jones. But even knowing that, it was hard to swallow the insult.

"What do you want from me, Moishe? Just say it."

"You want to treat the blacks like kin? Do it with your own money. Buy me out, Mick, all, the office, street money, juke warehouse, everything. The number's sixty-two."

"It's not worth half that and you know it."

"This ain't no fire sale, sonny, I ain't the one got burned out. It's a one-time offer. Take it or get back on the street, bustin' balls."

"I'll go forty-five, Moishe. Half today. I'll need a little time for the rest."

"You got a deal at fifty. And time's no problem. Your credit's good with me, Irish. Take a year if you want. Take two. But you'll pay full vig with the rest of the spades."

□   □   □

Except for the smashed glass and bullet holes in the front façade, the violence passed by The Casa Mayor. And it wasn't unique. Homes, businesses, even churches, were looted or burned, while most Motown saloons suffered only minor damage. Which only confirmed Moishe's view that Detroit blacks had gone collectively whack.

It was a season for madness. Despite the fiery riots in Newark and Detroit, Flower Children were still calling '67 the Summer of Love. The Beatles' *Sergeant Pepper* album exploded across America like a cultural H-bomb, transforming pop songs from disposable dance music to an instant, audible art form.

Suddenly, music mattered. Underground artists with no access to the press or TV could radio messages around the world in three minute sound-bites, Aretha demanding "Respect" for her sisters, Barry McGuire predicting an "Eve of Destruction."

Freaks in San Francisco held the Gathering of Tribes, a Human Be-in at Golden Gate Park to usher in a new Age of Aquarius. Adolescents wearing flowers in their hair were openly smoking dope, doffing their duds and fucking each other in public with juicy gusto, leaving their middle class parents utterly baffled. And envious.

Bras and incense were burning along with the ghettos. Inspired by the American fires, a onetime Hanoi lawyer, Vo Nguyen Giap was planning a new kind of riot. A surprise party set for the coming Vietnamese New Year.

Tet.

The Summer of Love was a busy one for General Giap, and for Mick too. When The Casa reopened, the Sultans found themselves playing to a half-empty house. The suburban white-bread kids who'd been filling the club abandoned the inner city to catch Question Mark or the Bob Seger System at the Hash Bash at Ann Arbor or Davison's Sherwood Forest.

But if the riots ran off much of The Casa's crowd, the fires heated Martika's career to a boil. In August, she scored a major hit single, "Love Lies." The soulful ballad broke into the Top Ten at number eight and became everybody's favorite make-out song that summer. Hippie kids loved slow dancing or slow screwing to the tune. So did their parents.

Tika's timing couldn't have been better. With The Casa bleeding red and the vigorish mounting on Moishe's street loans, they needed cash desperately and she went after it, touring the country with the Sultans as the opening act.

No chitlin' circuit dives this time. The Sultans were headliners now, and Martika was rapidly becoming a superstar. After a week in Chicago's Regal Theater, the Black Kats revue flew to New York for a ten day run at the Apollo in Harlem, then off to London, then back home to Atlanta, Biloxi, New Orleans, Dallas and on to L.A.

Being marquee names didn't change the game, though. Touring was still an endless parade of airports, buses and motels. A killer grind, and the performers paid the freight in blood. Benjy Jefferson crashed in London, hospitalized for alcohol poisoning and exhaustion. Bad news for the show but better luck for Benjy. While he was laid up, the Black Kats tour bus was rear-ended by a logging truck south of Atlanta, killing the two roadies sleeping in the back seat and crippling the drummer Jerome hired to take Benjy's place.

Varnell Mack was the next to fall. Onstage in Biloxi with Otis DeWitt belting out ""Motown Mama"", Varnell suddenly went pale, his face beading with icy sweat. Moving ever so carefully, the tall oldster shuffled gracefully offstage, to collapse in the wings. A mild coronary, a Mississippi doc said. Three month's bed rest and no stress.

Fat chance. Varnell had suffered through too many tough years to miss a single moment of the Sultans' success. He rejoined the tour two weeks later, bolstered by nitro, street cocaine and his own iron will, determined to carry on even if the road killed him.

Which it did. In Los Angeles, a few weeks before Christmas.

In their backstage dressing room at the Fillmore Auditorium, Otis DeWitt, the Sultans' bull-necked lead singer, noticed Varnell sitting quietly in the corner, watching the group joshing at the mirror, giving their perms and neckties a final check.

"You all right, Pops?" Otis asked.

"Fine as wine, boy," Varnell smiled. "I keep gettin' better with age." Otis finished straightening his collar, thought no more of it until the group gathered offstage for their entrance, and he realized Varnell wasn't with them.

Hurrying back to the dressing room, Otis found Varnell in his chair, still staring at the mirror. Smiling.

But gone. The burly singer lightly touched the older man's cheek to be sure, then slowly sagged to his knees, rested his bullet head on Varnell's lap, and cried like a child.

Varnell Mack's funeral was as dignified as the man himself, limited to family and a few friends. No reporters attended. The pop press was focused on Madison, Wisconsin that week, where singer Otis Redding and four members of his band died amid fire and ice when their plane smashed into a frozen lake in heavy fog. Compared to the death of a budding soul superstar, an old timer biting the dust barely raised a ripple.

The Sultans had intended to sing "A Mighty Fortress" at the graveside, but when the moment came, they simply couldn't do it. Afterward, they held a brief wake for their friend, then went their ways. Separately. Their street dream was over. Not one of the Sultans of Soul ever stepped on a stage again.

Martika didn't have that option. Varnell's death came in the middle of a sold-out tour with concerts booked a year in advance. She could only soldier on, mourning her fallen friend in her broken hearted blues music, missing him in lonely hotels and airport lounges, in nameless towns where she didn't know a soul.

Levi Stubbs and the Four Tops generously agreed to replace the Sultans for the duration of Martika's tour, a major surprise. The Tops had signed with Motown Records and Berry Gordy never allowed his artists to work for competing labels. Varnell's death was a special circumstance, of course, but the truth was, Gordy, the visionary master of Motown music, had seen the future.

And he was busy packing.

The rioters bypassed the Motown Studio, but the writing was on the wall. With Detroit's ashes still smoking, he was moving his company out of the city that gave his label its name. Running like a scalded dog.

During the months of madness, Mick caught up with the tour whenever he could, joining Tika for a weekend in Wichita, a one-nighter in Cleveland. Most of their time together was spent in bed or in backstage dressing rooms, fucking each other fiercely, talking in whispers afterward, then making desperate love again. Keeping the world at bay. Until the next morning, when the alarm rang early and she had a plane or a bus to catch, while Mick headed back to Detroit.

Inside 8 Mile, Mick nursed The Casa's shaky business along, auditioning new acts for Black Kats with Brownie while paying down his debt to Moishe.

When he wasn't in the club or the streets, he was in his garage, rebuilding his grandfather's Chevy, fine-tuning his Corvette or Brownie's Studebaker Hawk until he had them purring like Formula 1 racers. If a car took all night to tweak in, so much the better. Exhaustion helped him sleep without Martika.

The phone was no comfort. Mick wasn't much of a talker and hearing Tika's voice only reminded him they were apart. But gradually, the constant grind began to pay off. As the riots faded from the front pages, college kids began finding their way back to The Casa and Tika's nonstop touring was winning her new fans all over the world, making her a marquee name only a notch below Aretha or Diana Ross.

Five years flew by, but no matter how hard the performers in The Casa worked the crowds, they never quite recaptured the electric synergy of that first season. The fires altered the mood in Motown, perhaps forever. Tension crackled whenever the races came together now, an uneasy blend of resentment and fear that hovered over the city like industrial haze. And smelled like smoke.

CHAPTER 58

November, 1973

A blustery Tuesday night, city streets still wet from the day's chilly drizzle. After the sixteen hundred fires of the '67 riots, the rains in the fall of '73 felt like Satan's plan to drown the town.

Mick's office at The Casa was high and dry, though, with the heat cranked up to toasty. He was flipping through publicity folders at his desk. The Four Tops would be leaving the Black Kats tour in a few weeks, and with the Sultans gone for good, the show needed a replacement act, fast. Tika was pacing, sipping cappuccino as Mick called out possibilities. "The Drifters? The Coasters?"

"Great groups, but they're locked into the fifties," Tika said, frowning. "Keep going."

Over the past few years she'd added a few pounds but wore them well. Onstage, she favored glistening, gold lame' jump suits that camouflaged her hips and passed for high fashion in the pop world.

"Somebody psychedelic?" Mick went on, shuffling through the photographs. "The Parliaments?"

"Great showmen but stone druggies," Tika sighed. "None of their crew will see thirty."

"You said that about me once."

"You barely made it, sport," she said, continuing to pace. "Who else?"

Below them, the club was filling up. Tuesday was normally a slow night but Tika'd written two new songs for her next album and wanted to test them in front of a live audience. Word on the street was already spreading. It would be a happening night.

The sound system was pumping out Stevie Wonder's "Superstition," the dance beat thumping through the floor. Due onstage in half an hour, Tika was as edgy as a cat in a kennel full of Rottweilers, sipping the cold Italian coffee to lube her pipes.

After performing in theaters and soccer stadiums, a set at The Casa should have been like singing in her living room. It wasn't. Every show was a challenge. Varnell always said you can't step into the same river or onto the same stage twice. Every audience is brand spankin' new.

"How about The Family Stone?" Tika asked.

"Who?"

"Sly Stewart's group. You just flipped past them." Leaning over Mick's shoulder to show him, the coffee cup slipped out of her hand, slopping cappuccino all over the photographs. She danced back out of the way, avoiding the mess, but Mick wasn't as quick.

Grumbling, he was mopping coffee off his lap when a soggy napkin bounced off his head!

He nearly blew! "Hey! Get serious! We need a replacement act and— Another paper-wad whizzed past his ear! He caught the glint of mischief in Tika's eyes and the battle was on! Crumpled napkins, a half-eaten sandwich, wadded up invoices, all cannon fodder in the food-fight free-for-all as they dodged around the room pelting each other, laughing and jeering, making so much racket that Cephus stuck his head in to check out the noise.

When he'd gone, Tika yelped, discovering a catsup smear on her gold jacket with ten minutes to show-time. She shucked her shirt to wipe it off, but the combination of a black brassiere and caramel skin was too much for Mick. While she was erasing the spot he unsnapped her, spun her around, and for a moment, could hardly breathe.

"My god, girl," he said wonderingly, "look at you." He dropped to his knees, sucking her chocolate nipple into this mouth, pulling her down as she frantically slipped off her gold lame slacks

Their fracas finished on the office sofa, humping and groaning to a final juicy explosion fully ten minutes after she was due onstage. Still entangled, she reached up to caress his face.

"You and your 'hey, girl,'" she said, shaking her head. And then she squirmed from beneath him, scrambling back into her clothes, cursing the day she'd hooked up with a horny Irish punk.

Her band was already onstage, cooking her introduction, stretching their solos, pumping up the crowd. Heading for the door, she took a last gulp of cappuccino, fumbled her cup again and dropped it, breaking it this time.

Mick thought she was still kidding around.

The audience had begun an impatient, rhythmic clapping when Tika stalked onto the stage, grabbed the mike and ripped into her first tune. She still had the catsup smear on her blouse, her hair was a shambles and she was breathless from her orgasm. And she poured it all into her electric performance, galvanizing her audience, making the show as much a communion as a concert.

Up in the office, Mick got dressed, then began straightening up the mess, listening to Tika's voice over the house sound system. He was nearly finished when he heard her falter in the middle of a song. And then stop altogether.

Charging out of the office, he flew down the steps at a dead run. Tika was sitting on the stage, holding onto her mike stand for support, looking bewildered.

The dance floor was still full. One of the musicians signaled the house disk jockey to take over, and he promptly kicked off The Sultans' "Motown Mama", cranking up the sound level to cover the confusion.

Bulling his way through the dancers, Mick vaulted onstage.

"I'm sorry," Tika said sheepishly. "I...fell down."

"What's wrong?" he said, kneeling beside her.

"I don't know. My knees just went all wobbly and...I can't seem to make my legs work, Mick. I'm not hurt or anything. If can just rest here a minute— "

"Not a chance," he said, scooping her up in his arms. "Cephus, get my fucking car!"

With Tika in the red Corvette's shotgun seat, Mick blew through downtown traffic like a NASCAR racer to the Ford Hospital Emergency room. By then, Tika could walk, though she was still a bit shaky, and the intern on duty seemed more curious about her drug intake than her symptoms.

Taking him aside, Mick explained that Martika was a singer, not a doper, and if he didn't start diagnosing her medical problem, he'd need stitching up himself.

The intern ran a few preliminary tests, frowned at the results, then called down a consulting physician, a blocky little Jewish doctor named Kessler who also frowned. He told Mick Martika should stay overnight and scheduled more tests for the morning.

It was nearly one a.m. before they got her settled into a room. Mick nodded out in the chair beside her bed, holding her hand, drifting into chaotic dreams. Of the daughter they'd lost here, Wes Spivak tumbling through space. And Philly Savarese dying on his knees.

□   □   □

Around midnight, the crowd at Brownie's Lounge began thinning out. The joint had been busy earlier, jammed with shop rats and locals who came to knock down a few cold ones, hear some of John Lee Hooker's blues.

But as closing time ticked closer, the energy bled away. Shift workers had to hit the plant gates at five in the a.m., ready for another day, making Thunderbirds, making Fairlanes, making that overtime pay. Fastest way a black man can rise in this life without packing a gun.

Sure the UAW gave brothers the shit jobs, but working double shifts cranking out Fords for Cadillac money still beat hell out of choppin' cotton in Alabama.

By one a.m., Brownie's place was down to a few die-hards. Four white college kids, blues buffs from the University of Detroit, applauding wildly as John Lee closed out his set with "Smokestack Lightning." A few couples were still on the dance floor, rocking to the rhythm of their own hearts and loins, a tempo totally unrelated to the music.

Three working girls were gabbing near the door, drying themselves with bar napkins, too wet and windblown to stroll the Corridor for tricks.

And at the bar? One stone killer.

Moishe Abrams had limped in a little after one, parked his wide ass on a stool at the end of the bar, his back to the wall.

Brownie hadn't seen him since the war with Savarese, six, seven years ago? Hadn't changed much. Same old surly white dude, square as a cement block and just as hard. Not using a cane anymore, but still dragging a foot. Dated gray jacket with wide lapels, wet from the rain. Wide tie hanging loose, porkpie brim. He looked like a zoot suiter's ghost.

Carolina was behind the bar. Lush, milk chocolate skin, doe eyes, a smile warm as a Delta morning. She often dressed butch, wearing a tuxedo blouse and bow tie, like a man or a dyke, but nobody'd ever mistake her for either one.

Brownie stood in the shadows of his office doorway, watching Moishe guzzle down his first drink, then another just as quick. Didn't even blink. Dude had to be pushing eighty, still looked hard as a frickin' brick.

When Moishe swiveled on his stool to watch John Lee's band, Brownie motioned Carolina Shaw, his bartender/manager/part-time lover, over to the waitress station. Leaned in, keeping his voice low.

"The old white dude? He drinks free. On the house."

"You sure?" Carolina frowned. "He's already pig drunk and throwin' down bourbon like Tennessee's on fire."

"Just give him what he wants, no charge. And say yessir, nossir, he likes that."

"Fine by me, long as he knows I'm not on the menu. Who is he?"

"Moishe Abrams. Used to be the jukebox king 'round here. Irish Mick's old boss."

"A mob guy? That old gimpy dude?"

"Back in the day, Moishe *was* a mob, all by himself. He's meaner than a cross-eyed dog, so make nice with him, sugar. While I figure a way to get his honky ass out of here."

"Got it covered." Switching on her grand piano smile, Carolina sauntered down to sweeten Moishe's drink. Leaving Brownie wondering what the old thug wanted. Seemed like every time he saw Moishe, somebody ended up dead. Whose turn was it tonight?

Brownie wasn't short on sand. Running clubs, trouble comes with the territory. He'd handled countless drunks and brawlers, and he'd backed Mick against Savarese's crew. But Moishe was different. There was a primordial menace about the old man and down deep, Brownie was scared spitless of him.

Fuck it. If Moishe wanted trouble, might as well start the dance. Slipping off his tailored jacket, Brownie hung it neatly on the hook behind his office door. Wondering if he'd see it again.

Then he strolled casually down the bar to Moishe. And smiled.

"Mr. Abrams, how you doin' tonight?"

Moishe didn't look up. "Get lost, blood."

"You remember me, Mr. Abrams? I'm Brownie. Can I buy you one for the road? It's almost closing time."

"It's early."

No sir, it's almost two. Word is, beat cops are checkin' up and down the Corridor, writin' tickets for after hours."

"No beat cop's gonna roust me."

"I'm not worried about you, Mr. Abrams, just them. You bust 'em up in my place, it's bad for business."

Moishe glanced up, looking Brownie over for the first time. Frowning, trying to place him. "You trying to give me the bum's rush?"

"No sir, couldn't if I wanted to and we both know it. How about that drink?"

"I'll take it, but I ain't leavin'. I'm stuck. My damn Lincoln quit on me and I'll never get a cab this time of night."

"No problem, I'll drive you home," Brownie said. And instantly regretted it. "My car's out back, it'd be my pleasure."

Moishe considered the offer. "What kind of a car?"

"Studebaker. Silver Hawk."

"Hawks are for pimps," he grunted, knocking back the last of his bourbon. "Beats walkin', though. Let's go."

Grabbing his jacket from his office, Brownie thought about the gun in his desk. Decided against it. Old or not, Moishe was a stone pro. Might as well climb in the ring with Muhammad Ali, try to land a lucky punch.

Rolling through the city, Moishe kept glancing over his shoulder, checking every side street and the road behind them, his eyes flicking back and forth like a bat in a bonfire. Totally paranoid. The price of being a prick.

The night was blustery, wind off the river picking up, chasing newspapers down the alleys. In the car, neither man spoke, Moishe stewing in boozy silence, Brownie not about to try making conversation. Wasn't sure if the old man remembered him or not, best to keep it that way.

"Stop!" Moishe said suddenly. "Pull over here."

Surprised, Brownie eased the Hawk to the curb. Knew Moishe lived out in Grosse Pointe with his sister, a good five miles further on. Here they were only a few blocks from downtown in the dead of night. Empty streets, darkened windows. Brownie glanced the question at Moishe but he was already climbing out, grunting at the effort.

"Take off," he said, slamming the door.

"Yassuh, Massa Moishe, yo' very welcome, you hymie cocksucker, suh," Brownie said. But only to himself. Watching Moishe limp away down the empty street.

As he circled the block to head back to the lounge, a car came racing out of an alley, pulling up on his tail a few feet from his rear bumper.

Prowl car. But they didn't switch on their flashers. Hit him with the spotlight instead, checking him out.

Half blinded by the blaze, Brownie braced himself for the roust, wondering if they wanted grease money or were just busting his balls. Black man, slick ride, must be up to no good, right?

But maybe it was raining too hard. Whatever the reason, they didn't
bother pulling him over. Tailed him half a mile, their spotlight glaring
through the Hawk's rear window, reminding Brownie he was the wrong
color, wrong time of night.

Like he needed reminding.

CHAPTER 59

The scent of fresh coffee hauled Brownie up from the land of dreams.

Eyes closed, he breathed deep. Definitely coffee. His bedroom door
opened, Carolina stuck her head in.

"Brownie? You awake?"

"I am now. What are you doing here? What time is it?"

"Just after one. I opened the Lounge at noon, cops came looking for
you. Figured I'd best get my young butt over here, get you up."

"What's up?" Brownie asked, fully awake now. "What did they
want?"

"That old guy you left with last night? Moishe? He's dead, Brownie."

"What do you mean, dead? Dead how?"

"How you think? Somebody did him."

Brownie shook his head, trying to clear it. Felt like he'd been sucker
punched. "Carolina, tell me what the fuck happened to him. Exactly."

"Hey, don't be barkin' at me. I don't know squat about it, I'm just
telling you what they said."

There was something in her tone. He glanced at her sharply.

"Whoa up, you don't think *I* iced the old dude?"

Her hesitation said more than the shake of her head.

"No, course not. Coffee's ready, you want some breakfast?"

"Yeah. There's bacon in the icebox. Better fry up some eggs, too. Got
a feelin' it's gonna be a long goddamn day."

Showering quickly, he chose a dark blue pinstripe suit from his closet.
The vest and jacket fit a little loose, room enough in the shoulders for
the Smith. Which he wished like hell he hadn't left back in his office.

But it was for the best.

◻   ◻   ◻

Two men rose from their barstools the moment Brownie stepped into
the lounge. A huge black guy in an off-the-rack Sears jacket and a whip-
pet thin Latin in a trim Lord and Taylor three piece. Cops.

"Leo Brown?" Garcia asked. The black cop didn't say squat, just pointed to the wall.

Brownie raised his hands as Bennett, the black cop patted him down, found nothing, then spun him around. Up close he looked even bigger, half a head taller than Brownie, probably a hundred pounds heavier. Seamed face, bulldog jowls.

The Latin cop showed Brownie an I.D. Lieutenant Lupe Garcia. Metro Homicide, Organized Crime Division. The black cop didn't show him shit.

"Tell us about last night, Mr. Brown," Garcia said casually, like he was asking about the weather. "What was the beef between you and Moishe Abrams? You owed him money? Maybe got a little behind?"

"I had no problem with Moishe," Brownie said, brushing off his lapels. "He came in around one, had a few, hung around till closing. I gave him a lift uptown."

"To what address?"

"No address. He got out at a corner, Pingree and Second."

"Pingree?" the black cop said skeptically. "That time of night?"

"You know who Moishe was, right?"

"We know," Garcia nodded. "So?"

"Then you know he could get off any damn place he wanted in this town, any time at all."

"Maybe," Garcia conceded. "I understand he owns a piece of this joint."

"Moishe had pieces of a lot of places."

"That isn't what I asked you, Mr. Brown," Garcia said. "Did Moishe own a piece of your bar or not?"

"He used to, few years back. Not anymore. What bank do you use, Lieutenant? Detroit National?"

"Why?"

"Ten years ago, I was a bartender. Had six grand saved, needed a small loan to buy this place, fix it up. Do you think Detroit National fronted me the money?"

"Probably not," Garcia admitted. "So what went down last night, Brownie? You late with Moishe's vigorish?"

"I told you, nothing happened. Check me out," Brownie said, turning right and left, showing Garcia both profiles. "See this face? Do I look like I been alley dancin' with Moishe Abrams?"

The two cops exchanged a look, then Garcia shrugged. "No you don't," he admitted. "Too bad. In the old days we didn't give a shit when you mopes killed each other. Another one bites the dust, you know? But now we got a slave driver boss who takes her job serious. Loves lockin' up gangsters. And the since you left with Moishe after closing, you were the last one to see him alive."

"No way, man. I dropped him off around two. A prowl car pulled out of an alley on John R, tailed me a few blocks to make sure I got out of the neighborhood. You can check with them."

"We will, but even if that holds up, it won't get you off the hook with Moishe's boy. Was Mick Shannon having trouble with Moishe?"

"You want to know about Mick, ask Mick."

"I'm asking you."

"Right. Like I'm gonna talk to you about his business? Just shoot me in the head now, okay? Save me the wait."

"Might be doing you a kindness at that," Garcia smiled. "Shannon's a bad man to cross, I hear. You're better off talking to us than him."

"All I can tell him is what I've told you, Lieutenant. Moishe was half in the bag and he's a mean drunk. Mean sober for that matter. Way he was last night, I'm not surprised somebody got killed, I'm just surprised it was Moishe. What happened, anyhow?"

"Somebody cut him up bad," Bennett, the black cop said, his deep bass voice like coal rumbling down a chute. "Took their time at it. Like they were enjoying themselves."

"Enough already with this mutt," Garcia shrugged. "We've got two more homicides to check out before supper. That's why they call Motown Murder City, Brownie. Next one might interest you. A guy beaten to death over on Dequindre, couple blocks from Moishe's office. Want to take a ride, see your future?"

"I'm good here."

"Think so?" the black cop snorted. "Remember that ol' Jimmy Reed tune? 'Take Out Some Insurance?' If I'm you, I'd be buyin' a new policy. Big one."

As soon as they were out the door, Brownie hustled into his office, grabbed the phone, called The Casa.

"Cephus? Put Mick on. What do you mean he's at the hospital? What— ? Okay, listen up. You get your ass out there. Moishe Abrams bought it last night. Tell Mick the law's lookin' for him and they might not be the only ones. I'll find out what I can, call you when I got somethin'."

He hung up, stood there a moment, thinking. Then took his .38 Smith out of the desk drawer, spun the cylinder to make sure it was loaded.

Five minutes later he was in his Silver Hawk, retracing the route he'd taken the night before. From the Lounge to the corner of Pingree and Second. Easing the Stude to the curb, he scanned the area, remembering.

Moishe hadn't asked to be brought here. He'd been antsy as hell, then suddenly ordered Brownie to pull over. As though he'd remembered something.

Okay, what could Moishe remember about this corner? A newsstand in the next block carried the morning papers, the *Free Press* and the *News*, a few magazines. But it hadn't been open yet. Hell, it was after two a.m. Every damn thing was closed…

No. Not everything. Switching off the Studebaker's ignition, Brownie climbed out. The wind off the river hit him like a blast from a fridge door. Instant chill.

Dropping a dime in the meter, he strolled down the narrow service alley that led to the loading docks in mid-block behind the shops, holding his jacket collar closed.

There. The cast iron staircase led to a second story warehouse above a print shop. No lights showing, naturally. The windows were painted flat black. Fatback's blind pig. Where they'd ambushed Savarese's crew.

Trotting up the steps, Brownie rapped twice on the gray metal freight door, then twice again. The door opened. Just a crack. "What?"

"It's Brownie. Tell Fat I need to see him. It's important."

The door closed a moment, then opened again. Bass, Fatback's Muslim bouncer/bodyguard, waved him in.

Inside, the pig was empty, chairs stacked on tables while an ancient janitor mopped the hardwood floor. Gaming tables all under dust covers.

Fat was at the end of the bar, sipping single malt scotch, counting his register receipts, looking heavier than ever in a powder blue Full Cleveland jump suit, wide pimp collar, white belt. Brownie took the stool next to him.

"Po-lice been here, Fat?"

"Nah, they get greased on Fridays. Why?"

"I dropped Moishe Abrams in front of your place last night," Brownie said, shading the truth. "What the hell happened?"

"What always happens with the ol' jukebox king?" Fat said, jotting down the tape tally in a tiny notebook. "Shit happened. For openers, he claims the barstool facing the door is his, pushes some dude off it. Wouldn't drink from no glass, so I gave him a bottle. Figured he'd knock it down, maybe pass out. Didn't though. Just got meaner."

"Sounds like Moishe."

"Place was quiet, couple card games, some craps goin' on. Little Diddley was onstage playin' guitar, nobody payin' him no mind till Moishe yells at him to quit singin' them blues. Kid don't know Moishe from Bojangles Robinson, tells him to screw hisself. I told him to call it a night to save his damn life." Fatback shook his head, remembering.

"Then Moishe wants to play some cards. Butts into Bobby Cee's game. Them studs been at it all night, had serious money changin' hands, seven, eight hundred bucks every pot. Moishe antes up a grand, loses it in five minutes. He's too drunk to pitch pennies, say nothin' of playin' no cutthroat poker. Then he claims Bobby Cee's cheatin'."

"Jesus," Brownie whistled. "What happened?"

"All hell broke loose. Bobby grabs for him, ol' Moishe comes out his chair with a gun in one hand, straight razor in the other. Bass covers 'em all with the scattergun. I hauled Bobby Cee off, Bass took Moishe's gun and hustled his honky ass out the place. Might cost me my jukebox but it's better than havin' Moishe kill somebody or get killed his own self."

Brownie was staring at him.

"What?" Fat asked, annoyed.

"You haven't heard."

"Ain't heard nothin' about nothin', man. Just rolled in here ten minutes ago. What's up?"

"Somebody did Moishe last night, cut him up half a block from here. Law's all over it and I expect his people will be lookin' too."

"Aw, mama, you got to be kiddin'," Fat moaned. "Do they know he was here?"

"Not yet, but they damn sure will. Any chance Moishe waited outside for Bobby Cee, mixed it up with him?"

"Nah, we bounced Moishe around three. Cee's game didn't break up until seven-thirty or so, then me and Cee went to Greektown for breakfast."

"Cee was with you the whole time?" Brownie pressed.

"Yeah, the whole damn time, me and Bobby..." Fatback broke off, scowling.

"What?"

"On the other hand, a dozen people saw Moishe and Cee get into it. But I'm the only one can cover for Bobby after."

"That's cold, Fat."

"Hey, me and Cee ain't family. But Moishe and Mick Shannon are. And Irish is one *ofay* motherfucker I don't want comin' down on me. I ain't forgot what happened to Savarese and them. If Mick wants to bleed somebody out over Moishe, better Bobby Cee than us. Unless you got another candidate?"

"Not yet," Brownie said, rising. "You gonna be here?"

"Got nowhere else to be," the big man sighed. "Besides, I'm too wide to hide."

◻ ◻ ◻

Mick was in the center of the ring, circling counter-clockwise to stay away from his opponent's right. Big, white guy, tall as a silo, fists like anvils, the crowd roaring— somebody tapped Mick's shoulder. He didn't turn. It was some clown trying to distract him, give the silo a free shot— the tap came again.

This time Mick whirled to swing, but somebody grabbed his arms, pinning them to his sides—

"Wake up, Mick! It's me, Cephus! Wake up!"

Breaking through the haze, Mick realized he was in the Ford Hospital waiting room, wrestling with Cephus. A half dozen gawkers were staring, wide-eyed. A security guard hurried in, took one look at the two men, made a quick U-turn, headed the other way.

"You all right now?" Cephus asked.

"Yeah, lemme go. Sorry. Must've fallen asleep."

"You look like shit, man. How long you been here?"

"I don't know. Since last night. What time is it?"

"Three in the afternoon. How's Martika?"

"Sleeping. They've gave her tests all morning, got more scheduled for later. What are you doing here?"

"Are you all the way awake, Mick? Cause we've got trouble." Taking him aside, he told him about Moishe's death. Straight up. Mick barely blinked. But Cephus recognized the look. Like a fighter who's been rocked. To his socks.

"Do they ah…? Sweet Jesus. Any idea who did it?"

"Cops got no clue and probably don't much care. Brownie say he's lookin' into it."

◻ ◻ ◻

Brownie stood at the top of the stairway outside Fatback's front door, looking down and around. Remembering what happened to Savarese when he burst through this door. Did something like that happen to Moishe? Not likely. There were too many people around. And a man getting cut up doesn't die quiet.

According to Fat, Moishe got bounced around three. What would he do next? Where could he go without a car?

Nowhere. The answer came to him as surely as the turnaround in one of Hooker's blues tunes. Moishe would never accept being thrown out of a blind pig, by black men. With no ride, no place to go, he'd hang around. Looking to get even, to get his money back.

Waiting for Bobby Cee to come out.

Where?

The doorway at the foot of the stairs? Trotting down the steps, Brownie put his shoulder to the freight door. Couldn't budge it. Nailed shut now. Probably hadn't been opened since the shootout.

Which left the alley across the loading area. Same place Moishe staked out Savarese. Concealed there, he could watch the door, wait for Bobby to come down the stairway, then make his move.

Only Moishe didn't move so good anymore. With his limp, he couldn't rush anybody head on. He'd have to wait till the guy headed out the alley, try to take him from behind...

Circling slowly, Brownie scanned the ground. Signs weren't hard to spot if you knew what to look for.

Polka dots. Inky droplets more brown than red now, were spattered across the cardboard scraps littering the alley floor. Dried blood. Nothing dramatic, just a spattering. Easy to miss if you weren't looking. Fatback and Bobby Cee probably walked right past it.

Damn.

Some loose boxes were piled against the wall. Brownie nudged them aside, half expecting to find a body beneath them. Didn't. Instead he found a battered chipboard guitar case. The name Little Diddley was crudely lettered on one side in white paint. Spattered with bloody polka dots.

CHAPTER 60

"The kid's real name is Davonne Deveraux," Fatback said. "Calls hisself Little Diddley 'cause he plays guitar like Bo."

They were in Brownie's Studebaker, headed down Eighth as the gusty November dusk settled over Detroit, darkening the streets. Brownie at the wheel, Fat filling most of the back seat, Mick riding shotgun. He'd left Cephus at The Casa to get ready for the night.

"What do you know about this kid?" Mick asked.

"Not much. Alabama boy, cousin to Johnny Shines. Come up from Selma a few months back, scufflin' for gigs. Plays a mean guitar."

"And works cheap," Brownie added.

"It ain't like I'm rippin' him off," Fatback protested. "I gave him a gig singin' after hours, got him a room over at the Delmore Arms where most of the players stay. Figured he could make some connections there, line up more work. And this is how he pays me back. Gets jammed up with the fuckin' jukebox king, or used to was. Might as well head down to the morgue, pick out a slab for hisself. And us too."

"Might be there already," Brownie said, wheeling the Hawk into the Delmore Arms parking lot. "Cops said they found a stiff in an alley on the Corridor last night, beaten to death."

"Think it was Diddley?" Mick asked.

"They didn't mention a name. Let's find out."

Fatback slipped the Delmore desk clerk a five for a key to the kid's room. The three men rode six floors up, the rickety elevator rattling like a cattle car on the Rock Island Line.

Didn't bother to knock. Fat silently unlocked the door, letting Brownie and Mick slide into the darkened room. Brownie switched on the light.

"Aw man," Fat breathed. A body was on the bed, wrapped in a tangle of bloodstained sheets. Mick pressed a finger to the kid's throat.

"He's alive, but not by much."

"And not for long, any way you figure it," Brownie said, picking up a straight razor from the nightstand, handing it to Mick. Mick's lips narrowed. The pearl handled razor was crusted with rusty blood. And very familiar.

"Wake up, Davonne," Fat said, slapping the kid hard. "Come on, goddamn it! Wake the fuck up!"

Diddley's eyes snapped open, widening as they flicked from Fat to Mick and back again, terrified. He tried to sit up, then fell back, groaning.

"What the hell happened last night?" Fat demanded. "What'd you do?"

"Nothin', swear to God," the kid gasped. "I got jumped in the alley."

"Then why aren't you dead?" Mick asked reasonably. "Moishe is."

"Old dude's dead?"

"You oughta know," Fat growled. "You done him."

"No," the kid winced, remembering. "I came out the club, seen the old dude down on his hands and knees in the alley, two guys kneelin' by him. I figured old timer was pukin' up. He was damn sure drunk enough."

"Fuck that," Fat growled. "What happened?"

"Cats heard me comin' down the steps. I ask 'em if the old dude was all right, but they don't say nothin'. One comes at me with the razor, quick as a whisper. Musta zipped me five times before I got what the hell was happenin'. I swung my guitar at him, his razor stuck in the case. I grabbed it away and ran like a motherfucker, all the way here. Musta passed out."

"The two guys. Were they from the club?" Mick asked.

"Nah, I don't think so. I been workin' Fat's a few weeks now, know most of the regulars. I never seen these two before."

"Black or white?" Brownie asked.

"Could've been white. Wasn't much light and I only saw 'em a second, but... There was somethin' weird about 'em."

"How do you mean, weird?"

"Don't know, man, I never got a good look. But somethin' was— strange is all. Maybe it'll come to me."

"When you got time to think up a better lie," Fat snorted.

"I ain't lyin', Fat," Diddley protested. "Them two musta been cuttin' on the old dude when I come out. Damn, my guitar— "

"It's in my car," Brownie said. "Stay still or you'll start bleedin' again."

Stepping back, he motioned Mick and Fat away from the bed.

"He's cut bad," Brownie said. "Needs a doctor."

"We take him to a hospital laid open like that, the cops and Moishe's people will be on him five minutes later." Fat shrugged. "He's better off bleedin' out where he's at."

"One of Moishe's people already knows," Brownie said. "How about it, Mick? You and the old man were tight. What do we do?"

"I don't know. Think he's telling the truth?"

"Nah, he's lyin' to cover his own dumb ass," Fat said.

"Maybe," Mick nodded. "Was anybody around when you dropped Moishe off, Brownie?"

"I wasn't really lookin', Moishe was trouble enough. But... He was on edge, you know? Kept checking behind him. Like he was watching for somebody."

"How about it, Fatback? Anybody in your joint sound like the two guys Diddley saw?"

"Naw. All regulars. I knew everybody in the joint. Bass threw Moishe out and the kid split maybe twenty minutes later. Nobody else left. Kid's blowin' smoke. What you wanna do?"

"Hell, I don't know. Moishe was headed for that alley his whole life. The kid could be lying about the two guys, but the thing is? I can't see that punk takin' Moishe, especially not with his own razor. I'm thinking Moishe got jumped and Diddley walked into it. Tough luck for him, worse for Moishe."

"Bad for us too," Fat said. "Brownie dropped him at my place, he got cut outside my place. If the St. Clair crew hears about this, right and wrong won't matter. We could hand over Diddley tied up with a bow and still get capped."

Mick took a slow look around the seedy room, the terrified kid shivering under the bloody bedcovers. And the red-stained razor in his hands. Crusted with drying blood. Moishe's blood.

Couldn't make it add up. Knew Moishe's death might mean trouble with the St. Clair crew but that wasn't the worst of it. Somehow he couldn't shake off the feeling that every wrong thing he'd done in his life was coming back on him now.

"Fuck the St. Clair crew," he said abruptly. "Get hold of Tika's cousin, Calvin Oaks, the medic. Jerome will know how to reach him. Get this kid patched up on the quiet. No hospital, no law. Stash him someplace safe, for now. Gimme your car keys, Brownie. I gotta go."

CHAPTER 61

Whipping Brownie's Stude into the Henry Ford Hospital parking ramp, Mick left the car rocking, double parked. Racing into the hospital, he didn't know what was wrong, only that something was. Remembered the feeling from the alley behind the Regency, from Cooley's, and a dozen times since. Something heavy was in the wind, coming hard. His guts were in knots, every muscle tensed. Braced for a punch.

Didn't wait for an elevator, charging up the stairs two at a time to Tika's room.

Where everything seemed perfectly fine. Tika was tired and a bit groggy but otherwise felt okay. Mick sat with her, holding her hand until she dozed off, then went in search of the little Jewish specialist who'd ordered all the workups. Kessler.

When he gave the receptionist his name, she simply waved him through. A bad sign. And the minute he stepped into the room and saw Kessler's face...

The doctor was behind his desk, little sawed off runt, white fringe around his ears, white smock, black horn-rims. He waved Mick to the seat facing him.

"I'm sorry, Mr. Shannon, perhaps you told me earlier, but what is your relationship to Miss Daniels? Exactly?"

"I'm her husband."

"Legally or...? Forgive me pressing the matter but some hard decisions have to be made. I need to know I'm discussing this with the right person."

"I'm that person," Mick said, barely restraining his rage, "and you'd better start talking."

"Very well. There's no easy way to say this, Mr. Shannon. We've done a complete battery of tests and the results are conclusive. Miss Daniels has a thyroid tumor which is partially compressing her larynx and carotid artery. Thus, the sudden weakness and vertigo. "

"A tumor," Mick echoed, stunned. "Jesus. That's...bad, isn't it."

"I'm afraid so, yes. I'm very sorry."

"Okay," Mick said, taking a breath, "she has this... tumor. You can treat that , right? What has to be done?"

"I have already scheduled Miss— I'm sorry— your wife, for surgery tomorrow afternoon, but the outlook is troubling. In the X-rays, the growth appears to be engaged with her vocal cords as well. The operation is likely to be lengthy and difficult."

"But she'll make it?"

"The procedure is not without risk, but she's healthy and strong. She should make an... almost complete recovery." The little man glanced away. And Mick had been reading faces a long time.

"Almost complete?" he echoed dangerously. "Quit waltzing around, Doc. What the hell are you *not* telling me?"

"How long has your wife been showing symptoms, Mr. Shannon?"

"Not long. She's complained of some stiff necks— "

"When did her discomfort begin?"

"I'm...not exactly sure. She's been on tour the past few months so we've only spoken by phone. I noticed she sounded hoarse, and she said her throat's been a little sore. But hell, she sings her heart out four or five shows a week. Sore throats come with the territory."

"Unfortunately, that tends to confirm what we suspect," Kessler sighed. "Her tumor is particularly aggressive, but I believe we've caught it in time."

"You still haven't told me the bad news," Mick said, rising slowly, blood hammering in his ears, one second away from clocking Dr. Kessler or punching through the wall. "You said partial recovery. What the hell does that mean? Exactly?"

"Bear in mind, the diagnosis is still preliminary," Kessler said calmly. "I've asked for second and third opinions from the finest specialists available. For what it's worth, you have my deepest sympathy, Mr. Shannon. My wife and I have all of Martika's albums, we're both big fans. I give you my word we'll do our very best for her, but... "

"But what?"

"The tumor's involvement with her larynx appears to be extensive, Mr.

Shannon. She will almost certainly lose one of her vocal cords. Possibly both of them. I'm sorry."

Mick just stared. "What— are you telling me?"

"The loss of one cord means your wife will never sing again, Mr. Shannon. Or speak much above a whisper. If both cords are involved? It's possible she'll lose her ability to speak altogether."

"Sweet Jesus," Mick murmured, stunned. "Have um... have you told her?"

"Of course. Ultimately it's her decision, she has a right to know."

"Okay, let's say your... diagnosis is correct. What's going to happen?"

"We'll do the surgery tomorrow, and she'll be kept sedated afterwards. She'll need complete bed for at least a week, with absolutely *no* talking. If money is a problem, the hospital has programs— "

"I'll get the money! You just get these experts she's supposed to see. When will that happen?"

"I'll consult with them later today, and if they concur, we'll do surgery tomorrow. You can spend time with her now if you like, but please don't stay too long. She needs to rest."

□   □   □

"Hey, girl, look at you," he said, easing down on the white plastic chair beside her bed.

"They told you, didn't they?" Martika said, reading his face. "You look droopy as a blue tick hound. Damn it, Mick, you're supposed to be tough. And right now, that's what I need. Everybody else can piss and moan, not you. Okay?"

"Okay," he nodded, swallowing hard. "No moaning. How can I help?"

"For openers, Dr. Kessler's already told me I may lose my pipes. I'm done... " She swallowed, hard. "I'm done singing and maybe talking too. Did he tell you?"

"Jesuz, babe, I'm sorry— "

"Screw that. It don't help. But I need a favor."

"Whatever you need. Just say it."

"I want you to stay away after. They won't know what's what for most of a week. I don't want to see you before I know what's up. I need time to get my head around— whatever happens. All right?"

Hell no it wasn't all right! "Sure," he said. "Okay."

"No. It's not okay," she frowned, reading his face. "There's something else, isn't there? Something's up besides me, I mean? What is it?"

He tried to speak, coughed. Swallowed, hard. "Moishe," he managed.

"He was killed on the street last night."

"Oh," she said. She looked away absently a moment, then turned back to him, meeting his eyes dead on.

"Good," she said.

CHAPTER 62

The coffin looked like a packing crate. Laid out on a bier draped in rich maroon velvet in Lipinski's luxurious viewing room, the plain wooden box looked shabby and out of place as a beggar at a banquet. It was lidless, but there was nothing to see. Moishe's body was concealed beneath a coarse muslin sheet.

Mick looked around for somebody to ask about it, but the only souls in sight were Moishe's elderly sister, and the young usher in a dark suit standing with her.

"I need a word," Mick growled, seizing the kid by the bicep, muscling him aside to a corner. "Listen, I want Moishe out of that cheap ass box. You get him in the best coffin you've got, top of the line, understand? I don't care what it costs."

"Nor do I," the usher said dryly. "I'm not in the casket business. I'm Rabbi Eisenheim." He offered Mick his hand. "I take it you're Mr. Shannon?"

"You're a Rabbi?" Mick said doubtfully. The kid looked scarcely old enough to shave. Pale, bookish features, thick dark hair showing the tracks of a comb.

"More Rachel's rabbi than Moishe's, I'm afraid. Please don't be upset by the simplicity of the casket, Mr. Shannon. It's traditional, in our faith. We enter this world with nothing and leave the same way, rich and poor alike. No disrespect is intended to your friend. Not that he cared much about our traditions."

"How do you mean?"

"His gravesite."

"What about it? Look, if it's too cheap— "

"Quite the opposite, actually," Eisenheim smiled. "You didn't make the arrangements?"

"No, Mr. Lipinski said Moishe set it all up years ago. Why?"

"Let's just say that for an Orthodox Jew, Mr. Abrams chose a very unorthodox site." He moved off to greet a new mourner. Still smiling.

The newcomer was a surprise, Lieutenant Lupe Garcia, neatly turned out in a black suit. After offering Rachel Abrams his condolences, Garcia joined Mick at the bier.

He crossed himself. Mick gave him a look.

"Relax, Shannon, I'm not on the job," Garcia said quietly. "It may seem odd to you, but that old hood's half the reason I'm a cop. Growing up in Dearborn, I heard all the stories about the old days. When I was a rook, my big dream was busting Moishe, making a name for myself. I actually came close, a few times. Got called to crime scenes for guys we knew damned well he'd taken out. Forget about it. Roomful of witnesses, nobody saw a damn thing. I swear people would toss their babies into a bear pit before they'd rat out Moishe Abrams."

Mick glanced at his watch. Martika would be going into surgery soon. Dammit.

"Missing him must have chapped your ass some."

"A little," Garcia admitted, "but I understood why they were intimidated. To be honest, that old man scared hell out of me, too. What was it like, working with him?"

"Tough. He wasn't easy to get along with. But if you were jammed up, he'd be there. A standup guy. Aren't many like him anymore."

"Thank god for that. Were you two close?"

"Not so much. But I owed him. And learned from him."

"Mostly evil, I imagine."

"Mostly," Mick admitted. "Not all."

"Well, I can't say I'll miss him, but I'm sorry for your loss, Shannon. See you around." At the aisle, Garcia knelt to cross himself, then headed out. At the door, he met John Luca, Charlie Musso, the union goon and Fat Sal Benedetto, the crime boss from Pontiac, coming in. They eyed him a moment, then passed without speaking.

Mick joined Big John and the others at the back of the room. Luca and Fat Sal were wearing somber suits and ties. Charlie Musso hadn't bothered, still in his Teamsters leather jacket and work boots.

"What was that fuckin' cop doin' here?" Musso demanded.

"Came to pay his respects."

"Bullshit! Cops got no respect," Musso snorted. "Probably makin' sure the old Kike's really dead."

Mick slapped him! Hard! Totally on reflex. Didn't even realize he'd done it till Charlie's head snapped around. For a shocked second, everyone froze. Then Musso went for his gun!

Grabbing his hand, Mick bent Musso's thumb back in a bouncer's control grip, freezing him in place, paralyzed, gasping in pain.

"Chill out, Charlie."

"Let me go, cocksucker, or— "

Mick gave Musso's thumb a quick twist, snapping it like a dry stick, with an audible *pop!* Charlie gasped, going instantly ashen, his knees wobbling, would have fallen but his broken thumb was still locked in Mick's fist. Reaching inside Musso's jacket, Mick disarmed him, stuffing the thug's automatic into his own belt.

"One more word and I'll break your arm," Mick said quietly. "Get out."

Musso nodded, unable to speak. Releasing him, Mick thrust him toward the door. Charlie stumbled away, glancing back at Luca for help.

"Wait in the car," Luca said.

"Goddamn it, John— "

"In the car," Luca repeated, turning back to Mick without waiting to see if Musso would obey. "That was incredibly stupid!"

"I thought so. He should be more polite at funerals."

"Musso's got a big mouth," Luca conceded, "but this is no time to fight amongst ourselves. What happened to Moishe, Shannon? Did you two have a falling out?"

Mick just stared at him.

"You're young, ambitious, I get that," Luca continued, his eyes locked on Mick's. "So if you've got something to tell me— "

"I didn't do Moishe, Mr. Luca. He was..." Mick faltered, trying to think of the right word. But he didn't know one. "Moishe was my friend. He had nothing I wanted."

"Somebody must've wanted something," Fat Sal observed.

"No offense intended, Shannon," Luca said, "I had to ask. The Organized Crime Division is all over our union action. They've already indicted Hoffa and busted two shop stewards for taking payoffs, the last thing I need is more heat from a fucking street war. Do you think Moishe's killing was personal? Or is somebody trying to move in?"

"I don't know yet. But I'll find out."

"When you do, leave it to us. We'll take care of it."

"Not a chance," Mick said. "I'll settle up for Moishe myself."

"Is something wrong with your ears, Shannon?" Fat Sal Benedetto demanded, flushing dangerously. "John just told you we can't afford— "

"Sal," John murmured, touching Benedetto's sleeve, glancing pointedly at three plainclothes types who'd come in quietly, standing at the rear. "Cops. We better go."

But as he turned away, he leaned in close to Mick.

"Do as you're fucking told!" Luca hissed in Mick's ear. "Find out who did this! Give 'em to me!"

Mick didn't bother to answer. Watched the two old hoods offer their sympathy to Moishe's sister, then make their way up the aisle. The trio of lawmen trailed them out like an entourage.

"*Somebody wanted something,*" Sal's voice echoed in Mick's head.

But what? Mick glanced around the velvet draped room, the empty chairs, the crude casket up front where Moishe's shrunken corpse lay beneath the muslin shroud.

Whoever it was must have gotten what they wanted. Moishe damn sure didn't have it anymore...

Mick felt eyes on him.

At the back of the room, a tall figure was watching him from the shadows.

Mick didn't know him, but he definitely knew the type. A Mexican with a thin face, acne scars, wearing a camel sport jacket that didn't conceal the weapon at his waist, and wasn't meant to. Didn't even pretend he was there for Moishe, coolly scoping out the room. And Mick.

Another mug from the St. Clair? One of Musso's people? He didn't recognize this goon, but if he wanted trouble, Mick was definitely in the mood.

He was halfway up the aisle when a heavyset blonde guy followed the Mex in, looking around...Mick stiffened. Jesus. Was it Ronny Ducatti? If so, he'd put on forty pounds— and then Albert Luca stepped in and there was no mistaking him.

CHAPTER 63

Albert looked sleek, tanned and trim, wearing a collarless red Nehru jacket over black bellbottoms, a cluster of gold chains at his throat. His granny glasses were tinted blue, John Lennon style. Very hip, very L.A.

Albert said something to Ronny and the Mex. Ducatti stayed by the door, clearly on watch. Albert and the Mex came down the aisle, looking over the room like they owned it.

"Nice plush layout, Shannon, top drawer. Business must be good. Let's sit. Have a word." He eased down on a pew without waiting for an answer. Mick hesitated, then eased warily down beside him.

The Mex stayed in the aisle, watching Mick, his arms folded. Up close, he had a true Aztec face, hooked nose, high cheekbones, predator's eyes.

"Too bad about Moishe," Albert said.

"Even worse for you, Albert. I told you not to come back."

"It wasn't my choice," Luca said calmly.

"And people keep telling me how smart you're supposed to be."

"But you disagree?"

"Actually, I hear you've been scoring big out in L.A.," Mick conceded. "A *Variety* article said you own a half dozen record labels, party hearty with the stars. They left out the part about people dying whenever you're around. Cleavon Gates, Bobby Fuller, even Savarese. You're like one of those rats that carry the plague, Albert."

"Watch your mouth," the Mex said.

"Fuck yourself, Pedro. Or jump, if you feel lucky."

For a moment, Mick thought he might do exactly that. But Albert gave him a look, and the Mex relaxed. Just a little.

"His name's Paz Otero, actually. And you should be polite to him. You're going to be working for Paz and his brother Leon."

"Not in this life. Why are you here, Albert?"

"My Uncle John asked me to come back for Moishe's funeral— "

"No need. I know what you thought of him. And he liked you even less."

"A waste of time, I agree," Albert said coolly. "But the funeral's only part of it. My uncle tolerated Moishe because he was the last of the old timers. But you're just hired help, Shannon. You have no standing at all. And with Jimmy Hoffa in jail and the feds crawling all over the Teamsters, our union skim money is drying up. We need your action. You're out."

"You tried that once before."

"I was green then and Philly had five men. My uncle has thirty and I've got my own people now," he said, nodding at Paz. "You can't win a fight with us."

"It won't matter to you who wins, Albert. You'll be already be cooking in hell. Maybe in the next five minutes."

"Personally, I hope you try. I'd love to take you on. But my uncle can't risk any *agita* right now. So. He's willing to buy you out. A quarter mil for The Casa, the same for your interest in Black Kats."

"You gotta be kidding. The singers make more than that in royalties."

"Fuck their royalties, you're selling to us. We're not kikes, Shannon, I'm not here to haggle. If you take the offer, you can stay on and run the club for Paz, here. But that's the best I can do."

"Paz?" Mick eyed the Mex. "Not Ducatti?"

"Ronny's still with me, but he's strictly my driver now. You were right about him, he's not bright enough to be a number two. Do we have a deal?"

"I couldn't sell to you if I wanted to, Albert. My name's not on anything. I have partners who front for me."

"They're just spades, Irish. Cut them out."

"Jesus, you're really a piece of work."

"You can split your end with them or burn it for all I care," Albert shrugged, rising. "Our offer's final and the clock's running. You gave me three days once, Shannon, now I'm returning the favor. You've got three days to accept our offer. After that, we're coming after you."

"Fuck your three days, Albert," Mick said, unbuttoning his coat, showing the .45 in his waistband. "We can do this here and now. Tell your pal Paz to go for it. Maybe he'll get lucky. But you won't."

The Mex stiffened, his eyes widening. Mick rested his palm on the gun butt. Waiting.

"It's all right, Paz," Albert said, cocking his head to focus on Mick with his good eye, more wired up than spooked. "I've gotten so used to dealing with the ass kissers on the coast, I'd forgotten how serious a Detroit conversation can be, Shannon."

"That's not all you forgot."

"Don't be impatient," Albert said, rising to ease past Mick. "Enjoy your three days. And be smart for once. You can die in some alley like Moishe, or walk away with half a million. That has to be a no-brainer, even for you. Three days."

He strode up the aisle without a backward glance, cool as the wind off the Rouge. Too brave or too crazy to be afraid, Mick wasn't sure which.

Paz Otero paused beside Ducatti in the doorway, giving Mick a long, measured look. Memorizing his face.

Mick watched them walk out. Thinking a really smart guy would follow them out and cap them right now.

He didn't though. Instead, he returned to take his place beside Moishe's sister at the bier. Standing guard over his dead friend.

CHAPTER 64

Moishe Abram's gravesite, specified in his last will and testament, and paid off in advance years ago, was in the heart of Abyssinian Baptist, the largest black cemetery in metro Detroit. Four acres of weathered stones mark the final rest of the city's earliest African American citizens, many of them runaway slaves who risked everything to ride the Underground Railroad north to freedom. But here, even in death, they remained segregated from the same white folks who'd sacrificed their sons and brothers in the war to end slavery.

Race always matters.

At graveside, there was a brief memorial service, with Rabbi Eisenheim sharing the pastoral duties with Reverend C.L. Franklin, of New Bethel Baptist Church. Mick had no idea how Moishe hooked up with the good Reverend, who was widely respected in the city, but apparently he had enough pull to call in one last marker.

A single soprano from Bethel Baptist sang a hymn in a foreign tongue, Hebrew maybe. And even without meaning, it was beautiful beyond words.

After a life so fraught with violence, Moishe's trip to his eternal rest was surprisingly peaceful. A golden November afternoon, the grounds bathed in pale autumn light, perhaps the final clear day of the fall. To the west, towering, somber clouds, threatened snow by nightfall.

His grave was surrounded by family plots, Washington, Wallace, Johnson. Unrelated by blood or heritage, but for forty years, they'd been his people. He'd spent his life with them, and now he'd spend whatever came next. Exactly where he wanted to be, his grave marked with a pillar of hand-hewn granite, black as ebony and tall as a man. Incised with a simple inscription, in Hebrew.

Mick had no idea what it meant. It didn't matter.

Moishe knew. Or his God did. Or his demons.

The service was limited to immediate family and a few friends, a restriction enforced by Elijah Bass and a circle of Black Muslim brothers around the site. Fewer than a dozen folks were passed through the line. The only white faces were Moishe's sister Rachel and Irish Mick.

Until a black stretch limo pulled up to the rear of the cortege. The Reverend had begun his elegy when Ron Ducatti hustled around to open the door for Albert Luca. Heads turned, but only Mick rose, watching Albert and Ronny Duke climb up the gentle rise, the chilly autumn gusts riffling their lightweight Los Angeles suits.

As they approached the guard ring of Muslims, Mick stalked down the slope to meet them. Ronny swallowed, watching him come, focusing on Mick's hands. If the motherfucker reached inside his jacket—

But he didn't. Mick seemed to be looking past them. Ronny turned to follow his gaze. At the foot of the hill, Leon Otero had stepped out of the limo, standing beside his brother Paz, watching. The first time Mick had seen the Otero brothers together.

The Otero twins.

Identical. In similar suits.

Alike as peas in a pod.

'*Something weird about 'em,*' Diddley said.

But if the twins' oddness registered with Mick, he gave no sign. Instead, he had a quiet word with Bass, then escorted Albert and Ronny through the honor guard to seats at the rear of the canopy, sitting between them as the minister finished his remarks.

A few sobs. Carolina and Brownie dropped roses on the casket. The soprano sang "A Mighty Fortress," unaccompanied, but brilliant, with perfect intonation. Then the small gathering began to dissolve quietly, handshakes all around. No hugs.

Mick made no move to join the others or say any goodbyes. He waited until most of the mourners were halfway down the slope before turning to Albert.

"I'm glad you could make it."

"Simple courtesy, Shannon. Moishe was part of our family— "

"Fuck that, Albert, save the smoke. I know why you're here."

"Do you?"

"Sure. You're on pins and needles, couldn't stand the suspense. Wondering if I know you had Moishe killed. And I do."

Luca stared without speaking.

"Moishe warned me about you, years back. He said you were a stone psycho , and if I ever took a run at you? I should bury you deep. But I gave you a break. I let you walk. That was a mistake."

"Easy, Irish," Ronny Duke said, opening his jacket, flashing the automatic in his shoulder holster.

"Relax, Ronny. I don't want trouble here. But if I'd capped your boss with his pal, Savarese? Moishe'd still be alive."

"Keep your hands in plain sight and back away from him, Shannon," Ronny said uneasily, standing up with his hand on the gun butt—

Before he could draw, Mick clasped Albert in a tight embrace, swinging him around as a shield from Ducatti. Then he kissed him, hard, full on the mouth.

Shocked, Albert squirmed, struggling to break free, but Mick held the kiss a moment longer. Then, jerking him up by his lapels, he hurled Luca bodily toward the open grave, sending him sprawling, clawing at the dirt as he skidded over the edge to crash down atop the casket.

"Jesus, Albert, are you okay?" Ducatti asked, scrambling to the graveside. Grabbing Luca's wrist, he helped him clamber up out of the hole.

"Kill that bastard, Ronny!" Albert hissed.

"What? Here? You don't— "

"Do it, damn you!" Albert shrieked. "Do it now!"

Reading Albert's eyes was enough. Pulling his weapon, Ducatti turned to look for Shannon, but Mick was already halfway down the hill, passing through the ring of Black Muslims.

Risking a quick glance back over his shoulder, Mick saw Ducatti haul Albert out of the open grave, with Albert screaming at him the whole time, then yelling down at the Oteros who were still waiting beside the limo, too far away to hear him clearly.

Shaking off Ducatti's arm, Albert took off running, sprinting between the gravestones, heading for his car, with Ducatti only a step behind him.

Mick picked up his own pace as Albert made it to the stretched Cadillac still shouting orders at the Oteros. Ducatti scrambled in behind the wheel and fired up the limo. But to no avail. They were fifth in line and the cortege was parked bumper to bumper.

Dropping the long limo, into reverse, Ronny slammed into the car behind him, then popped it into drive, plowing into the car in front, hammering out enough room to pull free of the line.

Mick couldn't help smiling as the other drivers came running, ringing the Cadillac, yelling and cursing at Ducatti.

Then Paz Otero rose up through the Caddy's moon roof holding a shotgun. He didn't say a thing. One look at him and the drivers backed off. And the cursing stopped.

And Mick stopped as well. Dead in his tracks.

Because his battle plan had just gone south.

At the foot of the hill, Reverend Franklin's Imperial town car had pulled from the rear of the line to pick up the churchman and his entourage. And it was blocking in Mick's Corvette, with his backup weapons and the speed and power he needed to make a running fight.

With the driver at curbside assisting Franklin's people, there was no time to move the Imperial out of the way and Ducatti almost had the Cadillac free. Mick had to get out. Now!

Sprinting the length of the cortege, Mick piled into the lead car, a black Lincoln flower car, still half filled with wreaths and arrangements.

He heard somebody yelling at him. The car's driver probably.

Otero had warned them away from Albert's Cadillac, but a few had noticed Mick scrambling into the Lincoln and now they were coming on the run, after him.

The keys were in it, thank God. Mick cranked up the Lincoln and matted the gas, burning rubber as roared out of the cemetery, tires shrieking, bouquets scattering to the wind as he skidded the boxy funeral car into rush hour traffic.

CHAPTER 65

Shannon blew through the cemetery gates at fifty, cutting across four lanes, cars spinning out as drivers veered off to avoid the Lincoln. He barely noticed. Totally focused on his rear view, he watched Albert's stretch limo batter its way out of the cortege line, then come roaring out of the gates after him.

Good.

He didn't want to lose them.

This day had been coming since Ronny Duke traded him off to Moishe to settle a debt. And now he owed a much larger one, to Moishe, to Cleavon, to Aldo. Even to Albert's first kill, some high school kid who'd had his freakin' brains squeezed out in a machinery vise.

It was time to settle up. But first he needed to get clear of witnesses and bystanders. No more collateral damage. He'd buried all the friends he intended to.

Matting the gas, he pushed the Lincoln to the speed limit and beyond, flying low through city traffic, heading for the freeway directly into the teeth of a gathering snowstorm.

As if sensing his purpose, the big Continental stretched out like a thoroughbred kept too long in the barn. It was a great road car, powerful, with stiff suspension to counter its weight. It handled like a bit like a motorboat, with slack steering and spongy suspension. But he'd driven its older brother for Moishe for years, and this one wasn't much different.

Mick knew its quirks and flaws by heart, and despite them, the car felt like an old friend. And he was going to need a friend.

And a whole new battle plan.

Not that his original idea had been all that brilliant.

The moment Albert and Ronny Duke stepped into Lipinski's funeral parlor, Mick guessed what must have gone down with Moishe. Not why he'd been cut down so savagely, or who'd done the work. But the motive for it was crystal clear.

It was over turf. And the four hundred jukes that were still the key to the city. Albert had been run out of L.A., and now he was back, looking to reclaim his place in Detroit.

Seeing the Otero twins at the cemetery confirmed what Mick suspected, but down deep, he'd known it from the first.

Albert thought Moishe was a dinosaur. Old, and in the way. Probably assumed Moishe was still in charge because he'd remained the middle-man between Mick and the Lucas.

Which in Albert's mind, made Mick the hired help. Take Moishe out, then either sign Mick on, or drop him too.

But by now, Albert knew different. Knew that Moishe hadn't been the jukebox king for years. And killing him was a mistake.

He should have killed Mick first.

But better late than never.

□ □ □

Trailing behind Mick in a rented airport Cadillac, Albert was seething and Ronny's mood was just as dark. In the rear seat, only the Otero twins were cool. Savage as junkyard dogs, they didn't know why Albert hated Shannon, didn't care *why* he needed killing, or how it would be done. A bullet in the brain, or bleeding out slow from a hundred gashes. Like the old man in the alley.

Albert paid top dollar and kicked in big bonuses for inflicting pain. And after that scuffle at the cemetery? Taking Shannon down was going to be a serious payday.

But by the time Ronny got the big Caddy centered on Mick's taillights, Mick had led them out to the freeway, headed west on I-96 in the middle of the five o'clock rush, with dusk coming on and heavy, wet snowflakes beginning to fall.

No problem. All they needed now was a little patience. One short stretch with no witnesses—

"Slow down!" Luca barked at Ronny. "Don't get pulled over, for chrissake! And you two?" He swiveled in his seat to face the Oteros. "I want Shannon alive, you understand me? If we have to bust him up to take him, fine. But he'd better be breathing! I want his last five minutes to last fifty fucking years!"

He turned to the front again, totally focused on the Lincoln.

Paz and Leon exchanged a look. And a quick grin. This would be a fun gig. When the traffic thinned, they could pull up alongside the Lincoln, shove a shotgun in Shannon's face, force him off the road and they'd own his ass. Albert could take a week to finish him if he wanted. Just so they got paid.

Ronny Duke didn't say squat. After the scene at the cemetery, he knew something the Oteros didn't. Albert was totally off the rails. Stone freakin' insane, or close enough. He'd seen him like this before. Nothing but a hard, bloody death for Shannon would satisfy him now. If push came to shove, he'd gut Mick in the middle of Main Street. Land them all in prison for life. He wouldn't care.

Ronny'd been there done that with Albert. Seen more than he could stomach. Heard the screaming.

Being in The Life was a tough business. If somebody crossed you or needed doing, you cut him down quick, ditch him in an alley, or bury him deep. Then get far fucking away, as fast you can.

Simplest was best. Always. They should run the Caddy up alongside Shannon's Lincoln, Paz could take his fucking head off with the twelve gauge. End of story.

But that wouldn't cut it this time. Albert was foaming at the mouth and all the Oteros could see were dollar signs. The big bucks Albert would pay to take Shannon alive. They didn't understand how dangerous every second was now. How quickly Albert would turn on anyone who said 'no' to him, about anything.

Above all, Ronny knew he could *not* fuck this up. If they lost Shannon, Ronny'd be the one with his nuts in a vise.

So he played it safe, keeping the stretched Cadillac a few car lengths behind. The big Lincoln was easy to keep in view and Shannon couldn't run forever. He was a tough kid, dangerous in a dust-up. But by crossing Albert, he'd cut his own damn throat.

It was only a matter of where and when he'd make a stand.

But Shannon wasn't the one he was really worried about.

Albert was.

□   □   □

In the Lincoln, cruising at the limit with the stretch Caddy in his rear view, Mick was trying to rethink this, find a new way through it. At Moishe's grave, he'd been angry enough to take Albert apart on the spot. Ready for a war. Or thought he was. Had a full head of steam, a fast car and backup guns. He liked his chances against Albert's crew.

Not anymore. He was down to a single weapon, one of Moishe's army surplus .45s. Seven rounds. And traffic around him was already thinning out. They'd probably wait until full dusk to make their move—

Wrong.

They were making it now!

Behind him, the Caddy was picking up speed, gaining fast. The stretch limo had serious nuts, probably the 368 with a 4 barrel, more than enough horsepower to keep up with the Lincoln, maybe enough to run it down. Blow it off the road with its greater weight.

Matting the gas, Mick fishtailed the Continental's rear end, pushing it from seventy to eighty in seconds. Then eighty-five. Dangerously fast on the snow slicked road.

But not fast enough. Behind him, the big Caddy quickly closed the distance, its weight giving it better traction. Mick goosed the Lincoln to the outer limits of control but it didn't help. His lead kept shrinking as the Caddy came on. He braced himself, expecting to be rammed from behind at any second.

But they had other plans. The stretch limo's moon roof hummed open and one of the Oteros shouldered his way up into the wind. Holding a shotgun.

The windblast made it tricky to hold the weapon steady. Otero opened fire anyway, but not shooting at Mick. He was aiming for the rear of the car. Trying to take out one of the Linc's tires.

Mick heard the buckshot round slam into the Lincoln's trunk, saw his shattered taillight lens go flying off in the rear view! Jesus! If he blew a tire at this speed?

He had to shake them off!

Cranking the wheel hard left, then sharply right, Mick fishtailed the Lincoln across the lane markers, dangerously close to spinning out.

But it worked! Instinctively, Ducatti tried to stay on him, but the limo's greater weight made handling damn near impossible at this speed. It bucked hard, almost rolling over, forcing Ronny to jam on the brakes.

The sudden lurch nearly threw Otero out of the car. His shotgun went spinning off into the dark as he clung desperately to the window frame, until his brother grabbed his waist, hauling him back into the car.

The ploy gained Mick some distance, but it didn't change the math of the situation. Ducatti wouldn't bite on that swerve again. Next time he'd just ram him, blow him off the road.

Somehow, he had to get them off his ass! And fast!

Behind him, Ducatti switched on his headlight high-beams, making him squint against the glare blazing through his rear window.

Which actually helped. He wouldn't have to check his mirror to know the Cadillac was gaining. The headlight glare would give him a warning. And the big limo was coming on again, the lights blazing ever brighter as it closed the distance.

Damn! Otero was shouldering up through the moon roof again. No shotgun this time, he was holding an automatic, clinging to the roof with his free hand, with his brother clutching his belt from below.

Mick could hear the pop, pop pop of the handgun, the slugs thumping harmlessly into his trunk or whining off into the dark. With both cars running flat out, veering and rocking, he wasn't having much luck.

Until his sixth shot blew out the Lincoln's rear window.

Wind and snow came howling in out of the darkness, swirling madly around the dashboard. Mick's eyes instantly began watering in the wind blast. Snow was clinging to the windshield, and the leaves and stems from the wreaths in back were whipping his face.

Both cars were rolling past eighty now, careening at the edge of disaster. The big Caddy's power and extra weight gave Ducatti an edge on the straight-aways. Mick's .45 was on the seat beside him, but he was so focused on the road ahead he couldn't return fire. Otero was still popping away, likely to score a hit on a tire at any moment. And if he did, it would be all over—

But when you're fighting a guy who has an advantage, a longer reach or bigger punch? Find a way to use it against him.

The Caddy's extra weight made it harder to handle at speed, especially on slippery roads. It wasn't much, but it was all he had.

Up ahead, he spotted an overpass coming on. Some of them had turnouts for service vehicles.

Some didn't.

Another slug hammering into the trunk made the decision for him.

Now or never. Last chance.

Killing his headlights, he changed lanes, crossing all the way over to the right shoulder. Ducatti followed, thinking he was trying to dodge Otero's gunfire. Focused on staying close to the Lincoln to give the gunman a better shot, Ronny barely noticed the oncoming overpass, didn't spot the turnout until Shannon went for it!

Whipping the wheel around, Mick sent the Lincoln into a power slide, skidding across both lanes into the turnout, broadside. Behind him, the stretch limo's brake lights flashed cherry red as Ducatti crushed the pedal to the floor, throwing the Caddy into a wild skid, desperately trying to stay on the Lincoln's tail.

But he was too late! He'd already blown past the turnout entrance. For a split second, Ducatti almost saved it, kept the Caddy rocketing along the shoulder of the road... but then the ground dropped away and the big limo plunged head first into the median ditch!

Mick was still wrestling the Lincoln's wheel, struggling to keep the Continental upright as it bucked and plunged across the frozen gravel. Through the side window, he glimpsed Albert's limo veering wildly out of control, saw its nose drop into the ditch, and then the big Cadillac went airborne! Tumbling end over end, once, twice, three times, before crashing down to earth on the far side of the freeway. Upside down.

Skidding the Lincoln to a halt, Mick threw open the door and charged out in a blind fury, racing toward the wrecked limo.

Unarmed. He'd lost the .45 when the Lincoln spun out. But he was past caring.

His only chance now was to get to the limo before the gunmen recovered— *shit!* He tripped in the dark and, and went sprawling. Scrambling to his feet, he whirled to face—

Paz Otero. Or Leon. He couldn't tell which was which. And their own mother wouldn't know them now. Both men had been thrown out of the limo when it flipped end over end.

The shooter got the worst of it. His shoulders were already outside the moon-roof when the car crashed down the first time.

He'd literally been obliterated, his torso smashed into bloody shreds of torn flesh and rags that didn't resemble anything human.

His brother hadn't fared much better. Thrown a good thirty yards from the vehicle, he must have slammed down on the pavement at eighty miles an hour, breaking every bone in his body, his back, both legs, both arms.

And yet, somehow he was still breathing. Struggling to crawl, scrabbling at the earth with bloody fingers, dragging his shattered limbs and crushed torso forward, an inch at a time. Instinctively seeking the darkness, a place to hide. Mindless as a stomped insect...

And then he stopped. Dead. Mick didn't have to check the corpse. The vapor of the gunman's final breath rose like mist into the night. And no more came.

Moving more warily now, Mick edged up to the limo. In flipping end over end, the Caddy had hammered itself into scrap. Frame twisted, sides crumpled, it was barely recognizable as a vehicle at all. The roof had collapsed, blowing out the windshield. Trapping the driver and his passenger in the crushed cockpit.

Mick knelt to face them. Ronny Duke and Albert Luca were pinned in their seats by the collapsed roof and blown out dashboard, upside down. Ronny had been battered bloody by the Caddy's wheel. Dazed from the crash, he was clawing helplessly at the door latch, struggling to force it open. Not a chance.

Albert had come through the crash better. His face had been savaged by flying glass but he was fully conscious. When he saw Mick coming, he jerked an automatic out of his waistband, aiming it out the broken window, desperately trying to line up a clear shot with his good eye. One clear shot...

"You don't want to do that, Albert," Mick warned, not bothering to back away. "Take a deep breath. The crash ruptured the gas tank, fuel's pouring all over the ground. Fire that piece and you'll burn to death, whether you hit me or not."

His words pierced Ronny's daze. Or maybe Ducatti realized he was breathing the raw stench of gasoline. And grasped what it meant.

"Get us out of here, Shannon." He coughed. "Please."

"Tell Albert to lose the gun."

"Fuck you!" Luca shouted.

"You're the one who's fucked, Albert. Toss it! You can't use it anyway."

"You'll kill us. Or leave us to die! This way, I take you with me." He'd been edging the automatic around as he spoke, suddenly he raised it! Had Mick dead in his sights at point blank range.

Luca's face split in a crazy grin, the two men staring at each other across ten yards of torn ground. And ten crazy years.

Recognition. A momentary flash, of what they'd once been to each other. And what would happen now.

"Oh, hell no," Ronny pleaded, reading the murderous fury in Luca's eyes. "For the love of God, Albert!"

Mick dove hard to his left, rolling away from the car. Albert swung his weapon, zeroing in on Mick as he tried to roll clear—

Albert fired!

A slug plowed into the ground an inch from Mick's head. The second shot hammered his shoulder like a nine pound sledge— the Cadillac exploded!

With a fiery *whump*, the pool of gasoline went off like a napalm bomb, lifting the big sedan into the air, then crashing it down again, flames billowing out and around in a raging inferno.

The blast sent Mick sailing away from the car like a kick from a giant boot. Stunned, he managed to make it to his hands and knees, but couldn't do more. Crouched there, with his head down, panting like a dog.

Inside the crumpled cab, Albert and Ronny were writhing, engulfed in flame, shrieking like trapped animals. Burning alive.

Shielding his face with his bleeding forearm, Mick tried to edge closer. If he could reach Ronny... but he couldn't. A second blast drove him further away from the wreck as the flames and oily smoke roiled madly into the night sky.

Only Albert was screaming now. And not for long. There was a final gunshot... then nothing. Only the crackling roar and the foul stench of burning rubber and gasoline.

Backing away from the towering blaze with his face averted, Mick nearly tripped over the shattered Otero twin again. The gunsel's clothes were smoldering from the intense heat. As Mick knelt to check his pulse, one of Otero's boot soles burst into flame.

It didn't matter. He couldn't feel it.

□   □   □

Staggering to the Lincoln, he cranked it up, leaving the Cadillac and the corpses where they lay. Someone would spot the blaze and phone the police. He needed to be long gone when they came. Gunning the Lincoln around, he pointed its nose east, back to the city.

Had to drive one handed. His arm was numb and he was losing a lot of blood from the wound in his shoulder. Probably should have taken the first exit, sought help. But he couldn't seem to think clearly now. His only thought was making it home to Detroit. If he could.

It was almost full dark now, and the heavy snow made it hard to see the centerline. It was taking every iota of his concentration to maintain his focus on it, to stay conscious.

But images of Albert and Ronny, trapped in the blazing limo, screaming as they burned, kept flashing across his consciousness. Erasing the reality of the highway.

And then came images of Idlewild.

His life had gone violently wrong in that place and it wasn't done with him yet. A piece of his soul would be stuck in that swamp forever. Buried in the back of a jukebox Cadillac.

And for a moment he was there again, watching Mojo's big red machine sinking slowly into the swamp. Muddy water inching up the doors, then over the hood and finally the window ledges, gushing inside.

And Mojo seemed to move. Just a little. Was the water shifting his body, or was he still... ?

Mick peered hared, trying to get a better look, but he couldn't really see the Cadillac anymore. Or the centerline. The snow had covered it completely now. It was covering everything...

He felt the lurch as the big Lincoln rumbled off the road. It seemed to float for a minute as the earth had dropped away beneath its wheels.

He thought he might be flying... .

CHAPTER 66

Mick Shannon died at seven twenty-three in the Ford Hospital critical care unit. And again at nine fourteen. And a third time just after midnight. But only for a few seconds the last time, before the emergency surgery team restarted his heart. Again.

Four days later, he woke in a world of white. White sheets, white ceiling tiles, white walls. Even his pain was white. A searing ache every time he took a shallow breath. And deeper still, he sensed the throbbing numbness of agony held at bay. Circling him like a wolf. Knew he had to be cruising on serious dope.

He tried to remember where he was, how he'd gotten here, but his thoughts were slow as molasses in winter.

Realized someone was watching him. A trim Latin cop. Good suit, better haircut. Sitting in a white plastic chair beside Mick's bed.

"You're back," Garcia said mildly. "Thought you might be gone for good."

"I...feel gone," Mick rasped. "What happened?"

"A lot. We found four dead out on I-96. From the tire tracks and the bullet holes in the trunk of that funeral car you borrowed, it's obvious you were there. Not so obvious what went down. Want to tell me about it?"

"I'm a little foggy about... whatever it was. Did they do Martika's surgery? Is she okay?"

"I don't know, Mick, but I'll find out. Is she in this hospital, or... ?"

"I don't even know where *I* am. Christ, I can't think straight."

"You've been shot, wrecked two cars, You should probably be in the ground next to your old boss. Get some rest. I've got a man outside the door."

"To keep people out?" Mick asked. "Or keep me in?"

"Both," Garcia admitted. "But I doubt you'll be going... anywhere." He broke off. Mick was already asleep.

□   □   □

When he surfaced again, Martika was in the plastic chair beside his bed. Her dark eyes met his, but she didn't speak. And for moment he thought—

"Hey, Irish," she murmured softly. Her voice was husky, barely more than a whisper, but he understood every freakin' word. He closed his eyes against the overwhelming flood of relief.

"You... Can talk?" he managed.

"Try to shut me up," she said. "But ah... I can't sing, Mick. Or yell, or even raise my voice much above... this." She gestured toward her throat. "At least, not yet."

"Okay." He swallowed. "It doesn't matter."

"Yes it does. And maybe the docs are right, and I'm done for good. But I'm thinking, if I can carry a damn tune? Even a few notes? Maybe Jerome can amp me up, get me back in the game. But if not, there was always an expiration date on this life, lover. Ask Cleavon or Varnell. Hell, ask Elvis."

There was an "end of story" finality in her tone, so he let it pass. But he was sure of one thing.

If she was done with the Life, so was he. Or maybe he was just tired. Because the room had begun rocking, gently, like a ship at sea, shrinking down, fading out... .

CHAPTER 67

The day Mick limped out of Henry Ford Hospital, he truly *looked* like Moishe's boy, leaning on a cane with every step. His left arm was strapped across his chest in a blue sling, he was twenty pounds lighter, his leather jacket hanging loosely on his shoulders, his face was still blotchy with burn ointment, and seamed with new pain lines.

But he was on the mend. Deep down, he could feel his stamina seeping back. Like a truck battery on a trickle charge. And any day above ground is a good one.

The weather matched his mood, unseasonably warm for November, with a pale autumn sun high in a cloudless sky.

A long white, jukebox Cadillac convertible was idling at the curb. A '57, with its top down, gleaming with J-Wax from its hood to the chrome tips of its tailfins. A brown-eyed handsome man in a snap brim hat scrambled out of the car to hold the door for him. And in the back seat, an African queen in a faux ermine coat with a turban to match was waiting. Looking fine beyond words.

"Hey, Irish," Brownie said, taking Mick's arm, helping him in. "I tried to get in to see you, but the cop on your door said no visitors. How you doin'?"

"Better," Mick said, edging carefully through the door. "Thought the law might book me for the next ten years over what happened to Albert. Turns out I might get a medal instead. Where'd you get the ride?"

"Saw it in the police impound lot when I bailed out the Lincoln you 'borrowed' at Moishe's funeral. The Linc was a total, what with the bullet holes and all, but this one looked so fine I couldn't resist it. Got it for a song. Lean back on that leather and relax. We got business."

"We're out of the business, Brownie," Mick said, lowering himself carefully onto the back seat beside Martika. "You'd better find new partners."

"Who's talking about partners? I'm just lookin' for some advice. Your ears always were whiter than mine. Remember Little Diddley? The guitar player who got cut up the night Moishe bought it?"

"What about him?"

"The kid's been layin' low in New York, stayin' with kin up in Harlem." Reaching over, Brownie shoved a cassette into a boombox parked on the seat beside him. "He sent me a tape of a new thing happenin' in the black clubs there. Listen up."

A drumbeat kicked in, fattened by a barebones bass and guitar.

"That's the riff from 'Lickin' Stick'," Martika said.

"James Brown," Mick added.

"You two still got ears," Brownie nodded. "But that ain't James *or* the Famous Flames."

A voice broke in above the rhythm, shouting angry, machine gun rhymes, phasing in and out of sync with the beat. Mick straightened up, listening intently.

"What the hell is that?" he asked.

"It's a new style. Street poetry over a hard-ass rhythm section. No melody. Just the rhymes, the riff and the beat. They call it rap, Diddley says."

"It's barely music at all," Martika said, her voice a husky whisper.

"That's what they used to say about blues, lady. And about rock too, early on."

"I like jams with an edge, but this?" Mick said. "There's no... tune. No vocal."

"It's got energy, though," Tika noted. "And the rhythm's pedal to the metal. Okay, it's kind of interesting, Brownie. So? What about it?"

"Top 40 music is all about videos these days. Hair bands, white punks in leotards or brothers dancin' like the freakin' Village People. All flash. No truth to it, no soul. So I'm thinkin' maybe, just *maybe*, this rap stuff could be the next big thing. It's got power and its so new MTV and the big labels don't even know it exists. Pop radio won't play it, but what if it was all over the street? In the 'hood."

"On the jukes," Mick said.

"It'll hit like crack cocaine on the corners," Brownie nodded. "Our ticket back in the game."

"I don't want in, Brownie," Mick said. "We had one helluva ride, but I'm done."

"Are you done because *you're* done, Irish?" Tika asked. "Or because you think I am?"

Mick didn't say anything, watching her.

"Look, we paid some hard dues, lover. And lost good people along the way. But you saw the Sultans onstage. And you saw me. Loving every single second of it. I wouldn't have traded those times for anything. And neither would they. Even if we'd known up front what it would cost. Sure the price was too damned high. But it was worth it."

"Worth what?"

"We lived the life we wanted, Mick. And it wasn't easy. But the music we made? Maybe that will live on awhile. Maybe forever. And that means something to me. Maybe everything," she said, snuggling against his shoulder.

"A few years from now, nobody will remember Albert or them Dago gangsters. But the Sultans? They're gonna sing forever. They'll be young and strong, forever. And we helped that happen. You and me, Irish. We helped. And what could be better than that?"

"Nothing," Mick admitted. "Not a damn thing."

"All right, then," Brownie said, dropping the Caddy into gear with a flourish. "I know a place with the best barbecue north of the Arkansas line. I'll buy ya'll some lunch, we'll catch up, then talk some business."

As Brownie swung the Caddy into traffic, Mick reached over to turn on the tape deck again. Listening to the incandescent rhymes of a nameless rapper from New York.

Freed from the limits of melody, the street language crackled with anger, savage as a hook to the body. Music pared down to muscle and bone, like a fighter making weight.

The style was fresh. But the *feel* of it, was ancient. Bone deep. A hard man shouting about his hard times. It felt like...

The Blues. It had morphed into jazz, then rock, and now something new and fresh again.

Pumped up with inner city energy and tricked out in brutal rhythms, the message was still the same. I'm busted and battered and angry.

I'm down. But I damn sure ain't out.

With Martika nestled against his shoulder, Mick could feel the rhythm thumping in his chest like a pulse. Heard the rage ringing down the concrete canyons as Brownie goosed the big Caddy to the limit, rolling along 8 Mile Road.

Heading home.

Into the dark heart of Detroit.

THE END

Doug Allyn Bibliography

Novels

Lupe Garcia series
The Cheerio Killings (1989)
The Motown Underground
  (1993)

Mitch Mitchell series
Icewater Mansions (1995)
Black Water (1996)
A Dance in Deep Water (1997)
SuperSport (1998)

Dr. David Westbrook series
All Creatures Dark and
  Dangerous (1999)
The Burning of Rachel Hayes
  (2004)
Juke-box Cadillac (2010)
All Creatures Dark and
  Dangerous: The complete Dr.
  David Westbrook Mysteries
  (2014)
FrankenKat and Other Tales
  (2014)

Welcome to Wolf Country
  (2001)

The Lifeguard Lawyer (2017)
  [with James Patterson]

Short Story Collections

Hard Luck Klub (2002)
The Troubadour Tales: 5
  Mysteries Most Medieval
  (2014)

Stories

Final Rites *(Alfred Hitchcock's
  Mystery Magazine,* Dec.1985)
Firebomb *(Alfred Hitchcock's
  Mystery Magazine,* May 1986)
Wolf Country *(Alfred
  Hitchcock's Mystery Magazine,*
  Sept 1986)
The Puddle Diver *(Alfred
  Hitchcock's Mystery Magazine,*
  Oct 1986)
Homecoming *(Alfred Hitchcock's
  Mystery Magazine,* Dec 1986)
Death of a Poet *(Alfred
  Hitchcock's Mystery Magazine,*
  Apr 1987)
Witch *(Alfred Hitchcock's
  Mystery Magazine,* June 1987)
Supersport *(Alfred Hitchcock's
  Mystery Magazine,* Dec 1987)
The Ching Lady *(Alfred
  Hitchcock's Mystery Magazine,*
  Mar 1988)
Bloodlines *(Alfred Hitchcock's
  Mystery Magazine,* Feb 1988)
Déjà Vu *(Alfred Hitchcock's
  Mystery Magazine,* Jun 1988)
Night of the Grave Dancer
  *(Alfred Hitchcock's Mystery
  Magazine,* Sept 1988)
Lancaster's Ghost *(Alfred
  Hitchcock's Mystery Magazine,*
  mid-Dec 1988)
A Death in Heaven *(Ellery
  Queen's Mystery Magazine,*
  Dec 1988)
Evil Spirits *(Alfred Hitchcock's
  Mystery Magazine,* Jan 1989)
Debt of Honor *(Ellery Queen's
  Mystery Magazine,* Jan 1989)

The Last Reunion (*Ellery Queen's Mystery Magazine,* June 1989)

Cannibal *(Alfred Hitchcock's Mystery Magazine,* Nov 1989)

Star Pupil (*Ellery Queen's Mystery Magazine,* Oct 1989)

Mojo Man *(Alfred Hitchcock's Mystery Magazine,* Oct 1990)

Sleeper (*Ellery Queen's Mystery Magazine,* May 1991) **Edgar nominee**

Speed Demon (*Ellery Queen's Mystery Magazine,* Oct 1991)

Icewater Mansions (*Ellery Queen's Mystery Magazine,* Jan 1992)

Ten Pound Parrott (*Ellery Queen's Mystery Magazine,* Feb 1992)

Candles in the Rain (*Ellery Queen's Mystery Magazine,* Nov 1992) **Edgar nominee**

The Sultans of Soul (*Ellery Queen's Mystery Magazine,* Mar 1993)

The Meistersinger *(Alfred Hitchcock's Mystery Magazine,* Sept 1993)

Dancing on the Centerline (*Ellery Queen's Mystery Magazine,* Oct 1993)

The Ghost Show (*Ellery Queen's Mystery Magazine,* Dec 1993) **Edgar nominee**

Pageant (*Ellery Queen's Mystery Magazine,* mid-Dec 1993)

Fire Lake (*Ellery Queen's Mystery Magazine,* Apr 1994)

The Dancing Bear *(Alfred Hitchcock's Mystery Magazine,* Mar 1994) **Edgar winner**

Black Water (*Ellery Queen's Mystery Magazine,* Aug 1994)

Wrecker (*Ellery Queen's Mystery Magazine,* Nov 1994)

The Bearded Lady (*Ellery Queen's Mystery Magazine,* Dec 1994)

The Cross Wolf (*Ellery Queen's Mystery Magazine,* mid-Dec 1994)

Demons (*Ellery Queen's Mystery Magazine,* Feb 1996)

Frankenkat (*Ellery Queen's Mystery Magazine,* Dec 1995) **EQ Reader's Award**

Blind Lemon *(Alfred Hitchcock's Mystery Magazine,* May 1996)

Roadkill (*Ellery Queen's Mystery Magazine,* May 1996) **EQ Reader's Award**

Animal Rites (*Ellery Queen's Mystery Magazine,* July 1996)

Puppyland (*Ellery Queen's Mystery Magazine,* Sep 1996)

Green as Grass (*Ellery Queen's Mystery Magazine,* Nov 1996)

Money Face (*Ellery Queen's Mystery Magazine,* Dec 1996)

Beaches of Paraguay (*Ellery Queen's Mystery Magazine,* May 1997)

Bush Leaguer *(Alfred Hitchcock's Mystery Magazine,* Apr 1997)

Copperhead Run (*Ellery Queen's Mystery Magazine,* June 1997)

Thousandfurs (*Once Upon a Crime,* 1997)

Cedar Savage (*Ellery Queen's Mystery Magazine*, Mar 1998)
The Taxi Dancer *(Alfred Hitchcock's Mystery Magazine*, Nov 1998)
Crippen, Landru & Carlos Palomino (*Ellery Queen's Mystery Magazine*, Aug 1998)
St. Margaret's Kitten (*Cat Crimes Through Time*, 1998)
Unchained Melody (*Ellery Queen's Mystery Magazine*, Jan 1999)
Bad Boyz Klub (*Diagnosis Death*, 1999)
Saint Bobby (*Ellery Queen's Mystery Magazine*, Apr 1999) **Derringer Award**
Miracles! Happen (*Ellery Queen's Mystery Magazine*, Dec 1999)
Death Row Pet Show (*Ellery Queen's Mystery Magazine*, Apr 2000) **EQ Readers Award**
Country of the Blind (*Murder Most Medieval*, 2000)
Hitler, Elvis and Me *(Alfred Hitchcock's Mystery Magazine*, Oct 2000)
The Hessian (*Murder Most Confederate*, 2000)
The Turncoat (*Civil War Spy Stories*, Tor Books, 2000)
The Christmas Mitzvah (*Ellery Queen's Mystery Magazine*, Dec 2000)
The Saracen Curse *(Alfred Hitchcock's Mystery Magazine*, Nov 2001)
The Warlord's Widow *(Alfred Hitchcock's Mystery Magazine*, Jul/Aug 2001)
End of the Century (*First to Fight II*, 2001)
Sunlight Shining on Water (*Murder on the Ropes*, 2001)
First Love (*Foggy Windows*, 2001)
Custer's First Stand (*Alternate Gettysburgs*, 2001)
Black Irish (*Murder Most Celtic*, 2001)
Beer, Betrayal and Ho Chi Minh (*A Date Which Will Live In Infamy*, 2001)
The Murder Ballads (*Ellery Queen's Mystery Magazine*, Mar 2002) **Derringer Award**
The Jukebox King *(Alfred Hitchcock's Mystery Magazine*, Jun 2002)
Telephone to Forever (*Ellery Queen's Mystery Magazine*, July 2002)
The Prize Crew (*Submarine Combat*, 2002)
Valhalla (*Ellery Queen's Mystery Magazine*, Jan 2003)
The Blind Pig (*Ellery Queen's Mystery Magazine*, May 2003)
Palace in the Pines (*Ellery Queen's Mystery Magazine*, July 2003) **EQ Readers Award**
Secondhand Heart *(Alfred Hitchcock's Mystery Magazine*, Jan 2004) **Derringer Award**
What Child is This? (*Ellery Queen's Mystery Magazine*, Jan 2004)

Long Lost Love (*Ellery Queen's Mystery Magazine*, May 2004)

The Gin Mill (*Ellery Queen's Mystery Magazine*, Sept 2004) **EQ Readers Award**

Wolf Woman Bay (*Ellery Queen's Mystery Magazine*, June 2005) EQ **Readers Award**

The Timber Snake *(Alfred Hitchcock's Mystery Magazine*, Sept 2005)

The Top Ten List (*Ellery Queen's Mystery Magazine*, Mar/Apr 2006)

The Black Chapel (*Ellery Queen's Mystery Magazine*, Sept/Oct 2006)

Surviving Spouse *(Alfred Hitchcock's Mystery Magazine*, Oct 2006)

Stone Cold Xmas (*Ellery Queen's Mystery Magazine*, Jan 2007)

Dead as a Dog (*Ellery Queen's Mystery Magazine*, July 2007)

The Pig Party (*Ellery Queen's Mystery Magazine*, Mar/Apr 2008)

The Sonnets of September (*Ellery Queen's Mystery Magazine*, July 2008)

The Killing Farm *(Alfred Hitchcock's Mystery Magazine*, Mar 2008)

The Valhalla Verdict (*Ellery Queen's Mystery Magazine*, Mar/Apr 2009)

Famous Last Words (*Ellery Queen's Mystery Magazine*, Nov 2009) **Derringer Award**

Israfel (*On a Raven's Wing*, 2009)

The Digital Date (*Ellery Queen's Mystery Magazine*, Jan 2010)

Flashback *(Alfred Hitchcock's Mystery Magazine*, June 2009)

An Early Christmas (*Ellery Queen's Mystery Magazine*, Jan 2009) **EQ Readers Award**

Days of Rage (*Ellery Queen's Mystery Magazine*, Mar/Apr 2010)

The Hate Tapes *(Alfred Hitchcock's Mystery Magazine*, Mar 2010)

The Scent of Lilacs (*Ellery Queen's Mystery Magazine*, Sept/Oct 2010) **Edgar Award**

A Penny for the Boatman (*Ellery Queen's Mystery Magazine*, Mar/Apr 2011)

Thicker Than Blood *(Alfred Hitchcock's Mystery Magazine*, Sept 2011)

Bloodline (*Ellery Queen's Mystery Magazine*, Nov 2011)

Woodsmoke Boys (*Ellery Queen's Mystery Magazine*, Mar/Apr 2012) **Readers Award**

Downsized *(Alfred Hitchcock's Mystery Magazine*, Mar 2013) **Derringer Award**

Death of a Drama Queen (*Ellery Queen's Mystery Magazine*, Sept/Oct 2012)

Blaze of Glory (*Ellery Queen's Mystery Magazine*, June 2013)

Borrowed Time (*Ellery Queen's Mystery Magazine*, Sep/Oct 2013)

Hitler's Dogs (*Fiction River*, 2014)

The Bandit Ballads (*Ellery Queen's Mystery Magazine,* Mar/Apr 2014)
Message from the Morgue *(Alfred Hitchcock's Mystery Magazine,* Sep 2014)
The Snow Angel (*Ellery Queen's Mystery Magazine,* Jan 2014)
The Hobby Cop (*Ellery Queen's Mystery Magazine,* Sep/Oct 2014)
The Fury (*Ellery Queen's Mystery Magazine,* May 2015)
Claire's Mirror (*Ellery Queen's Mystery Magazine,* May 2016)

The Comeback (*Ellery Queen's Mystery Magazine,* Sept/Oct 2015)
The Dropout (*Ellery Queen's Mystery Magazine,* Mar/Apr 2016)
Puncher's Chance (*Ellery Queen's Mystery Magazine,* June 2016)
Coup de Grace (*Ellery Queen's Mystery Magazine,* Sept/Oct 2016)
The Belgian (*Ellery Queen's Mystery Magazine,* 2017)